"How thrilling would it be to get a summer job at the Cloisters, New York City's medieval art museum, in which your responsibilities included divining the future using tarot cards infused with dark magic? . . . An underhanded antiques dealer, a sexy Cloisters gardener with a side hustle in poisonous plants, a suspicious death or two, a mysterious centuries-old document written in an obscure language, the sense that no one, not even Ann, is telling us the whole truth—all this adds up to a dense forest of a plot . . . It's a question of discerning which clues Hays has laid out are worth paying attention to. Is this a story of the occult, or a story of ambition, or a tale of one (or more!) murderous psychopaths? The answer is a shock, and it sneaks up on you unawares."

—*The New York Times*

"A genre-blurring murder mystery/coming-of-age story . . . Hays's atmospheric descriptions of the exhibits, the gardens, and the interior spaces enhance the mysterious and menacing interactions among the characters."

—*The San Francisco Chronicle*

"Academic jealousy and Renaissance magic mingle in this hit US debut, a satisfyingly brutal tale of ambition set in a Manhattan museum."

—*The Guardian* (UK)

"Fans of the New York City art scene and the history of tarot will enjoy Katy Hays's dynamic mystery."

—PopSugar

"A tour de force by an important new voice, *The Cloisters* begins as a fish-out-of-water story. But as Katy Hays deftly weaves in layer after layer of the occult, art, and academia, it turns into a rich tapestry that speaks to issues of privilege, power, and ambition—and, more than anything, the darkness lurking just inside ivory towers. Virtuosic and incredibly compelling, *The Cloisters* grabbed me in a way that no book has done since *The Secret History*."

—Rachel Kapelke-Dale, author of *The Ballerinas*

"Prepare to lose your entire afternoon to *The Cloisters*, first for its atmosphere, a medieval museum at the tip of Manhattan; and then to pursuing a young scholar in her search for an ancient tarot deck, while keeping a sharp eye on the brilliant, attractive colleagues who may be out to help her or kill her. Good luck staying ahead of this one, and have a great time poring over the many treasures inside."

—Maria Hummel, author of
Reese's Book Club Pick *Still Lives*

"Like the moment before a thunderstorm on a summer afternoon, *The Cloisters* is sultry, lush, and trembling with menace."

—Julia May Jonas, author of *Vladimir*

"A tantalizingly clever tale, laced with surprises as devious as its cast of shadowy scholars, *The Cloisters* had me gripped from cover to cover. Hays's debut is diabolical and darkly entertaining, a masterwork of literary suspense that surges to an otherworldly conclusion."

—Mark Prins, author of *The Latinist*

"A sharply smart, engaging debut exploring art, desire, ambition, and privilege set in the mysterious, opulent, famed Cloisters museum in Upper Manhattan, with dark surprises through its final pages. Hays's

mooth narration deftly conjures the complex, sexy webs between her
characters—obsessives enmeshed in an obscure, cutthroat corner of academia, on the verge of a momentous discovery of the divination practices of the early Italian renaissance. A fun, seductive, intelligent read."

—Nicola DeRobertis-Theye, author of
The Vietri Project

"Hays's mesmerizing debut feels like the air before a summer storm—
thick and sinister, shimmering with tension. A seductive unfurling of
ies, envy, and the pull of the occult, *The Cloisters* does for tarot what
The Secret History did for Greek class. This sharp, shadowy book held
me in thrall from beginning to star-crossed end."

—Sara Sligar, author of *Take Me Apart*

"Whether you love tarot and the occult, dark academia, or even just
a gripping mystery thriller, *The Cloisters* is a mesmerizing and darkly
beguiling novel."

—The Nerd Daily

"Katy Hays's debut is dark, seductive, and captivating . . . Exploring
fate, class divides, magic and history, *The Cloisters* is a grand piece of
fiction that dark academia fans won't want to miss . . . Reminiscent
of *The Secret History*, *Ninth House*, and *If We Were Villains*, the plot
and characters are equally alluring. Each character makes you want
to dig deeper, uncovering their desires and motivations . . . Ideally,
this book would be read by candlelight in a grand research library,
but you'll do just as well tucked away in your home, reading in the
dark until all hours of the night."

—BookTrib

THE
CLOISTERS

THE
CLOISTERS

A NOVEL

Katy Hays

ATRIA PAPERBACK

NEW YORK   LONDON   TORONTO   SYDNEY   NEW DELHI

An Imprint of Simon & Schuster, Inc.
1230 Avenue of the Americas
New York, NY 10020

First Atria Paperback edition July 2023

ATRIA PAPERBACK and colophon are trademarks of Simon & Schuster, Inc.

For information about special discounts for bulk purchases, please contact
Simon & Schuster Special Sales at 1-866-506-1949 or business@simonandschuster.com.

The Simon & Schuster Speakers Bureau can bring authors to your live event.
For more information or to book an event, contact the Simon & Schuster Speakers Bureau at
1-866-248-3049 or visit our website at www.simonspeakers.com.

Manufactured in the United States of America

1 3 5 7 9 10 8 6 4 2

Library of Congress Cataloging-in-Publication Data
Names: Hays, Katy, 1982– author.
Title: The Cloisters : a novel / Katy Hays.
Identifiers: LCCN 2022020496 (print) | LCCN 2022020497 (ebook) |
ISBN 9781668004401 (hardcover) | ISBN 9781668004418 (trade paperback) |
ISBN 9781668004425 (ebook)
Subjects: LCSH: Cloisters (Museum)--Fiction. | Divination--Fiction. | Tarot--Fiction. |
LCGFT: Detective and mystery fiction. | Thrillers (Fiction) | Novels.
Classification: LCC PS3608.A9834 C58 2023 (print) | LCC PS3608.A9834 (ebook) |
DDC 813/.6--dc23/eng/20220502
LC record available at https://lccn.loc.gov/2022020496
LC ebook record available at https://lccn.loc.gov/2022020497

ISBN 978-1-6680-0440-1
ISBN 978-1-6680-0441-8 (pbk)
ISBN 978-1-6680-0442-5 (ebook)

For Andrew Hays
(and The Cheese)

The first day of human life already establishes the last.

—Seneca, *Oedipus*

PROLOGUE

Death always visited me in August. A slow and delicious month we turned into something swift and brutal. The change, quick as a card trick.

I should have seen it coming. The way the body would be laid out on the library floor, the way the gardens would be torn apart by the search. The way our jealousy, greed, and ambition were waiting to devour us all, like a snake eating its own tail. The ouroboros. And even though I know the dark truths we hid from one another that summer, some part of me still longs for The Cloisters, for the person I was before.

I used to think it might have gone either way. That I might have said no to the job or to Leo. That I might never have gone to Long Lake that summer night. That the coroner, even, might have decided against an autopsy. But those choices were never mine to make. I know that now.

I think a lot about luck these days. *Luck*. Probably from the Middle High German *glück*, meaning fortune or happy accident. Dante called Fortune the *ministra di Dio*, or the minister of God. Fortune, just an old-fashioned word for fate. The ancient Greeks and Romans did everything in the service of Fate. They built temples in its honor and bound their lives to its caprices. They consulted sibyls and prophets. They scried the entrails of animals and studied omens. Even Julius Caesar is said to have crossed the Rubicon only after casting a pair of dice. *Iacta alea est*—the die is cast. The entire fate of the Roman Empire depended on that throw. At least Caesar was lucky once.

What if our whole life—how we live and die—has already been de-cided for us? Would you want to know, if a roll of the dice or a deal of the cards could tell you the outcome? Can life be that thin, that disturbing? What if we are all just Caesar? Waiting on our lucky throw, refusing to see what waits for us in the ides of March.

It was easy, at first, to miss the omens that haunted The Cloisters that summer. The gardens always spilling over with wildflowers and herbs, terra-cotta pots planted with lavender, and the pink lady apple tree, blooming sweet and white. The air so hot, our skin stayed damp and flushed. An inescapable future that found us, not the other way around. An unlucky throw. One that I could have foreseen, if only I—like the Greeks and Romans—had known what to look for.

CHAPTER ONE

I would arrive in New York at the beginning of June. At a time when the heat was building—gathering in the asphalt, reflecting off the glass—until it reached a peak that wouldn't release long into September. I was going east, unlike so many of the students from my class at Whitman College who were headed west, toward Seattle and San Francisco, sometimes Hong Kong.

The truth was, I wasn't going east to the place I had originally hoped, which was Cambridge or New Haven, or even Williamstown. But when the emails came from department chairs saying *they were very sorry . . . a competitive applicant pool . . . best of luck in your future endeavors*, I was grateful that one application had yielded a positive result: the Summer Associates Program at the Metropolitan Museum of Art. A favor, I knew, to my emeritus advisor, Richard Lingraf, who had once been something of an Ivy League luminary before the East Coast weather—or was it a questionable happening at his alma mater?—had chased him west.

They called it an "associates" program, but it was an internship with a meager stipend. It didn't matter to me; I would have worked two jobs and paid them to be there. It was, after all, the Met. The kind of prestigious imprimatur someone like me—a hick from an unknown school—needed.

Well, Whitman wasn't entirely unknown. But because I had grown up in Walla Walla, the dusty, single-story town in southeastern Washington where Whitman was located, I rarely encountered anyone from out of the state who knew of its existence. My whole childhood had been the college, an experience that had slowly dulled much of its magic. Where other students arrived on campus excited to start their adult lives anew, I was afforded no such clean slate. This was because both of my parents worked for Whitman. My mother, in dining services, where she planned menus and theme nights for the first-year students who lived in the residence halls: Basque, Ethiopian, asado. If I had lived on campus, she might have planned my meals too, but the financial waiver Whitman granted employees only extended to tuition, and so, I lived at home.

My father, however, had been a linguist—although not one on faculty. An autodidact who borrowed books from Whitman's Penrose Library, he taught me the difference between the six Latin cases and how to parse rural Italian dialects, all in between his facilities shifts at the college. That is, before he was buried next to my grandparents the summer before my senior year, behind the Lutheran church at the edge of town, the victim of a hit-and-run. He never told me where his love of languages had come from, just that he was grateful I shared it.

"Your dad would be so proud, Ann," Paula said.

It was the end of my shift at the restaurant where I worked, and where Paula, the hostess, had hired me almost a decade earlier, at the age of fifteen. The space was deep and narrow, with a tarnished tin ceiling, and we had left the front door open, hoping the fresh air would thin out the remaining dinner smells. Every now and then a car would crawl down the wide street outside, its headlights cutting the darkness.

"Thanks, Paula." I counted out my tips on the counter, trying my best to ignore the arcing red welts that were blooming on my forearm. The dinner rush—busier than usual due to Whitman's graduation—had forced me to stack plates, hot from the salamander, directly onto my arm. The walk from the kitchen to the dining room was just long enough that the ceramic burned with every trip.

"You know, you can always come back," said John, the bartender, who released the tap handle and passed me a shifter. We were only allowed one beer per shift, but the rule was rarely followed.

I pressed out my last dollar bill and folded the money into my back pocket. "I know."

But I didn't want to come back. My father, so inexplicably and suddenly gone, haunted every block of sidewalk that framed downtown, even the browning patch of grass in front of the restaurant. The escapes I had relied on—books and research—no longer took me far enough away.

"Even if it's fall and we don't need the staff," John continued, "we'll still hire you."

I tried to tamp down the panic I felt at the prospect of being back in Walla Walla come fall, when I heard Paula say behind me, "We're closed."

I looked over my shoulder to the front door, where a gaggle of girls had gathered, some reading the menu in the vestibule, others having pushed through the screen door, causing the CLOSED sign to slap against the wood.

"But you're still serving," said one, pointing at my beer.

"Sorry. Closed," said John.

"Oh, come on," said another. Their faces were pinked with the warm flush of alcohol, but I could already see the way the night would end, with black smudges below their eyes and random bruises on their legs. Four years at Whitman, and I'd never had a night like that—just shifters and burned skin.

Paula corralled them with her outstretched arms, pushing them back through the front door; I turned my attention back to John.

"Do you know them?" he asked, casually wiping down the wood bar.

I shook my head. It was hard to make friends in college when you were the only student not living in a dorm. Whitman wasn't like a state school where such things were common; it was a small liberal arts college, a small, *expensive* liberal arts college, where everyone lived on campus, or at least started their freshman year that way.

"Town is getting busy. You looking forward to graduation?" He looked at me expectantly, but I met his question with a shrug. I didn't want to talk about Whitman or graduation. I just wanted to take my money home and safely tuck it in with the other tips I had saved. All year, I'd been working five nights a week, even picking up day shifts when my schedule allowed. If I wasn't at the library, I was at work. I knew that the exhaustion wouldn't help me outrun my father's memory, or the rejections, but it did blunt the sharp reality of it.

My mother never said anything about my schedule, or how I only came home to sleep, but then, she was too preoccupied with her own grief and disappointments to confront mine.

"Tuesday is my last day," I said, pushing myself away from the bar and tipping back what little was left in my glass before leaning over the counter and placing it in the dish rack. "Only two more shifts to go."

Paula came up behind me and wrapped her arms around my waist, and as eager as I was for it to be Tuesday, I let myself soften into her, leaning my head against hers.

"You know he's out there, right? He can see this happening for you."

I didn't believe her; I didn't believe anyone who told me there was a magic to it all, a logic, but I forced myself to nod anyway. I had already learned that no one wanted to hear what loss was really like.

Two days later I wore a blue polyester robe and accepted my diploma. My mother was there to take a photograph and attend the Art History department party, held on a wet patch of lawn in front of the semi-Gothic Memorial Building, the oldest on Whitman's campus. I was always acutely aware of how young the building, completed in 1899, was in comparison to those at Harvard or Yale. The Claquato Church, a modest

Methodist clapboard structure built in 1857, was the oldest building I had ever seen in person. Maybe that was why I found it so easy to be seduced by the past—it had eluded me in my youth. Eastern Washington was mostly wheatfields and feed stores, silver silos that never showed their age.

In fact, during my four years at Whitman, I had been the department's only Early Renaissance student. Tucked safely away from the exploits of major artists like Michelangelo and Leonardo, I preferred to study bit characters and forgotten painters who had names like Bembo or Cossa, nicknames like "messy Tom," or "the squinter." I studied duchies and courts, never empires. Courts were, after all, delightfully petty and fascinated by the most outlandish things—astrology, amulets, codes—things I, myself, found it impossible to believe in. But these fascinations also meant I was often alone: in the library, or in an independent study with Professor Lingraf, who lumbered into our meetings at least twenty minutes late, if he remembered them at all.

Despite the impracticality of it all, the overlooked edges of the Renaissance had grabbed me with their gilt and pageantry, their belief in magic, their performances of power. That my own world lacked those things made it an easy choice. I had been warned, however, when I began to think about graduate school, that very few departments would be interested in my work. It was too fringe, too small, not ambitious enough or broad enough. Whitman encouraged its students to reexamine the discipline, become ecocritical, explore the multisensory qualities of human vision. There were times I wondered if the things I studied, the overlooked objects no one wanted, had in fact chosen me, because I often felt powerless to abandon them.

In the shade, my mother moved her arms in circles, her silver bracelets jangling as she spoke to another parent. I looked around the party for Lingraf's shock of white hair, but it was clear he had declined to attend.

Although we had worked together for the better part of four years, he rarely made appearances at departmental functions or spoke about his own research. No one knew what he was working on these days, or when he would finally stop showing up on campus. In some ways, working with Lingraf had been a liability. When other students and even faculty heard he was advising me, they often asked if I was *sure* that was right; he so rarely took on students. But it was. Lingraf had signed off on my thesis, my major completion forms, my letters of recommendation—all of it. This, despite the fact he refused to be part of the Whitman community, preferring instead to work in his office, door closed to distractions, always shuffling his papers into a drawer when anyone arrived.

As I finished scanning the party, Micah Yallsen, a fellow graduating senior, came up alongside me.

"Ann," he said, "I heard you were going to be in New York this summer."

Micah had grown up splitting his time between Kuala Lumpur, Honolulu, and Seattle. The kind of grueling travel schedule that necessitated a private plane, or at the bare minimum first-class accommodations.

"Where are you living?"

"I found a sublet in Morningside Heights."

He speared a wan cube of cheddar off the paper plate in his hand. Whitman never wasted money on catering, and I was sure my mother's department had prepared the grazing trays in-house.

"It's only for three months," I added.

"And after?" he chewed.

"I don't know yet," I said.

"I wish I were taking a gap year," he said, spinning the toothpick in his mouth contemplatively.

Micah had been accepted into MIT's History, Theory and Criticism PhD program, one of the most prestigious in the country. But I imagined his gap year would have looked very different from my own.

"I would have been happy to go straight through," I pointed out.

"It's just so hard to find a place to study Early Ren these days," he said. "Our discipline has shifted. It's for the better, of course."

I nodded. It was easier than protesting. After all, it was a familiar refrain.

"But even so. We need people to continue the work of past generations. And it's good to be interested in something—be *passionate* about something." He speared another cube of cheese. "But you should also think about trends."

I was the sort of person for whom trends had always been intractable. By the time I caught them, they were already wiggling their way out of my grasp. What had appealed to me about academia was that it seemed like a place where I could be blissfully free of trends, where one settled into a subject and never left. Lingraf had only ever published books on the artists of Ravenna; he'd never even had to go as far afield as Venice.

"These things matter now," Micah was saying. "Especially since there's not much new to be done in the fifteenth century, is there? That's pretty well covered ground at this point. No new discoveries. Unless someone tries to reattribute a Masaccio or something." He laughed and took that as his cue to slip into another, more beneficial conversation. His advice doled; his obligation filled. *Here, Ann, let me tell you why those rejections came.* As if I didn't already know.

"Do you need help?" My mother leaned against the doorjamb of my bedroom, where I was pulling handfuls of books from my bookcase and stacking them on the floor.

"I'm fine," I said. But she came into my room anyway, peering into the boxes I had packed and pulling open the drawers of my aging dresser.

"Not much left," she said, so softly that I almost didn't hear her. "Are you sure you don't want to leave a few things here?"

If I had ever felt guilty about leaving her alone in Walla Walla, my own self-preservation had pushed those feelings aside. Even when my father was alive, I had considered my stay in this bedroom temporary. I wanted to see the places he brought home in books from the Penrose Library—the campaniles of Italy, the windswept coastline of Morocco, the twinkling skyscrapers of Manhattan. Places I could only afford to travel to on the page.

The day he died, my father spoke ten languages and could read at least five defunct dialects. Language was his way of venturing beyond the four walls of our home, beyond his own childhood. I regretted that he wasn't here to see me do the thing he had always wanted most. But my mother was afraid of travel—of planes, of places she didn't know, of herself—and so, my father usually chose to stay with her, close to home. I couldn't help but wonder if he had known, if he had known that he would die young, whether he wouldn't have tried harder to see a few more things.

"I wanted to be sure you could rent the room if you needed to." I finished filling a box with books, and the sound of the tape gun startled us both.

"I don't want anyone else living here."

"Someday you might," I said gently.

"No. Why would you bring that up? Where would you stay then, if I rented your room? How could I see you if you didn't come here, come back?"

"You could always come visit," I ventured.

"I can't. You know I can't."

I wanted to argue with her, to look at her and tell her that she could. She *could* get on a plane, and I would be there, waiting for her at the end, but I knew it wasn't worth it. She would never come visit me in New York, and I couldn't stay. If I did, I knew how easy it would be to get caught in the cobwebs, just as she had done.

"I'm still not sure why you want to go in the first place. A big city like that. You'll be much better looked after here. Where people know you. Know us."

It was a conversation I knew well, but I didn't want to spend my last night in the house this way—the way we had spent so many nights after my father died.

"It's going to be fine, Mom," I said, not saying aloud the thing I said to myself. *It has to be.*

She picked up a book that lay on the corner of the bed and thumbed through its pages. My bedroom had just enough space for one bookcase and a dresser, the bed wedged against the wall. "I never realized you had so many of these," she said.

The books took up more space than my clothes. They always had.

"Hazard of the trade," I said, relieved she had changed the subject.

"Okay," she said, putting the book down. "I guess you have to finish."

And I did, squeezing my books into the boxes that would be mailed and zipping my duffel closed. I reached under my bed, feeling around for the cardboard box where I kept my tips. I felt the weight of the money in my lap.

Tomorrow, I would be in New York.

CHAPTER TWO

I'm afraid we can't accommodate you at the Met this summer," Michelle de Forte said.

We were sitting in her office, a name tag with my department and *Ann Stilwell* still affixed to my shirt.

"As you know, you were assigned to work with Karl Gerber." She spoke in a flat, clipped way that had no discernible origin, yet could only have been cultivated in the best schools. "He is preparing for an upcoming exhibition on Giotto, but he had an opportunity in Bergamo and had to leave unexpectedly."

I tried to imagine a job in which one could be summoned to Bergamo on a moment's notice, and then again, to imagine the kind of employer who would allow me to go. On both counts I came up blank.

"It may take him several weeks to finish the work that needs to be done. All that is to say, I'm very sorry, but we no longer have a place for you."

Michelle de Forte, director of Human Resources at the Metropolitan Museum of Art, had taken me aside as soon as I arrived for orientation that morning, leading me away from the room full of carafes of hot coffee and sugared pastries, and into her office, where I sat in a plastic Eames chair. My backpack, still on my lap. She looked at me across the desk, her eyes lifted above the blue Lucite glasses that had slipped low on her nose. Her finger, narrow and birdlike, tapped out a constant metronome.

If she expected me to say something, I didn't know what it was. I was, it seemed, a careless oversight in their summer planning. An administrative inconvenience.

"You can see that we are in an unfortunate position, Ann."

I went to swallow, but my throat was dry. It was all I could do to blink and try not to think of my sublet, of the unopened boxes of books, of the other associates who would be allowed to stay.

"At this point, all our other departmental positions are filled. We don't need doubling up in Ancient, and frankly, you aren't qualified to work in our busier fields."

She wasn't unkind, just blunt. Matter-of-fact. Adding up her needs against my, now sadly, inadequate presence. The glass walls of her office revealed a trickle of arriving staff members, some with one pant leg rolled up, bike helmets still on, others with battered leather satchels and bright red lips—almost all carrying cups of coffee. I had spent the morning reviewing the few items my closet contained before deciding on something I thought was sensible and professional: a cotton button-up and a gray skirt with tennis shoes. My name tag could have read FLYOVER COUNTRY.

In my head, I calculated the loss of the Met stipend against my tips. I estimated I had enough money to stay in New York through the middle of July, and there was always a chance I could find other work, any work, really. There was no need to share the news with my mother. Now that I had arrived, it would take more than a dismissal from Michelle de Forte to make me leave. The words *I understand* were forming on my lips, my hands readying to push myself out of the chair, when a knock came from the window behind me.

A man cupped his hands against the glass and peered in at us. His eyes met mine before he pushed his way through the door, stooping to ensure his head didn't hit the top of the frame.

"Patrick, if you don't mind waiting. I just need to take care of this."

I was the *this*.

Undeterred, Patrick folded himself into the chair next to me. I stole a glance at his profile: a tan face, attractive creases around the eyes and mouth, a beard sprinkled with gray. He was older, but not old, late forties, early fifties. Good-looking, but not obviously so. He extended a hand in my direction, which I shook. It was dry and calloused, pleasant.

"Patrick Roland," he said, before even looking in Michelle's direction, "curator at The Cloisters."

"Ann Stilwell, Renaissance department summer associate."

"Ah. Very good." Patrick wore a thin, wry smile. "What kind of Renaissance?"

"Ferrara. Sometimes Milan."

"Anything in particular?"

"Most recently celestial vaults," I said, thinking of my work with Lingraf. "Renaissance astrology."

"The unlikely Renaissance, then."

The way he looked at me sideways, with half his face but all his attention, made me forget, if only for a moment, that we were sharing the room with someone intent on firing me.

"It takes some bravery to work in a field where the archive is still a necessity," he said. "Where things are rarely translated. Impressive."

"Patrick—" Michelle tried again.

"Michelle." Patrick brought his hands together and faced her fully. "I have bad news." He leaned forward and passed his phone across the desk. "Michael has quit. No notice. He took a job with a tech company's arts and culture division. Apparently, he's already on his way to California. He sent me the email last week, but I didn't see it until this morning."

Michelle read what I could only assume was Michael's resignation letter on Patrick's phone, occasionally flicking up and down.

"We were already understaffed before this. As you know, we haven't been able to find a suitable associate curator, and Michael had stepped into that role. Although he was by no means qualified. That left Rachel doing double duty on everything, and I'm worried we're putting too much on her. We have some extra hands in Education that can help, but it's simply not enough."

Michelle passed the phone back to Patrick and settled a stack of papers on her desk.

"I was hoping Karl could come help us for a few weeks until we can get someone," he said.

Throughout the exchange I had sat quietly, hoping that if I didn't move, Michelle might forget I was there, forget that she told me to go.

"Karl has gone to Bergamo for the summer, Patrick," Michelle said. "I'm sorry. We don't have anyone to spare. The Cloisters will have to make its own provisions. We've been quite generous giving you the budget to pay Rachel through the year already. Now if you don't mind—" She gestured toward me.

Patrick leaned back in his chair and gave me an appraising look.

"Can you send me her?" he asked, hooking a thumb in my direction.

"I cannot," Michelle said. "Ann was about to leave us for the summer."

Patrick leaned over the arm of his chair, his torso now so close that I could feel his body heat. It was a beat before I realized I had been holding my breath.

"Do you want to come work for me?" he said. "It wouldn't be here. It would be at The Cloisters. It's north, along the highway. Where are you living? Would it be an inconvenience?"

"Morningside Heights," I said.

"Good. You're right on the A train and can take it the whole way. Probably less walking than crossing the park, anyway."

"Patrick," Michelle broke in, "we don't have the budget to send you Ann. Rachel is already taking your summer associate budget."

He held up a finger and pulled out his phone, scrolling through the contacts until he found the number he needed. On the other end, someone picked up.

"Hello. Yes. *Herr Gerber*. Look, it's important. May I have your associate—" He looked at me expectantly and snapped his fingers.

"Ann Stilwell," I said.

"May I have Ann Stilwell for the summer? Who is she? I think she was meant to be your summer associate, Karl, but you left." He looked to me for confirmation, and I nodded. They switched to German for a few minutes until Patrick laughed and handed the phone to Michelle.

Mostly, she listened. But every few minutes she would say things like, "Only if you're sure" and "You'll lose the budget money." At the end, she was simply nodding and making agreeable sounds. "Okay . . . Mmhmm . . . All right." She handed the phone back to Patrick, who laughed loudly and repeated the word *ciao* two or three times with a wonderful trill.

"Okay." He rose from the chair and tapped me on the shoulder. "Come with me, Ann Stilwell."

"Patrick," Michelle protested, "the girl hasn't even agreed!"

He looked at me, a single eyebrow raised.

"Yes, of course," I said, the words tumbling out of me.

"Good," he said, brushing at a stray wrinkle in his shirt. "Now, let's get this over with and get you out of here."

While Michelle had been busy explaining to me why I couldn't stay, the room had filled with summer associates who could. The program had a reputation for selecting only a handful of graduating seniors from the best schools and working swiftly and silently behind the scenes to ensure their future successes. When my acceptance arrived, I had assumed it was a mistake, but by the end of that summer I would learn there were few mistakes in life.

The full-time staff had been pressed into attendance, and even though they did not wear name tags, I recognized a few of them: the young associate curator of Islamic art who had come directly from Penn, the curator of ancient Roman art who was a fixture on the ancient civilizations series produced by PBS. Everyone beautiful and sharp and inaccessible in person. The weight of my backpack hung more awkwardly against my hips when I realized I was the only attendee who still carried one.

"I'll be back in a few minutes," said Patrick. "Get some coffee"— he pointed at the carafes—"then we'll head up to The Cloisters." He scanned the room, tall enough to easily note everyone in attendance. "Rachel isn't here yet. But I'm sure you know a few of the other associates, right?"

I was about to explain that I didn't when Patrick walked off, throwing an arm around the shoulders of an older man in a worn tweed jacket. I could feel a prickle of sweat working its way down my side; I clamped an arm against my body to arrest its progress.

This was why I had arrived early, of course. So that I wouldn't need to break into a conversation. When you were the first to arrive, people had no choice but to talk to you. By the time a group gathered, I would have been happily ensconced in a circle of similar early arrivals. Instead, I hooked my thumbs into my backpack straps and looked around the room, trying to pretend I was looking for a friend. Although it was a welcome breakfast, it was not, I realized, a meet and greet. Looking at the circles of associates, the familiar way they spoke to each other, it was clear they had already had opportunities to get to know one another in various ways over the last four years—symposia and lectures that led to dinner parties and boozy late-night musings. I inched myself closer to a group so I could at least hear their conversation.

"I grew up in LA," one girl was saying, "and it's not what people think. Everyone assumes it's all celebrities and juice cleanses and woo. But we have a real arts scene. It's thriving."

People in the circle were nodding.

"In fact, last summer, I worked for Gagosian in Beverly Hills and we had both Jenny Saville and Richard Prince give artist talks. But it's not just big galleries," she continued, sipping from a hand-blown glass tumbler.

I used the pause to edge my shoulder into the circle and was grateful when the girl to my left took a step back.

"We have experimental spaces and community arts projects too. A friend even runs a food and contemporary art collaborative called Active Cultures."

Now, I could make out the girl's name tag: Stephanie Pearce, Contemporary Painting.

"When I was in Marfa last summer—" began another member of the circle. But the sentence died on their lips as Stephanie Pearce turned her attention to the entrance, where Patrick was in close conference with a girl whose hair was such a pale shade of blond, it could only be real. Across the room, the girl looked squarely at me before pinning a strand behind her ear and whispering something to Patrick. Whatever he responded caused her to laugh, and the way her body shook, all flat angles with a hint of softness, made me acutely aware of my own.

When I was younger, I used to imagine what it would be like to be that beautiful. All women do, I think. But breasts never arrived, my face never caught up with my nose. My dark, curly hair was more unruly than romantic, and the uneven freckles that spread across my face and arms were darkly colored from summers spent in the eastern Washington sun. The only thing I had to my credit were a pair of large, wide-set eyes, but they were not enough to make up for all the other plainness I enjoyed.

"Is that Rachel Mondray?" the girl next to me asked. Stephanie Pearce and a few others in the circle nodded.

"I met her during my prospective student weekend at Yale," said Stephanie. "She just graduated but has already been working at The Cloisters for almost a year. She was hired after spending last summer in Italy at the Carrozza Collection."

"Really?" asked someone else in the circle.

The Carrozza Collection was a private archive and museum not far from Lago di Como that was invitation only. It was rumored to contain some of the finest examples of Renaissance manuscripts anywhere in the world.

"Apparently the Carrozza offered her a full-time job after graduation, but she turned them down." Stephanie Pearce looked at me and added, "For Harvard."

While Stephanie talked, I watched Rachel make her way across the room. There had been rich girls at Whitman, of course. Girls whose parents had private planes and vacation homes in Sun Valley. But I'd never really known those girls, only known about them—rumors of impossible lives I dared not imagine. Rachel didn't need to be invited to join our circle, but rather materialized within it, naturally.

"I haven't seen you since spring, Steph," Rachel said, looking around at everyone. "What did you decide?"

"I ultimately chose Yale."

"You'll love it," said Rachel with such warmth it seemed she meant it.

"I'm going to Columbia," the girl next to me whispered.

I couldn't help but envy the people around me, their futures—at least for the next few years—secure in blue-chip graduate programs. Briefly, I worried that someone might ask me about my plans for the following year, but it was clear no one cared. A fact for which I was both grateful and ashamed.

"Ann," said Rachel, reading my name tag. "Patrick told me we'll be working together this summer." She stepped across the circle to give me a hug. Not a limp hug, but a tight one that allowed me to feel how soft she was, how citrusy she smelled, with notes of bergamot and black tea. She was cool to the touch, and again I felt the sweaty areas of my body come to attention, the coarseness of my clothes. When I tried to pull away, she held me for a beat longer, long enough for me to worry that she could feel the anxiety, imprinted hot and slick on my skin.

Everyone in the circle appraised the interaction, the way one might assess the performance of a racehorse under the command of a new jockey.

"It'll just be the two of us," she said, finally pulling away. "No one else ever gets up to The Cloisters. But it's a nice place to be abandoned to."

"I thought you were Renaissance?" said Stephanie, looking for confirmation at my name tag.

"Yes, but that's just what we need," said Rachel. "So Patrick made sure that we scooped Ann right up. Stole her from all of you at the Met."

I was grateful to not have to explain my situation in greater detail.

"Well, come on then," Rachel said, reaching out and pinching my arm. "We should go."

I clasped my hand over the spot, and despite the heat and pain that ran toward my collarbone, I was surprised to find myself enjoying the flush of it all—the attention, the pinch, the fact I wouldn't be here with Stephanie Pearce. All because I had decided to sit in Michelle's office just a moment longer, just long enough for Patrick to walk by and knock.

CHAPTER THREE

I don't think I'll ever forget what it was like to arrive that June day at The Cloisters. Behind us was the congestion of Museum Mile—that stretch of Fifth Avenue where the Frick, the Met, and the Guggenheim were packed with tour groups and waiting taxis, camp children and first-time visitors, all agog at the marble facades—and ahead of us was the greenery of Fort Tryon Park at the city's northern edge. When the museum first came into view, I did my best not to tumble into Rachel's lap as I leaned across the car to get a better look; it never crossed my mind to feign indifference. Here, it was as if we had left the city entirely, taken an unmarked exit and found ourselves under a collaged network of downy maple leaves. The road to The Cloisters curved up a gentle hill, revealing a gray stone wall, overgrown with moss and ivy, that unspooled through a staccato of tree trunks. A square campanile with slender Romanesque windows peeked above the canopy of trees. I had never been to Europe, but I imagined it would look something like this: shady and cobbled and Gothic. The kind of place that reminded you how temporary the human body was, but how enduring stone.

The Cloisters, I knew, had been brought into being—like so many institutions—by John D. Rockefeller Jr. The robber baron's son had transformed sixty-six isolated acres and a small collection of medieval art into a fully realized medieval monastery. Crumbling remnants of twelfth-century abbeys and priories had been imported throughout the 1930s from Europe and rebuilt under the watchful eye of architect Charles

Collens. Buildings that had been left to the ravages of weather and wars were reassembled and polished to a new-world sheen—entire twelfth-century chapels restored, marble colonnades buffed to their original gloss.

I followed Patrick and Rachel up a cobblestone path that snaked around the back of the museum, and under a natural hallway of tumbling holly bushes whose prickly leaves and dark red berries snagged at my hair. Like a true cloister, it was silent save for the sound of our footsteps. We walked until we found ourselves on top of the ramparts, where our progress was blocked by a large stone arch that framed a black metal gate; I half expected an armored guard from the thirteenth century would greet us.

"Don't worry," Patrick said. "The gate is to keep people out. Not lock you in."

On the roughly hewn stone blocks that made up the building's facade I could just make out the places where they had been cut, riffles where the bronze head of an axe had sliced through. Patrick pulled out a key card and swiped it against a thin gray pad of plastic that blended in so well with the existing stonework, I hadn't noticed it. Hidden in the stone wall was a small, rounded door that Rachel held open; we had to duck to enter.

"Normally, you'll enter through the front, but this is more fun," he said from behind me. "You'll discover more hidden passageways and overlooked corners the longer you're here."

On the other side of the door was a garden courtyard that teemed with pink and white flowers, delicate brushes of silvery sage. It was one of the green spaces, one of the cloisters, for which the museum had been named. There was a hush in the air that even the insects seemed to respect, the only sound a soft buzzing and the occasional slap of shoes along the limestone floors. I wanted to pause and take in the plants that spilled out of pots and over beds, reach out and touch the stone walls that ringed the space, to feel with my fingers the realness of this world that looked like a dream. I longed to close my eyes and inhale the mixture of lavender and thyme until it erased the smell of Michelle de Forte's office, but Rachel and Patrick were already moving.

"Typically," said Rachel, "any square medieval garden surrounded by walkways like this one was called a cloister. This is the Cuxa Cloister, named for the Benedictine monastery Saint-Michel-de-Cuxa in the Pyrenees. The footprint of the garden was originally laid out in 878 BCE, and when the cloisters were built, the builders in New York maintained the original north axis. We have three other gardens like this."

The walkway was flanked by marble columns, each topped with carved capitals that revealed eagles unfurling their wings, lions poised on their haunches, even a mermaid holding her tail; between the columns, framed arches were decorated with palmettes and bits of stone lattice. And despite the number of pictures I had seen of medieval cathedrals, I was unprepared for The Cloisters' overwhelming scale, for how intricately everything was carved, for how many sculpted and painted eyes were peering back at me, for the way the stone kept the garden cool. It was the kind of world that would continue to offer up surprises, no matter how familiar I became with it.

I followed Rachel and Patrick through a set of doors at the end of the cloister into the museum itself. The room, a shocking medieval world in miniature: thirteenth-century wood beams crisscrossed the ceiling and massive stained glass windows were set in the walls. Cases full of goldwork glinted with precious stones—blood-red rubies and sapphires as dark as a moonless sea. An enamel miniature caught my eye—its colors vibrant despite its age—and I studied its case, my fingers at the edge of the glass. These were the objects, so small in execution, that I had always believed might make me bigger by association.

"Come on," said Rachel, pausing to wait for me at the top of a set of stairs. Patrick was already out of sight.

There was no way not to be overwhelmed by the jewel box that was The Cloisters—it wasn't like the Metropolitan, where your eyes could rest. The entire space was the work. I was grateful when the stairs led down to the lobby and main entrance, where visitors handled maps and audio guides, pointing out which galleries housed the most well-known works. Admission to The Cloisters, like the Met, was free for New York residents.

"Moira," said Patrick, walking toward a woman whose black hair was feathered gray around the temples. "This is Ann. She's joining us for the summer."

"You should know," Moira said, coming out from behind the information desk, "that Leo was smoking in the garden shed again. I could smell it. And if I could smell it, I'm sure visitors could too. He's still on museum property. Smoking isn't allowed. It's the fourth time already this month."

Patrick brushed off Moira's concerns with the skill of someone used to brokering institutional peace. "Ann, meet Moira, our front desk manager."

"And docent program coordinator," she added, barely looking at me before turning her attention back to Patrick.

"She does an excellent job," said Patrick.

"I was thinking," said Moira, placing a hand on Patrick's sleeve, "that we could install smoke detectors in the garden maintenance area. That might—"

"She's always like this," said Rachel, leaning in to whisper in my ear. "If you're late, just know she'll remember by exactly how many minutes."

It felt good to be conspiratorial with someone, even if only for a moment, her breath hot on my neck, burning the words just between us.

"Moira," said Patrick, "we're on our way to security. I just wanted to introduce Ann. Do you think we could—"

"Talk about this later?"

Patrick acquiesced. "I'll have someone talk to Leo."

"See that you do."

We continued to the security office, a drab metal door where Patrick finally left us. But not before he offered me a rueful smile and a wink. For a moment, I thought I saw his hand come to rest on the small of Rachel's back, but it happened so quickly—as had the morning, our arrival, our trip through the galleries—I couldn't be sure. I didn't have time to smile before my photograph was taken, a key card issued, and Rachel moved on, down the hallway, deeper into the staff offices.

"You're coming, right?" she asked over her shoulder while I was still struggling to clip my key card to my skirt. I tried not to run after her.

The offices of The Cloisters were a labyrinth of stone passageways and Gothic doors, darkly lit by wall sconces that were placed a little too far apart, leaving shadowy gaps. Rachel introduced me to the Education department, where leaded glass windows overlooking the Hudson were propped open. From there, she showed me the staff kitchen, which was surprisingly modern and full of European stainless-steel appliances.

Next was the conservation room, where a team of preparators in smocks and white gloves were absorbed in the slow process of scraping away centuries of varnish from a painting whose gold, filigree frame had been removed and set aside. Then, there was a room full of fluorescent lights and storage drawers—*accessions*, Rachel said—where thousands of smaller artworks were housed like scientific specimens. I filed away as much as I could: faces, the number of doors between the kitchen and the education offices, where I had last seen a bathroom. And finally, after we curved back around toward the lobby, Rachel took me into an additional room full of stacks, all tightly closed, their crank wheels ready to be sprung open.

"The stacks adjoin the library through a back door," said Rachel, "but the library, where we work, is separate from the staff offices."

We walked through the stacks, the rubber soles of my shoes squeaking on the terrazzo floors. She leaned on a heavy wooden door that opened onto the library—a long, low room with rib vaults that intersected above huge oak tables and chairs upholstered with green leather and big brass buttons. It was the kind of library that belonged in a lavish country house, with stained glass windows and walls of bound books, some titles written by hand onto the fabric bindings.

"Patrick's office is the door at the end." Rachel gestured at a wooden door decorated with curved ironwork depicting two deer, their antlers locked in combat. "But you and I will work here, in the library itself. The Cloisters doesn't have enough office space to accommodate us elsewhere."

Looking around the library, I couldn't imagine having to work within the four white walls of a regular office when this was a possibility. For years, I had lingered over the images, not just of paintings, but of archives—dimly lit rooms full of books and papers, the material history I was desperate to hold in my hands, see with my own eyes. And here was the Cloisters library in person. True, there were no rare manuscripts—although there were plenty on display in the galleries, and still more conserved in accessions—but it was a space, full of first editions and rare titles, that revered the dead as much as I did, and in that, I felt like it was home.

I could feel Rachel watching me take it in. It was impossible to affect the nonchalance she had shown throughout the whole tour, as if all of this—the rib vaults and leather—were simply normal. De rigueur. I pulled out a chair and set down my bag.

"Don't you want to see the collection?" she asked. "This"—she waved her hand at the library—"is just the workroom."

She didn't wait for me to say yes—maybe the answer was already plain on my face—but opened the library's main doors, where I was instantly blinded by the sunlight.

"This is the Trie Cloister," she said.

The garden was anchored by a stone crucifix at the center and surrounded by a profusion of wildflowers, some so small and unassuming that they had found their way into the creases between the brick walkway that circled it.

"It was planted to resemble the carpet of flowers you'll see on the fifteenth-century unicorn tapestries," she explained. "And there's a café at the far end. They'll open for lunch in a few hours. Excellent coffee and salads."

"Do we get a discount?" I asked, immediately regretting it.

Rachel looked at me as we headed toward another door. "Of course."

I let myself exhale, realizing that I'd been afraid to breathe since arriving at The Cloisters, worried that if I took up too much space, they might change their minds.

"Patrick told me what happened with Michelle," Rachel said, lowering her voice as we walked into a room whose soaring ceilings revealed an entire medieval chapel in miniature. The red stained glass windows cast pink illuminations on the sand-colored floor. "I can't believe she did that. Brought you all the way out here, from where was it? Portland?"

"Washington," I said, hoping I wasn't flushing with the embarrassment I felt correcting her. Something about Rachel made me desperate for her approval; if I could have made myself from Portland in that moment, I would have. Maybe it was the way she carried herself, always pushing forward. Even when one of the restorers had told us we couldn't come in, Rachel just shrugged, holding the door open so I could see it all—the gallon-size bottles of turpentine and linseed oil.

"I had a friend from Spence who went to Reed. Sasha Zakharov?"

"I don't know anyone from Reed. It's pretty far from Whitman," I said.

"Oh."

Rachel didn't seem embarrassed by her mistake, and I wondered how it must feel to be so secure in a position that it didn't matter if you listened to your colleague's corrections. We had stopped in front of two stone caskets, nestled into niches in the wall.

"I want you to know," I said, perhaps a little too breathlessly, "even though I came to work in the Renaissance department, I have a lot of background in medieval. And anything I don't know, I can set aside the time to learn."

I didn't know why I was desperate to get this out. Rachel hadn't asked what I studied, nor had she expressed any doubt in my skill set.

Rachel dismissed my concerns. "I'm sure you'll be fine."

I didn't say anything, hoping she would continue.

"Patrick doesn't take on just anyone." She looked at me, for the first time, assessing what she saw, registering my shoes, my clothes, my freckles. "He must have known you would work out for us."

We were standing in front of the tombs while visitors milled around, inspecting wall labels.

"Is it your first time in New York?" Rachel asked, her eyes meeting mine.

"Yes." Although I wished in that moment it weren't true.

"Really?" she said, arms crossed. "Any initial opinions?"

"I don't know that I've seen enough to have opinions. I've only been here for three days."

I had spent the first day unpacking my bag and washing a sticky substance off all the dishes and pans in my sublet. The next day, I learned the commute I would never again use—taking the subway from uptown to the Eighty-First Street Station, and walking across Central Park. Despite the fact that Manhattan was known for its soaring concrete and glass skyscrapers, I had spent most of my time in lush parks.

"You must have had opinions before you arrived, though?"

"Well, yes—" My mother's concerns replayed silently through my head—the bigness of the city, the impersonality of it, my inability to handle it.

"And is it living up to those?"

"To be honest, it's totally different."

"That's the city. Both everything you imagine it to be and nothing at all what you expected. It can give you the world or take it away in an instant." She smiled at me, glancing down at my shoes, which had been squeaking on the floors since we arrived, before making her way to the next room and motioning me to follow.

"What do you think of the city?" I said, trying to keep the conversation going and trailing in her wake.

"I grew up here."

"Oh, I didn't realize."

"That's okay. Spence? I thought you would put two and two together."

"I don't know what Spence is."

"That's probably for the best," she said with a laugh. "We all have complicated relationships with our hometowns."

We had entered a room with a glass case full of enamel miniatures. Shiny renderings of Jonah being swallowed by the whale, Eve biting into an apple so red it glistened. These little masterpieces, over eight hundred years old.

Rachel waved at the guard, who was moving to his next station. "When does Matteo's summer camp start, Louis?" she called after him.

He stopped shy of his post. "Next week. I think he's driving his mother insane. Thank you again for watching him last Saturday."

Rachel waved him off. "We just walked around the park. Spent a lot of time with the boats."

I tried to imagine Rachel babysitting but couldn't.

"He loves those boats," said Louis.

"So do I," said Rachel. "Louis, by the way, this is Ann. She's going to be here through the summer. Louis is the head of security."

Louis walked toward us and extended a hand. "Just filling in today in the galleries."

I shook it and said hello.

"We have one more stop," Rachel said, wrapping a hand around my wrist and pulling me away from Louis.

As soon as we were out of the room, she whispered in my ear: "Louis's son was such a shit. I only agreed to do it because he covers for me with Moira when I'm late, or when my smoking accidentally sets off the fire alarm."

We moved through another set of galleries, already full of visitors who were drinking in the cool, dark interiors where depictions of magical beasts mixed with the severed fingers of saints. I was drawn to these objects, to their strangeness. I stopped in front of a reliquary of Saint Sebastian, a statue of his torso painted cream and red, his sides shot through with arrows. In a little glass box in the center of the statue, his wrist bone—or someone's wrist bone—was visible.

Rachel had stopped at a glass case full of individually painted tarot cards; one depicted a skeleton on horseback, decorated with gold chains—Death. Another showed a plump, winged child—a putto—carrying the sun above his head, its gold rays cutting across the card. The deck was incomplete, but the wall label next to it indicated they were from the late fifteenth century. And although they were unknown to me, their imagery was familiar—a set of symbols that had haunted the fringes of my research over the years. Images I had always been curious about but never had the time or resources to pursue.

"I've been bouncing between The Cloisters, the Morgan Library, and the Beinecke for years now," Rachel said, "studying the history of tarot. So, like you, I'm not strictly a medievalist. After all, the history of tarot doesn't really begin until the early Renaissance." She didn't bother to look at me before continuing. "The Cloisters makes an effort to elevate works of art like this. Down at the Met, it's all big paintings and big names. But to work in anonymity and produce something this exquisite"—she closed her eyes for a moment—"is real artistry."

It struck me as romantic, the way she talked about the cards, as if squares of painted vellum were simply dormant, waiting for us to shake them awake. When she opened her eyes, I quickly looked away, hoping she wouldn't notice I had been staring.

"This is what Patrick needs help with," she said, glancing at the tarot cards. "We're preparing an exhibition on divination. On the techniques and artworks that were used to tell the future."

I looked down at the Queen of Staves. Clothed in deep navy, her bodice dotted with gold-leaf stars, she sat upon a throne, a knobby stick raised in her hand. I ventured, "It was a period when everyone was fascinated with the idea of fate."

"Yes. Exactly. Was your fate already written? Was it predestined? Or, could you alter its course?"

"And, did you have the free will to do so?"

"Right. The ancient Romans were so afraid of the power of fate that they worshiped the goddess Fortuna. Fortuna—fate, fortune—was the center of civic, private, and religious life. Pliny always said, 'Fortune is the only God whom everyone invokes.' The Renaissance never got free from that obsession, either."

"Because," I said, "in a period of constant conflict, knowing the future, or believing that you could, was wildly powerful."

"That belief can be a burden, too," said Rachel, so softly I almost didn't catch it. Then she moved away from the glass case and looked over her shoulder at me. "You coming?"

CHAPTER FOUR

During that first week at The Cloisters, filled as it was with the gentle patter of afternoon rains, the scent of wet stone and blooming herbs, Patrick made it clear how much would be expected of us, of me. His exhibition was only in its planning stages, which meant that the bulk of research—the foundational material that Patrick required to identify artworks and request loans—fell to us. We had only through August to assemble it all, a heavy ask I was eager to prove I could answer. And while Patrick was firm about deadlines, he was patient in the way he introduced me to the material, to the place itself.

"These are the lists you'll be working with," he said, setting down a sheaf of papers and pulling a chair close to mine at the library table where we worked. "Rachel, of course, already has copies."

I leafed through them. They contained divination practices known in the ancient world, everything from cleromancy, or the casting of lots, to pyromancy. Some terms on the list, like augury, I only knew as a word used to describe something that portended or foreshadowed. I would learn, however, that the original definition of augury was the practice of using bird formations—flocks and migrations—to tell the future. There were lists of documents and authors that needed to be pulled from the library and scoured for mentions of divination, as well as a separate section that listed artworks Patrick was considering for the show. I noted several of the works were tarot cards.

"We'll meet once a week to go over your progress. In the meantime, Rachel should be able to help you with any questions you might have."

I paged through the material again. Even dividing the work between the two of us, there was no escaping the fact that there were thousands of pages to read, hundreds of works of art to review, dozens of divination practices to explore.

"Ann," he said. He was still sitting next to me, the arms of our chairs touching. Across the table, Rachel worked her way through the diaries of Girolamo Cardano, the famed Renaissance astrologer. Although every few minutes, she stole a glance across the expanse of rough-hewn oak that separated us, to where Patrick and I were in conference. "I don't bring people into The Cloisters lightly. We're like a family here, and your success is our success. If you do a good job here this summer, we can help you."

I was facing Patrick, but could feel Rachel watching us at the edge of my vision.

"What do you want us to help you accomplish, Ann?"

I'd never had someone ask me so bluntly about my goals, let alone so clearly offer to help me attain them. While I scrambled to find the right thing to say, Patrick sat companionably with the silence, hands folded in his lap, his eyes watching my every fidget.

Finally, I said, "I'm here because I want to be a scholar."

It was the truth, after all. And more palatable than the other truths I wasn't ready to share: that after last year, Walla Walla would always feel like death to me, that I didn't have any other options, that I wasn't confident I would be able to survive in a job that demanded I live in the present. That, on some level, I was doing all of this for my father, for us.

"We can help with that," Patrick said, starting what he was about to say by deliberately drawing out his vowels. "Introduce you to the right people. Get you the right letters of recommendation. I'd even be happy to read your work before you submit it and offer suggestions. And while scholarship is a valuable and important thing, it cannot be the only thing. It does not sustain us. Not really. Even though we wish it could. I've seen you out in the galleries, Ann. The way you spend your time with just one work; you look lovingly, slowly. You are more than a scholar."

Patrick, I realized, had a way of stripping away the pleasant surfaces of human interaction. There was an intensity to the way he spoke and observed, but he was unfailingly polite, always ensuring you were at ease. So while I felt like he was probing beyond the professional facade I wanted to present, it wasn't uncomfortable. There was a relief in laying it bare to him. To Rachel, even. And of course, he was right. All of this—the place, the objects, the magic of the past, the scholarship—was about more than the work. It was transformation I was after. A way to become someone else.

Before I could say as much, he continued, "You know, Ann. After you came up here, I decided to take a look at your application. Just to be sure that we were using your skills in the best way possible, of course. And I was very surprised. You say you grew up in Walla Walla?"

"Yes."

"But you speak six languages?"

"Seven," I said. "Although three of them are dead. Technically I read Latin, ancient Greek, and a thirteenth-century Ligurian dialect from Genoa. I speak Italian, German, and Neapolitan. And English, of course."

"Nevertheless, this is remarkable."

"There wasn't much else to do in Walla Walla," I said with a shrug. "Besides study. And work."

I was used to downplaying the influence my father's fascination with language had had on my life. Parsing long-lost languages and learning their secret codes was something we had shared, just the two of us. It was never in the service of advancing my career. Or his. And in moments like this, our love of languages felt like a secret I wanted to keep for myself, even if Patrick was intent on teasing everything else from me.

"And you worked with Richard. Didn't you?"

I had never heard anyone call my advisor by his first name, and for a moment I struggled to place who Richard might be. But of course Patrick had read my application materials, had seen Richard Lingraf's letter of recommendation.

"I did. All four years."

"I knew Richard, once. Long ago. When I was a graduate student at Penn, he was doing some very daring work at Princeton. You were lucky to have a mentor like him. So curious and so talented." And then, more to himself than to me, he said, "I still wonder why he went to Whitman. What an odd place to end up for him."

"He always said he preferred the weather."

"Yes, well," said Patrick, his fingers quickly drumming on the table. "I'm sure that was part of it." After a beat, he added, "I can't guarantee you anything, Ann. But if your work is as good as I expect it to be, then I've little doubt that The Cloisters can help you end up somewhere you're happy to be."

"Thank you." I hesitated. Throughout the whole conversation Rachel had been there, listening. I wanted to let it go at that, to thank Patrick for his offer of support, but I needed to ask just one thing, even if it would put paid to the nonchalance I had been trying to affect around Rachel since arriving at the museum.

"What about after this summer? I don't yet have a job lined up, but I would love to stay in the city. And here, if you need me." I looked across the table and met Rachel's gaze, trying my best to lift my chin a little higher, hold her eyes a little longer.

"We'll see what happens," Patrick said. "Who's to say what the future holds?"

I noticed then that Patrick was weaving something between his fingers, something he must have pulled from his pocket—a piece of red ribbon—a kind of reflexive habit, a meditation.

I took another look through the lists he had handed me.

"We need you here, Ann. We need the help," he said, searching my face. "Don't forget that. You're not charity."

I was, I think, a little in love with him right away. The way he solicited our opinions on his research, the way he valued my language skills, often handing off translations to me, fully confident in my abilities. Even the way he held the door for us and brought us coffees in the afternoon; it was the first time anyone in a position of power had been genuinely kind to me. And already, he paid me more attention than most of the boys I had known in college. When I finally got around to reading his essay on medieval calendrical systems, I shouldn't have been surprised to find it completely groundbreaking, but I was. I tried to control the color that came to my cheeks every time he talked to me, but there was little I could do. I tried, in those early days, to figure out if he was involved with anyone—romantically. But the only evidence I ever saw was a soft arm on the metal windowsill of his car's passenger seat. Just an arm, no face.

My mother's voice came through the phone, edged with a familiar thinness.

"There's no way I can manage like this any longer."

The death of my father had unmoored her. After he was gone, the tight structure of our daily life got looser: the milk expired and was not replaced, our small patch of lawn overgrew, my mother stopped changing her sheets. And then, there would be a day during which she would whip everything back to the way it was before, a sudden tightening. But the loosening would come back. A slow easing at first, and then a swift, remorseless undoing—again and again.

Those days, the days of tightening, were preceded by my mother despairing over the state of the house. *Why are there coffee cups here? Doesn't anyone put anything away? How can you expect me to live like this?* Only, my mother did expect me to live like that. Anytime I picked things up she would cry from the other room: *What happened to that water glass?* or, *Why did you throw out the milk?* It was as if, by leaving things, she could slow time, rein it in. But that was the hardest thing about death: the unrelenting march of time forward, away from the person you've lost.

"It's everywhere, Ann," she said, the pitch in her voice getting higher, tighter. "His stuff. His shirts, his clothes, his shoes, his papers. I can't do it. It's too much. This place is a mess. He left it a mess, you know?"

I was doing my dishes and drying them with the only dish towel that my sublet had provided, the phone cradled against my cheek. I was too cheap to buy paper towels.

"Maybe it's time to donate some of it, Mom?" I had ventured this before. And while she always said yes in the moment, in the coming days, she would back away, leave everything as it had been the day he died. A memorial of half-used shaving creams and dirty socks.

"That's what I'm going to do. I'm going to donate it. All of it. And everything else, I'm going to throw away."

"Mm-hmm." I walked over to my air conditioner, which had developed a deathly rattle, and hit it on the side, hard. The force seemed to settle the frequency back to white noise.

"I don't want you to complain when it's all gone. When you come home and it's all gone. I don't want to hear about it."

"You won't, Mom, I promise." I never wanted to see the house again.

"Maybe I'll send you a few things in New York." She was mostly talking to herself now. "I don't even know what to send. It's all junk, you know? He just left us with junk. Do you really want that? What do you want? Any of it?"

I thought about my dad's things and how most of the time my mom moved through them silent and oblivious to their presence. It was only in these moments, when the house seemed to startle her awake, that she even noticed his books and papers and clothes, the way he still clung to our space.

"Sure, Mom. I'll take some of Dad's stuff. Send me whatever you think I'd like, okay?"

I could hear her on the other end of the line rummaging around: glass, paper, plastic, all pinging together somewhere in the house that had once been a home before it became a mausoleum.

It hadn't always been this way. There had been a time when the house was full of conversation and warmth and my father's low chuckle, full of humor and surprise. But my father was like the putty that had filled in the sharp cracks between my mother and me, the places where we didn't fit, and without that putty, we kept running up against each other, all hard angles and brittleness.

"Mom, I have to go. It's getting late. We're three hours ahead, remember?" I waited for her to respond. But all I could hear was the rustling, her constant movement, her breath distracted and fast into the phone, and so, I hung up.

By the end of my second week, it was clear that no matter how much I tried to emulate the way Rachel dressed and the conscientious way she handled old texts, I wouldn't measure up. For every beautifully unwrinkled linen jumper Rachel wore, I could barely pull together two items that matched. Against the luxury of her fabrics and accessories, everything of mine felt like a dull imitation. Even the gentle deference she showed to Moira and Louis, I couldn't match without it ringing false in my own ears.

I imagined that when museum visitors saw the two of us together—as we almost always were that summer—they pitied me, her effortlessness rubbing up against my desperation. How could they not? Rachel two steps ahead, Rachel confidently redirecting people who had lost their way, Rachel whose movements were silent, while the cheapness of my slacks made chafing sounds every time we walked through the galleries. And if the sound was loud to me, I couldn't help but wonder if others noticed it, too.

It didn't help that I usually arrived at work already sweating through my shirt and sometimes even my pants, my hair working to escape my simple efforts at containment. My commute wasn't long—Patrick was right, it was faster than going all the way to Fifth Avenue—but by the time I had walked the streets of Morningside Heights on my way to the A train, stopping only for a coffee at the corner bodega, and then up the winding paths of Fort Tryon Park, to one of the highest points in Manhattan, the humidity had done its damage. My body, unused to a heat so cloying, reacted violently, profusely, almost in apology.

At the end of my first week, Moira had looked me up and down upon arrival and told me that I could always take the shuttle that ran every fifteen minutes from the station to the museum. Also, it was air-conditioned. As grateful as I was for the tip, the way Moira had taken a step back when she saw me, flushed and sweating, my hair growing increasingly wild, did not go unnoticed. Rachel, of course, emerged untroubled from an unobtrusive town car that deposited her at the top of the upper driveway, in front of the metal gate, every morning at nine.

But even if the humidity was overwhelming—particularly for me, a girl whose skin was used to the arid fields of eastern Washington—the museum itself was full of cool breezes that made their way off the Hudson River, and ruffled the canopies of elm trees, like a giant carpet being snapped in the air. It felt more like working on a private estate than in a public institution. One that Patrick oversaw from the privacy of the library.

"It was his first job," Rachel told me at the end of that second week, "right out of grad school. Not that he needed one. A job, of course.

"Patrick's grandfather was involved in quarrying upstate," Rachel continued. "The stones they used to build the ramparts and fill in the gaps at The Cloisters were all quarried by his grandfather's company. It was the largest private quarry operation in New York. Until the 1960s, when Cargill bought it. Patrick still lives in the family home, in Tarrytown. He drives in every morning."

I tried to imagine a young Patrick at his grandfather's quarry, his glowing tan a stark contrast to the damp and darkly terraced hillsides. Sometimes a child's resistance to the legacy of their family was almost molecular, as if their body became allergic to the landscapes and environs of home; other times they settled in, sinking back into the fabric, the familiar warp and weft of tradition. I had always been the former, and perhaps Patrick was too.

Rachel interrupted my reverie. "Should we get a coffee, then?"

I had been packing lunches and not eating them after I noticed that Rachel rarely took lunch, but rather, only took two cigarettes and caffeine. It surprised me how quickly my hunger passed, and how much money I saved as a result.

"They're my vice," she had said once when I caught her at the edge of the garden, a thin tendril of smoke rising from the cigarette in her hand. "Well, one of them, anyway."

We left the library behind and took two seats at the café nestled alongside the columns at the edge of the Trie Cloister, which was overrun with blooming wildflowers, between which bees buzzed like drunken men, almost colliding into one another. The afternoon so warm and full of the gentle sounds of nature's humming that I believed, for a moment, I was the poor relation in an Edith Wharton novel, ushered into luxury for the first time, already terrified of the day it might fade but desperate to experience it to the fullest while I could.

Rachel let her arm lie on the low stone wall that ringed the garden and pulled off her sunglasses, a sandal dangling from her foot. Although we'd been spending almost all our time together, there had been little casual conversation. Mostly we'd had our heads diligently bent over texts, searching for mentions of people—witches, shamans, saints—who might have told the future in the thirteenth or fourteenth century. Often, without much success. Weathering the silence, I studied the sculptures that were set in niches around the walls of the cloister. Rachel watched the garden with the kind of idleness enjoyed by only the most confident—those who refuse to bring their phone or a book to dinner alone.

Our cappuccinos arrived, each with rough cubes of sugar. When the waiter had gone, Rachel pulled a short brown biscotto out of her pocket. It was the type they had for sale at the cash register, the type I hadn't seen her pay for when we ordered.

"Here." She broke it in half and offered me some.

"Did you steal that?"

She shrugged. "You don't want it? They're really good."

I looked around. "What if someone notices?"

"What if they do?" She bit into the cookie and pushed the other half at me a second time. I took it from her and held it in my hand. "Go on, try it."

I took a bite and left the rest sitting on my saucer. She was right, it was delicious.

"Well, was I wrong?"

I shook my head. "No. Not at all."

Rachel leaned back in her chair. Satisfied. "They taste even better when they're free."

I looked around again to make sure the waiter wasn't there to notice me eating the rest of the half she had given me, but instead my eyes lingered on a carved figure set in the wall—a winged woman holding a wheel, the relief mottled and softened with age. At each cardinal point of the wheel, figures had been lashed, Latin words engraved on the body of each figure.

"Can you make out those words?" Rachel asked, following my gaze. "*Regno,*" Rachel said, pointing to the figure at the apex of the wheel.

"I reign," I said reflexively.

She nodded. "*Regnavi.*"

"I have reigned."

"*Sum sine regno?*"

"I am without reign."

"*Regnabo.*"

"I will reign."

Rachel slipped the sugar cube into her cup and looked at me appraisingly. "I heard that last week, you know. That you read Latin. And Greek, too. Any other secrets, Ann from Walla Walla?"

What is life without secrets? I thought. Instead, I said, "None that I can think of."

"Well, we can fix that." Rachel reached across the table and took the rest of my cookie, revealing a flash of red, a satin ribbon around her wrist that cut against her pale skin. I knew where I had seen it. In the library, wound around Patrick's fingers.

We began to take breaks together more often after that. While Rachel smoked at the edge of the gardens, I would keep her company, sitting on the cool stone of the ramparts, my feet swinging through the tufts of lush summer grass, tickling my ankles. It was then that she started quizzing me. First about my love life—uneventful, save for a few guys in high school and even fewer in college. Then about my mother—what she did, where she had grown up. And also, about Walla Walla and Whitman— what it was like, what was it known for, if we had county fairs. The enthusiasm of her questions surprised me. She wanted to know how big the town was (small), how long my family had been there (four generations), what it was like (hot, until it wasn't, then boring), and what Whitman students were like (like Bard students, but from the West Coast).

"I'm obsessed with places I've never been," Rachel said by way of explanation. "And with people's relationships. There's so much space to imagine how a story might unfold when you don't know anything about the setting."

But whenever I asked about her relationships and family, she always changed the subject, stubbing out her cigarette and saying, "Oh, far too boring," or "I'd rather you tell me about yourself," before walking back into the library.

One afternoon, I waited for her on a stone bench in the Bonnefont Cloister, the entire garden flanked by Gothic arches and stained glass. In the terra-cotta pots next to me, frankincense and myrrh grew from gnarled trunks to culminate in feathery white flowers, their scents warming in the late-afternoon sun. I leaned into the flowers and felt them brush my cheek.

"It has thorns, you know."

He held a bucket of gardening tools and had a pair of worn, tan leather gloves tucked in the front pocket of his jeans, which were smeared with mud, and torn.

"Myrrh," he said, "it has thorns." He pushed back the branches to reveal a sea of long black points.

I moved farther away on the bench.

"It won't come after you."

"I know that."

Although I wasn't sure I believed it. There was something about the things that were housed at The Cloisters—the artwork, even the flowers—that made them seem like they might come alive.

"The Egyptians used it for embalming."

"Excuse me?"

"Myrrh. It was used to prepare bodies for embalming in ancient Egypt."

"It was also worn around the neck during the Renaissance to repel fleas," I said, coming back to myself.

He laughed. "It hasn't managed to repel me yet. Leo," he said, pointing a dirty finger at his chest.

"Ann."

"I know," he said, reaching down and flicking my ID card. "I've seen you around. The new girl."

I nodded, and he kneeled next to me, holding the leaves of frankincense to the side and pulling out a pair of rusted, creaky shears that he used to trim the dead leaves.

"You working with Rachel?"

"And Patrick."

"Seems like they're a package deal these days."

There was an edge to the way he said it, glib and hard as he placed the clippings in a bucket.

"I like them," I said, unsure why I was being defensive.

He sat back on his heels, and I noticed for the first time his sturdy work boots, and the way his arms were sinewy without being too muscular.

"Everyone likes Rachel," he said, searching my face. "What's not to like?"

It didn't surprise me that someone like Leo might find Rachel attractive. I imagined the way he watched her in the gardens, surreptitiously smoking, rubbing herbs between her fingers before dotting their oils on her neck. I resisted an overwhelming urge to ask him everything he knew about her.

Instead, I said, "How well do you know her?"

He gestured around us. "She started working here in the fall, during her senior year at Yale. Weekends only until she graduated."

"They let her work around her school schedule?"

He shook his head. "Don't you know? Girls like Rachel Mondray get whatever they ask for." He bit off a piece of brown tape and used it to wrap a broken branch of myrrh. The tender way he held back the leaves at odds with the rest of him. "What about you, Ann Stilwell? Are you getting what you ask for?"

The question, and the way he had positioned his body, made me feel trapped against the bench, but I didn't want to be free.

"Do you know what butcher's-broom is?" He pointed at the pot on the other side of me.

"I don't."

"It's a member of the asparagus family, but if eaten in large quantities, it can rupture or destroy your red blood cells."

I looked at the plant with its glossy green leaves and bright red berries.

"We grow a lot of poisons at The Cloisters," he said. "You'll have to be careful. Some of them are incredibly beautiful and look edible. They aren't."

"Can you show me?" I said, feeling a surge of confidence to ask for what I wanted. Being close to Leo was like holding a hand above an electric current—a sharp, animating pulse—that I had never had the bravery to touch. Now, I yearned to tap my hand against the live wire.

He pushed off his heels and stood up, walking toward a bed of herbs that tumbled and fell over each other; I followed.

"In this bed, we grow hemlock and belladonna, both of which you've probably heard of. But we grow others, too, henbane and hound's-tongue, vervain and mandrake. All herbs found in medieval medicine and magic. In fact, this whole cloister is planted with poisons and remedies you might find in the eleventh or fifteenth century. Those urns over there"—he pointed to a pair of tall stone vessels full of waxy green leaves and pink flowers—"oleander. Very deadly, but also very popular as a poultice in ancient Rome. If you push the leaves aside, you'll be able to see the labels."

I leaned forward as he held back a shower of hemlock flowers, revealing a ceramic tile on which was neatly engraved the Latin for hemlock, *Conium maculatum*.

"Here we have *Catananche caerulea*," he said, holding a blue flower between his fingers.

I pulled aside the sinewy vines to find the plaque, which read CUPID'S DART.

"It was believed to cure the love-sick," he said, his voice low and so close to my neck that I could feel the baby-fine hairs on my nape stand up. The urge to lean in closer surprised me.

He led me toward another bed, a calloused hand on my arm. I felt a blind welling of attraction growing inside me, a feeling that didn't abate even when I noticed Rachel standing beneath a pointed arch that led out to the garden, her eyes following us. There was something about being watched that made me braver, that made me close the gap between our bodies when Leo moved his hand from my arm to the small of my back, that made me bite the inside of my lip in antic- ipation. We arrived at a bed full of lemon balm, its warm citrus notes mixing with the lavender and sage that surrounded it.

"It's even more powerful if you close your eyes," he said, closing his and taking a deep inhale. Across the courtyard I watched Rachel raise her eyebrow.

"I have to go," I said.

He followed my gaze to Rachel on the other side of the cloister.

"Of course," he said. "Rachel always gets what she wants."

I wanted him to say more, but Rachel held up her wrist and pointed at her watch. Already I had been with Leo for almost a half hour.

"I'm sorry," I said, not sure how to break away from the strange inti- macy of the moment.

When I joined her, Rachel put an arm around my shoulder, casual but possessive. "Having fun?"

"Just learning about plants."

"And the teacher, too?"

I didn't look back until we were walking down the passageway toward the library, but when I did, I noticed him trimming a thick hedge, cov- ered in shiny black berries. Belladonna, Leo had said.

CHAPTER FIVE

The night was hot, so hot that my window unit couldn't keep pace but just heaved and sputtered against the still summer that clung to the streets outside. I lay in bed, resenting every inch of sheet that touched my skin until the sky began to lighten, and thinking of the only place I knew in the city that was reliably cool, with its heavy stone chapels and vaults, decided it was not too early, at quarter to five, to leave for work.

If security was surprised to see me arrive, they didn't show it. Instead, I was passed a fresh page of the after-hours sign-in book without fanfare, and made my way to the library. In the galleries, the statuettes cast narrow shadows that spidered up the walls. With only early-morning sun for additional light, the precious stones from the reliquaries left watery, colored pools on the floor. My footsteps, the only sound that echoed through the twelfth-century hallways. When I passed a guard slumped in his chair, eyes closed, I didn't blame him. It was cooler and more comfortable than my apartment, too.

The door to the library was unlocked, but when I pushed it open, there was something different about the space—a thickness to the air and the sulfur smell of matches. I fumbled along the rough stone wall for a light switch before the door closed, taking with it what little light there was. In the dark, I put my hands out in front of me and inched forward until I hit one of the study tables and grasped for the reading lamp, pulling its string until the green glass shade lit up, a sad beacon that sent its illumination onto the oak table, not the room as a whole.

I hadn't noticed that, in the darkness, my breathing had ratcheted up; I only noticed now that it had returned to normal.

Around the library, the curtains had been pulled against the Gothic windows, windows that usually filled the space with enough natural light that the table lamps felt like redundant accessories. I walked to the windows and began pulling the curtains back, letting in the weak sunlight and watching motes of dust dance across the room. Perhaps security closed them every night and I had simply arrived before their routine reopening? I cracked a window and the morning songs of birds sifted into the room, chasing away whatever I might have imagined in the dark library.

At the table where Rachel and I usually worked, I began to unpack my bag, setting down my computer and notebook, and pulling out a few texts I had been using as reference—monographs on medieval approaches to astrology and oracles, a thirteenth-century handbook on how to interpret dreams. But on the table I noticed smooth red dots. When I wedged a fingernail under one, it resisted. I pressed until I could feel it pinching the nail bed, when it released from the table with ease. I rubbed the red disk between my fingers. Wax. Wax drippings from candles? I pulled the drippings off the table and set them aside, a neat little pile on a sheet of paper.

I liked being in the library early and alone. At a time when the only sounds were my footsteps and the guards', when the lighting was low and I could move around unnoticed. Alone, after all, was my default way of being, one of the main reasons that academia had appealed to me in the first place: the ability to be unchaperoned with captivating objects and ancient histories. This, I preferred to the idea of working in an office with small talk and endless meetings, the forced intimacy of team-building exercises. Academia did away with all that. And for that, I was grateful.

By the time Patrick arrived I had made my way into the storage stacks, cranking open two sets of shelves just wide enough that I could wedge my body between, hoping the book I needed wouldn't be on a lower shelf, as I hadn't left enough space to bend down. I heard his footsteps before I saw him pass through the sliver at the end of the stacks, like an apparition. And then, he paused, retracing his steps to where I stood.

"Looks tight," he said, letting his hand rest heavy on the crank arm. The stacks inched closed. It was only a hair, but I instinctively put my hand up to brace against the movement. Tight spaces made me claustrophobic, and there was something about being squeezed while Patrick stood out in the open that caused my heart to kick up into my throat.

"I'm not going to crush you, Ann," Patrick laughed. "I saw the sign-in log. Early morning?"

"Couldn't sleep," I said, plucking the volume I was looking for off the shelf and scooting out of the narrow confines of the stacks, back to the cart I had been filling with books.

Patrick used his finger to read the titles. "A very fine collection you've pulled together here."

I held the book to my chest, embarrassed by how quickly my anxiety in the stacks had turned to eagerness. I longed desperately to please him, so much so that I lingered on his words, on his praise for the way I conducted research. As if all the books were for him, the early morning, too; I could feel the flush on my cheeks, the heat.

"Tell me, Ann," he said, reading the last title, "did Richard talk to you about the divinatory practices of early Renaissance Italy?"

I was well versed in the essential role at least one divination—astrology—had played during the Renaissance. The way it had guided little decisions like when to shave a beard or take a bath, as well as big ones, like when to go to war. The way aristocrats and popes had believed that their painted ceilings—known today as celestial vaults, decorated with constellations and signs of the zodiac—could have as much impact on their fates as the stars themselves. I had even briefly worked on geomancy in Venice—the city's passion for using a handful of thrown soil to tell the future. The courts of the Renaissance loved magic and occult practices, and they were surprisingly adept at fitting them into their Christian worldview. Lingraf, I knew, had a kind of soft spot for this work, a romantic and fanciful interest I had always attributed to personal passions, not academic rigor. And to a certain extent, he had encouraged it in me, and I had let it blossom.

"He did," I acknowledged. But Lingraf had never been keen to share his work. He was avuncular. Encouraging. Never open.

"That's right. You mentioned in Michelle's office some of your work." I wondered again how deeply Patrick had gone through my application materials. If he had reached out to Lingraf to learn more.

"And what do you think of it all? This exhibition we're working on?" he continued. "Broad strokes."

"I think it reflects the extent to which, although the Renaissance is often considered an era of logic and science, it was easily seduced by ancient practices that didn't include geometry and anatomy, but rather a belief in oracles and mystical traditions. In some ways it was also very"—I paused—"anti-science. Broad strokes, of course."

"Of course," said Patrick, looking at me.

I was struck again by how handsome he was. Even in the fluorescent light of the stacks, his jawline and cheekbones seemed to gleam with health. During my first week I had tried to figure out his age by looking up the date of his dissertation. He was, I had confirmed, in his late forties, maybe early fifties. Young to be a full curator anywhere, but particularly at The Cloisters.

"Why do you suppose," he said, pulling out a volume I had selected on medieval visions and paging through it, "they were so seduced by these things?"

"We long to explain the world around us," I said. "To make sense of the unknown." Or, at least, I knew I did. The impulse, on some level, universal.

"Have you ever considered," said Patrick, looking up, his finger on the page, "that maybe there is something about these practices, though difficult for us to believe now, that might have some"—he met my gaze—"truth?"

"What do you mean? That by studying the position of planets, we might be able to predict the best day to"—I searched for the strangest thing I remembered reading in an astrological manuscript—"treat gout?"

Patrick nodded, the shadow of a smile at the corner of his mouth.

"I don't think so," I said, considering the question. The idea that humans might be able to tell the future by watching planets migrate across the night sky had captured the imaginations of scholars and mystics for centuries. But to my mind, it was impossible to believe in astrology. I had seen firsthand how unforgiving, how random fate could be. It was something, I was sure, we could never fully know. Nevertheless, I didn't want to disappoint him, to reveal myself as too much of a cynic, so I added, "Of course, people still believe in astrology today."

"We have a tendency to discount things we don't understand," said Patrick. "To dismiss them out of hand as antiquated or unscientific. But if you take one thing away from your time here, I want it to be that you gave these belief systems their full due. You don't have to believe in divination for it to have been true for an aristocrat in the fourteenth century." He put the book down. "Even, for it to be true again."

By the time I returned to the library, the paper, with my pile of wax drippings, was gone. I checked the trash, but it was nowhere to be found; Patrick and I were the only two to have arrived.

"Looking for Leo?" said Rachel, taking a drag on her cigarette. The heat of the morning had given way to a cloudy afternoon, rain threatened on the other side of the river, and we were taking advantage of the cooler air by sitting at the edge of the Bonnefont Cloister, Rachel holding her hand over the ramparts so no one would notice her smoking.

"Not really," I said, although it was a lie. I'd been looking for him all day, even going so far as to linger in the kitchen, the gardens, around the staff bathrooms, hoping he might walk by.

"You're a terrible liar," said Rachel, watching my profile as she stubbed out her cigarette. "On Monday he usually works in the garden shed, not out in the cloisters. Not that you care."

She took in the scene: visitors reverently wandering the brick paths of the garden, their hands clasped behind their backs. I imagined it might have been the same five hundred years earlier.

"Thank god the heat broke," she said. Not that Rachel looked touched by the heat or the humidity.

"I came in early," I said. "I couldn't stand it. But when I got to the library this morning, there were wax drippings on the tables. Or at least I thought it was wax. What do you think could have caused that?"

Rachel looked out over the ramparts, toward the river. "I don't know," she said.

"Do you think someone would light candles in the library?"

"Maybe there was a donor function over the weekend. You wouldn't believe what I've found in the library—even the galleries—after one of those."

It seemed plausible. And it wasn't like there was much communication between the Events department and Curatorial at the museum. "It was just strange. Why would anyone bring candles into a room full of rare books?"

"Monks used to do it all the time," said Rachel, getting to her feet.

The day moved quickly after that, but despite the bruised sky, the city never received anything but humidity and stillness. I was sad to leave the library at six, its cool stony confines having quickly become more familiar than my studio; the beauty of my daytime surroundings somehow made the reality of my nights all the worse.

As I walked through the galleries and under the lofty vaults of the hallways on my way to the shuttle, my mind drifted to the heat. I hadn't been prepared for it, for the wetness. And I began to wonder if I had enough money for a new window unit; there was a hardware store two blocks from my apartment. But as I started to do the math of cool air against the realities of my budget, I realized the margins were so slim, I needed to be sure. I moved to open the calculator on my phone, only to realize I had left it on the chair in the library. It was a quick walk back, but on my way around the Bonnefont Cloister, I saw the two of them—Rachel and Leo—standing by the arch that led to the garden shed, deep in conversation. Rachel leaned against the wall, her arms pinned behind her back, Leo's hand positioned above her head.

Without thinking, I paused behind one of the columns and watched from across the garden. I could hear her laughter as she shook out a cigarette, lit it, and held it out to him. He didn't take it from her, but slowly lifted her hand to his mouth, where he took a drag. Annoyed, Rachel wrested her hand free and slid off the wall, leaving Leo alone.

I took the opportunity to duck into the library, unseen. It took me a few minutes to locate my phone, difficult as it was to focus through the mix of jealousy and desire that made my palms ache. Phone in hand, I went to lean my weight against the wooden doors of the library when I heard Patrick's voice coming from the other side.

"I think it's time to bring Ann in."

"It's too soon, Patrick," responded Rachel.

"She's here to be an asset."

Patrick had lowered his voice, which required me to lean my whole body against the door, my ear to the seam. When Rachel spoke again, I could sense the frustration in her voice through the thick, damp wood:

"We don't know that we can trust her yet. Although she's already curious. You know she found the wax? Did she ask you about it?"

"I took care of it."

Then silence, save for the sound of my pulse beating through my ears.

"Come on," said Patrick, his voice in a soft tone I hadn't heard before. "Let's not fight about this. You wanted her."

"I think she can help," Rachel conceded, and I sensed that this conversation was not only about the exhibition but something more, something I couldn't yet see.

"Sometimes we have to take risks," Patrick insisted.

Then a beat.

"Don't you trust me," he said.

Rachel must have nodded because he added:

"That's my girl. You know I don't think she ended up here by chance, right?"

The handle of the door began to turn, and I hurried to the end of the library, then slipped into the stacks before it had a chance to open. I made my way through the staff hallway, past the kitchen. My head down in the poorly lit hallway, I nearly made it to the lobby before I ran, literally, headlong, into Leo.

"You okay?" he asked, holding my shoulders and looking me up and down.

"Yes. Sorry. I'm—" I was too flustered, too out of breath from hurrying to focus on the words I wanted to say.

"Slow down, Ann. It's a museum. No one's saving lives here."

"Right. I know." I exhaled. "I was just trying to make the shuttle."

"It just left," he said, taking a step back.

"Shit."

"Why don't we walk?" He motioned for me to go ahead of him. The way his arm moved reminded me of the way he had stretched it above Rachel's head—the strength of it, the possessiveness. I wanted to feel it above me, wrapped around my waist, my shoulders, hard and tight.

We traded the darkness of the museum for the canopy of the park, where the winding paths crossed the grassy expanses with dizzying rhythm. Leo walked next to me, occasionally humming a few bars of a song I didn't recognize.

After we passed a group of children being led hand in hand like a tiny toddler daisy chain, he turned to me and said, without preamble, "Why are you here?"

"What kind of question is that?" It was sharp, his question. And it reminded me, as if I didn't already know, that I was new and inexperienced, even unwanted.

There was some part of me that knew it would be best to ignore the things I had seen and heard that day, to build a barrier between myself and Leo and Rachel and Patrick. Between the world of the museum and the things I needed it to accomplish—an acceptance to grad school, a life outside Walla Walla. Contained in Leo's question was an implication that had begun to worry me, too: *Why are you meddling in our world?*

I must have been quiet for a moment too long because he added, more gently, "I mean, why not Los Angeles or Chicago or Seattle? Why here?"

I gestured around us, relieved. "I hear it's the greatest city in the world."

Leo laughed. "Give it time."

The last, trailing child trotted by us, dragging their free hand through the knee-high grass.

"It's the art, I guess," I said, looking up at his profile. Although I kept the other reasons to myself: it was thousands of miles from the Lutheran church where my father was buried, it was a city that never faulted you for your ambition, even if others might. We walked side by side, Leo's hands deep in his pockets, a shoulder bag across his chest. "It's the only place I can do the work I want to do," I settled on.

"What are you willing to give up for the work?"

There was an edge to the question, and I pushed my hands into my own pockets and shrugged, not ready to let him know more when I still knew so little about him.

Leo bumped his shoulder against mine. "Not everyone is sensitive around here," he said. "You shouldn't take questions so personally. And if you do, and don't want to answer them, just tell people to fuck off. I'm just trying to figure out if you'll like it here. Most people here don't care if you do, by the way. So long as you do the job. But I like it. I like the gardening, at least. The work, like you said. Even if I hate the visitors. Sometimes, on the quiet days, I can pretend it's the way it was meant to be. Pre–tourist-industrial complex. Pre–experience economy."

"To me, The Cloisters always feels a little that way. A world apart."

We had reached the subway station, its entrance built into a rock outcropping, ivy cascading down its flanks. It looked like a station that belonged in Rome, not the northern tip of Manhattan.

"This is your stop," he said, nodding at the stairs.

"Thanks for walking with me," I said, embarrassed by how juvenile it sounded, as if he had held my hand like the children we had passed.

"I like walking with you, Ann Stilwell." He hesitated. "It's an incredible place—the city, The Cloisters. Just don't let it wear you down. Make it sharpen you instead."

The next day, a constant patter of rain tapped out its rhythm on the glass windows of the library where Rachel and I worked. The speed with which she managed to consume texts still astonished me, her reading quick and incisive. When the rain finally stopped, Rachel stood and excused herself from the table, knocking on Patrick's door. For almost an hour I watched the door out of the corner of my eye, pushing down the thought that, if five more minutes ticked by, I might have time to get closer, perhaps catch a word or two of the conversation unfolding inside. But just when I was about to peruse the shelves closest to his office, Rachel reemerged, holding the door behind her until it closed with only a whisper.

"Patrick wants to know if you would come to dinner at his house on Friday," she said, sitting down across from me.

I couldn't help but think about what I had heard through the library door the day before, but if there was a thread of resignation in Rachel's words now, I couldn't parse it.

At Whitman, I had never been invited to a faculty house for dinner. Even though the school was small, a division between students and staff persisted. Such dinners, after all, were fodder for speculating about inappropriate relationships. But I had been curious about Patrick's house since Rachel had first mentioned it, and the invitation felt like the initiation I had been waiting for.

"It's a tradition," she continued. "I usually go up once a week. Sometimes there are other guests. More like an intellectual salon. This week it's going to be Aruna Mehta, the curator of rare manuscripts at the Beinecke Library."

"I don't know how to get to Tarrytown," I said, beginning to worry about the logistics of arriving in a presentable way, not damp from walking or riding an airless Metro-North.

"We can drive together," Rachel said, holding up a hand. "I'll pick you up at five."

CHAPTER SIX

On Friday, Rachel picked me up in a black town car, her driver at the wheel.

"I brought you a few things," she said, holding out an oversized, stuffed lilac bag. "I hope you don't mind. It's clothes."

"You bought me new clothes?" I said, pulling a skirt from the bag, its tags still attached.

"No. Of course not. I was cleaning out my closet and thought you might be interested in some of these things. I never wore a lot of them. I was going to donate it."

The way she said it, off the cuff, made me think there was nothing more to it than that, but part of me wondered if she was tired of looking at my drab outfits every day, my sensible cotton/poly-blend life. I looked through a few of the pieces, feeling the fabric between my fingers. No wonder Rachel always looked incredible.

"Thank you," I said.

"Do you want to change into something now—?"

It was a gentle prod, gentle enough that I didn't feel an immediate sense of shame, but enough for me to look down at the slacks I had selected for the evening. Even the word—*slacks*—made my mistake clear.

"Would you mind?"

"Not at all. John, can you circle?" Rachel asked the driver, who replied in the affirmative. "I'll come up with you."

"No!" The thought of Rachel in my cramped studio, seeing my clothes pinned to the clothesline I'd run across the fire escape, just as my neighbors had done, the dirty dishes—her trying to squeeze onto the single square of my couch that was not covered with books and notes—made me dizzy with panic. "I mean, I'll be super quick. There's no need."

"There's a black dress in there that would be perfect. Just a simple shift. That's what I would wear."

As I pawed through the bag upstairs, I was glad Rachel wasn't there, taking in the single room that made up my sublet. To make it look more like home, I had mounted a framed photograph of my parents, as well as a few postcards of paintings I'd never seen in real life, but which had occupied the bulk of my time and effort at Whitman: a suite of frescos from the Palazzo Schifanoia in Ferrara. The name Schifanoia, derived from the phrase *schivar la noia*, or, to escape boredom. A pleasure palace on the outskirts of Ferrara where Borso d'Este, the eccentric ruler of an influential duchy, had an entire banquet hall painted with scenes from the zodiac. There was a procession of Venus being drawn on a carriage by swans. Beneath her, a resplendent Taurus, a tan-colored bull whose flanks were dotted with gold stars, blessed her passage. Borso had designed the hall to impress his guests—astrology as a performance of power, as a totem of good fortune. But some scholars had argued it ran more deeply than that, that Borso and the Renaissance astrologers who had designed the room believed *paintings* of celestial bodies could have as much impact on an individual's fate as the actual stars above. As if the drawn image of Leo could affect the viewer's—or in this case, Borso's—horoscope in felicitous ways. Art at its most powerful, perhaps. It was an argument that Lingraf had always encouraged me to take seriously.

I changed into the black shift and pulled my curly hair into a low pony, using the newly arrived box from my mother as a footstool so I could gain enough vantage to see more of my body in the small mirror in the bathroom. The difference was striking: my hair slightly romantic in its chaos, the neckline drooped just enough to look sexy, while the silhouette itself was loose and comfortable, falling at just the right place on my thighs so that it was still appropriate for a salon—the first I'd ever been invited to. Rachel couldn't have worn it more than once, maybe twice; it had the feel of something that had never been laundered. I resisted the urge to go through the rest of the bag and see what other castoffs Rachel had gifted me. Instead, I ran back down the stairs. I didn't want her to wait.

"Oh, I knew that would be perfect," she said when I slid into the car next to her. The compliment felt as natural as the fabric of the dress on my skin.

We drove north, or rather inched, along the crowded parkway, Rachel tapping out something on her phone, me watching the high-rises slowly give way to the leafy exits of the exurbs, until the driver hugged the curve of an exit, and then the easy back-and-forth of quieter streets. Rachel said nothing through it all, and I, not wanting to appear too eager, too desperate, kept quiet. Finally, as we pulled up a long gravel driveway, Rachel slipped her phone back into her bag and said, "We're here."

The house came into view—an orderly collection of gray flagstones and leaded glass windows, separated by crosshatched metal into a tiny patchwork of frames. The circular driveway was flanked by balsam firs and beech trees; the front door, a Gothic arch framed by manicured boxwood. In so many ways, it reminded me of The Cloisters—the color of the stone, the faux-Gothic aesthetic, the way the driveway built anticipation, teasing the driver with the slow reveal of a stone chimney here, an aged copper weathervane there. I wondered if John would wait for us the entire time, just sitting in the car, a sandwich packed away in the trunk, like he did every week.

No one met us at the door. Rachel simply let herself into the oval foyer, anchored by a stone staircase. To our left was the library, and as Rachel led me through, I did my best to commit the details to memory. It was my first glimpse inside an academic home: there were framed manuscript pages and an encaustic triptych on display, a table covered with oddly shaped white dice, shelves filled with leather-bound books. It was a richly and carefully curated collection, one that extended well beyond Patrick's salary at The Cloisters, I was sure. I wanted to linger, to touch the thick fabric of the couches, feel the cool mahogany of the tables, but Rachel had already crossed the space, as if it were commonplace, and was waiting for me at a pair of French doors, thrown open onto the summer evening.

From the flagstone patio off the library, views stretched down to where the Tappan Zee bridged Rockland and Westchester Counties across the Hudson. The air was hazy and thick with the constant hum of insects. Beneath a striped awning, Patrick and a woman sat holding drinks sweaty from the humidity. Her small frame barely filled the chair, but her dress, a vibrant coral with woven gold accents, made her presence outsized. With only four attendees, it was too small a number to be considered a salon; it was more an intimate dinner party.

For whatever reason—likely our surroundings, the library, the glass windows oily with age—I expected someone to come take our drink order, so I was surprised to see Patrick get up and walk into a door at the far end of the patio—the kitchen, I would learn—and fix our drinks himself.

"Negronis," he explained, handing me a heavy, etched crystal highball.

The woman sitting in the chair, I learned, was Aruna Mehta. Punjabi by way of Oxford. She and Patrick had been graduate students together—almost twenty years of friendship, she said. Aruna wore her glossy hair piled elegantly on her head, a pair of reading glasses around her neck. Rachel kissed her on both cheeks before sitting down. Even if it was a casual greeting, the intimacy of the gesture and Rachel's confidence at executing it surprised me. No faculty had ever invited me to enjoy such familiarity.

"Your first time?" Aruna said to me, gesturing at the view.

"It is," I said. "It's incredible."

"Thank you," said Patrick, lifting a glass. "I take no credit for it."

"You can take credit for its masterful restoration." Aruna touched her glass to ours. "Cheers."

"That I can." Patrick smiled.

"Most curators don't live like this," said Aruna, leaning in my direction with faux confidentiality. Her closeness felt like a lifeline. "Patrick is alone in that distinction. As he is in many others."

Patrick laughed, and I noticed for the first time that he had shallow dimples beneath a layer of stubble. I wondered why he didn't have anyone here with him in this house—a wife, a family, even a housekeeper. There had to be dozens of rooms.

"Aruna, stop," Patrick said, no trace of warning in his voice.

"Rachel knows." Aruna winked.

It was a reminder of how on the outside of things I was. Perhaps a purposeful reminder of how many times Rachel had drunk Negronis on Patrick's patio, how she may have known what the house looked like before the restoration. How she had known Aruna, she'd told me, from her years at Yale. And while I had spent my time as an undergraduate being overlooked by the faculty who mattered, she had already been identified as something special, one to watch. I reminded myself that was why I had come to New York in the first place, to remake myself into someone like Rachel. Someone people took seriously, someone *I* could take seriously.

"You've heard about the thing at the Morgan?" said Aruna. "This year they've proposed the topic will be the history of the Renaissance occult."

"Yes," said Patrick. "I suggested they have Rachel moderate the panel on tarot."

Rachel leaned toward me and whispered in my ear, "They said no."

"I'll be presenting instead," Patrick added.

"So interesting that after so many years of claiming it's a subject not

worth examining, they decide to run this at the same time you're working on an exhibition about divination. Isn't it, Patrick?" Aruna bit off the
end of her orange rind and chewed it thoughtfully.

"Something in the air," said Rachel, taking a sip of Negroni, the enormous ice cube clinking against the side of her glass.

"What about you, Ann?" Aruna dabbed at a bit of condensation that
had dripped from her glass and onto her dress. "Have these two made
you a believer yet?"

"Not yet, I'm afraid." I struggled to read the tone of these conversations, to understand the way Patrick and Rachel, and now Aruna, talked
about tarot cards and divinatory practices like they might be real. It
seemed like a joke. One, I worried, that would only be revealed when
I finally agreed to believe the unbelievable. All of it at my expense, of
course.

"Ah, not yet," said Aruna. "Meaning there's still time to convince
you?"

"One need not be convinced," interjected Patrick, now leaning forward in his chair, elbows on his knees, hands wrapped around his glass.
"One must be open to the process. To attempting to understand why
these practices mattered. And how they still might. We're talking about
belief systems that shape the way we talk about fate, even today. Take
tarot—"

"Yes, but tarot," Aruna interrupted, "only became part of the occult
in the eighteenth century. Before, it was a trump-taking game. Something like bridge, played by the aristocracy. Four people, sitting around
a table, shuffling and dealing a simple deck of cards. It wasn't until that
charlatan Antoine Court de Gébelin got involved that tarot cards were
transformed into something more"—she waved her hands—"mystical."

"Gébelin," said Rachel, facing me, "was a notorious eighteenth-
century rake of the French court. And he suggested that Egyptian priests,
using the *Book of Thoth*, not fifteenth-century Italians, were responsible

for the creation of the tarot deck, which consists, of course, of four suits like our regular deck, plus twenty-two cards that we now call the Major Arcana. Things like the High Priestess card, for example. Which used to be the Popess."

I had begun to notice flashes of light that zigged and zagged, leaving trails of neon as the twilight became darker. Fireflies, illuminating our conversation with the tangible magic of nature.

"Between the Egyptomania of eighteenth-century France," Rachel continued, "and the atmosphere of a court that loved secrets and mysteries, tarot developed an entirely different use. But I think there's still an argument to be made for occult use in the fifteenth century, especially somewhere between Venice, Ferrara, and Milan. An area that was a bit of a golden triangle for experimental, magical practices. You see, we know that aristocrats in the early years of the Renaissance were fascinated by ancient practices of divination. Things like geomancy and cleromancy. So why not cards? The Dominicans were staunchly opposed to tarot decks. We know that Henri III taxed them in France. We know that someone was arrested in Venice in the early sixteenth century for cartomancy. And we have numerous indications in the historical record that tarot cards gave rise to *public scandals*, a phrase I think we could parse in different ways."

I looked between her and Patrick, who had returned to sitting back in his chair, his fingers steepled.

"And of course," Rachel said, "we cannot look at the imagery of the Major Arcana—the Moon, the Star, the Wheel of Fortune, Death, the Lovers—without acknowledging that a pervasive interest in the occult in the fifteenth century in Italy may have influenced the imagery, if not the function, of tarot cards."

Growing up, it had been impossible to believe that something like a horoscope or a tarot reading might give me an advantage, might show me the outlines of my future. That kind of belief was a luxury I didn't have. And I found it too painful to imagine that the stars could have warned me about my father's death, although I knew that the ancient Romans would have disagreed. Perhaps the three of them would, too.

"But of course," said Patrick, "Rachel hasn't yet been able to marshal all the resources she needs to prove this theory. And many of us have tried."

There was an edge in that, in the way he said *tried*—clipped and hard and resentful. And in it I realized that it wasn't Rachel's project alone, but his as well. Perhaps a failed project. Patrick, at every opportunity, seemed to be implying it was something more than research, something real and tangible, while Rachel still harbored reservations. Although I had noticed she chose not to voice them around Patrick.

"Just think of the legitimacy it would give the practice today—if we knew that there was a deck of cards from the fifteenth century, an early deck, maybe even *the* earliest deck that was used for the same purpose," Patrick concluded.

"But there are few arrest records," Rachel said. "And even fewer mentions of the practice."

"There probably wouldn't be arrest records," I said, finding my voice. "I can't imagine Borso or Ercole d'Este arresting someone for something like that in Ferrara." The d'Este family had set up shop in Ferrara in the thirteenth century, where they ruled over a libidinous and mystical duchy that was as superstitious as it was ambitious. "I can't imagine them writing something like that down."

"Neither can I," said Rachel.

As the sun dipped into the Hudson, making the river look golden and black, Rachel didn't look away, but kept an appreciative smile on her lips while she examined me, as if for the first time.

"Let's go inside and show Ann how it works," Patrick said, clapping his hands on his knees and turning his attention to Rachel.

They all rose, but I stayed in my chair for a moment, wondering what awaited me inside and whether I wanted to know what they were about to show me. Patrick's words from the other day haunted me—*it's time*. I felt a strange mix of disbelief and credulity—fear that I would not be able to believe what they so clearly wanted me to believe, and then again, fear I would. Easily, in fact. When Rachel reached the door to the living room, she turned back to where I sat and just like that, as if on command, I stood and followed her.

Inside, they had gathered around a low coffee table that Patrick had cleared of books. He held a deck of cards, taller than the usual playing deck, and thicker, with frayed edges and a backing that showed a series of yellow suns, set in deep orange hexagonal tiles. Patrick placed the deck on the table and looked at me expectantly.

"Shuffle," he said.

The urge to laugh from nerves was overwhelming. I wanted to laugh so that they would all understand that I, too, was in on the joke. Because it had to be a joke, didn't it?

"Go on. Shuffle," said Rachel.

I kneeled next to the coffee table and took the deck in my hand. It was pleasantly worn, but when I went to fan the cards, they resisted.

"No," said Patrick, "spread them around. Touch them. Get your energy on them. Then pull them back into a pile and cut the deck in three."

With the cards spread across the table, I did my best to touch them. I was sure they were old—not hand-painted or made of vellum, but still, they had seen at least two hundred years of use. They were the first deck of tarot cards I had ever handled, and however briefly, I wondered if the cards might feel that in my energy before I realized the outlandishness of the thought. But there was something there, as I crouched on the floor of Patrick's living room, surrounded by collections of medieval artifacts and rare books, watched carefully by my three mentors, that made me wonder, if only for a moment, if it *was* possible. To believe. The cards felt electric and entirely at home in my hands.

When I finished cutting the cards, Patrick laid out five in a grid, face-up. The illustrations were spare but full of arcane symbols—the ouroboros on the Fortune card, a lion on the card labeled *la force*, power. The pip cards showed a graphic restraint—a Three of Wands thinly executed on a robin's-egg-blue background, and a Five of Coins with the symbols of the zodiac against a eucalyptus green. And a card that read *protection* illustrated with a watery horizon, full of sea creatures that writhed and frothed in the foreground. I was embarrassed to find myself so drawn to the imagery that I reached across the table and picked up one of the cards—a Three of Wands—to get a closer look at the inscription.

"It's an Etteilla deck," said Rachel. "An original. One of the first occult decks ever printed. This edition is from 1890."

"What does it mean?" I asked, returning the card and looking up at Patrick.

He studied the spread in front of him. "We can see here," he said, pointing to the card full of sea creatures, "an ocean of opportunity, of power, of exploration but also, self-consumption. The ouroboros, of course, a symbol of rebirth, death, and self-empowerment. The lion, a powerful card tempered by the pip cards that remind us about balance and desire."

As he spoke, I found myself trying to place the cards in my life, trying to create meaning out of their darkly sketched imagery. In the body of the ouroboros—forever forced to devour itself—there was an echo from my past I wasn't ready to hear.

"This is a deck," said Rachel, breaking my reverie, "that we know was used for divination. But what we need is to find a set of cards from the fifteenth century that would tell us it was used for the same thing. A deck whose imagery is distinctly culled from other divinatory practices, or archival material that would allow us to make that argument about existing decks."

"There are many loose, single cards around from the fifteenth century," added Aruna, "but complete tarot decks from then, or mostly complete tarot decks like the ones at the Beinecke and the Morgan, are incredibly rare. It's much more common to have complete decks from this vintage. Printing, after all, allowed for a master deck and multiple copies. That was less true when decks were handmade by artists."

"And there would probably only be a handful," I said, dragging my gaze from the deck. I couldn't imagine that the pragmatic Florentines or residents of Rome would have indulged in such ideas, but I was surprised to find myself, when confronted with the imagery here, feeling the pull of possibility.

"It would be a major breakthrough," said Rachel, "not only in the history of art but also the history of the occult to locate a deck like that. It would give legitimacy to a practice that so many people use today. To this." She gestured to the spread between us.

If I had often been told that there was nothing new left in the Renaissance to study, then this certainly felt new. Not only new, but arcane and delightfully mysterious. And although it was an idea that under other circumstances I might have been inclined to dismiss, here, I could feel myself being seduced. That, for once, the thing academic researchers had stripped of its magic was about to have its magic restored. Wasn't that, after all, why we had become academics and researchers in the first place? To discover art as a practice, not just as an artifact?

We decamped back to the patio for dinner, an unfussy mix of grilled vegetables, cod, and slices of campagne bread that Patrick brought out from the kitchen. Despite my initial impression that Patrick must have a full staff to run such a large house, it was clear that he happily made do on his own, and we ate tucked around a small table, not in a large dining room as I had initially anticipated. When we had eaten everything and were falling back in our chairs, the night still warm from the heat of the day, Rachel stood and cleared her plate and my own before Patrick joined her with the rest. I watched their bodies recede into the kitchen, the dim interior light revealing only the faintest shadows inside. We could hear the clatter of plates and pans making their way into the dishwasher and sink.

"They might be a little while," said Aruna, who pulled out a cigarette and offered me one before hers sprung to life in the darkness, our table lit only by the flame of a single hurricane lamp.

"Should I go help?" I said, moving to stand.

"No," she said, placing a hand on my arm. "They don't want your help." The way she said it, with the barest edge of warning, caught me off guard.

"Oh."

"Do you know what you're getting yourself into here, Ann?" Aruna blew out a cloud of smoke.

"I think so." I had watched Aruna drink at least four glasses of wine, and I wondered if that was factoring into her willingness to share with me as we sat alone on the patio.

"I don't think you do." She tapped some ash off the tip of her cigarette and onto the flagstones. "You must stay out of this." She gestured at the door to the kitchen. "The rest of us, we stay out of it. We know better. It's not a place for you or me, Ann. Our place is out here, on the patio. Not in the house. We don't need to know what happens in the house."

Of course, I knew what Aruna meant. Had known it, I realized, since I saw the red piece of ribbon wound around Rachel's wrist. Inside, the sound of dishes clanging and the sink running had stopped. They had been gone for at least ten minutes.

"Don't let Rachel get you involved," she said. "Make sure that you remain yourself. That you keep a piece for you, apart. Because this"—she gestured down toward the Hudson and back to the house—"can be too much for some people."

We sat in silence while the chorus of crickets grew louder and louder, a humming I could feel at the back of my throat, until Rachel and Patrick finally returned to the table. I noticed, as they walked side by side, that Patrick reached out once to touch Rachel's arm, their bodies silhouetted by the kitchen light.

When we finally drove home, it was late, and the thought of my studio apartment seemed foreign and cold. The lights on the parkway flicked by outside, an orangey, otherworldly glow.

"I'm glad you're here," said Rachel quietly from the other side of the car. She reached out and put a hand on my arm, and let it linger a beat too long.

CHAPTER SEVEN

After that night, we stopped taking days off, Rachel and I. When the weekend came, we found a reason to be at The Cloisters even when Patrick wasn't. And while I thought the magic of walking beneath its coffered ceilings, endlessly decorated with rib vaults and the occasional gold leaf, would wear off, it never did. The beauty was intoxicating, and I wondered if I would have felt the same down at the Met on Fifth Avenue, where the summer associates worked at rows of adjacent computer monitors. The Cloisters had taken me instead to a world of damp stone and a surfeit of flowers, where the artwork itself, in glossy encaustic and enamel, burned hot.

And as my urgency around the work grew—every waking minute occupied with the occult, every waking minute devoted to proving I was worth the risk Patrick and Rachel had taken—I started missing calls from home. At first, my mother's messages were *just to check*. Checking I was doing okay. Checking on my summer. Checking to see if I had received the papers she sent. Checking in on my plans for fall. And then they became *just to see*. Just seeing if I had time to call her back. Just seeing if I was around. Just seeing if I had received her messages. In one, I could tell she had been crying, and it was as if I could see her, standing in the kitchen, wearing his clothes, clutter and sadness everywhere. I texted her: *alive and well, just busy at work*.

And it was true, we were busy, but not so busy that I couldn't have called her back, couldn't have checked in on her. I think, perhaps, I leaned into the work at the museum, even into the city itself, to hide from guilt I felt about not being there to guide her back to the business of life. As if I might have been able to persuade her to leave the island of grief she had created for herself. But it was better here, in New York, and I was finding it increasingly difficult to move between my new reality and my old nightmare. I didn't want my mother, Washington, the apple orchards that surrounded town, to pull me out of the reverie I had tumbled into.

I was drunk on the city itself, desperate, in some ways, to drown in it. To let the sounds and the people and the constant movement draw me into its tides and send me out to sea forever. I never felt as alive as I did when I was being tossed around by New York. Even the fact that the city, under the summer sun, smelled of hot garbage and metallic exhaust enticed me. Already the idea that I might not be here to see the light change as it filtered through the maples in Fort Tryon Park in September—a month without Rachel, less luminous, less strange—filled me with dread.

Rachel, it turned out, was a remarkable person to work with. She was on a first-name basis with most major scholars in the discipline, the contact information for each tucked away like so many little secrets in her phone. When we needed to make appointments at the Morgan Library or Columbia, she charmed the librarians with her disarming questions and overt flattery. But she was also shrewd: always ready with the right reference, an arcane historical tidbit. She had a way of making every discovery seem vital, as if it could be the one to break the case. I felt that I was no longer an academic or a researcher, but a detective one clue away from greatness, because that's how working alongside Rachel made me feel—like the artwork or document that could change my life was just around the corner.

But I started to notice stranger things as well—little tics and lies that slid off Rachel. She took great joy in lying to Moira, who had a frustrating way of inserting herself into everything at The Cloisters. If Moira came looking for Patrick, Rachel would say he had just left, even if he was in his office. I watched her move Moira's things around the kitchen, just shift them from one shelf to another, enough of a difference to make a person begin to doubt themselves. When we were asked to update the docent training manual to reflect a change in the works on display, Rachel marked it up, filling it with false information Moira had supposedly missed. I thumbed through it one day, standing at Moira's desk, and went back to tell Rachel.

"It's a joke," she insisted.

"You should go tell her," I had said, worried Moira would take it seriously, but it took days for Rachel to make the corrections, a delicious slowness she seemed to enjoy. I wondered if she might have skipped telling Moira entirely if I hadn't noticed.

Then there was the day all the enamel tiles identifying the plants in the Trie Cloister went missing. During a staff meeting, Leo came in just to address the issue. *Unfortunately, it's probably one of the visitors, maybe a child*, Patrick had suggested. But Leo had kept at it, bringing it up until one day, they were found, thrown in the fountain at the center of the Trie Cloister, broken into shards. No one thought any more of it, except for me, and maybe Leo. Almost certainly Leo.

They seemed like games, these little things. Games overrun by a dark playfulness that only seemed natural amid the funerary sculptures and mummified saints' bones that filled the galleries. And of course, I could never be sure it wasn't a game, nor could I be sure it was. Rachel, I think, liked it that way.

But she never played, I noticed, with Patrick. With him, she was always straight, especially during our weekly meetings when we sat in his office and reviewed our progress. We were, Patrick once said, his eyes and ears in the archive. It was our responsibility to see and hear everything, especially those things that might have been missed over the centuries.

This meant reading and rereading material we were familiar with, creating indices of occult and divinatory practices we turned up, and chasing down other, small leads, no matter how tedious or tenuous. Every week, Patrick went over our work and set us after a new batch of material, a new trove of letters or diaries or manuscripts he suspected—although could never be sure—might reveal something of importance, something he could *use*.

It surprised me that after the tarot reading, we all pretended as if it had never happened. As if we hadn't gathered on our knees around a table to take fortune-telling seriously. As if I hadn't started, in my daily life, to look for the kinds of changes the cards had predicted—the watery expanse of the protection card, the force of the lion. All while Rachel and I were straining under the load, even if Patrick didn't see it. Every week, we were combing through thousands of pages of writing, translating from scratch or switching between three or four languages per day, often staying late into the evening.

Which was why, perhaps, almost two weeks after the tarot reading, I was surprised when Rachel declined Patrick's invitation to stay late that evening as we were packing our things.

"Fine," he said. A whiteness spread across his knuckles as he gripped the edge of the door to his office. "And this weekend?"

I looked back and forth between them and had the feeling I was intruding on something very intimate even though the words themselves were unremarkable.

"I don't know," she said. "We might be working. I might go up to Long Lake. I haven't decided. But I don't think I'll be here."

"Well, we can talk about it—"

"Ann," Rachel said, "would you mind giving us a minute? I'll meet you in the lobby."

When I closed the door behind me, they were still in their corners, not speaking, and I wondered what it was like, navigating power and lust and the work, all at once.

After the dinner at Patrick's house, I had found myself scrutinizing every interaction between Rachel and Patrick—the way she let her hand linger on his arm or his back, the way he followed her with his eyes even in crowded galleries. But I had always been good with languages, and over time I had begun to translate theirs into a call-and-response of desire, a complicated syntax of pursuit and capture.

I walked through the gardens on my way to the lobby, letting my hand drift along the big white yarrow flowers and feeling the softness of the mint. The sunbaked smell of the stones was a pleasant break from the dusty volumes we had pulled from the stacks. I let my eyes close for a minute, only to open them and see Leo across the garden, knees in the dirt, watching my face.

"Ready?" said Rachel, coming up behind me. "I want to show you something."

"If you need to stay—"

"I don't. Sometimes Patrick forgets The Cloisters isn't my whole life. Even if it's his."

I nodded, letting myself touch the flowers one last time.

We walked down the winding paths of Fort Tryon Park, past runners and older couples on benches, past toddlers lying on patches of grass and children using the thick shrubbery to play hide-and-seek. Like schoolmates, we held books to our chests and walked two abreast. Our steps steady, even, synchronized. It was us, I realized, against the world. An arrangement we had hashed out silently during our meetings with Patrick.

If we had been at the Met, maybe we would have gone to a small chic bar with a French name and a select clientele, but this far north, Rachel led me to Dyckman Street, where we walked through two graffitied concrete underpasses until we found ourselves on the Hudson, where a bar sprawled alongside a public boat launch and sailing dock. The tables were plastic, and white umbrellas offered shade to the handful of people who enjoyed their drinks, skin pinkened from the sun and wind. There was no fanfare, no hostess, no formal menu, just a place to order and a place to sit and wait. It delighted me that places like this could exist in a city like Manhattan, where I had once imagined everything cheap and beautiful had long ago been remade into something trendy and expensive.

Rachel ordered our drinks, and I watched her lean over the bar to chat with the bartender; he didn't seem to mind her body in his space and kept returning to hover near her. In between the conversations she shared with the bartender, the man sitting on the stool next to her kept trying to edge his way into her attention. When her head tipped back in laughter—from whose words I couldn't be sure—I noticed, again, the undulating way her body moved, all softness and curves, no sharp points like the ones I had begun to develop. When she returned, she put down two pale beers. I could feel the late-afternoon sun tanning my arms, baking them in a way that reminded me of my childhood in Washington. But the call of the seagulls, the constant motoring along the river, was entirely new.

"What do you think of Leo?" she said, finally, taking a sip, the foam clinging to her lips.

"The gardener?"

"Mmm," she said, "yes, the gardener."

"I don't know him."

"I didn't ask if you knew him. I asked what you thought of him." She paused and considered the question. "If you think of him?"

"I think of him," I said, trying to keep the heat out of my cheeks when I remembered the way he had touched me that day in the garden, the weird intensity with which he held my gaze, even the way his hand had rested above Rachel's head.

"He seems to be thinking about you," she said, looking out across the river.

"He's not why I'm here." Although I wanted to believe that they had talked about me. That the day I saw them in the garden, I was the topic of conversation, and nothing else.

"Well, that's the best way, then, isn't it?"

Out on the Hudson, sailboats waited to catch the breeze in their miniature triangle sails, the wind shuddering against their white canvas, the loose snapping audible from shore.

"I'm only here for the summer," I said.

"That's what I thought, too," she said, looking at me over her sunglasses. "But there's something about this place." She gestured out at the Hudson. "You know, Leo is the one who showed me this bar. I never would have found it otherwise. He knows so many little spots in New York like this."

I felt a surge of jealousy, thinking about Leo and Rachel here, maybe even at the same table. But I couldn't tell who I was jealous of.

"So you've known him for a long time?" I asked.

Rachel shrugged and changed the subject in that way she had—final, closed. "Do you want to go sailing?"

I didn't have a chance to answer before she added, "Let's go." She drained her mostly full glass. "Come on."

She was already pulling me toward the marina where the sailboats were tied up with colorful ropes in slips, a kaleidoscope of clanging hulls and bumpers, her hand wrapped around mine. I couldn't help but notice that whenever I asked Rachel personal questions she changed the subject, or even the scenery. And yet, it was clear there were things she wanted me to know—clues about her life before me. I knew we would get there someday, and so I tripped behind her, happy to let things unfold in the way they were meant to.

"I don't know how to sail," I said.

"I do."

I looked down at the thin cotton dress I had worn to work, the soft leather flats that Rachel had handed down to me, and the sailors on the dock, all in long-sleeve shirts and shorts, sensible shoes. But Rachel didn't look behind her. She trotted down the dock until we came across a boat tethered near the end and began expertly untangling the lines, her long fingers working on instinct, coiling, throwing them into the boat and holding on to the deck so that I could slip in.

"Hurry up," she said, and I noticed her glance over her shoulder. The boat was small and unsteady, and it took everything in me to grip the edges of the hull, what tiny bit of railing there was. The whole thing so shallow I thought I might just slip into the Hudson. Rachel leaned her body against the boat and gave us a surprisingly forceful shove before angling the bow out to join the current. As she lifted the main sail, pulling confidently on a rope and cleating it down, the wind caught up and lurched us forward. I finally spared a look back at the dock, where the man who had been sitting at the bar was cupping the sun out of his eyes and yelling. But the sound was lost to the rustle of the main sheet. I turned and looked toward the open stretch of water, a smile playing on my lips.

CHAPTER EIGHT

The box from my mother had been waiting for me in the kitchen of my sublet for nearly two weeks. Because of its size, I had moved it around, using it as a stool, a coffee table, a doorstop, wanting to keep my past contained for as long as possible. I wasn't sure I was ready for the contents of Walla Walla to spill into New York; I worried that it might close the distance I'd worked hard to build. But I was tired, too, of tripping over the box, of seeing my mother's handwriting on the exterior, of the way it had a presence in my little studio, taking up more space than I was willing to cede. So I used my keys to roughly strip away the tape, pausing only to add cream to my coffee and wedge open my front door with a book in a desperate attempt to increase the breeze.

There was no note. Nor was the box organized in any reasonable way. It looked as if—and I was sure she had—my mother had simply grabbed fistfuls of paper and thrown them in, occasionally pausing to push down on the stack, and then fill in that space again. There were bits of torn material and scrunched up paper. A notebook, now bent down the middle, beckoned from the bottom.

For a moment, I considered throwing the entire thing away—carrying it down to the dumpster behind the building and just heaving it in. A closed chapter. But at the sight of my father's handwriting—a narrow scrawl where all the consonants made the same sharp uplift—I found myself pulling the papers out of the box and stacking them reverently on the floor. I made piles for translations, vocabulary, and etymological lists.

Two additional notebooks surfaced, and nothing in the box revealed any kind of logic or order or filing system. I wondered where my mother had found these in the first place, and it struck me that she probably had kept stashes of my father throughout the house, stashes I didn't know about because I had spent so little time there after his death. My last year at Whitman, I did my very best to spend only nights there, a time during which my eyes were closed to the realities I might otherwise have to face.

With all the papers out, I began to comb through them, trying to find their mates and fellows. There were translations my father had done and their original texts. In some cases, photocopies of books, in others, hand-copied passages from manuscripts. As a janitor, it had been my father's job to go into the offices on campus in the evening and empty the trash cans. He always kept an eye out in the humanities and language buildings for passages he could bring home and translate. Often, he would be late coming home from work because he had spent too long going through the paper waste of the tenured professors who thought nothing of throwing out material they had already incorporated into their research. But to my father, those discarded pages were his textbooks.

They were also how I learned. We would sit down with the leftover fragments of articles or books or letters and piece together translations. I always thought that these partial bits of writing made us, made me, a better translator because they lacked context, lacked clues. Often all we had to work off was a page of abandoned text. A page from a German academic article on Goethe, a letter from Balzac, transcribed manuscript pages from fifth-century Parma. This trash was our joy. A little project we could do in our spare time, just a page or two of work, before he left to clean offices and I left for my shift at the restaurant.

And these were the papers my mother had sent. The odds and ends we often worked on together. They should have been mementos, cherished items of little value to anyone but me and him. But now, looking through them, I could also feel the familiar blurring at the edges of my vision, a dizziness that only increased the more watchful of it I became. It was the panic. The break. The thing that had overtaken me the afternoon of my father's memorial, the thing I had been fighting, had been afraid of, ever since. A kind of thick, deep welling of vertigo that had overwhelmed and broken me. And left me, on the worst days, unable to tell the difference between the fabric of reality and the power of my nightmares.

I left the pages on the floor and walked to my window, where I let the sounds of the street below filter up to meet me, anchor me in place. I breathed, as the school therapist had told me to do during our one meeting after the incident—in through my nose on a count of five until the feeling passed. And that day, it did pass. It passed after a few minutes and a glass of water. But the day of my father's memorial, it had not passed. I could almost smell that day on the pages in front of me—a mixture of frozen meals and zinnias, a thick sourness.

I had held it together the afternoon of the memorial, with just the edges of my vision going in and out, just my breath catching in my chest, until my mother stood to speak. We were in our backyard, really just a square of grass and four fenced walls, where friends, family, and colleagues from the school had gathered. It was full, that square of grass, and my mother ascended a stool to thank everybody. When she did, sobbing through her words, I could no longer stand the tightness in my chest, no longer ignore that I was going to be sick. I could feel the dizziness of the unconscious coming for me, and so I turned and walked as quickly as I could back into the house, only to walk right through the glass door. I didn't even see the blackbird stickers my father had put on the glass when I was still a child.

Mostly, I remember the blood. But my mother remembers the screaming. And although they never talked to me about it, I think that's what most of those in attendance remember too—my bloody body, my lungs expelling every breath until there was nothing more to give; everything was gone. I had needed stitches. Almost thirty of them at various points on my body: my hands and cheeks, my stomach and arms. There was still a scar, just past my hairline, by my ear that had healed keloid and hard, and sometimes I worked it with my fingers, unthinking, until I remembered. They placed me on a seventy-two-hour hold when it turned out I was having difficulty distinguishing between the real events of the recent past—my father's death, my injuries—and the world as I imagined it: dark and false and haunting. At least, that was what they told me. But it was also the reason I couldn't be in the house any longer: My mother wasn't the only one who had broken. She wasn't the only one who had lost her sense of which way was up. At least I knew which way was out.

I took a steadying breath and continued to sort through the papers until something caught my eye. Handwriting I recognized but could not place. Not my father's, but someone else's. I focused past the looping letters to read the text. It was written in the Ferrarese dialect of Italian, and as I read the transcription, I realized to whom the penmanship belonged and why it looked familiar: it was written by my advisor, Richard Lingraf. The man still copied archival material by hand in the era of the digital phone scan. He didn't, as far as I knew, even own a cell phone. My father had probably fished the pages out of Lingraf's trash one evening, but had never gotten around to sharing them with me.

I made slow progress with the document. A few of the words I couldn't make out due to the tendency Lingraf had to string words together in haste, but the rest started to come into focus. It was a record of household contents on the eve of someone's death. Clearly, whoever's household it was had been of significant means: gold coins, books, hunting hounds, porcelain, and frescos. There were also listed, I noticed, *carte da trionfi*. Tarot cards. I picked up the page and flipped it over, but there was nothing on the back. Lingraf had abandoned the transcription midsentence. I set it aside and continued to look through the rest of the papers, searching not for my father's script, but Lingraf's. I turned up another half dozen pages, some of which my father had already provided translations for; those I set aside.

During my four years at Whitman, Lingraf had once joked that I was his only student. Only it wasn't really a joke; it was largely true. Lingraf had been hired in the nineties from Princeton. I always imagined him as an anchor for the department, a hire that conferred the kind of stable, long-term legitimacy a liberal arts college in the wheatfields of eastern Washington so desperately needed. But he hadn't taught much at Whitman, nor had he researched very much after his early publications. And even if he had, he never shared that information with me. Mostly he enjoyed the view from his office and offered me vague suggestions about where I might decide to take my work on the Schifanoia Palace. He did, I realized in retrospect, truly love the strangeness of the work—he liked to linger over the iconography, to talk through the symbolism, to delight in the arcane associations. I thought little about his obsessions, because we were all too preoccupied with our own. That was, after all, what being an academic was all about.

I was surprised to find that the pages my father had translated talked in detail about playing cards and tarot. They talked about a character in Venice whose gender was unclear, and who had been known to use cards for telling the future. The documents spoke, too, about the work of a man I knew well—Pellegrino Prisciani, the astrologer of the d'Este family—and the images he was developing. Lingraf had never mentioned any of this to me, even though the connection to my own research was obvious—Prisciani had also designed the astrological banquet hall at the Schifanoia Palace. If my father had lived, I was certain he would have shared it with me, but I never had a chance to talk to him about the d'Estes or their pleasure palaces.

Outside of those details, however, there was little else the pages revealed. There was some evidence that tarot had been in and around the d'Este court, something we already knew and something that could have been reasonably assumed anyway. But when I turned to the final page of Lingraf's handwritten notes, I could not make out the words. They were written in a language that looked like it should have been Ferrarese or even Neapolitan, but all the suffixes were inverted and appeared as prefixes.

It was, I realized, something like a code: a carefully inverted series of letters that I couldn't decipher. A code for which my father had not attempted a translation.

I tested a few scenarios, to see if I could make a sentence work, a technique my father had taught me when a dictionary was not handy. A way to rely on the Latin I knew so well, but nothing clicked. I put the page aside and tried to find a note or a word from my father or Lingraf that might identify where the transcriptions had come from—an archive, a private collection, anything. There was only—at the top of one of Lingraf's rare photocopies—the edge of a watermark, half of an outstretched eagle's wing, the sharp fragment of a beak.

Without knowing the archive or library from which the transcriptions had come, there was little more I could do. Of course, I could guess at the location, I could confirm my father's translations, although they already looked very clean, but there were hundreds of prefectures and archives and libraries and personal collections. The options, overwhelming.

Around me, the papers were strewn across the floor—echoes of the past that were calling me back—and it suddenly felt like too much, like they were blanketing not just my floor but my life. I needed to escape those four walls the way I had my bedroom at home. I hastily grabbed my bag and found myself on the street, walking south, finally breathing.

⌐

I didn't have a destination in mind, but it soon became clear I was walking in the direction of Central Park, down the big blocks of the Upper West Side where prewar brick buildings boxed out views of the river and occasionally the sun. The neighborhood changed in subtle but marked ways with each block, getting leafier, richer, more boutique as I went. I wanted to walk the papers out of my system, walk long enough that I might be able to go back in time and throw them away. It bothered me that Lingraf had never brought up this aspect of his research with me. All the afternoons we had spent together in his office, full of loose papers and handwritten lectures, and he had never implied that tarot was a topic he might be interested in. If Patrick had hoped, upon reading Lingraf's letter, that I might have shared in some of his research, I was sad to disappoint him. If it hadn't been for my father's willingness to sort through discarded materials, I might never have known that Whitman connected me to The Cloisters.

I stopped for a coffee among the wealthy neighborhood shops, a few blocks from the park, and sat outside for a few minutes to watch the flow of people come and go, baskets in their arms full of produce and fruits.

"There's a greenmarket today," the woman who delivered my coffee said when I asked where they were coming from. A greenmarket, a place where I might buy a bouquet of flowers, something to restore the mood in my studio.

Coffee in hand, I wandered along the row of stalls set up on Seventy-Ninth Street, surprised to discover a wealth of produce that spilled from baskets and down the fronts of tables. There were sellers of honey and lip balms, pole beans, and even a small bunch of ranunculus that I purchased, and some sachets of lavender that I wished I could have. There was something about window shopping that I had always equally loved and resented. It was a joy to be in a group of people, to take in beautiful things, but the feeling of knowing you couldn't afford anything but a handful of stems was restrictive, dark.

Toward the end of the row, people were gathered around a small card table that lacked the protective tent other vendors enjoyed. It was largely bare, without the extravagant display of the other sellers. And then, I heard him before I saw him.

"Ann?" said Leo, coming around to the front of the table and taking my wrist in his hand. "What are you doing here?"

"Just walking." I was so flustered to see him that I didn't even notice he was pulling me around to his side of the table and pointing me toward a chair.

"Sit there," he said as he took cash from a woman dressed in a chic, structured dress. She tucked whatever he handed her into a leather hand-bag and walked off.

I watched Leo make a few more transactions, sometimes selling items off the table, sometimes pulling them from a basket underneath, until finally there was a break in the activity, and he faced me.

"So just walking?"

I nodded. It was, after all, a coincidence, wasn't it?

"No one sent you down here? Rachel didn't tell you to come find me?"

I wondered that Rachel would have known where Leo was on a Sat-urday morning, but simply said, "No one. It's just me."

Leo handed me something off the table. It was a string of black seeds, delicately held together in a necklace. I fingered their shiny exterior.

"You'll want that," Leo said, motioning at the string. "Put it on."

I looked up at him and noticed again how he dwarfed the card table. It was almost comical, Leo's torn jeans and black T-shirt with holes along the neck, his legs and torso both so long that everything he wore looked a little too small, as if it had been made for a child.

"What are they?" I asked.

"Peony seeds. Said to ward off evil spirits and nightmares."

"I haven't had trouble sleeping."

"Yet," he said.

I slipped the strand over my head while he made another sale, the business brisk.

"What else are you selling?" I walked over and consulted the table. There were amulets of woven grass and strings of peony seeds. A handful of crushed things in small plastic packets, each with a shockingly high price sticker. The strand of peony seeds I wore was tagged for $40.

"Remedies. Remedies for the malaises of the rich."

I turned over one of the grass amulets to see the price—$60. I held it to my nose.

"Lemon verbena," I said.

"Very good. We'll make you a horticulturalist yet. But mostly it's vervain. Same family. I add the lemon verbena for smell. "

Everything on the table I realized was also grown in the Bonnefont garden at The Cloisters, the garden that contained the magical and medicinal herbs most commonly used in the Middle Ages.

"What about this?" I asked, picking up one of the plastic packets.

"Henbane. Dried and pulverized. Two grams." When I didn't say anything, Leo continued, "It's a narcotic."

He said it with a shrug, as if selling organic narcotics to richly dressed women was no big deal.

"Have you tried it?" I asked.

He nodded.

"Can I?"

He looked at me appraisingly. "You can, but I have some better stuff you might prefer." From under the table he pulled out a box of labeled herbs. There was mandrake and absinthe. He offered me a packet labeled sea holly.

"What's it for?"

He leaned in to my ear and whispered, his other hand holding my upper arm, "It's an aphrodisiac, a stimulant." He took the packet from my hands and licked his pinky before dipping it in. He held his coated finger in front of my lips. I took him up on the offer and licked the dust off. It was grainy and bitter, tinged with the salt of his skin.

"How long does it take to work?"

"You'll find out."

I watched him go back to the table, where a line of people were waiting for his help. I didn't want to leave. Being around Leo's energy made the papers seem very far away.

"Could you help me?" a woman asked, attempting to squeeze behind the table, past where Leo was now exchanging an amulet for cash.

I looked to Leo for direction, but when he didn't say anything, I stood and threw myself into the business of it all, saying, "Of course. What were you looking for?"

We must have continued like that, selling herbs and necklaces, mixtures and potions, for at least two hours. Leo, always reaching out to touch me as he passed behind, brushing up against me, lingering sometimes a little too long over me while I made change. A delicious dance that made me hope the sun would never go down, that the day at the greenmarket would never end.

But it did end, and after the women were gone—because it was mostly women—and Leo's inventory was depleted, he pulled out the till and counted out $200 in twenties and handed it to me.

"Commission," he said.

When I went to take the money, he pulled it back.

"But you can't mention you saw me today, okay?"

"Okay," I said slowly and reached again for the cash, this time snaking it from his hand. "Why is that?"

Leo raised an eyebrow. "Really?"

"Yes, really. Why?"

"Because everything I sold today came from the gardens at The Cloisters. All harvested. All stolen. All rebranded to appeal to white women who don't believe in modern medicine but are the only ones left who can afford it. You know what I mean?"

"Do you really think anyone would care? What are a few snips of herbs from the garden?"

Leo tilted his head back and laughed.

"Oh, Ann, no. This isn't a small operation. I'm not snipping a few herbs. I'm growing an entire second garden in the greenhouse behind the Bonnefont Cloister full of herbs I harvest for this," he responded, gesturing at the table. "I'm selling more than a few trimmings."

He was, I thought, proud of it—the money, the hustle, the covertness.

"Why would I tell anyone?" I said, pocketing the cash.

"You'd be surprised what can come up in casual conversation."

"I'll make a note to keep your illegal grow operation out of rotation."

"Illegal grow operation?"

"What? Isn't that what they're called?"

Leo laughed, and I found the hearty and rich way he let it all out delightful. I couldn't believe I had been the one who caused him to make that sound. I loved it.

"I can't imagine you're familiar with them," he said. "Grow operations, that is." I was going to admit that I wasn't, he was right, when he said, more seriously, "You've got to just take what you can from the situation you're in, you know? Make it work for you."

That *was* something I was familiar with, something I had been doing since I was old enough to realize what my situation was.

"It's just—" He took a step closer, closing the distance between us, and reached up to grab a curl that had slipped loose from my topknot. "One of the things I have going right now. But an important one."

I could feel his calloused knuckles graze the edge of my cheek, and I turned my whole face so that his open palm rubbed against my lips. I wanted it to smother me, but as I breathed him in—all soil and body odor and lemon balm—Leo looked up sharply and said:

"Shit. Time to go."

He hastily packed up his things, revealing how little had been there in the first place, folded his table, and passed me the cashbox.

"Come on, now." He grabbed my wrist and pulled hard.

At first we were just walking briskly, and I noticed a man behind us, closing in quickly.

"Leo," he called out. "Leo—"

"Pick it up," Leo said, transitioning to a trot.

My shorter legs struggled to keep up.

"Who is that?" I asked, looking back over my shoulder.

"Local constable," Leo said. "Gets bent out of shape when I sell without a license."

"You don't have a license?"

"Hey. You were selling today, too. So hurry."

Ahead of us, I could see the park.

"We gotta get you a cab," Leo said, lifting a hand and waving one down. "You're too slow."

When a cab pulled up, Leo folded me into the back seat and threw a twenty at the driver. "Take her home," he said.

"Leo, wait. No—" I was confused, but he had already closed the door. The window didn't work, and I yelled his name against the glass, watching as he looked behind him to see the officer, because it was, in fact, a police officer, on his tail before he broke into a sprint and entered the park.

CHAPTER NINE

Rachel barely waited for the library door to close behind me before she said, "Patrick needs us to go downtown."

It was Monday, and I had spent the rest of the weekend curious about Lingraf's tarot research, wondering if it was appropriate to reach out to him, if he would even respond. But then, I would have to explain how I had ended up with so many of his papers; he wouldn't believe it was by chance. I had fingered the shiny black peony seeds that I had worn around my neck since seeing Leo and decided to keep my father's secret, at least for now.

"I don't know how long it will take," Rachel continued, "but it might be a good day to be out of the library anyway." She hooked a thumb in the direction of Patrick's office. "He's not interested in having us underfoot at the moment."

It was true, Patrick had been increasingly on edge during our meetings. His expectations growing unreachable as we continued to encounter dead ends in our research.

"I don't know when we'll be back," Rachel said. "Later, I guess. If you need a time."

It didn't matter to me. If anything, it solved the problem of Leo, of what our next interaction would be like, the first after I had seen him that weekend.

In the town car on the way downtown, Rachel said, "We're going to see Stephen Ketch."

I didn't know if I was supposed to know who Stephen Ketch was, but I stayed quiet, hoping she would continue and I wouldn't have to reveal my ignorance.

"It's a personal errand for Patrick. Not for the museum."

At this, Rachel seemed annoyed, and it struck me that things between her and Patrick might have become more strained since the dinner with Aruna, since he had brought me in. I wondered what it was like for her to have the balance upset. When I didn't respond, Rachel looked up at me sharply, expectantly.

"I'm sorry," I said. "I don't know who Stephen Ketch is."

Rachel sighed and watched the buildings flash by outside the window of the car. "You'll see," she said.

John drove us past doorman building after doorman building in the direction of the Queensboro Bridge before stopping. We could see where Sutton Place ran along the East River, and it was one of those rare places where the city gave you space to breathe, let the buildings recede into the background, and the sky take over. I followed Rachel down the block, but before we could reach the river, she stopped in front of an iron gate flanked by two brick alcoves and topped with a wrought iron filigree. A Victorian light dangled from a black chain.

It was an alleyway, almost. A small notch between the buildings that I might not have noticed were I not on foot, and were I not being brought there by someone who knew where to look. It was inconspicuous and beautiful. Hidden, but once noticed, it refused to give up your attention—narrow and historic, and a departure from the busy blocks we had passed on our way south. Rachel rang a bell to the left of the gate, and deep in the alley, behind another door, I heard the bell sound. No one came out to meet us, but the gate buzzed, and Rachel pushed through. We walked until we came to a glass door with the words KETCH RARE BOOKS AND ANTIQUES, hand-lettered in gold, on the front.

The interior was not what I had expected. It was dark and the ceiling was low. Everything appeared hemmed in by clusters of vintage glass bottles and paintings stacked on the floor. Every spare inch of wall space was occupied with books, some in glass cases. The air-conditioning sputtered at the back of the shop, and whirring fans had been placed in the corners to assist in moving the cool air around. Everywhere things were in the way—a Louis XIV chair, a blue-and-white vase, a sculpture, a tin knickknack.

A short, wide man who I could only assume was Stephen sat behind a large oak desk in the deepest recess of the room, making notes in a ledger. I paused to look at some of the glass cases where cheap spotlights were trained on the more expensive pieces: a handful of antique rings with genuine precious stones in them, all with their tags flipped over, prices obscured. I lingered over a gold ring with a smooth red stone set in the center, uncut, simple. It looked like it could have been ancient, Roman in origin.

In Walla Walla, the antique stores had been full of dusty farm equipment and furniture baked by the hot western sun. Every now and again, you would find an item that had made the trip east with its original owner, a chest painted with flowers, or a mirror, darkened with age. But mostly, the things that were considered antique were actually quite new. Fifty years old, a hundred maybe. Here, there were pieces from the seventeenth century, paintings that were dated before the emigrant trails were first opened west from Independence, Missouri.

I hadn't spent money since arriving in New York—aside from my MetroCard and groceries—but in the antique store, I found myself wondering what amounts lay hidden on the underside of the tags. Out of the corner of my eye, I watched Rachel follow Stephen through a door at the back of the room, and I could hear them, through the thin, prewar walls, going up a short flight of stairs. Alone in the shop, I idly pulled a book off the shelf only to discover it was a first edition of *Oliver Twist*. I put it back and made my way closer to Stephen's desk.

At the end of the shop, the clutter became even more overwhelming, and I imagined Stephen living like an animal in his burrow, a cozy nest of antiques and rare books for batting and comfort. I peeked down at his ledger, where objects and prices were recorded in a blocky script—*reliquary, St. Elijah, $6,800*, I read—just as the door opened and both he and Rachel reappeared. She was holding a box wrapped with green ribbon.

"Is there something here you'd like to see?" Stephen asked. It wasn't an unkind request, no hint of reprimand despite the fact he had just caught me snooping.

"You have some lovely pieces," I said.

He looked at Rachel and she nodded.

"Let me show you a few."

I realized then that he had a wildly short frame and that the majority of his presence came from his girth, which he struggled to fit back behind his desk, and then back out again, a ring of keys jangling in his hand.

As he passed me, he grabbed my hand and felt around the base of my ring finger. His touch was pleasant: warm and dry and soft; and he motioned that I should follow him, while Rachel stayed behind to browse a few books on the shelf next to his desk.

"Looking has its pleasures," he said, leading me to a glass case, "but there is no replacement for feeling the real thing."

He pulled out a ring from the case and handed it to me. It had engraved vines and the smallest of diamonds that sparkled fiercely despite the lack of sunlight in the store and their diminutive size.

"A platinum engagement ring, circa 1928," he said.

It slid onto my finger perfectly, its scale delicate.

"It's lovely," I said, allowing myself to imagine what it must have been like to own such a clear marker of wealth on the eve of the country's collapse. A beacon in the dark days that would have been ahead. I wondered if it had been pawned in the wake of the stock market crash, and then passed around from shopkeeper to shopkeeper until it landed here, with Stephen.

He pulled out a small square-cut emerald ring with etched decorations at the corners.

"Even older," he said, passing it to me.

I slipped it on. I had never had jewelry growing up. I didn't even buy cheap pieces as substitutes, but I had always coveted a single piece my mother wore—a beautiful gold bracelet with one charm, a wax press made of amber. It had been my grandmother's, she explained to me, and someday it would be mine. And despite the bracelet's beauty and the fact I loved how it hung, like a pendulum, from her wrist, the thought filled me with an ineffable sadness. These pieces of jewelry that had ended up here instead of living on someone's body. The same way the pieces of jewelry at The Cloisters were relegated to a lifetime of coldness.

"What about that one?" I asked, pointing at the gold band with the smooth red stone in the center. I noticed that the small curlicues of gold that held the stone in place were actually serpents, their scales minute and worn with age.

"Ah, you have excellent taste." Stephen pulled out the ring and held it in one hand while he used the other to shake out his handkerchief with a flourish before placing the ring in his palm, now covered with a simple cotton square.

It was tiny, this ring. Much too small to fit on any finger but my pinky, which it barely fit. On the interior the words *loialte ne peur* were engraved. Old French, probably from the thirteenth or fourteenth century, meaning *loyalty without fear*.

"Very old," he said. "Very old," as if repeating it to himself.

I flipped over the tag, which read $25,000. How such an item could be lost in this crowded stretch of shop, wedged between rare books and other items, shocked me. I pulled it off and examined the band, which was clearly hand-hammered.

When I went to return the ring, I noticed behind the rows of jewelry a handful of minted coins, their edges cracked where the original die had worn thin. On one, the head of Medusa—her eyes pinpricks, her hair made of serpents—was clearly visible.

"May I?" I reached for the coin and Stephen nodded.

In my palm it was heavier and thicker than a regular coin should be, and I realized it was an amulet with an inscription on the back.

"For settling the womb," he said as I began to make out the ancient Greek inscription.

"Such unusual things," I said, almost to myself.

"You should show her, Stephen." This from Rachel, who was watching us from the end of the shop. "I think she'd like to see."

Stephen made his way past Rachel to the door through which they had disappeared. He held it open for me to pass.

There were a few stairs, and then a brief hallway that opened onto another room, this one more sparsely populated with glass cases and a handful of manuscripts displayed open to illustrated pages. The curtains were drawn against the potentially damaging light of the day. And arranged within the cases was a wild collection of beautiful objects: brooches and rings, sets of antique playing cards. Older things, even: a set of papyrus, an enamel scarab, a reliquary. It was a museum in miniature.

"Stephen cultivates collectors," Rachel said from behind me. "He works with a lot of people interested in items that are . . ." She paused to look down at an open manuscript. "Hard to acquire on the open market."

"Provenance is not our expertise," said Stephen, gesturing at the items around him. "Acquiring, however, is. We get all kinds of sellers and buyers in here. Sometimes things come from overseas. Often, the things that come through need to move quickly. I can offer them a home."

"And does The Cloisters?" I asked.

"Oh no," said Rachel. "Never. But Patrick, his standards are a bit lower."

She put the box down on one of the glass cases, and Stephen unwrapped it, pulling out a single card from the stack.

"They're from Mantua," Rachel said.

Stephen nodded. "Yes, from a dealer who thought they might have originated in Ravenna. You know how those Byzantine cities were, such liberal use of gold."

"They're striking," I said, looking down at the card that Stephen had laid on the glass—the *Mundi* card, the World. A card that signified wholeness and completion, a sense of totality. It was the final card in the modern trump sequence.

"A family had found them in the attic of an old country home, in this same box, wrapped with this same ribbon."

"Is that true?" I asked.

Stephen shrugged. "It is the story."

"Patrick has been collecting," Rachel said. "Usually little things: fragments, pages pulled out of manuscripts, small devotional paintings. Sometimes things that are a little more"—here Rachel met my gaze—"unusual. Last year, he came home from Greece with a set of astragali, the knuckle bones of sheep that the ancient Greeks used to tell the future. Over the winter, he purchased a manuscript supposedly written by a haruspex, someone who used the entrails of sacrificed animals to look for omens." She pointed to the card on the table. "These fall into the latter category of his collecting."

I thought back to the items in his library as Stephen slipped the *Mundi* card back into the box and retied the ribbon.

"Perhaps you would like to think about collecting?" he asked me.

I resisted the urge to laugh. There was nothing in the shop I could afford.

"He's been working on me for months," said Rachel, coming up alongside me. "Can we try those?" Rachel pointed down at two bands of hammered silver, each decorated with a ram's head facing the opposite direction, so that when worn together they would be symmetrical. Only when the rings were pulled out did I notice that the entire ring took the shape of a ram's body.

Rachel slid them on her finger. They were surprisingly delicate.

"Here," she said, handing one to me. It fit beautifully. Rachel leaned in close to me and held her hand out so that it matched mine and the rams' heads mirrored each other. Our hands were noticeably different, her fingers long and angular with manicured nail beds, mine with larger joints and torn cuticles. It struck me as curious that the same-size ring would fit both our fingers so easily.

"We'll take these," she said to Stephen, holding out her hand to admire the carving.

I slipped the ring off and held it out to her, curious what number the tag read. Just how much of an investment this was.

"No," she said. "That one is yours."

"Rachel, I can't accept that."

"Of course you can, don't be silly."

"They're friendship rings," explained Stephen, writing the receipt by hand. "Meant to be split between two wearers. From the 1930s. Silver. Sterling, of course."

"But it's such an extravagant gift." I slid the silver band back on my finger.

Rachel looked at me. "Ann. What's extravagant to some is not to others. Learn to accept a gift."

I looked down where the ring was already exerting a delightfully heavy pull, and realized I needed to stop fighting the things that had been brought unexpectedly into my life since I had arrived at The Cloisters.

"Thank you," I said.

Rachel nodded curtly, and we walked back to the main room where Stephen recorded the sale in his ledger in large, looping script.

"A beautiful pair," he said. "Take care that they are never separated."

"We will," said Rachel, looking at me.

On the way back uptown, Rachel and I sat in silence, each of us watching out opposite sides of the car as the city unspooled: Central Park, the Henry Hudson, until finally, the campanile of The Cloisters was in view.

"You can drop us at the bottom here, John," said Rachel, motioning for the car to stop well below the entrance to the museum.

As soon as we were out of the car, Rachel turned to me and said: "Don't tell Patrick that Stephen showed you the cards."

We were walking through stretches of manicured grass. It was mid-afternoon, and the sun hit us squarely as we went.

"But he sent me with you—"

"He didn't," Rachel interjected.

"Then why—"

"I thought it was important that you came. That you knew. I don't want to keep things from you."

I hadn't planned on telling her, on telling anyone, really, about what I had discovered in my father's papers. But Rachel wasn't the only one who had secrets to share.

"I came across some unusual mentions of tarot over the weekend," I said, looking up and seeing the ramparts of The Cloisters ahead of us.

"Oh? In which volume?"

"I can't be sure."

I explained to Rachel about the papers my mother had sent, about my father's translations, and about my advisor's transcriptions.

"And Lingraf never shared any of this with you?"

"No. I had no idea he had done any research on tarot."

Rachel stopped. We had reached the roundabout in front of The

Cloisters, and on the walls of the museum, colorful red banners rippled in the breeze.

"So he never mentioned it? Over the four years you worked together. Not a word?"

"None."

"I see." Rachel waited only a beat before adding, "Would you be willing to bring the papers in? So we could take a look at them?"

"Sure, but without knowing where they came from, I'm not sure how much use they'll be."

We entered The Cloisters and I let the cool air wash over me, felt the reassuring echo of my footsteps on the stone floors.

"I suppose we could ask Patrick," I said.

Rachel put a hand on my arm, a light one, nothing too urgent. Then she said, "Let's not. Let's keep it just between us. For now."

CHAPTER TEN

The flowers were so fully in bloom that their heads drooped toward the ground by the time mid-July arrived at The Cloisters, bringing with it a heavy blanket of heat and haze. But the library and galleries remained a refuge. Some days, despite the appeal of the gardens, I hewed to the gilded and vaulted interiors, walked close to the vents, and lived a life inside the walls. I was, in a word, cloistered, but mostly because of the appeal of air-conditioning.

Perhaps part of the appeal, too, was that Leo rarely came inside, and I felt myself caught between my desire to spend time with him and my commitment to Rachel. My attraction to him was, I feared, a distraction from the work. And the work had to come first; the work was my future. And so, while we had seen each other in passing—him across the garden in cuffed jeans and work boots, face obscured by a straw hat, or him leaving conservation and storage, hands in his pockets—I had done my best to make myself invisible in those moments. Done my best to be smart and put my head down, no matter how hard it seemed, no matter how easily I knew I might fold if given the chance.

If Rachel had noticed any of this, she didn't say. We had, at this point anyway, our own secrets to keep together. It was true; the transcriptions I had shared with her didn't reveal anything radical, but they did reveal that the conversation around Renaissance tarot was more robust, or at least more nuanced, than that of a simple card game. But I held one paper back, even from Rachel—the page that contained the language I couldn't decipher, that nevertheless seemed to be part of the same collection of translations that bore the partially visible eagle insignia. That one I kept for myself.

I had already been in the library for two hours when Rachel arrived and looked at the door to Patrick's office.

"Is he in yet?"

I shook my head.

"I was hoping he'd be able to help get us out of this docent tour with Moira." Rachel looked around, searching for something. What, I wasn't sure. A second later, Moira pushed past Rachel into the library.

"Oh good. You're both in. The tour starts in five minutes, so you should probably wrap this up." Moira looked at me, bent over the table, papers spread around. "For now at least."

"Moira—" Rachel said, but Moira turned on her heels and left before we could protest further.

Docent tours were funny things. Usually staffed by retirees, the docent program at The Cloisters worked with the Education department to offer tours to schoolchildren and visitors alike. But it was never the collection the docents were most interested in seeing—it was always behind the scenes. When we led them through the offices, they lingered longest against doorjambs and at windows, each committing the private topography of the museum to memory. And when we took them through Storage and Security, we fielded more questions than we ever did standing in front of the Mérode Altarpiece or the twelfth-century sarcophagi.

When we arrived at Storage, a woman, a scarf whipped around her neck despite the summer heat, asked, "How many pieces do you keep in here?"

Rachel pulled out a tray, where bits of fragmented stonework and small enamels were numbered and catalogued. "There are over five thousand works like this in The Cloisters' storage. Works we can draw on to support exhibitions or rotate into the main galleries."

"There are even more at the Met," someone next to me whispered, and I smiled politely. "Have you been on the tour of their storage?" she asked me, placing a hand on my arm.

"I haven't."

"Oh. You really should. Not to be missed. You can see the way they hang paintings on wire racks."

Rachel and I were used to these kinds of comments, the way the docents saw fit to tutor us on our own material. And later, after the docents had all dispersed into the galleries, Rachel and I would sit at the table and laugh, rather cruelly, in fact, about their condescension and imparted wisdom.

So while I hadn't been through the storage facilities on Fifth Avenue, I knew from my brief time at The Cloisters that precious items were stored in all sorts of ways. So long as the room was climate controlled and protected from harsh sunlight, very little else mattered. But of course, visitors to museums don't see works of art in that way, as functional objects to be rotated and deployed to create meaning. They see each one as a treasure, something they imagine finding in their attic, among their family storage, something they give immense value to out of sentimentality and lack of true research.

At Security, Rachel introduced each of the guards by name.

"We're excited to have you join us," said Louis, a bank of television screens lighting up the back of his head.

"Do you have camera footage everywhere?" asked one of the women, raising her hand somewhere in the back.

"Almost," said Louis.

"But don't you need every angle in the event of a robbery?"

"Museum robberies are incredibly rare," he explained patiently. "And we have staff on twenty-four hours a day to ensure the security of the collection."

"Which areas don't have cameras?" the woman asked.

"You planning a theft?" Louis asked. He was jovial about it. Most of the artworks at The Cloisters were impossible to move—frescos, massive tapestries, statues fixed into niches, art that weighed several hundred pounds.

The woman drew out the word *noooo* a little too long, clearly a bit offended by the implication. At the front of the group, Rachel caught my eye, and we both did our best to repress the smiles that were trying to work their way across our faces.

"The interiors of the offices, the library, and parts of storage are not fully covered by video," said Rachel.

"And most of the gardens and work sheds," added Louis. "We have a lot of the garden on camera, but not all of it. After all, plants are replaceable."

"I don't know if that's true," said Leo. He was attempting to make his way, coffee mug in hand, through the knot of women, some of whom eyed his outfit with concern.

"Leo," said Rachel, "please introduce yourself to our new summer docent class."

"Hey," he said, lifting the empty cup.

"Leo is one of our gardeners," Rachel continued.

"In case you couldn't tell from the mud stains."

"If you have any questions about the types of things we grow in the garden, he is a great resource."

"I was on a tour once and heard that you grow poisons? Is that true?" a woman interrupted.

Leo nodded. "But you need to remember that many things we consider poisons today had medicinal properties in the Middle Ages and Renaissance. Take belladonna, for example," he said. "It's called the beautiful woman because women used to take small amounts of it to enlarge their pupils."

His eyes found mine, his face dimpling through the stubble he hadn't bothered to trim for several days.

"What were some of the other uses?" asked a voice from the back.

"Well, mandrake was used as a sleep aid. Although we now know that taking too much can easily result in death—"

"We can discuss all of this when we're out in the garden," Rachel interrupted. "I'm sure Leo needs to go."

Leo raised the mug in thanks, and as he slid his body past the group filling the hallway, he brushed up against me as he went, a single, calloused hand grabbing my wrist. That was all it took for the blood in my body to rush and burn. But by the time I looked over my shoulder he was already walking down the hall; he didn't look back.

"Okay," Rachel said, clapping. "Who wants to see the statue of Saint Margaret of Antioch?" And we shuffled on.

After we left the docents to their free coffee and pastries in the kitchen, where Moira clucked over them attentively, Rachel and I stopped in the chapel. I loved the way voices sounded in there—a collection of quiet whispers that came together into something else entirely, a monastic hum or meditative chant. Footsteps in the stone hallway outside gave a welcome percussive structure to the space. It was how I imagined the churches and cathedrals of Europe must feel, as visitors shuffled around the stations of the cross painted by Italian, Flemish, or French masters, while a real Mass was prepared nearby.

Rachel sat on a bench and leaned back on her arms, her fingers curved around the edge, her face cast toward the ceiling, where light came through the stained glass and spread pools of red, blue, and green on the blond stone walls.

"So. You're going to do this, aren't you."

She didn't pose it as a question, but a statement of fact.

"What do you mean?"

"You and Leo."

"I haven't decided."

"Oh, but you have." She let her head loll in my direction until our eyes met. "You look hungry around him."

"I don't even know him." I could feel a heat spreading not just across my cheeks but throughout my whole body.

"Do you need to?"

I didn't know. The majority of my experience with men had either been men I barely knew—the stray one-night stands of my sophomore and junior years, a customer I met waiting tables who was in town for the weekend, a senior about to go to law school—or men I had known my entire life. There was no in-between, and already, Leo was somewhere in between.

We walked back through the galleries, stopping in the early Gothic hall where the walls were lined with brilliant examples of stained glass from the cathedrals of Canterbury, Rouen, and Soissons. One showed a woman in a golden dress clutching two bottles; the title read: *Woman Dispensing Poisons from the Legend of Saint Germain of Paris*, 1245–47.

I stayed late that night, but looking back, I don't know why. An afternoon rainstorm had come through and broken the heat, if not the humidity, leaving the gardens heavy with moisture. When five o'clock came and went, Patrick and Rachel left, asking only in passing how long I planned to stay. *Just another hour*, I had said, but I knew I wanted to wait until it was dark. I wanted to feel myself fully alone in the space, to hear nothing but the slight echo of my own breathing or the shush of paper under the pad of my finger.

Once the sun was down, I closed my books and went to sit at the edge of the Bonnefont Cloister, where I watched the moon rise above the tops of the trees. And while I watched, time slipped away from me, and the day eased deeper into the night. My face tilted up at the sky, I couldn't help but believe the night sky in New York was different from the one I had seen back in Washington. I imagined that here the constellations hung differently, the moon waned more slowly, the earth spun more quickly on its axis. Even though I knew no such thing was possible.

When the moon crested directly overhead, I decided to make my way back to the library. Two hours, perhaps, had elapsed, and when I leaned on the door, the interior was dark. Supposing that security had simply turned the lights off when they found the room empty, I reached instinctively for the switch. But as the door closed, I realized the space was not entirely unlit, but rather illuminated at the end, by two large candelabras that dripped with wax and liquid yellow light.

At first I didn't see the bodies, cast as they were in shadow. But I did see the cards laid out on the table, their gold leaf flickering and catching the candlelight. It was only when Patrick moved that their silhouettes became clear, the flex of his arm, the fall of her hair, familiar specters.

"Ann—" he said, and I could see, as my eyes adjusted to the dim light, that he had crossed the space toward me, had closed the distance so that his hand could reach out and touch my arm, steady me.

Rachel remained rooted on the other side of the table, and none of us seemed capable of finding the right words. All the questions I wanted to ask seemed unnecessarily redundant—it was clear what was going on. There was no doubt they thought they were alone; my books, after all, were closed. The experiment, the reading, whatever they were about to call this, was not supposed to involve me. It struck me that my presence was a mistake, an error, and that we all had secrets to keep from each other—I from Rachel and Patrick, Leo from us all—and some part of me liked that, as it meant every ounce of information and intimate knowledge was hard-won.

"Ann," Patrick said again, sliding his hand up my arm toward my shoulder. "I'm sorry. We should have invited you."

I don't know what I thought he would say, perhaps that I shouldn't be there. That I was fired. But I hadn't expected to be invited in, and although I should have been frustrated that, yes, I had been left out, my heart swelled with appreciation at his words.

He motioned me to follow him to where the deck of cards we had picked up at Ketch Antiques was laid out in a complicated grid.

"With a new deck, Patrick likes to"—Rachel paused as if searching for the right way to phrase it—"break them in here."

"Atmosphere," he said, "helps one fully tap into one's intuition."

I knew not to ask if we could turn on the lights but joined Rachel on the far side of the table, where she reassuringly took my hand and squeezed it. Whose decision it had been to leave me out of the evening crossed my mind, and I wondered if Rachel had played the protector or the gatekeeper. As much as they had welcomed me in, there was a relationship, a connection between Rachel and Patrick, I would never be able to access.

The reading was set up for Patrick. He had dealt the cards and was untangling the meaning of the spread, running a finger below each card, pausing only to touch the corners of the cards themselves. After several minutes had gone by, he gathered them in a pile, taking care that they didn't rub up against one another, and handed them, the entire stack, across the table to me.

Out of the corner of my eye I watched Rachel observe the gesture. Something flashed—as if she were pulling away—and then she softened, took a step closer.

"Start by holding them in your hand," Patrick said, "and think about the question you want answered, then lay out three cards in a row."

I did as I was told, keeping my eyes closed through the entire process. Not shuffling, of course, for fear of damaging the oil paint and gold leaf. I was beginning to dare to hope that they might show me the shape of my future—the days still ahead at The Cloisters and those beyond.

It was impossible not to be struck by the beauty of the cards as I laid them out, not to be captivated by their brilliance and unusual symbols, not to read into what they might be saying. In front of me were the Moon, the Hanged Man, and the Two of Cups. I knew that the Moon, facing me as it did, square and upright, meant deception or obscurity, trickery. The Two of Cups, though, spoke of love or friendship, of new relationships, of cooperation and attraction. The Hanged Man was a symbol of transition and change, but also, traditionally a sign of Judas— *the traitor*. Together, they told me of a shifting landscape, of newness and danger. And there was something more, something prickling at the edges of my vision that felt like an older warning I couldn't quite pin down. An energy coming off the cards that made my pulse beat faster and my eyes swim and burn as if I were underwater.

Because Rachel already knew the symbolism of the deck inside and out, I had begun to study the meanings of individual cards on my own, the way I had once studied Latin flashcards. I had learned the way the suits spoke of different tendencies—the cups of intuition; the swords of diversity of direction; the wands of primal energy. I had discovered that the Major Arcana could be interpreted differently depending on the orientation of the card, whether they were upside down or right side up. But mostly, I had learned that there wasn't a one-to-one correlation between the cards and events; it was more a feeling, a sensation that they gave.

"What do you see?" Patrick asked, his eyes meeting mine. And then again, he asked, this time with an edge, "What do you *see*, Ann?"

In them, I could see my future, even echoes of my recent past, but what I saw was private, for me alone—they were a semaphore that things were shifting, beginning to shake loose, even if I couldn't see exactly how they would come back together for me. I resisted the urge to mess them back into a pile and pretend I hadn't laid them out at all.

"I'm still new to all of this," I said, gently setting the cards aside. "Why don't you read, Rachel?"

"I can't," Rachel said. "I don't do readings."

"Why?"

"I just don't. I study them, but no, I don't do readings. I won't."

"You've never had a reading?" I asked.

She looked across the table, pinning her gaze on Patrick. "I have. In the past. It's complicated. Unlike Patrick, I don't want to see the future. I'd rather be surprised."

At that, Patrick pushed himself away from the table, and the heavy wooden chair he had been occupying fell backward, clattering against the stone floor. He did not bother to right it. Rather, he walked out of the library, leaving both of us standing there, alone, in the candlelight.

CHAPTER ELEVEN

Three days after I thought I saw it in the cards, Leo invited me to a gig in the Bronx.

"I play bass," he explained, chewing a toothpick and leaning against one of the columns that ringed the Trie Cloister. "You can take the subway. Just one stop past Yankee Stadium. I'll meet you."

There had been no small talk, no explanation of what happened that day at the greenmarket or after. He simply stopped me and asked. It was less an invitation and more an inevitability. At least that was how I felt about it, even though I didn't have his phone number—and he wasn't offering it now, either. Just a promise to meet me.

"Okay," I said. "Yes."

The decision, I knew, would save me from another night in my studio, which, over the past couple of weeks, had deteriorated further: clothes piled on the bed, dishes lining the sink, papers everywhere. I didn't consider myself a slob, but that morning I had stepped on some coffee grounds that had spilled from the filter I'd thrown out the previous night and not even bothered to brush them off the soles of my feet. The similarity to the home I had left behind in Walla Walla had not escaped me, but I chose not to examine the impulse I shared with my mother, to let things spiral when stressed.

The truth was, I had dedicated my kitchen table to books, articles, my laptop, and a deck of tarot cards I picked up from a local bookstore. I read scholarly articles about tarot, or *carte da trionfi*, as they had been called during the Renaissance. I learned that the earliest extant record of tarot cards came from a 1442 accounting record from the d'Este family in Ferrara, and that Marziano da Tortona, the secretary and astrologer to Duke Filippo Maria Visconti of Milan, had been one of the first to write about the symbolism of the deck. I also discovered that while it was true that tarot had originally been a card game, it had been recorded as a divinatory device in Venice by 1527.

And while few scholars had written about tarot—rarely did historians or art historians bother with the topic—all agreed the early modern period was obsessed with divination and telling the future. Astrologers, of course, were on every payroll in Italy in the fifteenth and sixteenth centuries. Marsilio Ficino, astrologer for the influential Medici family, had believed in the wisdom of the planets so thoroughly he had even predicted, at the birth of Giovanni di Lorenzo de' Medici, that he would become pope. He did—Leo X. Moreover, places like Ferrara, where the ruling family was both fabulously rich and darkly fascinated with occult methods that might advance their reign, seemed like the ideal place for tarot cards to be used as a fortune-telling tool. Then there was the tradition of tarot itself—the imagery so distinctive, so unlike any other deck of cards that had come down to us, that it was hard to imagine they had been used for anything outside of the occult. And finally, there was the way the cards felt in my hand when I laid them out—electric, alive.

After I agreed to meet Leo, I left him in the garden and made my way to the library. Ever since the night we had read the cards by candlelight, I'd been surprised to find Rachel sitting at the same table, fully illuminated, surrounded by work papers and research materials, and not in shadow. She seemed to move so seamlessly between the world of the cards and the world of rational research, but for me, I was finding it increasingly difficult to keep the boundaries clear. And as I joined Rachel, we could hear Patrick through the thick door of his office, voice raised but words muffled by the old oak grain.

"It's Aruna," said Rachel, not looking up from where she was transcribing notes. "He took the cards up to her and she thinks they're fake. He was hoping to present them at the Morgan, but that won't be happening anymore. He'll be relegated to moderating instead."

It was hard to believe. I had felt something the night I held them, the night I laid them out, here, on this very table. But wasn't that how magic worked? Distract the audience with the setting, the atmosphere, the flashy production, so that no one noticed the sleight of hand, the falseness of it all?

We could hear him through the door, a dull roar of anger, disappointment. It was a setback, and Patrick was becoming increasingly intolerant of setbacks.

"What do you think?" I asked her.

Rachel looked up from her work and shrugged.

"They're beautiful, but they don't feel right. They're stiff. Vellum is much more flexible usually. And it's true that there's something a little rough about the illustrations. Childish, maybe?"

I nodded. I'd only seen them twice, once at Ketch Antiques and again in the dim light of the library. Rachel, I assumed, had had more opportunity to view them.

"Aruna agreed?"

"She did. I told him, of course. But he didn't want to hear it coming from me. I think he'll have to show them to a few more people before he really comes to terms with it."

"I didn't think people were in the habit of forging fifteenth-century tarot cards."

"Personally? I think they're a seventeenth-century copy. Not a contemporary forgery. A bad attempt to reproduce what the Viscontis were doing in Milan." Rachel leaned across the table and lowered her voice to a whisper, almost a hiss. "You know what he's looking for, don't you? He's looking for an ur-text. The earliest deck. The most clearly occultist.

He's looking for something we don't even know exists. Just something he"—she waved her hands—"dreams about."

"But don't you think we'll find evidence of it? At some point?"

"Probably, yes. I wouldn't do this work if I didn't think that was possible. But what's the likelihood it comes through Stephen? Stephen doesn't sell anything that good. The things that are that good he keeps for himself, or ultimately passes off very quietly to institutions whose acquisitions policies are more lax."

Rachel was right; the cards were stiff, lacking the supple quality of vellum, and some of the illustrations looked rough. But there was something different about the way the cards felt, something intuitive I wasn't ready to dismiss.

"I just think Patrick was willing to overlook so many of these issues because the deck was almost complete. And complete decks are impossible to find. It was going to be such a coup, sharing it at the Morgan. In fact, Patrick wants us to go pick up a few remaining cards down at Stephen's tomorrow. I guess several had to be acquired from another source."

"Sure," I said. "I'm surprised he still wants them, considering Aruna's opinion."

The sounds coming from Patrick's office had stopped, and the library returned to stillness, save for the sound of visitors passing along the corridor outside.

"It might be best not to be around Patrick right now anyways," Rachel whispered.

The 125th Street platform had little standing room and the subway car even less. Everywhere, people were dressed in pinstripes and Yankee caps: young families, drunk college kids, Japanese tourists, a guy hawking bootleg hats—a sea of bodies, suffocating and idiosyncratic, that moved me around, despite my attempts to stand my ground. I was squeezed in before the doors closed, my face pressed up against the glass, slightly scratched and worn, only to be spit out three stops later when the car emptied at Yankee Stadium; it was fifteen minutes before first pitch. Afterward, the only people left on the train were myself, a man who had inexplicably slept through it all, and a young mother, infant on her lap. That the city swung wildly between these two extremes—joyful chaos and the workaday—made me desperate to experience it all, to feel the polarity of the two.

I met Leo one stop later at the entrance to the subway. I was wearing a short baby doll dress from Rachel's castoff collection, and was gratified when Leo looked at me and then performed a dramatic double take.

"You look good," he said, appraisingly. "Come on. We're going to eat before the gig."

He didn't take my hand, but held my upper arm and walked very close to me, the way a hostage taker might lead a victim if he had a gun. It was an unusual way to walk, but I liked how close he was, how intimate it felt.

It was my first trip to the Bronx, and it was vibrant and loud—car stereos and music spilling out of bodegas, people on stoops laughing and playing music of their own, a cacophony or a symphony, I couldn't decide. And despite the long, leafy streets and low-slung apartment blocks, only four or five stories high, it felt more densely packed than Manhattan, where the view was dominated by skyscrapers. If Leo seemed occasionally brittle and often biting at The Cloisters, here he seemed loose. Even the way he walked was lighter, more off-kilter, like he didn't have complete control of the way his feet moved or their cadence.

"That's where I live," said Leo, pointing to a brick apartment building. "On the third floor, in that corner window."

I could feel his breath on my neck. The way he inhabited my space was always a little unnerving, taking up too much of it, like it wasn't mine, but his. And while it should have made me nervous, it only made me excited. It made me want to unlock all the carefully compartmental- ized qualities in my life and let them loose.

We kept walking toward the sun until a hot orange twilight spread across the pavement. Neither of us spoke. I was worried that anything I might say could give me away, reveal me as a fraud. But Leo simply led me into a bar, walking quickly through the dark interior until we reemerged on a back patio, where the umbrellas were emblazoned with beer logos and a single rotating fan blew stale, humid air back and forth between makeshift fencing.

Leo threw himself into a plastic chair, then quickly got back to his feet to pull out mine, but the gesture was too late. He only managed to reach the arm and knock it back a bit, but I appreciated the effort.

"Sorry," he said. "Out of practice."

"Putting me in cabs, pulling out my chair," I said. "I wouldn't have pegged you as chivalrous."

"Chivalry was very big in the Middle Ages, wasn't it?" he asked.

We ordered beers that wept condensation and a plate of tacos. I was overdressed.

"Did you get in trouble?" I asked. "The other day?"

"Oh. Officer Palko? He only catches me now and then. Technically you need three fines to be banned. He's only managed to give me two so far."

I nodded, and we both fell silent until finally he asked:

"Will this be your first punk show?"

"Yes."

It was actually my first concert of any kind. But I wasn't ready to admit that.

"When we go on, you can come backstage." Leo offered me his pack of cigarettes, but I declined. He pulled one out for himself and lit it. The sulfurous smell from the match found me across the table.

"Is this what you want to do?" I took a sip of my beer, fizzy and filling, grateful to be talking about something else. "Be a musician?"

"You don't think being a gardener is a career?" He leaned back in his chair and tapped his cigarette on the table; there was no ashtray.

"No. I mean, if you want it to be."

"What if I told you," he said, striking a match and lighting it idly, a reflex, a habit. "That I had zero ambition. That I just wanted to plant and trim and weed all day. What then?"

"What do you mean, 'what then'?"

"Would that be it? Would you be over this?" He drew a line in the air between us. "Are you looking for someone who's always trying to transform themselves into the next thing? Because that can get exhausting."

I still struggled to get a bead on when Leo was kidding and when he was being serious; I suspected it was often a combination of the two.

"I don't know who I'm looking for," I said after a minute, both to fill the silence and because it was true.

"Let me warn you away from artists, you know. They can be assholes. Real jerks, psychologically, you know." He pointed at himself. The way he sat in the plastic chair, making it flex and tilt with every movement of his tall, lanky frame. He was never not moving, jiggling his leg or tipping back in his seat. But despite the frenetic energy, he was watchful; he eyed the way I ate, the edges of my eyes, my lips.

"I guess it's good you're just a gardener then," I said.

"I knew I was right about you," Leo said, blowing out a thin stream of smoke. "And I'm a playwright, if that's what you were asking. I write plays. And play pickup bass in a punk band in my spare time."

"So you don't want to be a musician?" It felt like every time I pinned down a fact about Leo, the landscape shifted. I liked that, the feeling of being off balance.

"No," he inhaled. "Must be a relief, huh?"

"I don't have anything against musicians."

"But how many of them do you know? Personally?"

"None," I admitted. "You're the only playwright I know, too."

"That's because there aren't many of us left."

We ordered another round and I asked him how he got into play-writing: college. And why he loved it so much: the structure, the pacing. We talked about our college experiences, him at NYU, me at Whitman. He was five years older than I was, and I wondered how many more years it would take me to give up on my dream and go home, try something else. More than five, at least.

"Do people ever ask you what you'll do if it doesn't work out?" I asked.

He paused. "What will *you* do if it doesn't work out?"

"What?"

"Museums, *academia*." The way he said it, drawing out the word, thinning it through his teeth, was a dare, a tease.

"It hasn't worked out," I said. "I was the orphan Patrick adopted, remember?"

"Yeah," he said, exhaling cigarette smoke and studying the fringe on the umbrella above my head. "Rachel always told me that if it doesn't work out, I should just convert everything to screenplays."

"Why don't you?"

"Because I believe in the integrity of the process."

"So Rachel knows you're a playwright," I said, sipping my beer. I wanted to sound nonchalant, but I couldn't help but wonder about the number of conversations they'd had, if they'd been to this bar before, and why she hadn't told me.

Leo nodded.

"Has she seen you play?"

"Are we going to talk about Rachel all night? I could have just invited her."

It was hurtful, and he knew it, because a second later, he reached across the table for my hand, and although I tried to wrestle it back into my lap, he held on to it, his long fingers wrapped around mine, exerting the same kind of pressure he did on everything. A little too hard, but easy to respect in its conviction.

"Were you two together?"

I don't know why I asked, but I did. I asked because I needed to know.

"No," he said, pushing his hair behind his ear. "Not my type. Plus, as far as I know—as far as everyone knows—she and Patrick have been doing something for a while."

I didn't want to push it further; it was, after all, the answer I wanted.

"Am I your type?" I asked, emboldened by the two beers I had drunk and the fact he was still holding my wrist, running his thumb across my skin, across its soft blue veins.

He didn't answer, but leaned across the table and kissed me. Not gently, not the way you do at first, but big and hard, his hand in my hair. And it was *that* I couldn't resist about Leo: the urgency, the disorder, the chaos, his unabashed enthusiasm for doing things differently. Not just differently from everyone around us, but differently from what I had always known: the timid advances of boys, the clammy hands in the car, the unanswered texts. It was like Leo's attraction to me was expansive and hungry, like it might eat the table, the bar, my life. I wanted it to.

I watched him play that night, from the wings of the stage. The sound so loud, it transformed into noise—a banging and an aching. In the crowd, bodies collided frantically, but I barely spared a glance for what was happening in the dark of the room, fixated as I was on the way Leo's hair fell into his eyes, the way a slow trickle of sweat spread down the front of his chest. And despite all that had happened that summer, that year, the devastating months around my father's death, I thought of none of it in that moment. I thought only of Leo. Of his long torso and his meanness. Of the energy from the crowd and how my body was moving on its own, independent of me, to the sound.

Afterward, we crammed into the guitarist's apartment, where the light was yellow and the air smoky. He had a balcony that overlooked the water and a tiny girlfriend, Mia, with wild, curly hair that she claimed she hadn't brushed in six years. A claim I believed. When I went out on the balcony to escape the crush of people, the stale smell of cigarettes and liquor, Leo joined me, pushing his body against mine.

"You liked it, didn't you? The show?"

I murmured in agreement.

"I knew you would. There's something a little punk about you, Ann. Even if I'm not even sure you know it yourself. But I like it. It reminds me of myself."

I let my body lean back against his, until his cheek brushed the nape of my neck and he whispered, "I have something for you."

"What is it?" I said, spinning around. Our bodies were so close I had to tilt my face up to see what he held above me: a battered deck of cards.

"Mia's tarot," he said. "Here, pull a card."

I frowned. "That's not how you're supposed to do it."

But he held it up, the top card already partially pulled out. I snatched it from him and held it to my chest.

"What is it?" he asked, a smile on his lips.

I peeked down and peeled it away from my chest, the card damp with sweat after only a second against my skin. The Lovers. When I looked up at him, he was laughing. Leo leaned in and whispered against my ear: "I like telling your fortune."

I woke up the next morning in the Bronx to a paper cup of coffee and a bagel on the bedside table. Leo's apartment was shared with the drummer—who was actually an aspiring mixed-media artist from Brown. By the time I peeked my head out of Leo's bedroom, the drummer had already gone for the day, and Leo was bent over the kitchen table, scribbling in pencil. There were clothes and bits of weed and sticky specks of resin, but also a worn collection of Sam Shepard plays, a few loose-leaf essays by David Mamet on the coffee table, a scattering of *Playbills* with dates scrawled on their covers.

"Thanks for the coffee," I said.

"Full service." He didn't look up.

"I had fun—"

"Dinner later this week?" he said, still scribbling.

"I don't have your number." I stood, searching for my cell phone or a scrap of paper, while Leo continued to write. Finally, he pointed across the apartment.

"Get me a pen. I'll give it to you."

I walked to the corner where a collection of ink pens and notepads was carelessly heaped on top of a bookshelf. I was scanning for one that was relatively normal when I saw them—a pair of dice. Not just any dice, but astragali like Patrick had in his library. I resisted the urge to palm them and ask Leo where they had come from, if they were replicas or the real thing, and returned with the pen.

"Give me your arm," said Leo, and I held it out obediently, enjoying the way he embossed the number on my skin, onto the softest part of my arm. "There," he said, looking up at me. "Now you have it."

CHAPTER TWELVE

Even after the ink marks had worn off, I could feel his numbers crawling on my skin. But the busy high season at The Cloisters proved a distraction, and every day, I found myself surrounded by buses of camp kids, international tourists, and native New Yorkers looking for an escape from the midday sun. A constant flow of bodies moved through the galleries, steady and lymphatic, pumping energy and heat into the Gothic building; so many of them that the temperature sensors began to tick up and the system itself began to groan. Children stood on the big metal grates set in the floor, enjoying the novelty of the cool air running up their legs. The sound of echoing footsteps was inescapable as people made their way from the bejeweled reliquaries to the frescos of lions and dragons, and on to the paintings of martyred saints.

And as the sun dragged slowly across the skyline, and the heat seemed like it might never leave us, it all was beginning to get to Patrick. His avuncular smiles had given way to hollow cheeks; his flawlessly pressed shirts were now rumpled. And when he spoke to Rachel and me, there was an edge to his questions, an urgency that had been brewing but that now reached a fever pitch alongside the crowds of visitors. Where previously Patrick had put Rachel and me to work on the same material, I noticed that he was now breaking us up. Parceling out archival resources and dividing them between us, and then, much to our frustration, always checking our work, treating us like school children instead of trained and seasoned researchers. As if the lack of information in the archive were our fault, as if we were hiding from him what we really found.

It was for this reason, I assumed, he decided to take me, alone, down to Ketch Antiques that day and leave Rachel in the library, awash in books and translations.

"I need this done before the symposium at the Morgan," he said to Rachel while he waited for me to gather a few of my things. It was, I realized, a punishment, but I wasn't entirely sure for whom.

In the cab downtown, however, with The Cloisters behind us, he seemed restored to the Patrick I had known at the beginning of the summer, eager to show me how entangled I was in the mystery of the cards.

"Rachel," he said, "does excellent work. Truly excellent. But she doesn't always believe. Not in the way I do. Or, I think, you do. It's not something that can be taught, that instinct."

I wanted to protest, to say Rachel shared it too. Or that he was wrong, I still didn't believe. But I thought back to the night Leo and I stood on the balcony, me holding the Lovers card against my chest, of the spread at The Cloisters that had warned me of a shifting, of a transition, maybe betrayal. I looked across the cab at Patrick, but he was facing the window, a hand along the sill, the tips of his fingers white from pressing down. I knew he still hoped that this deck might be the discovery he had long sought.

"You have seen it, haven't you, Ann?" he said, now turning to face me. "In the deck. That night. You noticed something different, too. I saw it in you, you know."

The way he searched my face, desperate and haunted, made me want to assure him that they were just cards, just a parlor trick. But he was right. I had felt it. And it had been following me, too, like a specter of something I couldn't explain, something beyond the research and citations.

"Yes," I said. "I think there's something there." And then I added quickly, "But Patrick, you need to remember that I might be wrong. These cards—it's all still new to me."

"Of course. But doesn't that make it better? Make it proof that you—someone who isn't experienced—can feel it too?"

"Sometimes," I said gently, "we can't trust what we feel. Intuition, a sensation—they're not proof."

I didn't add the thing that had been troubling me, which was that I was starting to struggle to distinguish between what was real and what was imagined within the walls of The Cloisters. Some days, under the Gothic arches and among the funerary sculptures, it seemed as if the eyes of the statues were following me, as if the gold and the glitter were filling my vision and blurring it, as if, for a moment, my very body was dissolving in the space and becoming a feeling, a sensation, an intuition.

I knew where that instinct had come from, that insistence that the outlandish was worthwhile. It had germinated at my kitchen table in Washington, across scraps of paper and bits of language, across the pads of paper my father and I often filled together. Although sometimes, he worked alone. It was that instinct that had led me here, had led me in everything I did. Always. I was beginning to realize it when he died, but some of my belief had gone with him. Only now was it beginning to return. Patrick wasn't wrong that I believed more than Rachel. Because perhaps one needed a little magic to make a narrow childhood more bearable.

Down at Ketch Rare Books and Antiques, we discovered the scene had not changed. If anything, it seemed that the antique bottles and books had grown in quantity, multiplied in the intervening time, as if they had copulated in the dark.

Despite having buzzed us through the gate, Stephen wasn't in the main room. Patrick rang a bell on his desk, the echo of which I could hear in the upstairs room.

I pulled out a first edition of Émile Zola and sat in one of the free chairs to wait, opening the pages to where the first few lines of French began. Patrick browsed the shelves, waiting for Stephen, until he came around to where I sat, and placed a hand on the back of my chair, his body angled into my space.

"Ah," he said, looking down at the text in my lap. " 'If you shut up the truth and bury it underground, it will but grow.' Zola."

I looked up at him and felt, for a moment, very young. As if I were looking up at my father as he leaned over my translation, checking that I had chosen the correct cases. The image so startling, it moved me to close the book, to stand up, to put some distance between myself and Patrick. Something that was maddeningly difficult in Stephen's shop.

"You know," he said, turning in a circle to take it all in—the rare books, the jewelry, the paintings. "We'll find it. Eventually, we'll find it. The deck, the document. The truth. The thing that will unlock it for us. We'll find it."

There was something in his voice, a pushing thinness that belied what every researcher knew: the thing may no longer exist. That was the reality of an archive—they were always incomplete despite their depth, made up, as they were, of fragments.

"Always a believer," said Stephen from the end of the room. He had entered through the back door and now pawed through the papers on his desk until he came across a thick packet that he passed to Patrick, who absently handed it off to me.

"I have a few other things you might like to see?" Stephen said to Patrick, inclining his head toward the door. When I went to follow, Patrick held up a hand.

"We'll only be a few minutes."

I returned to my seat among the antiques, the packet in my lap, the image of Patrick standing above me morphing into an image of my father standing above me replayed in my mind. After more than a few minutes had passed, it was clear that they would be longer, and looking for a distraction, I stood and began to pick up objects and guess their age, their value, before consulting their tags. I did this until it felt like the only thing left in the shop I hadn't examined was the packet Patrick had handed to me. I lifted it up in the dim light and looked at its closure. It was just a fold, one that I was quickly able to slide my finger beneath and shake the contents out into the palm of my hand. There were three cards: two pips and the Major Arcana card the Popess.

I set down the two pips and flipped over the Popess card to examine its back. It revealed not just stars against a blue sky, but delicate gold lines that connected the stars—constellations. There was Scorpio and Libra, the Pleiades and Cancer, as well as twinkling motes of gold leaf suspended above an outline of the earth, the world as black and unseeing as the night. I looked down at the card in my hand and felt its stiffness with my fingers.

I flexed it instinctively, just a test, to feel what Rachel and I had talked about, the strange stiffness of the cards, and as I did so, I felt one of the edges pop. At the top right corner, something had pulled away from the delicate blue and gold backing of the card, a piece of paper. And there, underneath, I could see something unusual—a strand of hair blowing against a pale blue and pink landscape. I wedged my nail gently into the gap and watched as the stiff card of the Popess fell away entirely, revealing a different card—the Huntress, Diana. Recognizable because of the bow she carried in one hand and the moon diadem on her head. Across from her, a stag drank from a pond. Above her, putti held a collection of arrows, and the constellation of Cancer—the astrological sign associated with the moon—hung in the sky.

The false front, I realized, had been held in place by a dab of flour and water in each corner, a drying substance that flaked off when I brushed it, gently, with the pad of my finger. The card I had revealed was lyrical and dramatic in its execution. Its color pale but saturated, the imagery diverse and arcane. But a word—*trixcaccia*—written on the card was indecipherable to me. Not because of the lettering, but because of the language. It was almost recognizable: a Neapolitan-Latin hybrid perhaps, that had an air of the familiar.

The card I held in my hand had the uncanny character some works of art have, the ability to draw you in, an absorptive quality. The first time I'd experienced anything like it was actually with a reproduction. A careful copy of Botticelli's fresco of the graces that is housed at the Louvre, but that had been copied, in painstaking detail, for an exhibition in Seattle. I could have looked at that fresco for the entire day, its graceful figures and washed-out colors. The card in my hand had the same quality, as if I were falling into it, a pool of beauty.

The sound of footsteps from upstairs brought me back to the present, and I quickly set about getting the false front to re-adhere to the card I had revealed underneath. I stopped short of wetting the flour again for fear that I might damage the paint, but there was no way to reunite the two. In the moments that followed, it never crossed my mind to return the card to the packet, or share my discovery with Patrick. Instead, I pulled out my bag and emptied everything from my wallet—all cards, coins, dollars, anything that might scratch the surface of the card—and then, I zipped the card inside.

As I set my bag back on the floor and reopened the copy of Zola I had been reading, now to a random page a little ways in, the door at the end of the room opened and Patrick and Stephen came in, still in close conference.

"You'll let me know if you hear of anything else?" said Patrick.

"Of course, of course," said Stephen. "You'll be the first one I call."

I watched Patrick hand over a thick envelope and Stephen pass him a slip of paper.

"Don't keep that," he said. "Best not to have receipts in easy reach if anyone has questions. But I realize you might want something for right now."

Patrick nodded, and having walked back to where I was sitting, handed me the receipt and reached for the packet.

I looked at it and read: three tarot cards. I slipped it into my purse, wondering how long I might have before Patrick realized there were only two in the envelope.

For the rest of the day I feared Patrick would notice the card's absence. Sitting in the library, I tried, unsuccessfully, to push away the fear of him coming out and demanding to know where it was, the card, the discovery. I found it impossible to focus, and even when I walked through the gardens and tried to force myself to breathe, the smell of lavender and the brush of the grasses against my skin could not calm me.

Rachel joined me at the edge of the Bonnefont Cloister.

"What happened downtown?" she said, shaking out a cigarette and lighting it, her movements quick and sharp.

"Nothing," I said. "We picked up a few more cards."

"And that's all?"

"That's all." I wasn't ready to tell Rachel, tell anyone, what I had discovered, but I could feel in her questioning something urgent, something that made my skin feel tight and my face flush.

"Okay." She paused to exhale a stream of smoke. "Because he's in there on the phone, and he sounds furious."

What could I say? That the thing Patrick was angry about was sitting only a few feet from his office, tucked safely into my bag. No. And so, not wanting to reveal my secret, I said the one thing Rachel and I had been leaving unspoken between us, though we both had observed it.

"He's been so on edge, so desperate to make this work, to have something ready for the Morgan. Do you think, maybe, it's all beginning to get to him? The fact we've found so little? The fact it seems like nothing is there?"

Rachel looked at me from the corner of her eye, just a glance, and nodded.

"What do you think about getting out of here for the weekend?" she said. "I think we should go together."

I had wanted to spend the weekend with the card, alone. To maybe have that dinner with Leo. But she continued:

"The Morgan symposium starts on Monday. That gives us almost three days if we leave today. Can you leave today?"

"Where did you want to go?" I asked.

"Long Lake," she said. "To the camp."

I had never heard the term *camp* used to describe anything other than places where children learned the basic skills of archery and spent slow afternoons making friendship bracelets, but I was certain Rachel was referring to something else entirely.

"Yes," I said. "And Patrick?"

"I'll tell him. I'll go tell him right now. Just pack a few things for the weekend and meet me at my apartment. I'll text you the address."

"Right now?"

"Unless you want to stay and see how this all plays out?"

She was right. I pulled out my phone and texted Leo—*rain check?*—even though he had yet to follow up about his passing invite. Briefly, I watched the three gray dots bounce on my screen, but I didn't wait for his response. I needed to put some distance between Patrick and myself. If the card was a life raft, I knew there would not be room for all three of us.

That I expected we might drive to the Adirondacks showed how little I understood about Rachel's wealth. When I met her in front of her building, a car was already waiting for us. Her doorman carried a neat, cream leather bag behind her and placed it ceremoniously in the trunk, next to my backpack into which I had shoved two paperback novels and my computer. It was, although I wouldn't admit it to her, the first time I had gone on a girls' trip or slept over since elementary school.

We were deposited at a heliport along the West Side Highway, where another porter collected our luggage and stowed it before the blades of the helicopter began to beat rhythmically. I assumed we would take it all the way upstate, but when I mentioned this to Rachel, she laughed and said into her headset, *It doesn't have that kind of range.* When the pilot turned around and grinned at me, I did my best not to let the embarrassment spread from my cheeks to my neck and chest.

After landing at a Long Island floatplane center, we boarded a yellow plane with two large pontoons and relatively small wings. Two small props would power us all the way to Long Lake as the sun set. Rachel expertly hauled herself into the back seat and was already buckling her seat belt when I took my first, tentative step aboard. The pilot handed me a pair of headphones and offered me a thumbs-up. It was the smallest plane I had ever been on. Once my headphones were on, I heard the pilot say to Rachel, *Our time in flight will be approximately two hours and fifteen minutes.* Only a few minutes later, we were in the air; gradually, the skyscrapers of Manhattan receded behind us into the haze.

As we flew, the pilot would occasionally call out landmarks—the wide, flowing Hudson, the swell of the Catskills, the racetrack at Saratoga, Lake Placid, twice home of the winter Olympics—until the channel became quiet while he piloted us down onto a dark patch of earth that turned out not to be land at all but the inky expanse of Long Lake. I had imagined, during the flight, what Rachel's camp might look like, but I was ill equipped to understand the reality.

Our pilot motored some distance until the house came into view, its dock lit by bright white lights that jutted into the lake; they were the only lights for miles. On the dock, a man gestured with a green wand until the floatplane was fully snug up against the dock; the door opened and we disembarked. Rachel hugged the man, and although I could see her lips moving, I couldn't hear what she was saying.

The floatplane pilot tapped me on the arm and gestured for me to take off the headphones. When I did, the sounds around me came roaring back, and I was surprised to feel my arms blooming with goose bumps as I registered a chill in the air. Since moving to New York, I had yet to experience a truly cold summer night. Usually I slept without covers, my window unit always out of service.

As our bags were unloaded, I looked toward the house. Two chimneys with crenellated tops, black against the dark sky, graced either end. Lights were on inside, and I could just make out the curves of the veranda that wrapped all the way around the structure, the delicacy of the trim; here and there, a chandelier was visible through the windows. I couldn't understand why it would be called a camp; it was a manse with a complex of matching outbuildings and boathouse. Everything so clearly historic that the light that came through the float glass windows was tinted and watery. We made our way down the dock and up a sloping lawn, and as we got closer, taxidermies of deer came into focus on the walls and above the mantels of the home; there were antlers everywhere.

When Rachel stepped onto the stairs that led to the front door, there was a heavy creaking, and I could see, even in the thin light, the thickness and width of the boards that had been used to construct the house. Rachel didn't pause at the front door, but blew through into a living room that was paneled, floor to ceiling, with clear lacquered pine. The small, delicate strips of wood were polished to such a shine that being in the room was like being inside a tree—it even smelled of pine pitch and campfire smoke.

Everywhere there were shelves bursting with books: foxed paperback copies of *The War Between the Tates* and *Valley of the Dolls*, clothbound copies of Zane Grey novels, old boxes of checkers and board games whose corners were worn with use. There were couches that sagged in the middle, only a little, and thick cashmere throws on each one. Everything casual, but only in the most studied way of the monied class.

"Rachel?" I heard a woman call from what turned out to be the kitchen.

If the rest of the house was decidedly historic, then the kitchen was radically modern. A butcher block island and ten-burner stove anchored the space. There were peonies in various states of bloom in vases on the breakfast table and windowsill, bowls overflowing with bananas and onions, and the delicious smell of lemon and peaches.

An older woman with steel-gray hair and a pleasant thickness embraced Rachel in a hug.

"The flight was okay?"

Rachel nodded and settled onto a stool at the counter.

"And Jack got your bags?"

"Mm-hmm."

"I'm Ann," I said, holding out a hand, but she batted my hand aside and wrapped me in her arms.

"I'm so excited you two are here. The house used to be busy all summer, but it's slower these days." She looked at Rachel and patted her hand. "I'm so sorry, sweetie."

But Rachel waved her off. "It's been a long time, Margaret, since the house was like that."

"Some things never get easier."

We sat in silence for a beat before Margaret said, "Well, I prepared a few things for you in the fridge. But I assume you can fend for yourself.

We can get more from the market if you want, but Jack won't be going into town until tomorrow afternoon."

"Thank you, Margaret. I don't think we need anything else."

"I'll be off for the night then." She slipped out of the apron she was wearing and circled back around the island to give Rachel another hug and leave a solicitous hand on my shoulder.

"You know where we are."

After she was gone, I said, "I thought that was your mother."

Rachel shook her head. "Margaret. Our caretaker. She's worked here as long as I can remember. Come on," she said, getting up from her stool. "I want to show you your room."

Rachel led me through the front foyer and up an arcing staircase with a heavy pine banister to the second floor. The hallway ceiling was curved and made of the same pine that decorated the rest of the house; it crested overhead, like a wave. Rachel took me as far as the third door to the left and opened it.

"There isn't anyone else up here except us. There's a matching staircase and wing of rooms on the west side of the house, too, but they're only used when there are big parties at the house, or we have a lot of guests."

I memorized every detail: the way the pine paneling nested together, the way the brass switch plates were polished, the fact there were fresh flowers in every room and most hallways. I'd never stayed anywhere as nice as Rachel's house at Long Lake, neither a hotel nor someone's home, and I found myself struck by how casually Rachel moved through a space I was desperate to savor.

Rachel stood inside the room, which had a four-poster bed and a brick fireplace, a bank of windows and a glass door that opened onto a second-story deck. Outside, the area around the house was completely dark except for the sliver of moon, hung low, that lit the lake.

"It's quiet up here. Not like the Hamptons or Long Island," she said. "Really quiet. And dark. Intimate. And up here, no one asks any questions about who your parents are or where your house is. The house belonged to my maternal great-great-grandparents," she said by way of explanation. "Back when no one wanted to go to the Hamptons and everyone came up here. They built it in 1903. My grandfather liked to sail the little boats on the lake. Every year there's a regatta. It's named after him: the Henning Summer Regatta."

I had seen the little boats at the end of the dock when we arrived, their white hulls gleaming in the reflected moonlight as they hung in the boathouse.

"And because of how much my mother loved this place, we always came here, nowhere else, for the summers."

While it sounded lonely, I was grateful for the solitude, for the space Rachel had been able to put between us and the city. And there, on the bed, were my bags. And inside them, the card, which had made the long journey from downtown to upstate in less than five hours.

At the floatplane center, I had noticed that Rachel had silenced her phone. When she pulled it out, Patrick's name had flashed across the top of the screen. And in that moment, I was grateful to have Rachel to stand between us, to have her absorb the growing friction between Patrick and me. The length of the day suddenly hit me, and I couldn't help but look longingly at the bed—its carefully folded quilts and fluffed down pillows.

"I'm right next door," Rachel said, reading the exhaustion on my face as if it were her own. And then, after she closed the door, I sat on the bed, looking out into the darkness of Long Lake. The big house, silent save for the creaking wood, contracting as it released the heat of the day.

CHAPTER THIRTEEN

For all the time Rachel and I had spent together, we had never been alone, unstructured hours unspooling ahead of us. Every moment had been spent at work on something. We had never gone out to dinner or lunch, as friends do, only grabbed a few cappuccinos, a beer, a stolen sailboat. But all those moments, it turned out, had added up to a friendship. And so, in the kitchen, the next morning, we sat at the counter, drinking our coffees black with our bare feet curled under us.

"In the 1920s the secretary of state used to fly up from Albany for summer weekends. And for a while, my parents lent it to the director of MoMA for the Fourth of July. I think Dorothy Parker may have stayed here once because I found a copy of Nancy Mitford's *Love in a Cold Climate* with her name inscribed inside of it. And in any case, I've decided that she was here," she said, taking a sip of coffee, "for a weekend, or something, and must have left it behind."

The idea that the house used to be filled with parties and laughter left me with a kind of nostalgia, and I wondered what strange games had been played in the shadow of the Adirondacks. Save for our conversation and the gentle lapping of the lake against the shore that filtered through the windows, the kitchen was quiet. It was easy to imagine what it must have been like with music and people littering the veranda on a cool summer night, music drifting into the hardwoods.

"Have you often brought friends here?" I asked, imagining groups of girls clustered around the counter where we sat, bacon crackling on the stove.

Rachel shook her head. "You're the first. I haven't had many girl-friends."

In that, at least, Rachel and I were the same.

"And Patrick—" It was barely out of my mouth before Rachel stood and walked to the refrigerator, pulling it open.

"Do you want breakfast?" she asked, changing the subject.

"I'm actually not that hungry."

"Neither am I. Beach?"

I hadn't seen a beach the night before when we had landed in the darkness, but I was eager to feel the sun on my thighs and a book in my hand. "The beach sounds great."

And so, together, we changed into swimsuits and carried towels and books and umbrellas, awkwardly wedged under our arms, down to the sliver of sand that curved alongside the lawn of the house. At the end of the lake, puffs of white clouds lolled across the sky. We napped and read and lounged like that until Rachel rolled over and made clear the reality that had been settling into my bones since the dinner at Patrick's house by asking:

"Has Patrick convinced you about the fortune-telling yet?" She was lying next to me, her head propped on her hand; a bit of sand lingered on her cheek.

I didn't want to put down my book, the thing that I had been holding between my face and the sun for the better part of an hour, grateful for the distraction. I wasn't ready to accept what awaited me back at The Cloisters, even what awaited me in my room.

"I want to say no," I said, letting the implication drift between us.

"My mother once had her fortune told," Rachel said. "She went to a place on lower Lex where they read her tea leaves. The woman who was doing the reading looked at her leaves and told her she wouldn't give her the reading. That whatever was in there was too dark and too sad. My mother always said she laughed it off, but I don't think it ever left her, that fear."

"I don't know what will become of my life," I said, "and I'm the one living it."

"I think, if it's real at all, that women would be better at it than men," said Rachel, looking out across the lake. "And not because women are intrinsically more intuitive—we're all so obsessed with the idea of a woman's intuition. No. It's because women can see new patterns better than men. Think, for example, of textiles. For centuries, women have been weavers. And those women have been able to see patterns and make inferences that create beautiful things. All we're doing is weaving together a life. Trying to see where the different threads take us."

I thought of the Moirai, the Greek weaving goddesses who were said to assign our fate at birth. Clotho spun the fabric of our lives, while Lachesis pulled the thread out. Atropos, the cutter, decided when it would end. The three, it was believed, decided a baby's fate within a few days of its birth.

"Did you know that my parents died here?" said Rachel, not looking away from where the wind was gently pushing the surface of the lake into unfurling crests and valleys.

"No," I said. But the image of Rachel alone, orphaned, didn't seem jarring or surprising. There was something about her, a kind of self-sufficiency, occasionally a kind of weariness, that made her revelation make sense.

"I often wonder if that tea reader knew. I tried to find her afterward, but I couldn't. I had my tea leaves read by dozens of women below Lex. None of them had ever seen my mother. I carried a photo of her to each appointment. And now I don't carry any photo with me at all."

"How long ago?" I knew there were no good questions in this situation.

"Three years."

"I'm so sorry." It was a deeply inadequate statement. "My father passed away last year."

Rachel sat up and looked at me.

"So you know," she said.

I nodded. The clouds hung low in the sky, kissing the tops of the Adirondacks in the distance.

"I think I do believe that people can tell the future," I said quietly.

"But I don't know why anyone wants to know how their story ends," she replied.

By late afternoon, a thunderstorm had come through Long Lake, wiping away any trace of the heat that had burned the tops of my thighs a rich pink. And in the coolness that spread through the window screens and made me reach for a sweater, I found the desire to be out there, in the bracing summer air, away from everything in the house—Rachel, the card, even myself.

I threw on the pair of running shoes I had brought with me and heard the screen door hinges creak as they closed behind me. From the beach, I had seen it—a narrow trail, maybe nothing more than a game path, that wound its way north, away from the house, which occupied the southernmost edge of the lake. It was overgrown by a network of lacy green leaves and delicate white flowers. Roots gnarled their way onto the path and caught my feet at odd, slippery angles. Everything was wet from the rain, and the stones along the trail glistened with damp, bright green moss. It was, I couldn't help but notice, a far cry from the trails I had grown up using, trails that were open and dry and grassy, full of big vistas that allowed you to chart your progress using a few distinct landmarks.

Here, there were no landmarks, just a continually knotted thicket of hardwoods and a canopy so dense that I quickly lost any ability to see the sky. And in time, the trail moved away from the shore of the lake and deeper into the forest, where the terrain shifted back and forth from mostly dry and passable to water-logged and boggy. Still, I continued on. Feeling in my aloneness and the steady movement of my body the distance I needed from the day, the summer even.

There was no denying the position I had put myself in by concealing the card from Patrick; the risks to my job and my future were enormous. And yet, I wasn't sure if the choice had been mine to make. In that moment at Ketch's, I had felt as if I were possessed by something outside my rational self, as if instinct had overwhelmed logic. It was, I realized, as another group of roots tugged at my feet, a feeling that I had only ever felt once before. During a day when everything seemed automatic, instinctual—the day I had come home from campus to find the phone in the kitchen ringing and ringing and ringing, my mother never having set up the answering machine, until finally, I answered it, and heard the words on the other end. *I'm so sorry to tell you this, but Johnathan Stilwell is dead.*

Nothing else from that day ever came through, just the feeling of acting on instinct, of being unable to distinguish between what had really happened and the dreamlike reality I had entered. I could remember the clunk of my car as I shifted it into park, the faint ring of the phone audible even from outside, the feeling of the phone in my hand. But there was nothing else besides the inevitability of it all.

This time, the hardwoods that flanked the path reached out and tripped me, and I found myself, knees scuffed, palms muddy, face-to-face with the damp soil and hard shale that made up the trail. I wasn't sure, at that point, how long I had been walking. Long enough to realize I was no longer certain of my surroundings, nor even of the route the path had taken to get me there. Under the canopy, it was impossible to tell how quickly the sky had darkened, or if it had done so at all.

I picked myself up and brushed the twigs and dirt from my hands and knees, and decided it was time to retrace my steps back toward the house. As I walked, I thought about the card sitting in my bag, about the strange inscription—*trixcaccia*—that had been painted across its front.

If the word looked unfamiliar, the language did not, at least not entirely. And I searched my memory—that thin, imperfect archive—for where I might have seen it before. But while I worked on this, it was becoming clear that the temperature was dropping and that the light was waning. I should have, by then, reached the shores of the lake, but all I saw was the same tangle of hardwoods, the same undulating stone and loamy soil, the same ponding water where the sound of beavers, their tails hitting the surface in warning, echoed through the forest.

I had never been afraid of the wilderness, at least not in the West, where I could overland, where I could see my destination. But here, the forest was so thick I could only see twenty feet in any direction. The hardwoods were like a hall of mirrors, always receding into sameness. I stopped moving and took a moment to listen, hoping to hear the roar of a boat motor or the occasional rush of a highway, but the only sound was the water dripping from the leaves of the trees, a steady and maddening break to the silence. In front of me, the trail continued; I had not noticed it branch or loop back, and so, I kept moving, waiting to see the stretch of lawn in front of the house, the boathouse, the lake, anything.

Before long, it grew dark. Dark enough for me to be sure that it was not simply the shadow of a passing storm, but nighttime, with its concomitant coldness, working its way through the tree trunks. And although my eyes had adjusted some, I still found myself tripping every few steps and reaching out to catch myself, on a rock, a shrub, anything that might help keep my balance. But the cold and the darkness weren't the worst of it. The worst of it were the shadows, the deeper blacks that darted along the edges of my vision like apparitions, so quickly, I couldn't be sure if they were real. And with them came the fear. Not just the fear of the night and the cold and whatever else might be in the forest with me but the fear of my decisions—to hide the card, to leave Washington behind with its open, grassy rangeland, to agree to come to The Cloisters at all. And then, the fear that none of it had been mine to decide in the first place.

I paused and realized that in the darkness I had lost the trail. There was no way I could continue on until the morning, until the sun came back and allowed me to get my bearings. Out of options, I sat on the damp ground, my knees pressed against my chest, my back against the flaking bark of a tree, and waited until the dampness seeped into my bones, and my teeth began, every few minutes, to uncontrollably chatter. There was no space, then, to worry about anything other than keeping warm enough to make it through the night.

I still don't know how long it took her to find me, but by the time she did, I was so cold I couldn't work my jaw open to call out. It didn't matter. She had brought a jacket and a flashlight, and she saw me immediately, my white shoes now caked with mud and splashes of green.

"Oh my god, Ann." When she reached me, Rachel wrapped the jacket around my shoulders and slipped an arm around my waist. "Can you stand?"

It turned out I could, if unsteadily. The jacket was helping, but it was Rachel's body heat, which came off her as she worked to help walk me back toward the path, that warmed me the most. Within a few minutes, I was able to take more confident steps, so long as she stayed by my side.

"It's okay," she said as we followed the trail of her flashlight. "This is the way. You can trust me."

Even when I felt better—warm enough, well enough—to walk on my own, I didn't want to let go of her. As if she, herself, were a ghost who might disappear if our bodies ceased to touch. But then, after about thirty minutes maybe, I could see it—the lights of the house, the trim on the veranda. And most importantly of all, the difference between what was real—our bodies, the card, the house—and what wasn't: my memory of the shadows from that night, maybe even my memories from nights before.

∽

"I need to show you something," I said. I was running a towel over my hair, and had spent what felt like an hour in the shower scrubbing the dirt and grit out of my hands and knees.

Rachel was sitting on the bed in my room, having started a fire in the fireplace while I was in the bathroom. It was well past midnight, and the only noise in the house came from the popping of sap as it was licked by the flames.

If I could pinpoint the moment that my loyalty to Rachel became stronger than my loyalty to Patrick, it was then, that night. The moment when I decided I needed her to confirm what I had already begun to work out in the forest. From my bag, I produced the card and its old fake front. I set them down on the bed next to her where the word on the card, *trixcaccia*, stood out. It seemed, in so many ways, to be nonsense. A collection of consonants and vowels, but already I could see the way the suffix had been turned into a prefix, the word cut up and reassembled. It was a code. One I had already seen. I returned to my bag and felt around until I found the folder that contained the transcription from Lingraf, the passage neither my father nor I had been able to decipher, and set it down next to the cards.

Rachel didn't say anything, picking up the card and turning it over to look at the back before turning her attention to me. "These were what Patrick was picking up the other day?"

I couldn't miss the accusation, the implication in her question—that he hadn't told her what we were picking up at Ketch's, and then again, that this might be why he had been so angry.

"Not exactly," I said. I placed the old false front on top of the card. "All the cards Patrick picked up looked like this. While they were in the upstairs room, I was looking at this card, the Popess, and just flexed it in my hand. I knew I shouldn't, because it could crack the paint, but the stiffness had always, like you said, felt wrong. Like it was manufactured. When I did, the top corner of the card came loose. I could see something else underneath but didn't want to damage it. So I separated it with my fingernail. It was held together with flour and water, and this is what was revealed." I removed the false front as I spoke.

"Diana," said Rachel, looking down at the card. "The huntress."

I nodded.

"And the others?"

"I didn't have a chance to get to them."

Rachel kept her eyes focused on the card, as if she were committing it to memory.

"Does he know?" she asked, finally looking up to meet my gaze.

"No. Only you."

"Good. If he hasn't figured it out by now—" She shook her head. "It only took you minutes of feeling the card to notice. How could he have them for this long and still not know?"

"Do you think he already knows one of the cards from Stephen is missing?"

Rachel shrugged. "He told me Stephen was working on getting him a complete deck. And that Stephen had located a few loose cards that matched the descriptions of the deck he had sold to us. They would be coming in over the next few days. So I don't know if this is all of them, or if there are more still coming. When I went in to talk to him on Friday and let him know we were leaving, it didn't sound like Stephen on the phone. At least not that I could tell."

I was grateful, then, that Patrick had passed off the receipt to me. He had no record of what Stephen had sold him, although, no doubt, Stephen would know. Stephen with his ledgers and his records.

"The huntress," Rachel said again, this time more softly. "*Diana Venatrix.*"

I looked down at the card, Rachel's words echoing in my ears. *Venatrix* was Latin for huntress, while *cacciatrice* was the Italian word. I had always, when looking at the transcription written out by my advisor, thought I could see bits of Latin here or there. But translations without a key were impossible. The card, I realized, was that key—an image of Diana as the huntress, and the word, spelled out in the same strange way, was something we could use.

I reached into my bag and pulled out a notepad, on which I wrote the word on the card: *trixcaccia*. And then the Latin, *venatrix*, and the Italian, *cacciatrice*. There, in the word on the card, I could see the way the Latin suffix, the ending of the word—*trix*—had been combined with the prefix of the Italian—*caccia*. In order to translate Lingraf's transcription, all I needed was to watch for standard Italian and Latin prefixes and suffixes.

This kind of parsing wasn't mine; it was my father's. It was how he had pieced together other languages for years. By finding an original text and then working his way out, starting with only a single word and painstakingly building sentence by sentence. And here I was, using the same method to translate a language that had eluded him, eluded Lingraf too.

"The huntress," Rachel said again, picking up my notepad.

I turned to the transcription and got to work. Even collaborating, it took us until the morning to translate the one page. We sat next to each other on the floor, progressing word by word, just as my father and I had done. We assumed throughout that the grammar was romance-language-based in origin and the code had been crafted by a Renaissance aristocrat interested in secrecy. And we were right. Between Rachel's superior Latin skills and my strong Italian, we finished translating the document—a brief letter from someone, probably a member of a ruling family, to his daughter—which read:

My dearest daughter. I have sent to you a set of cards that I have had in my possession for some time. They will, I hope, give you the illumination they have given me. With these cards you may see more than you like. You may believe that we have been granted free will, but these cards will remind you that our fates are written in the stars. Be warned, my daughter, that I send these cards along to you, fearing, as I do, that they will not only show you the future but will ensure that it is so. You must be prepared, be accepting of this. And may your desires align with the will of the cards, for only one will reign.

CHAPTER FOURTEEN

We were so exhausted from the night that we slept until noon. And then, when the sun was overhead, we finally pulled ourselves out of the bed in my room, where we had fallen asleep together surrounded by notes and books. We lay in chairs on the lawn, letting the sun warm our bodies while we watched the breeze work the lake into stiff whitecaps.

There was a joy to being in a place where we could speak openly about the discovery, where no one like Moira or Patrick or even Leo could overhear our wildest theories about the card and its origin. What was clear, at least, was that we had found it—*I* had found it—the tarot card, the deck that proved divination had been an original purpose of the cards. What we didn't know, however, was where the deck had come from, or when. The document in Lingraf's hand had no attribution, no notes. The illustration on the card was almost certainly Renaissance—everything from the subject matter to execution testified to that fact. But it could have come from anywhere—Milan, Rome, Florence, Venice. The only evidence we had was the partial seal, the wing and beak of an eagle in black-and-white photocopy. Even Stephen saying the cards had come from Mantua meant little, so many centuries later.

But it was okay. We were, for a moment, deliciously happy in our discovery. And there was a security in sharing it with Rachel, a lessening of my vulnerability: we were together in this secret.

I stood up from the lawn and stretched. "I'm going to get something to eat. Do you want anything?"

Rachel simply shook her head, never looking up from her book, which cast a long shadow across her face and into the grass. The ring she wore, the ram that matched my own, glinted in the sun.

Rachel was lighter, more relaxed here. The past two days had been the only time I had seen her truly enjoy herself, except, perhaps, for the day we sailed on the river. Around Patrick she was always watchful, professional. I wandered into the kitchen through the wood-paneled library to find Margaret filling a ceramic vase with blooms of white hydrangeas.

"From the farmers' market," she said, trimming a few stray leaves off the stems with a paring knife. "Can I help you find anything?"

Growing up, there had never been anyone to help me navigate the kitchen, just foiled-over remainders of residence-hall dinners my mother would bring home after her shifts at Whitman. It was always my own trial and error, opening cupboards and drawers, trying to piece together a meal before and after school. There were never labeled containers of cut fruit and sliced vegetables. And there was certainly never a Margaret, a motherly figure who would put down her own work to help you.

"I don't want to bother you," I said. "I was just going to get a little something to eat." We had never managed to adequately feed ourselves after waking, neither of us wanting to make the effort to pry ourselves off the lawn. Rachel had lit a cigarette, declaring it *good enough*.

"What about a sandwich?" Margaret said, looking in the fridge. "I picked up some bread from the farmers' market this morning." She started pulling ingredients out, stacking them on the counter.

"I can do it. I don't want to put you out."

"I know you can do it. But wouldn't you rather I do it?"

Already, the way she expertly cut the loaf in half, with a firm hand and an assured thrust of the knife, made me realize she was right, I would rather have her do it.

"Thank you," I said, sliding onto a stool.

"It seems like you girls have been enjoying yourselves, sunbathing and reading." Margaret dipped a knife into a marbled jar of mustard. "It's nice to see Rachel enjoying herself again."

I wasn't sure if I should mention anything that had happened between us in the brief time we had been there. That Rachel had saved me, that I knew about her parents, but something about Margaret made me want to confide in her. Maybe it was the way she spoke, as if every sentence were confidential, a communication just between us.

"She told me about her parents' deaths," I ventured.

"She did?" Margaret looked surprised, almost resigned. "I thought she would give up this place forever after it happened."

I wanted to know the details. I had found details helped give a solidness to the event, a body to the horror. Even if, for me, the details of some of my own worst days were still elusive. Margaret looked at me from across the counter and wiped her broad hands on the smock she wore before picking up a head of lettuce and plucking a few leaves.

"Rachel's parents liked to sail north in the evenings," she said, "and have dinner at this little restaurant on the water. It's still open today. And then, afterward, they would sail home. Those little sailboats"—she shook her head—"well, they're barely big enough for two people, but that night, all three of them decided to pile into the boat and head out. The wind wasn't that strong. In fact, I watched them tack back and forth up the lake, but of course, that happens a lot around here before the thunderstorms move in and the winds come. After dinner, the wind was starting to gust. I still don't know why they got into that little boat, but they did. All of them, and they sailed back to the camp. When they hadn't arrived by ten, I sent Jack out on the motorboat to see if he could find them. After a few hours he found the boat. Flipped over in the middle of the lake. No sign of Rachel or her parents. Well, of course, he radioed the Hamilton County sheriff—"

"Rachel was with them? And survived?"

Margaret nodded. "It was a massive search. They found Rachel, unconscious on the shore not far from the boat the next morning. But the search for her parents took days. They closed the lake and dredged with nets. Finally, they found them floating in an inlet not far from the camp. The wind that night—" She paused. "The storm had been so fierce that waves swamped the boat. There was only one life jacket on board. Rachel was found wearing it. There was speculation they had removed the other two to fit all three of them in the cockpit. And Rachel, it seems, remembered very little. She remembered the boat flipping, but that was all. The sheriff thought she might have been struck by the mast, or that they may have been closer to shore when she was tossed overboard. No one really knows. It was the first drowning in Long Lake in almost five years."

I thought of how dark the water looked, and the remote location of the camp—at the far end of the lake, miles from town and other homes. Of course, it had to be an accident: she had lost both of them at the same time. But I remembered the look on Rachel's face the day we stole the boat, the masterful way she cast off the lines and helmed us into the Hudson, the wind whipping the ends of her hair against her sunburned cheek, creased from smiling, and I wondered if I could continue to enjoy the same sport that had taken the lives of my parents.

"Is this the first time she's been back since the accident?"

"No. She's visited a few times. At first, just to handle the reports with the local police. But then, she didn't come for a very long time. Last fall, she came with an older gentleman who she was working with."

"Patrick," I said.

"Yes. Patrick. He's a lovely man. A little old for Rachel. But, of course, with the loss of her parents and everything, who could judge a decision like that?"

The choice of Patrick did seem to make more sense. He offered her the security she had suddenly lost.

Margaret leaned across the counter and lowered her voice. "And it's all in a trust, you know? Rachel can't have any of this until she's thirty. It came as surprise, that. Her parents and her, you know, they weren't really that close. She argued with them that night, and I think the memory of that always weighed heavily on her. Her thirtieth birthday is only a few years away, but we're all wondering what she'll do with the camp. If she'll keep it or if she'll sell. The same with her parents' apartment. She can't sell it until she turns thirty, so it just sits empty, a few floors above her in the city. I would have moved, poor thing," Margaret said confidentially. "It's a lot of money, you know. Her mother was what we used to call an *heiress* and her father, well, he did very well for himself, too. Right now, she's on an allowance. It's managed by the family attorney. He's the one who pays us and pays all the property expenses currently. We're all just in a holding pattern, waiting for Rachel to decide what she wants to do, sometime in the future."

Margaret pushed the sandwich in my direction. It was taller than I had expected, full of bright crunchy lettuce and layered with roast chicken and heirloom tomatoes.

"Thank you," I said.

Back out on the lawn, Rachel was watching the water; clouds were amassing at the end of the lake.

"That looks good," she said.

When I put the plate down, she promptly took half and bit into it—a streak of mustard smeared her cheek.

"Another summer storm," I said, sitting down across from her. We chewed in silence until there was a crack of thunder. The hazy, high clouds had coalesced into a nighttime darkness that was spreading toward us.

"I miss this about upstate," she said.

"Isn't it hard?" The words were out before I could stop them.

"Margaret told you, didn't she?" Rachel sighed. "I try not to share the details. I don't like to. Every time I do it's like I'm reliving it. Sometimes I can still feel the cold, the bone-deep chill that came for me that night."

I reached out to put a hand on her arm, to offer her some comfort. I knew there was nothing to say. Words weren't made to fit these holes. But I knew what it was like to lose a parent. And after yesterday, to feel that cold.

"That's the only thing I remember, you know? The cold. People always ask me for details, but our memory protects us from the worst traumas. Were you and your father close?" she asked.

I, too, only remembered a few things from the day my father died. "He was the most like me," I said. "Or maybe I was like him. Sometimes I think my mom was frustrated by it. She didn't always understand us."

"My parents didn't always understand me, either," Rachel added. "I always hoped we might get there, though. Even though I don't think I was what they were hoping for. Not really. They wanted a child who was lighter, more fun. Less serious."

"I think my mother wanted a child who was less ambitious," I said, because it was true. I had always felt that she saw my ambition as an indictment of her. Maybe it was.

"Those expectations can be heavy," said Rachel. "Mine always thought I would grow out of the tarot, the world of academia. They even tried to incentivize me—that's what they called it—to quit. To go work in fundraising, get married young, do what they couldn't: have more children."

"They wanted to pay you?"

"More like they wanted to be less supportive if I continued. Financially, of course. Life after parents is like a clean slate."

"But at such a high cost."

Rachel nodded and turned her attention across the lawn toward the lake. I wondered if every time she saw this view she could see the broken boat, the storm that blew her life open. But I knew that time made it possible to revisit even the hardest places.

Just as we finished eating, the sheet of rain marched closer to the house, the damp downdrafts whipping the pages of our books. The storm came upon us quickly, the branches of the larger elms scraping against the shingled roof of the house. And although Rachel and I took shelter inside, we both knew the storm would pass swiftly, swiftly enough that there would be no problem when our floatplane landed in an hour to take us back to the city, through the orange spray of sunset.

Looking back, it would have been wise to have ended my summer at The Cloisters then. To have never gone back to the city, to have packed my bag and left what remained in my subleased studio. But it's clear to me now that it wasn't my choice to make.

As the floatplane landed on Long Island, Rachel turned to me and said, "Why don't you stay the rest of the summer with me?"

And so, because it seemed like we weren't just in this, but in everything together, I said yes without hesitation. And after all, why would I have declined? To stay in my cramped apartment when Rachel was offering me a way out?

"I have plenty of space," said Rachel, as we slipped into the waiting town car, "and we're going to the same place every day for work. I've seen your building, you know. It looks like you don't even have air-conditioning. I know it's already August and I should have asked you earlier, but—"

Rachel didn't need to sell me on the decision. In many ways, we already felt like roommates, like twins who had been through the same experience, thousands of miles apart.

"Take the car and grab what you need," she said, looking at me. Behind her head, the West Side Highway unspooled. "I'll have our doorman make you a set of keys."

Even though we had only known each other for a little over two months, it struck me that I had spent more time with Rachel than I had with anyone outside my own family. Family that I would have happily spent less time with if I had been able to afford living in the dorms. And friendships throughout college had always been elusive, particularly when it became clear I'd rather spend more time learning languages that were of little use than going to parties or gathering in claustrophobic dorm rooms, ten girls to a bed. Rachel didn't care about that. Because we were the same. We were different, in so many ways, but the things that animated us were the same.

And so, I took the car north to my studio, where I packed my clothes and books into the duffel I had brought with me from Walla Walla and slipped the rest of my father's translations into a notebook. I threw out the remaining food in my dorm-room-sized fridge, slipped the key in my pocket, and, then, I stood in the hallway under the flicker of the fluorescent lights, not sure if I would ever return.

When the driver deposited me back at Rachel's apartment, an Upper West Side two-bedroom, I was reminded again of what I had experienced at Long Lake: Rachel was rich. There were sweeping views of Central Park, a terrace with overflowing planters, parquet floors, and a light blue glossy refrigerator with vintage pulls. The space wasn't enormous, but it was still large enough. And she lived alone.

I appreciated that she didn't make excuses for the place. She didn't say, *Oh, don't mind the mess, I didn't have time to clean up*, or, *I know it looks like a lot but it was my grandmother's*. She let me into the apartment and simply pointed me to the dish where I could drop my keys and the spare bedroom where I could drop my bag.

The kitchen and living room were both part of one large, open entertaining space divided by the dining table, an older wooden piece with intricate inlay and more than a handful of scratches. I appreciated that even though everything in the apartment looked immaculate, there were a few places where imperfection was welcome. I found myself letting my hand linger on the materials: the smooth wood, the soft leather, the delicate silver of her picture frames—everything cool to the touch. Until

I arrived at the glass windows that looked out over the park. Below, I could see the ever-present line of taxicabs and people making their way in and out of the green canopy of Central Park. The air-conditioning in Rachel's apartment hummed quietly.

"Before you ask," she said, "my parents lived in the same building. On the top floor. I grew up here. And, no, I didn't buy it myself. They bought it for me when I was still in grade school. As an investment."

"I wasn't going to ask."

"People usually want to know."

"It's up to you, Rachel, what you want to share."

"I know," she said, and then, crossing the space between us, she reached out and hugged me, harder than she had the first time we met. Almost desperately. "I just don't want us to have secrets from one another."

CHAPTER FIFTEEN

The next morning was my first visit to the Morgan Library on Madison Avenue, a nineteenth-century brownstone mansion whose gilded interiors housed rare manuscripts, original drafts of Mozart's symphonies, and drawings by Rubens. In 2006, a major fundraising campaign had paid for the addition of a contemporary building behind the brownstone, including a glass atrium and auditorium. That day, the atrium was crowded with a mix of academics and art world figureheads for the Morgan's annual symposium, which this year was titled *Art and the Occult: Divination in Early Modern Europe.* We had come together, Rachel and I, after Patrick told us he would meet us there.

The Morgan was closed to the public, and the clubby atmosphere was unmistakable—everywhere people raised hands or cups of coffee in greeting. There were clusters of women in chic black pencil skirts, statement necklaces and bow ties, and various levels of studied deshabille. Everywhere, people gathered with those they knew, gossiping about those they didn't. If I had been able to listen in on a single conversation, I was sure it would have been like a private language, an insular list of names, places, and courses meant to exclude any individual brazen enough to try to break in. From the coffee bar rang out the sound of a La Marzocco milk frother.

I recognized some of the faces and realized within a few minutes that I had been rejected by at least ten people in attendance. Rejections from doctoral programs being quite personal, I wondered how many of them would be revising their earlier opinions of me, of my work, after this summer, after Rachel and I found the best way to break the news of our discovery.

The list of speakers that day was full of luminaries and up-and-coming faculty, an invitation to the Morgan a sign that you had made it. There were faculty from Chicago and Duke giving lectures on prophecy in the Carolingian gospels and on medieval mysticism as female cult worship. There were talks on the history of dice and Isabella d'Este's childhood horoscope, the role of astrology and geomancy, superstitious omens and dream interpretations. And we had come, in particular, for Herb Diebold's lecture on tarot, the question-and-answer session for which Patrick would be moderating.

Aruna was in attendance too, and she made her way over to us on arrival to lean in conspiratorially and say, "I thought I might see you two here."

"Yes. We wouldn't have missed it," I said.

"Nor would Patrick have let us," Rachel added, so softly I wasn't sure Aruna had heard.

Aruna smoothed the front of her dress. It was white silk crepe, with big square pockets at the front. A style that would have made anyone else look frumpy, but on her looked simple, elegant.

"Have you had a chance yet to talk to any of these other gossips about what we might be able to expect today?" Aruna said.

"I think they prefer to be called scholars," said Rachel.

Before Aruna could respond, we were interrupted by a deeply tanned, olive-skinned man who kissed Rachel on both cheeks and said, "She's right, you know. We prefer 'scholars.' Although 'gossips' is perhaps more accurate."

"I thought you were supposed to be in Berlin all summer?" said Rachel, her words muffled against his cheek.

He was, I knew, Harvard professor Marcel Lyonnais, best known for his groundbreaking study that created a typology of symbols in early modern Italy, and also, for having left his wife and three children for one of his graduate students, Lizzy, who was a few decades younger.

"I was. Actually, I am. Just here for a few days. Spending some time with Lizzy. She feels a little left behind . . ." He drifted off. Marcel reluctantly turned his attention to me. "You must be?"

I held out a hand and he gripped it, his palm soft. "Ann."

I wanted to say more than my name, to make it clear to him that I was on the inside too, was a valued asset, but around us the sea of bodies began to shift toward the stairs, an indication that social hour would be postponed until after the talks. And as shoulders jostled past me, one set struck me as familiar. At first I didn't recognize her, the way you don't immediately recognize familiar faces without context, but after a moment I reached out and put a hand on her arm and said, "Laure?"

Laure had been two years ahead of me at Whitman and the closest thing I had to a friend, and sometimes, a mentor. Although I imagined she had been the same to other students as well. Laure had been a student of contemporary art and someone whose ineffable style and quick comprehension made it clear to everyone that she wouldn't be constrained by Walla Walla, or even by Seattle, where she had grown up. Back then, she had been trailed by the constant scent of weed and a coterie of emo boys who nipped at her heels.

"Ann!" She threw her arms around me as soon as she saw me. "You're in New York?"

We were being elbowed and squeezed into the stairwell. "At The Cloisters," I said, following behind her.

"That's great. I had no idea. We should get a drink. And next year?"

I shook my head.

"That's okay. I know it'll happen for you."

We had made our way down a flight of stairs while talking and lost Aruna in the process; Rachel was behind me, huddled up against Marcel.

It always seemed that adults were eager to impress her, while for the rest of us, the dynamic was often reversed.

"Do you want to sit with me?" Laure said as we walked into the auditorium.

"Actually, I'm with—"

"We're together," said Rachel, coming up next to me.

There was a coldness to the way Rachel greeted Laure, and I noticed that Laure looked to me immediately. There was an edge in the way her eyes searched my face.

"I'll find you at break," said Laure, quickly squeezing my arm and walking between a row of seats.

The auditorium had been designed with acoustics in mind. It was warmly finished with curved cherrywood panels, under which red seats rose toward the back of the room with a slow, marching gravitas. Already, several of the presenters had settled themselves into chairs on the stage, with Patrick in the middle. Rachel and I chose a row halfway up and took our seats.

The academic world, I knew, was small; full of friends and enemies, lightly smoldering conflicts that had been stoked by years of offhand remarks about one's work, and sometimes, one's character. Just a survey of the room identified the different cabals: tenured faculty who still sat with their aging dissertation advisors from ten, twenty, thirty years ago, ringed by their own current graduate students who, no doubt, imagined how their own acolytes would someday gather around them. Each group was like a constellation, intertwined, but also circling each other, always trying to gauge the size of the other orbits, the power of individual gravitational pulls.

Unlike me, Rachel could have seamlessly merged into one. She could have been swept up into these constellations—a bright star in the academic heavens. But instead of joining one of the groups, we sat together while the lights dimmed, and I couldn't help but prefer our exclusive group of two. At the back of the stage, the screen lit up with an image from a Renaissance tarot deck, one of the many examples of fragmented decks, incomplete save for a card or two. It was the World card. Against a gold-leaf background, a miniature painting of late medieval life—a boat being rowed, a knight moving between two castles—all curved into the shape of a sphere. Above this little world ruled a woman, a scepter in one hand, an orb in another.

Herb Diebold took his place behind the lectern. He was older than I expected, and shorter, but tidily dressed in a cheerful checkered button-up. An expertly groomed gray mustache set off his round cheeks and fully bald head.

"When I was in Pontegradella last summer," he began, clearing his throat, "in a stuffy little municipal archive trying to find the arrest records of Alfonso, Ercole d'Este's nephew, who many believed was his bastard, I came across something unusual. Yes, I found Alfonso's arrest record of course, but there was something listed below it that caught my eye."

Diebold paused and advanced the image on the screen to show a photograph of the arrest log, and there, in the upper corner, was an image I knew well, if only because I had seen it before leaving the apartment that morning—in Lingraf's papers. Here was the complete image, an eagle, wings outstretched, the full watermark that we had only seen as partial: the municipal archives of Pontegradella, a commune of Ferrara.

I was just about to put a hand on Rachel's arm when she whispered in my ear, "The watermark."

I nodded as Diebold continued:

"It said, *Mino della Priscia, arrested for speaking to a non-member of the court about the Duchess of Ferrara's oraculum*. At first, I thought this couldn't be right, so I made some space on my research table and pulled out my handy Latin dictionary. Even after all these years, I still need some help translating."

Here, a light smattering of polite laughter filled the auditorium. Everyone in attendance knew that Diebold did not, in fact, need any help translating.

"Of course, *oraculum* is very close to 'oracle.' But I didn't believe that could be right because as far as I knew—and I know quite a bit about early Renaissance Ferrara—the Duchess of Ferrara was extremely devout."

I looked at Rachel and she met my gaze. Around us the faces in the audience were lit by the light from the screen, their attention rapt.

"So what am I to make of this?" Diebold let the question sit while he took a sip of water. "That the mother of Isabella d'Este, Italy's most prominent female patron of the Renaissance, was consulting oracles? I checked my dictionary a second time, but the etymology was clear. This is what we have come here today to talk about—oracles and seers, cards and dice, to determine what role they played."

Here, Diebold paused and looked around the room before adjusting his glasses and returning his attention to the notes in front of him. I turned to Rachel and mouthed the opening line of the document we had translated: *My dearest daughter*.

"The question shouldn't be Was divination in use? Of course it was. Astrology, we know, was everywhere. We also know that the aristocrats of the Renaissance were obsessed with whether or not their fates were fixed or mutable. They wanted to know what they could change, what was left up to chance, and what they couldn't escape. They got this fascination from the Greeks and Romans, who were always turning to oracles to parse the fates of men. And if the medieval Christian world failed to consult oracles, it was only because it was an era besotted with apocalyptic thinking, a tendency handed down by the most important oracle of all—Christ."

Diebold flipped over a page on the lectern and continued. And although I knew we had to stay, had to sit through the question-and-answer session during which Patrick's voice was so thin I worried he might abandon the ordeal all together, through more small talk and coffees, I longed to leave the auditorium and return to the papers that I kept next to my bed. To see again with my own eyes, even though I knew it to be true, the matching mark on the page.

"And so the question becomes: How do we know? How do we know what fate awaits us? This was a question that preoccupied men and women of letters throughout the Renaissance. They wanted to know the future—the good, but especially the bad. The question was always: Could they change those futures, or were they predestined? Were they fate? This is the question that underlies what we are doing here today."

Rachel leaned across the armrest as if to whisper something, but stopped when Diebold began again, "Of course, I went searching for that oracle of Ferrara, but I never found another reference to it. I asked Ferrarese scholars at the Università di Bologna about it, and they all shrugged. What could it be? they asked. Perhaps a temple, I said. Maybe a room in the Palazzo Schifanoia? A painting, a—"

He pointed up at the screen behind him.

"Tarot card?"

An expectant hush had settled over the audience. Diebold shook his head.

"Alas, I found no such record of a tarot reading in the municipal archives that summer. Nothing in the surrounding towns, either. But then I returned to my trusty Latin dictionary and began to trace the roots of the word *oraculum*. It turns out it comes from *orare*, which means to pray or beseech. And I went back to the line in the arrest record, the one that I thought might indicate the Duchess of Ferrara had an oracle, and I realized it could also be read as someone outside of the court overhearing, or being told about, the duchess's prayers. And it was then that I realized how thin the line is that separates what we know as fate and what we think of as choice—just an interpretation, really. Nothing more."

Herb Diebold went on for the next thirty minutes, explaining that even if they weren't used for divination, it was time art historians gave the iconography of tarot cards their due. He compared cards from the fifteenth century to examples of Roman and Greek statues, to frescos and mosaics in Ravenna. When he finished to applause, and the lights in the room came up, Rachel and I simply looked at each other, long enough that people in the neighboring seats began to brush up against our knees, asking us to move out of the way.

We lilted back up the stairs to the atrium but were split up by the crowds and spun into separate orbits. The planned coffee break had tea sandwiches and macarons, but I wasn't hungry. I wanted to hold the card in my hand, to know, tactilely, just how wrong Herb Diebold had been. That not only did the duchess have an *oraculum*, not only had she passed it down to her daughter, but that we had found it; the deck of tarot cards *was* her *oraculum*.

Laure came up alongside me and said, "Do you want to go outside and have a cigarette?"

"I don't smoke."

"You can enjoy the fresh air then."

"Actually," I said, looking around to where Patrick and Diebold were standing together near the stairs, Patrick gesturing forcefully, frantically, while Diebold rubbed a hand across the back of his neck, "I'd love some air."

We walked down a set of stairs that led to Madison Avenue, where the maples planted in front of the Morgan were heavy with waxy green leaves, the day having grown so hot that even the breeze from passing cars was a relief. As at all academic symposiums, there were several dozen people outside smoking. Laure took a pack of cloves from her bag and tapped one out. Even unlit, their sticky sweet scent was cloying in the heat.

"Okay," she said, fixing her gaze on me, "how do you know Rachel Mondray?"

I was hoping that we would catch up or even chat about what happened with my applications, have a minute of commiseration about the heat—I did not expect her to talk about Rachel. She hadn't even acknowledged her in the lecture hall.

"I work with her at The Cloisters."

"Just the two of you?"

"And Patrick."

"Mmm." Laure cupped her hand in front of her face and deftly lit her cigarette. "How long have you been working together?"

"Since June."

She took a drag and then let her arm drop to her side. The other arm folded under her breasts; she looked like a figure in a Balthus painting, wan and very thin.

"And what has happened? I mean, what has happened at The Cloisters since you started working with her?"

"Nothing. We just work. How do you know her?"

In a previous life, I would have confided everything in Laure. I would have told her about the card. About moving into Rachel's apartment. About Ketch Antiques and the late nights at The Cloisters. About how uncanny it was to work among aging skeletons and people who believed in the persistence of the occult. But I was a different person, one who had learned the importance of keeping a secret, the value of information.

"I met her last year," Laure said. "She was sitting in on one of my graduate seminars. Most of the grad students found it really frustrating, but the professor made a big fuss about how good she was. It's clear Rachel was a *thing* for them—talented, you know." She made a circle with her hand, a wisp of smoke tracing the shape.

I nodded because I knew exactly what she meant.

"And she was nice enough. It was pretty clear that Yale wanted her to stay, but she went with Harvard."

"That's what I heard."

Laure looked at me appraisingly. "Did she say anything else?" Around us, people were beginning to make their way back into the building.

"Like—"

"Do you want to get brunch with me?" Laure interrupted with an edge of urgency in her voice, stubbing her cigarette out beneath her shoes, a pair of tasteful leather flats.

"I'd love that."

"Good," said Laure. She slung an arm over my shoulder as we walked back into the atrium. "I want you to take care of yourself, okay?"

I looked up at the facade of the Morgan rising above us—centuries of treasures collected and preserved within its walls.

"Okay," I said, although I felt confident that I was already doing a better job taking care of myself than Laure would have, given the chance.

When the symposium was over, I waited for Rachel on the steps of the Morgan, leaning against one of the nineteenth-century concrete urns that had been planted with white, trailing annuals. She had been detained inside by Marcel, who wanted to be sure she had an opportunity to meet some of the presenters. I longed to be the kind of scholar people cornered at the end of events to introduce their students to, if only so I could make excuses as to why I had to leave: lunch with the director of the Frick, a waiting town car, a library full of books desperate to be read. Rachel, it was clear, was going to become one of those people.

"Did you enjoy yourself?"

It was Aruna, who had appeared soundlessly at my side.

"I did."

"I find these sorts of things exhausting now," she said. "Almost sad. All these aging obsessives, still fretting over the same works that have vexed scholars for centuries. Have you ever wondered why you want to be here, and not"—she pulled out a cigarette case and held it out to me—"on Wall Street, making real money?"

I declined, wondering if one day I would just say yes. Become a smoker too. Some days it seemed inescapable.

"Don't idolize it," she said.

"I don't."

"Don't lie, either."

She tapped some ash off the end of her cigarette, and I laughed.

"So many of us here just wanted to spend our lives studying *something*. To be in libraries and classrooms, to be in archives and museums, to *feel* history through the things it left behind. But to do that is not to be with the living, Ann. You must remember that. And some of us survive all this death better than others."

"To me," I said, "this seems very much alive."

"Yes. But that's a fiction. It's dead. All of it. That's the real task of the scholar, to become a necromancer. Do you know what I mean, Ann?"

"I do." But I wasn't sure I did.

"Good. Because so many of us forget the true purpose is to reanimate the thing, even sometimes at the cost of animating ourselves."

Standing on those stairs it was hard not to feel the weight of the past around us. After all, weren't museums just mausoleums? Quite literally in the case of The Cloisters.

"Have you considered law school?" asked Aruna.

I looked at her and she just laughed.

"It might not be too late," I said.

"Well, if this summer still hasn't dissuaded you," she said, "please feel free to come to me for advice in the fall. It helps to have someone on the inside."

"Thank you," I said, meaning it.

"And good for you. Not making a fool of yourself by attempting to pander to every faculty member in attendance. Desperation. Always a bad look. Particularly in academia, where we reward effortless achievement, not years of struggle." She stepped on the end of her cigarette and pressed a cool hand on my arm. "That's what Rachel has learned faster than most," she whispered.

A quick squeeze and she was gone, seamlessly mingling between the last remaining groups of academics before making her way to the edge of Madison Avenue, where she slid into a cab and offered me one last wave goodbye. I began to lift my hand, but then noticed the number of people who also raised a hand, so instead, I inclined my head, the small gesture setting me apart from the others.

I waited until I was the only one left standing on the stairs and settled into the sound of the cars on the street, a steady stream of activity, the sound of things alive.

CHAPTER SIXTEEN

I t was better, arriving at The Cloisters in a town car. And I quickly
forgot what it was like to worry about being jostled on the subway,
coffee in hand, or timing my arrival so that I might make the shuttle.
Living together opened up pockets of time with Rachel we hadn't had
before: the commute, the breakfasts, the time after dinner. And in those
pockets, I found myself finally able to unfold, to let Rachel see me fully.
I liked to believe she felt the same way too.

Patrick, it was clear, did not.

During our first day back in the library after the Morgan symposium,
he said to us, "Living together and working together can be a strain on a
friendship. Best not to push too hard and see if it breaks. No?"

"It's different with girls," was all Rachel had said to him.

But we could see his discomfort that we were always together now.
The way he watched us, always hoping to trace the origins of some inside
joke along the contours of our faces.

That day, the gardens of The Cloisters hummed with the energy of
visitors and pollinators, and I, unable to forget the secret that hummed
inside me, inside Rachel now too, walked the perimeter until I got to
the Bonnefont Cloister with its bright green quince trees and gnarled
branches. I didn't want to sit, so I stood, overlooking the edge of the
garden, which gave way to steep stone ramparts and the ground, nearly
one hundred feet below.

My palms placed on the top of the stone wall, I leaned out just to feel the precariousness of my situation, to let the adrenaline surge through my body until I could feel it again, the same feeling I had had when I revealed the Huntress card, the quick sprint of fear, the bite of urgency. If only so I could enjoy the wave of relief that followed. The moment when nothing happened, when I didn't fall, when Patrick didn't catch me, when Rachel and I, ultimately, would get away with it.

New York had shown me how hungry I was. Hungry for joy and risk, hungry to admit, aloud to everyone around me, my ambitions. Hungry to realize them. Instead of being filled with fear, I was filled with a kind of giddy joy. And the knowledge that in a city like this, it was possible to start over, to make the memory of my father something that drove me forward, not something that held me back. Beating Patrick to the discovery of the tarot deck would be the biggest accomplishment of all. I wasn't immoral; I simply understood the lesson the city was teaching me.

As I leaned out over the wall again to the see the cobblestone road below, I felt two hands around my waist give me a quick push forward. I screamed, loudly and sharply.

When I turned around to see Leo, I also saw a garden of visitors watching us, concerned, trying to decide if they should intervene.

I batted at Leo's arms, but he just smiled and held on to my waist. "Gotcha."

"That was terrifying," I said, looking around. I smiled reassuringly at a few of the more worried faces.

"You shouldn't lean out like that. What if something happened?"

"You mean like what if someone came up behind me and pushed me?"

"That, or what if you tripped and fell. There's a reason we don't allow sitting along this wall."

"Oh?"

He pointed to the sign that I had somehow, for weeks, missed. DO NOT LEAN OR SIT ALONG THE PARAPET.

"Come on," he said. "I have something for you."

He led me by the hand across the Bonnefont Cloister and through a gate that read STAFF ONLY BEYOND THIS POINT. I had never been in this section of The Cloisters. It was grassy and walled off from the rest of the museum, containing two small sheds and a long greenhouse full of sprouts. There were garden items like grass trimmers and cutting shears littered in piles, stacks of empty pots and bits of errant stonework tucked out of public view. There were trash cans full of trimmings, and a clump of leaves had been spread across the composting bed.

Leo led me into one of the sheds, which had wide potting shelves lining the walls, each dotted with glass canisters filled with dried seeds. I picked one up as we entered.

"Hyssop seeds," he said. "I dried flowers from last year's garden."

There was a tenderness to how carefully everything was arranged, from the handfuls of flowers tied up and drying from pegs on the wall, to the way the cutting shears were all tucked, sharp end down, into terra-cotta pots. And it smelled of Leo, or maybe, Leo smelled of it: earthy and grassy, a hint of body odor.

He took down a handful of dried lavender from the wall and handed it to me. "These are for you."

Their scent filled my nose—herbaceous and sunny and complex.

"I cut them after that first day in the garden and hung them up to dry. They last longer than fresh," he said. "And when you're tired of looking at them, you can break the flowers up and leave them around your drawers." He reached out his hand and used his thumb to break the lavender flower into smaller parts. I watched them scatter to the floor below us.

If I hadn't noticed how small the garden shed was when we entered, I did then. There was barely room for the two of us to turn around, and so, our bodies were already pressed close together when Leo put his hand behind my neck and kissed me. Looking back, it wasn't he who lifted me onto the shelf, but me who hopped up, wrapping my legs around his waist and pulling him close enough that I could feel myself against him.

He matched me, sliding a rough hand under my shirt, past my bra, then, lifting the shirt off, over my raised arms.

There was something in my movements that I found surprisingly confident and assured. As if, for the first time, I was leading and Leo following. No longer was I waiting for those around me to welcome me or offer approval; I was taking it, and the feeling thrilled me. So much so that I reached for the waistband of Leo's jeans and began to unbutton them. But even over the rustle of our clothes, our bodies, an unmistakable cough could be heard outside.

"Sorry to interrupt," said Rachel.

The strap of my bra had been pulled down. Leo didn't turn around to greet her, but I slid slowly off the shelf and stepped into the sunlight that lit the threshold and pulled up my bra, slipped back into my shirt. And then, I walked out to where Rachel was waiting.

"You can finish," she said. "I can wait around the corner."

"We're fine," said Leo from inside the shed. "I'll call you, Ann."

As I walked away with Rachel, I didn't say anything, didn't even bother to brush away the creases on my shirt or cool my skin where it had become damp with sweat and anticipation.

"I didn't realize it had become this serious," said Rachel, looking at me as we walked back toward the library.

"I don't know if I'd call it serious."

"Taking these kinds of risks at work? It must be," she said.

"How did you know that's where we'd be?" I wasn't sure I wanted to know the answer, but Rachel shrugged.

"I looked everywhere else."

Then, as we passed through the Gothic arch into the galleries, she held the door and said, "Don't let Leo ruin what we're doing here."

I walked through the door and stopped. We were in the tapestry room, where massive, thickly woven textiles depicted scenes of idyllic medieval life—a carpet of flowers sprung to life, a unicorn at rest.

"Why would you say that? Leo has nothing to do with what we're doing."

"Right now, you're compartmentalizing. But what happens when that gets harder? When instead of focusing on the situation at hand you want to go to shitty punk shows and drink warm beers in the Bronx?"

Rachel's words stung. Not just in their accuracy, but because I'd given her no reason to think I would put Leo ahead of her, ahead of our work, our discovery. The work was why I had come, but the tarot ensured I stayed, not Leo. Even if I occasionally found it hard to disentangle my relationships at The Cloisters from the place itself, as if my personal relationships and passion for the work had all become as knotted as the grapevines that grew in the gardens.

"Leo isn't my priority," I said.

"Then act like it. This is huge, Ann. What we've found—what you've found—is big. And now that we know where the cards came from. With that proof, we can accomplish so much. We need to accomplish so much."

Rachel started to walk away, but I grabbed her arm. A handful of visitors were watching us, and although our voices were lowered, they were still louder than one would normally hear in The Cloisters' galleries.

"I *am* acting like it," I hissed. "I've only been out with him once. Every spare minute I spend with you. I've told you *everything*. Isn't it clear we're in this together?"

I didn't consider myself confrontational, but in standing up for myself I felt the same rush I had felt leaning over the wall in the garden.

Rachel held up her hands. "Okay. Okay. I get it. Maybe I just don't want to share you right now. I really need you. We need to stay focused. I just don't want Leo taking that away from me."

"I'm not leaving you," I said. And then, I was surprised to find myself hugging her, feeling her slight frame relax against mine.

"I just want to make sure we can get ahead of this before Patrick does," she said, pulling back.

I nodded. "I want that too. I need it."

"I know you do," she said.

"He'll ask us soon," Rachel said the next day as we sat in the library, surrounded by loose papers and notes, the chaos actually a carefully orchestrated curation of material. "He's been talking about doing another reading. A reading here. At night again. Now that the deck is more complete. We'll have a chance then."

Rachel and I needed an opportunity to view the rest of the cards ourselves, an opportunity, at least, to photograph them so we could begin our research. The discovery, we both knew, would cement our careers, our stature in the academic world. It was an opportunity neither of us could risk by sharing what we knew with Patrick. Both of us understood how easily, how quickly the narrative of the discovery might shift, from us—two young women at the beginning of their careers—to Patrick, an established researcher of the occult. And so, we had decided to keep quiet and bide our time.

When Patrick finally asked us to stay late two days later, Rachel and I were out in the gardens, sitting on the far wall, where we enjoyed the waning afternoon sun, Rachel smoking, me allowing the grass to tickle my ankles and the mossy stone to pad my palms. The visitors who filled the walkways admired the carved capitals, the sculptures of frocked friars tucked into their niches. Rachel and I, however, went unnoticed. We had become, it seemed, part of the scenery.

It was Leo I was watching for when I saw Patrick make his way across the cloister, slowly, taking in the scents of lemon balm and lavender, casually dipping his hand in the fountain and then shaking off the water, the beads clear in the sunlight.

"You're not smoking, are you?" Patrick asked when he reached us, his hands fisted in his pockets. I didn't bother to look, but I instinctively felt Rachel release her cigarette off the edge of the rampart and into the grass below.

"Never," she said.

I repressed a smile.

"Smoking is strictly forbidden on the grounds. But you are always welcome to smoke outside the back gate."

"That's usually where I do it," Rachel said.

Patrick looked over our heads, toward the river, before asking us, still not meeting our gazes, "Do either of you have plans for later this evening?"

Rachel and I did our best not to look at each other, but I could feel the blood moving faster through my fingers as they gripped the edge of the wall.

"No," I said, my mouth dry.

"Nothing really," added Rachel.

"Would you mind staying late?"

"Not at all," I said. "Is there anything in particular you want us to prepare?"

Patrick shook his head. "All you need to bring is yourselves. And an open mind."

Rachel and I both nodded, and Patrick took his leave, this time crossing the garden in a few quick steps.

After that, the end of the day felt like it might never arrive, but we waited, continuing to do the research tasks Patrick had set before us, tasks that now felt futile in light of our secret, until security came through the library to perform their sweep as the sun set.

"We're going to work late tonight," Rachel said.

Louis nodded. "We're short-staffed, if you want to fill in later for us."

We both laughed, and I thought to myself again how remarkable it was that we were rarely bothered by security, that we were allowed to work, to walk, to pass through the spaces of The Cloisters whenever and however we wanted, despite the value of work on display.

Less than an hour later, Patrick came out of his office, the box of cards in his hand. Outside, the tile roofs had turned a dark terra-cotta as the light of the sun was replaced with the glow of the city. The hanging lanterns that lit the gardens at night swayed in the gentle breeze that worked its way up from the Hudson.

Patrick set the cards on the table and checked his watch. "He should be here soon," he said.

"Who?" asked Rachel. But she needn't have asked, because Leo pushed his way into the library, his jeans still dirty from an afternoon spent in the garden.

"What is he doing here?" Rachel said.

"Leo is going to help us with a very important experiment."

At this, Leo offered me a quick smile before pulling a handful of plastic packets out of his pocket. He threw them on the table, and I recognized them immediately. They matched the packets he had been selling at the greenmarket, the ones he had sold exclusively from under the table—bespoke herb mixtures and tinctures, carefully mixed in the greenhouse of The Cloisters.

"I've been thinking," said Patrick, approaching the table and picking up a small, clear packet, "that maybe we've been going about this the wrong way. I think we should consider approaching the cards differently, in an entirely new state, if you will."

"You think we should take drugs." Rachel said it without emotion, bluntly, as if it were a request for us to pull an old book from the stacks. But it struck me that she knew what Leo was offering in these packets, maybe had opportunities to try them herself.

"No. Not drugs. Not in the narrow sense. Not as we understand them today," Patrick said. And in that moment, he sounded like himself, like the curator who had hired me, like the curator who felt a deep sense of curiosity about the things that had come before us, and not the curator who was frustrated by his lack of progress, by the slow unraveling of his own passion.

"As you both know," he continued, "medieval mysticism has been widely studied. And we know that those who experienced visions had some help. Henbane and mandrake may have played an important role in helping facilitate the visions of medieval mystics. But this is not—was not—drug use for recreation. But for research, for understanding. So that we might get closer to our own intuitions, our instincts. It's a process of understanding, not intoxicating. I've been talking about doing this for a while now, and Leo has been a great help."

Leo picked up and shook one of the plastic packets. "Thirty percent henbane, sixty-five percent mandrake, and very small amounts of belladonna and thorn apple. None of this is enough to hurt you," he explained. "Both henbane and mandrake have hyoscine in them. It's a hallucinogen, a psychotropic. Belladonna and thorn apple both have atropine, it works like a muscle relaxant. It will help to even everything out."

Rachel looked at Patrick. "You've got to be kidding, right? You want us to take poisons Leo has prepared?"

"We thought about that, about your concern. So—" Leo pulled a thermos out of his back pocket and set it down on the table. "Here, they're all the same." He mixed up the packets on the table. "Pick one and I'll take it right now."

Rachel selected a packet and handed it across the table to Leo, who emptied the contents into his thermos and swirled. Then he drank, the thermos tipped back and his throat working methodically until he showed Rachel an empty container.

"It's safe," he said. "I promise. Everything in here is fine in a small quantity."

I had already seen Leo selling these mixtures to women on the Upper

West Side, women who were looking to escape their own lives, looking for their own kind of revelations. And perhaps it was because of that that I felt safe drinking the herbs Leo had prepared for us. Or perhaps it was my desire, like Patrick's, to go deeper. To see what else we might be able to open up in the cards, in ourselves, with a little help. Patrick procured three cups and a carafe of hot water, pouring us each a cupful and handing them out with the packets.

"How long will it take to kick in?" I asked Leo.

"Around twenty to forty minutes. It has to be processed into your bloodstream. It comes on slowly, not fast. You'll only notice by accident."

Rachel took a sip of her tea. "It's really foul, Leo."

"Bitter," he said. "Not foul."

I took a sip, and it was bracing. A dark slurry of pungent, grainy liquid, and part of me wished there had been an option to take it in one swallow, so that it might be done and over with.

"Thank you, Leo," said Patrick, sipping from his cup delicately.

"I'll be in the garden shed if you need me." Leo moved to leave.

"Why don't you come check on us in two hours," Patrick said. "Just to be sure everything is going okay."

Leo nodded. "I'm sure you'll be fine. But I'll come back."

While we waited for the drugs to take effect, we cleared our worktable and propped the windows open. Patrick brought two candelabras from his office and lit them, their flames flickering in the gentle drafts that sifted into the space. A silence had settled in between the three of us, and no one dared break it. Perhaps out of fear that the next words might be those we couldn't take back. The red wax quietly dripped pools onto the oak table.

And it was these pools of limpid wax that first made me realize something unusual was going on. At first, they seemed to shimmer and shake, to swirl on the table without any direction from us. I kept blinking and rubbing my eyes in an effort to clear whatever it was that was making my vision hazy and unstable. But when I was unable to arrest the movement in the wax, I noticed that the things in the room around me—the books and lamps, the Gothic windows and curved beams—seemed to take on a brighter quality, too, as if lit from within.

Rachel, I could tell, had begun to feel the effects, and when she grabbed my wrist, I could see it in her eyes—the belladonna, her pupils dilated to shiny black dimes.

"Why don't you lay out the cards," she said to Patrick. And although her voice sounded very far away, as if she were at the end of a long hallway, Patrick began to do just that. Card after card placed on the table. And as they were laid down, it was as if my mind were doing the work my fingers ached to do: each front dissolved to reveal another card underneath—the Magician for Mercury, the Lovers for Venus accompanied by the constellation of Taurus, the Queen of Cups for a woman who looked like Rachel, her long blond hair set against a gold crown of olive leaves, a one-shouldered toga bound at the waist.

Panicked, I looked from Rachel to Patrick in an attempt to figure out if they were seeing the same thing, but clearly I was alone. When I looked back down at the table, the cards, like everything else in the room, had begun to throw off their own otherworldly glow, and as Patrick's fingers traced the outlines, they left golden trails on the table, as if part of him had stayed behind where his finger had once been—hundreds of traced fingerprints.

And even though we had candlelight, the room itself began to feel darker still. As if we all, as if the library itself, were being pulled deeper into the belly of The Cloisters. As if the ceiling, with its rib vaults and crisscrossed beams, were slowly folding down on us. But rather than being terrifying, there was something about it that felt delicious, as if I were finally becoming one with the building. As if we were always meant to be crushed beneath the power of the work itself.

I still cannot remember the exact spread Patrick laid out, but I do remember that he did more than one reading, that he kept restarting in an effort to reach a resolution that continued to elude him. In fact, everything I thought I could see in the cards seemed to dissolve into a haze before I could grasp it. And I realized that rather than enhance my intuition, the drugs had dulled it, muddied it, so that I could no longer see, no longer feel as clearly.

But through the darkness that was kicking up around me, there was still an electric feeling. A beacon that came from the cards as Patrick slapped them down on the table, flashes of a heavy, dark future that I couldn't explain but that nevertheless felt certain. The more I tried to tap into those flashes, however, the more overwhelming they became. Surging into and over me like a dizzying cloud that left as quickly as it arrived. Through the drugs, I didn't notice that I had stopped breathing, that lightheadedness was quickly progressing to unconsciousness.

And although it only seemed like minutes had passed, there was Leo, standing at the door of the library, asking if I was okay. Walking around the table and putting a hand on my shoulder and looking me in the eye. I wanted to tell him that I couldn't see what I needed to in the cards, that the herbs we had taken had cast a veil over my eyes. But when I looked up to meet his gaze, the movement proved too fast and the room around me spun violently, casting me out of the darkness and into a blinding light. And while Leo said something to me as he steadied me, an arm under my armpit, and while I could see Rachel's and Patrick's mouths moving, it was as if my ears had been stuffed with cotton, as if I were underwater and watching them all from a distance I couldn't close.

Even though it felt like my legs might not work, Leo nevertheless led me out into the garden. But before we went, I glanced back into the library. And there, I saw Patrick and Rachel, both craned over the table, Rachel's hand reaching for a card, every movement made slow by the candlelight.

The gardens, however, were not an improvement on the library. The carved capitals and statuettes, the twisting vines that wrapped their way around the Celtic cross that adorned the center of the Trie Cloister, the shadows and pockets of darkness, all seemed to reach out and grab me, pull me in. When Leo walked with me through the galleries, the glittering stones were blinding, and the lion fresco moved before my eyes as it stalked us down the wall. Everything, it seemed, aimed to do us harm.

"I want to go back." It was my voice, although I could barely recognize it.

"You need to sober up a bit," said Leo, and I realized he was leading me down the staff hallway toward the kitchen. "I'm going to get some food in you, then you can go back." He didn't look at me, but dragged me, supporting me with his long arm and strong back. "What have you eaten today?"

"I don't eat much anymore," I said. It was the truth, and in my mind, an image of Rachel as a skeleton, as someone who slowly melted from flesh into bones, came to me.

"You should fix that."

Leo set me down on a chair in the kitchen and offered me a slice of cake from the fridge, but I pushed it away.

"You have to," he said.

"I'm going to be sick."

"No, you're not." Leo was close to me now, and I could feel his hands on my hair, stroking it, and running his fingers through it. Consoling me, petting me.

"I want to go back," I repeated.

Leo pushed the plate back in front of me, but I shook my head. "Sick," I said again.

He brought me a glass of water, which I drank, slowly, and it was as if I could feel every molecule of water pass down through my throat and into my stomach. Even the industrial light in the kitchen hadn't been able to dull the high. Everything seemed to work on its own schedule, in wild new ways. I tried to imagine how long ago I had taken the mixture.

"How long will it last?" I asked.

"Longer if you don't eat anything."

Begrudgingly I picked up the slice of cake with my hands and took a bite. But it didn't matter that I ate. It didn't matter that I drank. Because the drugs only became more powerful, as if they were only just amassing their forces in my blood, gathering strength for a full, final run. And as Leo led me back through the halls of The Cloisters, this time the light closed itself off to me, and I saw only darkness. It was coming from within me as well, a darkness I saw echoed in the saints' fingerbones and ankle fragments, the wilderness of the unicorn tapestries and the open mouths of the gargoyles that sat along the edges of the cloisters. The whole museum, I realized—although perhaps I had always known it, always wanted to believe it—was struggling to come alive.

CHAPTER SEVENTEEN

I'll never forget the way that morning appeared, the way Leo's apartment was dark because of the cloud cover, the way I kept hoping for a clap of thunder, the release of rain. Instead, the bruised sky darkened everything below. Leo was already gone when I woke, but he had left a note—*I'll see you there*—so I saw myself to the subway, where the ride was hot and my coffee bitter. Still, I was early, the drugs in my system having left my sleep fitful and restless, and I caught the first shuttle up to The Cloisters, reshouldering the weight of my backpack as I reached for the door of the staff entrance. Inside, the hallways were empty of people, but full of half-remembered events from the night before, shadows of memories I couldn't trust. The drugs, it seemed, had caused an erasure of fact, of real events, and replaced them only with sensations, fragments of memories I had no confidence in.

I made my way to the library. Gone were the candelabras, the telltale pools of wax, the cards. Instead, Rachel's bag sat on the table, its contents strewn at odd angles, as if hastily dropped. The door to Patrick's office was ajar, and through the crack, I could see a foot, and only a foot, shaking rhythmically, like it was experiencing a slow tremor. Breaking the silence were racking breaths and a repeated sound, like the beat of a hollow drum.

Why I didn't call out Rachel's name, why I didn't run immediately for security, I don't know. Maybe I couldn't see the clues for what they were—the foot, the bag, the shaking—adding up to a grotesque accident. Maybe, in that moment, I couldn't have been sure of what was real in the wake of that night, if the drugs truly were out of my system. Instead, I was pulled to the door of Patrick's office, where everything was as it should be but for a coffee mug that had been knocked to the floor, where it had bled an inky puddle into the carpet.

Nearby lay Patrick's body, still dressed in the suit he was wearing the night before, now lifeless.

And there was Rachel, performing chest compressions, breathing air into his lungs, although they neither rose nor fell with the effort—his skin shiny.

In that moment, everything left me—my sense of time and action, my ability to understand the scene in front of me. All I could do was stand in the doorway, watching Rachel, her face emotionless and hard, her compressions mechanical and labored, like a pump jack. Her focus so intense, she hadn't even noticed me arrive.

When she finally looked up at me, both hands on Patrick's chest, all she said was, "I haven't had time to call an ambulance. Can you call an ambulance? I'm afraid if I stop, he—"

She trailed off, her face damp with sweat, drained of color despite the effort, and looked down at the body.

"Rachel," I said. "He's dead."

You could smell it in the room, the stale sweetness of death—like overripe Concord grapes. I managed to walk toward the body and touch my fingers to his neck. He was cold. No blood pumped through his skin, nor had it for hours.

"I've heard that as long as you keep the blood and air moving, there's a chance," she said, almost to herself, not meeting my gaze.

I knelt across from her and wrapped my hands around her forearms.

"Rachel. It's over."

Finally, she met my eyes. There was a milky quality to them, almost unseeing. As if the entire event might be an apparition, a spell from which she simply needed to be awoken. I wondered if we both looked that way, our pupils still enlarged from the belladonna.

"No," she said, breaking away and holding back a sob. "Call an ambulance."

I pulled my phone out of my backpack and dialed 911, reporting the scene to a dispatcher who asked me several times if I was sure Patrick was deceased. I answered *yes* every time. Rachel, listening to the conversation, had finally stopped pushing against Patrick's chest; she sat on the floor next to his body, her face wet, her knees tucked under her chin, shaking, as if from the cold. Where normally Rachel's arms seemed lithe and strong, now they seemed weak and wan, and I wondered where she had found the reserve of energy to keep performing compressions.

The questions I might have asked in that moment—how long she had been here like this, pushing over and over into a dead body, what had happened, how she had found him—seemed impossible to articulate. All I could do was join her on the floor, where we held each other, our knees pushed together, hoping that no one would come in and find us for a very long time, until we had at least been able to adjust to a world that didn't have Patrick in it.

We didn't know how long it would take for the police to arrive or even the other staff, but we sat together on the floor for what felt like hours, though it could only have been minutes, watching Patrick's unmoving body, until finally, Rachel pushed herself to her feet and walked around to the front of Patrick's desk. I watched her as she began to pull open the drawers and lift papers and notepads.

"Rachel, what—" I stopped. There was something worn openly on her face—determined and hard—that made me stop. Instead I stood, the sudden movement causing my vision to swim. The surreality of the scene—the body on the floor, the speed with which Rachel was looking through drawers—made me realize I needed to keep checking the door of the library for any sign of movement, keening my ears to hear the sound of sirens. When she got to Patrick's bag, she dumped it out on the floor—its contents spilling across the room, Patrick's address book coming to rest against his polished shoe.

Rachel was on her knees now, sorting through the items and shoving them back into the bag following an inspection, until I realized, through the haze of the scene, what she was looking for. I saw it, on the far side of the room, having skittered across the floor, its green ribbon slightly frayed and bleached. I moved to where it had come to rest, but my movements felt slow. Slow enough that there was time for Moira to arrive at the door, where she screamed—a high wailing noise. And while Rachel put Patrick's bag back on his chair during the commotion, her eyes came to meet mine as I slid the box silently into my backpack, all while Moira crouched by the body and started weeping, repeatedly asking the same thing I had been silently asking myself since arriving that morning: *What happened?*

The police took our statements, and the coroner took the body. Moira had to be sedated. In front of the museum, the blue lights of police cars illuminated the gray stone of the building. And as I stood among the staff, I noticed that the entire building was eerily quiet. None of us knew what to do. I had never witnessed death, only lived its aftermath. And in its wake, I found myself adrift, knowing there were no good decisions, no good next steps, only the awful certainty that time would continue, no matter how much I wanted it to stop, rewind. The only thing that grounded me sat heavy in my backpack: the leather box, its green ribbon.

There was no opportunity, then, to ask Rachel how she found him or how her night, the evening before, had ended. But I was grateful that Rachel had found him before the museum opened, before visitors to The Cloisters walked from the lobby to the Mérode Altarpiece and back again, while Patrick's unhearing ears lay just beyond the stone wall, unnoticed.

A heart attack, they seemed to think. *At least he went quickly. Died in a place he loved.* These were the platitudes that I knew meant nothing, and every time I heard someone repeat the sentiment, the humming in my ears grew louder.

"We need to call Michelle," said Rachel quietly, appearing at my side. I had been standing at the edge of the entrance to the museum, watching people come and go, a crush of forensic and janitorial staff. Onlookers had begun to gather in the park.

I knew she was right, but I also knew that sharing the news would make it real. That in losing Patrick, I had also lost my benefactor, the person who had brought me to The Cloisters. Rachel was already holding the phone to her ear, and I realized that as much as I feared what Michelle might have to say, I was also desperate for someone to tell me what to do. Only after Rachel hung up did I realize that despite how it looked, we were the ones who had to find our own way.

"What did she say?"

"That she's going to call me back in a little bit with instructions, but that we should close the building to visitors for the day and the staff should go home."

"Do you think she'll make me leave?" I finally ginned up the courage to ask.

Rachel's eyes narrowed. "Why would you have to leave?"

"Because with Patrick gone—"

"With Patrick gone—" The words died on her lips, and I could feel Rachel's exhaustion, the amount of effort it took her just to speak. It was a feeling I wished I didn't remember, but I did. She tried again. "With Patrick gone there's even more to do. You'll be fine, Ann. We're both going to be fine." And then she paused, gripping my arm so tightly that I could feel the half-moons of her nails cut into my skin, and said in a hard whisper: "And now. And now, some things will be easier."

I wished, then, that we were alone. But around us staff members huddled at the entrance, their faces periodically lit by the blue rotating lights of the police cars. All of it, a sudden, unwelcome intrusion—the contemporary world puncturing the peace of The Cloisters.

On the drive home, neither of us spoke, but the weight of the box in my backpack felt much heavier than it had previously. I was desperate for a shower, having come straight from Leo's, the sweat from the night before still on my body, salty and rough. I didn't remember seeing Leo after he pulled me out of the library. Even though he had taken me home, beyond the slice of cake and the harsh lights of the kitchen, I had no other memories from the night before. And Leo—where was he? I hadn't seen him arrive at the museum that morning.

Inside Rachel's apartment, I threw my bag on the table and went into the bathroom as much to shower as to think. I needed the hot water to scrub off the scene of the morning. Only when I got out did I realize that it was imprinted more deeply, against my bones and not along my skin, and was not so easily washed away.

By the time I returned to the living room, my hair wet and falling below my shoulders, Rachel had already stripped each card of its front and set it down on the table, next to its false twin. Beneath all the Major Arcana cards were iconographically complex cards that represented both Roman deities and the astrological signs and symbols. Already I could see patterns emerging among the cards, a dense web of symbolism that seemed to connect each card to its namesake constellation. Above Venus and the Lovers card, Taurus hung in the sky; the Pope card depicted a constellation of Sagittarius, with Jupiter, Sagittarius's ruling planet, in the foreground. As quickly as I could make out connections, another set would emerge. I counted them silently; there were seventy-seven cards. The deck was complete, save for one: the Devil was missing. It might, I imagined, depict Hades with the sign of Scorpio. After all, Pluto was the Roman name for Hades, and also ruled the sign.

But as much as I was drawn to the cards, was desperate to hold them, even lay them out in a grid to see what they could tell me, I needed to know what had happened last night, this morning, to me, to Rachel, to Leo, to Patrick, to all of us. To the world of The Cloisters.

"Can you believe this?" Rachel said, looking at the cards. "Have you seen these?"

"Rachel—what happened last night?"

"First come look at them."

I walked to the edge of the table, taking in the cards' refined swirls of paint and the feathery features of the figures. In the corners of each card, I noticed the distinctive shape of a white eagle crowned in gold. The imprimatur of the d'Este. The same eagle that appeared on the archival documents we'd seen at the Morgan, and again, in Lingraf's papers. And as much as I wanted to talk about what happened last night, I couldn't look away from the scene on the table. Nothing, I knew, was as powerful as curiosity. I had always considered it more powerful than lust. After all, wasn't that why Adam bit into the apple? Because he was curious? Because he needed to know? For *research*. I picked up the World card, which showed the full heavens with Saturn in the center, his mouth agape, a child in the palm of his hand.

"They're incredible."

"Can you imagine what we'll be able to do with these?"

I folded my arms. "What happened last night?" I asked again.

Rachel was still dreamily gazing at the cards, and it took her a minute to shake herself back into our world.

"I don't know," she said. "I woke up here. I don't remember much after the second spread. It's like my memory has a big black spot. There's almost nothing from midnight until six a.m."

It was the same gap I had. "But when you left?"

"When I left, Patrick was fine. You and Leo were fine."

"Leo and I, we were still there?"

Rachel shook her head and pulled out one of the chairs. "I think so? Honestly, I don't know for sure. All I know is that in my last memory of Patrick, he was alive. And that I woke up here this morning. And that you weren't here."

Rachel let it hang between us. Not an accusation per se, but a way of tempering her involvement with my own. An acknowledgment, again, that whatever had happened, it was shared, that we had participated together, willingly.

"I woke up at Leo's."

"And what do you remember?"

"About as much as you. The reading. And then I was sick, and Leo tried to feed me. Whatever it was, it was more powerful than I expected it to be. But Leo didn't seem that overwhelmed."

"Tolerance," said Rachel, adding, "learned tolerance."

I hadn't considered that Leo might have done the drugs before, more than once even, but it made sense.

"Do you think it was an overdose?" I asked Rachel, wondering if I remembered what had happened to the cups we had used, even what we had done with the little plastic packets.

"A bad reaction maybe?"

"But we all took the same dose, the same mixture."

"It could have just been bad luck."

I didn't respond. There was no way to articulate the darkness I had felt that evening, and I was certain it was more than just bad luck.

I wanted the days after Patrick's death to be different, but The Cloisters opened every day except Wednesday at 10 a.m., and the visitors who streamed through the galleries surely didn't read the small article that ran in the *New York Times*, commemorating the untimely passing of a celebrated curator of medieval art. No one else used the library on those bright summer days, preferring instead the glitter of sun on their skin, the dampness of grass under their thighs. But Rachel and I remained in the green leather chairs, at the large oak tables, surrounded by volumes on art and architecture.

"Just keep doing what you've been doing," said Michelle de Forte when she made her way up to The Cloisters for a visit the following week. "The new curator may simply want to move ahead with Patrick's work. Both of you should continue under that assumption."

"How long until you find someone?" asked Rachel.

We were standing in the library, surrounded by books, some of which Rachel had propped open, one revealing a medieval manuscript that illustrated the signs of the zodiac and which bodily functions they oversaw—Libra, the small intestine, Scorpio, the genitals.

Michelle looked between us and the door to Patrick's office.

"We're doing our best," she said, "but we don't want to hire fast and make a mistake. Until then—" She shrugged and made her way back out into the sunshine of the garden.

That was all she told us. Until Rachel's phone rang the next day.

"It's belladonna, the coroner is certain," Michelle said.

There was a thinness to her voice, a tightness that couldn't release, except, perhaps, explosively, a result she was working to head off. We were sitting at the edge of the garden, the phone held between us, the volume as low as we could manage.

"When they completed the autopsy," Michelle continued, "they found it in his tissues and blood. Large amounts. Potent amounts of poison."

"A suicide?" Rachel mused.

"Of course not," said Michelle. "How could you say that?"

Because, I thought, both Rachel and I knew the alternative was much worse. I studied Rachel's profile, looking for a flicker of anything—surprise, guilt—but she only looked stunned.

"What can we do?" I said, filling the silence.

"Well, there's an investigation. The police will be contacting you. They've already contacted me and are making the rounds through the staff at The Cloisters."

"Could it have been an accident?" Rachel asked. It was there, in the question, that I heard a quaver of devastation. The edges of another violent loss she would have to process. That we both would have to process.

"They're considering it a homicide." Michelle paused before adding: "At this time, we're recommending that every staff member cooperate with the investigating detectives, but of course if you would like an attorney present, that is up to you."

Two days later the detectives at the Thirty-Fourth Precinct in Inwood wanted to speak to us separately, and I still hadn't heard from Leo.

One, a Detective Murphy, met us at reception and informed Rachel: "We'll send a car up to The Cloisters when we're done with Ann to come get you."

Rachel nodded and gave me one last look before beginning her walk toward the museum, leaving me alone in the flickering yellow light of the precinct.

I had imagined that the interview would take place in a spare room with a metal table and uncomfortable chairs, perhaps a one-way mirror. But I was led to Detective Murphy's office, a cozy space that reminded me of a faculty office, full of stacks of papers and faded family photos in lightly tarnished frames. She gestured at a leather chair in the corner and sat facing me behind her desk. There was a second detective too, one I hadn't met. He leaned against the filing cabinet, occasionally checking the clock that was hung above Detective Murphy's door.

"I'm sure you're upset to hear about Patrick," she began. "We're talking to everyone who was in the building that day. It's procedure."

I wondered fleetingly if she had ever been to The Cloisters prior to this, if on her lunch breaks she liked to wander through the galleries and think about the mummified bodies that were entombed in our sarcophagi.

"Let's just start with the basics. You saw Patrick the day he died, right?"

"Yes."

"And how did Patrick seem that day? How did he seem in general?"

"He seemed fine. A little stressed. It's been a busy time for him. For us."

"Okay. Stressed. Did he seem angry or uncomfortable?"

"Not that I noticed, no."

"Have you seen anyone around The Cloisters recently? Anyone unusual? Anyone that you don't know?"

"It would be difficult for someone to go undetected in the staff area of The Cloisters," I said, "and the library has barely been used this summer. All those visitors are logged, and you can contact them. As for museum guests—" I shrugged. "We see thousands every day."

"What about a relationship?" The detective checked her notes. "Did he have a girlfriend? A boyfriend?"

The image of Patrick grabbing Rachel's wrist passed quickly through my mind, their bodies silhouetted through the door of his home, the way Margaret had talked about their time together at Long Lake.

"Not that I know of," I lied.

"What we're trying to establish," said the other detective, "is a motive. Right now, we can't figure out why someone would want to murder Patrick."

"I don't know," I said. "I really don't. Everyone loved him—the staff at The Cloisters, the staff at the Met. He was well respected. Sometimes things don't have a reason. A motive. Sometimes it's just bad luck."

"Generally, poisonings aren't bad luck," said Detective Murphy.

"We worry about accidental poisonings all the time at The Cloisters," I said. I didn't know if it was true, but it seemed entirely plausible given the number of children that came through the museum and the number of poisonous plants we cultivated.

"So you can't think of anyone who might have had a motive to murder Patrick? No bad blood? No workplace disputes?"

"None."

"When we brought Leo Bitburg in for questioning," the other detective said, "he mentioned that Rachel and Patrick had had a thing. Did you ever see anything that would indicate that?"

I tried to sound as casual as possible, doing my best to mask my concern that Leo had already been to the precinct but had neglected to talk to me. "I've only been there since the beginning of summer, so I don't know."

"Leo Bitburg said, and I quote, 'Rachel and Patrick have been together for almost a year. It was common knowledge at The Cloisters. They were together all the time.' But you never saw this?"

Both detectives watched me closely, but I shrugged.

"I'm still new," I said.

"Do you consider Rachel to be a close friend?" asked Detective Murphy.

"Yes," I said. "I think so."

"And she never talked to you about Patrick?"

"No."

"Okay." Detective Murphy made notes. "What about you? Did you and Patrick have any relationship outside the museum?"

I thought of the day we had gone down to Ketch Antiques, of the way he had stood above me, looking over my shoulder, just as my father had done when he reviewed my work. But I shook my head and said, "No."

"And what do you know about belladonna?" Detective Murphy continued.

"That it's poisonous. That The Cloisters has been growing it since they opened in the 1930s."

"Are you aware that the root is the most poisonous part of the plant?"

"I was not."

"Right now," Detective Murphy said, tapping a pencil on the desk in front of her, "we believe that Patrick was given a strong dose of belladonna root, likely ground into a fine consistency. Something that could easily have been added to a beverage or food. The flavor is very bland, so it would have been easy for Patrick to miss. Did you ever see anyone bring him food? Did you ever see anyone around the kitchen at work acting suspicious?"

I wondered if it had even happened in the kitchen at all, or if Patrick had gone to look for more of the tincture we had taken. If, with Leo tending to me, he had administered his own dosage. Even though we hadn't spoken about it we all knew—Rachel, Leo, and I—that we could not share the events of that night with the police.

And so, instead, I said, "It's a communal kitchen. We share the space. Like any office, people are always mixing things up—accidentally eating someone else's lunch, drinking their coffee." The cake Leo had pushed in front of me that night came to mind. I wondered now whose it was.

"Are you saying that it's possible someone else was the intended victim?"

I thought about how easy it was for things in life to go off the rails, for mistakes to be made, for accidents to occur. My firing, my father's death—the way we all lived, on a knife's edge, so easily pushed by fortune onto one side or the other, success or failure, life or death. These were the caprices that the ancient Romans tried to rationalize with their philosophies and gods, but deep down, they knew the truth: fate was as brutal as it was providential.

"I'm just explaining the kind of kitchen we have," I said.

"And what about you," asked the male detective. "Are you involved in any personal relationships at the museum?"

"Intimate relationships," clarified Detective Murphy.

"What would that have to do with the investigation?"

"We're just trying to get an accurate picture of the work environment," he said.

"Well, Rachel and I are friends. And I've been seeing Leo, but I wouldn't describe it as anything more than casual."

They both made notes.

"And what about Rachel. What's your impression of her"—the detective waved her hand—"in general?"

"In general, she's been very welcoming and professional. I don't think she's capable of anything like this, to be honest."

"And you're sure that—since you're still new—you know her well enough to make that assessment?"

"I know her as well as I know anyone," I said. It didn't seem necessary to share that we were now living together, and spent all our time together. I wanted to keep myself apart from what had happened as much as I could; the instinct of self-preservation came naturally to me.

"Okay," said Detective Murphy, standing to usher me toward the door. "We may have questions in the future. Please ask Rachel to let us know when she's ready for a car when you get back to The Cloisters."

They offered to drive me, too, but I wanted to walk. I followed the winding concrete paths in the direction of the museum, past groups of people sprawled on picnic blankets and knock-kneed girls reading books on their backs. An urban pastoral. And in that minute, I longed to see myself among them, a sandal dangling from my toe, my mind somewhere else. Worrying about whether the ants had gotten into the sandwiches from the deli on West Twenty-Fourth Street. Not worrying as I was about Patrick's death, about my potential role in it. Perhaps it had been an accident; perhaps he had misdosed after Leo left; perhaps the coroner had missed something in their pursuit of the poison as a cause?

I knew why I had decided not to tell Detective Murphy everything I knew. It was because what Rachel and I had discovered was so rare it was worth the risk; it was worth the choices we had made. Wasn't this what the city taught you? That it was your job to climb to the top, to hustle, to take chances? When I had arrived in New York, I was eager to forget myself, to become someone new, the kind of person who believed in tarot. Someone who was happy to be pulled into the uncanny and dark world of The Cloisters. Into a world where it was possible to get away with things. And Rachel had helped me become that person.

At The Cloisters, I went up the back drive and through the metal gate, feeling the cool iron on my fingertips before I let go and let it swing closed behind me. I found Rachel sitting at our table in the library, her head bent over the book in front of her.

I sat down across from her. My cheeks felt hot from the walk uphill, my body tight with excitement over the interview. Our eyes locked across piles of books and bits of notes.

All I said was, "I told them nothing."

"I knew you would," she said.

CHAPTER EIGHTEEN

Patrick's memorial took place on a cloudy Saturday afternoon, an hour after the doors of The Cloisters had closed to visitors. I didn't know who arranged it, but everyone was in attendance: not just staff, but the curator of the Morgan, the staff of the Frick, faculty from Columbia, Yale, Princeton, and Penn. And there were tables of tasteful charcuterie and glasses of champagne, extra chairs arranged under the shade of the quince trees. I overheard Moira saying that they had planned the memorial before they learned that Patrick's death had been a murder, information that was still only selectively shared—a trustee of the Metropolitan had been successful at keeping it out of the press. At least for now.

Guests wandered through the gardens or took their flutes of champagne into the galleries to escape the late-afternoon sun that had finally decided to make an appearance. I marveled that there was no security on hand, no one to remind them not to spill on the frescos or altarpieces, not to leave hors d'oeuvres on the windowsills. Later, when I walked through the galleries, I picked up paper napkins with half-eaten bits of charcuterie and carried them to the trash in the staff kitchen.

Rachel wore black. A shift dress with a long gold chain that ended in a painted enamel pendant, all green and red. I had borrowed a demure and appropriate dress from her, but it was clear from others in attendance that I could have opted for something more expressive. Everywhere there were splashes of color and texture.

We had changed in Patrick's office. Peeling off the clothes we had worn to work and sliding into our dresses together, as if it were a high school locker room, not the place where Patrick's body had lain almost two weeks ago.

"I don't want to do this," Rachel had said, turning so I could zip her up.

"None of us do."

"I still expect to find him in here."

"I know."

"I really mean it. Almost like he never left. Just his body left."

She grasped my hand, hard, before we bunched our clothes into our bags and walked out into the fading sunlight of summer. And in facing Patrick's memorial, I realized that The Cloisters, perhaps even Rachel, had given me one thing—it had given me a fresh start, away from Walla Walla, from the memory of my own father's memorial, from the old instabilities I had faced over the last year. And in that, I found some comfort.

Under one of the architraves at the back of the Bonnefont Cloister, I noticed Leo standing, the top half of his body in shadow, the bottom in sun. His worn jeans brightly stained with bits of green, his face hidden. He hadn't bothered to change for the event. I wanted to go over and stand with him, on the periphery of all this, but when I took a step away, Rachel grabbed my arm, the other hand shielding her eyes from the sun. "Don't leave me," she whispered.

And so, Rachel and I stood together, shoulder to shoulder next to the flowering yarrow, listening to Michelle de Forte speak, and then the curator of the Morgan. Aruna told stories about Patrick, her eyes fixed, almost the entire time, on Rachel and me. When the final eulogist was done, a string quartet that had been set up under the loggia began to play, and for the first time I realized how wonderful the acoustics of The Cloisters were, even outside.

Prior to the memorial, Michelle had told us that they would have a replacement for Patrick in place by the end of August, which was only a week away, and as I watched the figures move around the paths of the garden, I wondered who among them was already planning where to host their first farm-to-table trustee dinner, how to design improved signage in the galleries, when to start proposing their own exhibitions, after, of course, they saw if Patrick's loans could be undone, our research put to other use. I was sure there was no shortage of interest in The Cloisters' curator role.

Aruna joined us with a flute of champagne in her hand. " 'God keeps all things in order,' " she said.

"Boethius," I responded. "Patrick would have found that fitting."

" 'My fate circles on the shifting wheel, like the pale moon's face that cannot stay,' Headlam," said Rachel in response.

"I think Patrick's fate is no longer on the wheel, Rachel. He has fallen off."

"But ours still spins," she replied, looking past Aruna at the gathering of curators clustered around a bed of herbs that included henbane and mandrake.

"We are all obsessed with our fates," said Aruna, dreamily. "For they are the one thing we cannot control. The one thing we are blind to. Wouldn't you agree, Rachel?"

I glanced at Rachel, who had refocused her attention on Aruna.

"There are ways of seeing," I said.

Aruna raised an eyebrow. "Do you think there are ways of knowing how the wheel of fortune might turn, Rachel?" Aruna spun the olive that dipped low in her drink and cocked her head. "Perhaps you have found some already?"

"I don't know what you mean, Aruna."

"You should be careful what you put your faith in, of course," she continued. "Humans have a tendency to be easily romanced by the promise of knowledge." Aruna didn't wait for me to respond but lifted a hand in greeting and said, "I'm sorry, I must say hello to someone." She backed out of our circle and moved on.

"She tries so hard to be a riddle," said Rachel.

But for the first time it struck me that Aruna wasn't a riddle, but an oracle. After all, who were oracles if not women who guarded temples of knowledge?

I shook my head. "We know better than most how easy it is to be seduced by the mysteries of the past."

"Don't get too seduced, Ann. Sometimes it's better not to know what the future holds."

I thought of Rachel's survival and her parents' deaths, of Patrick's. It was easy to see why she wouldn't want to know what the future might hold, why it was easier to believe Patrick was still here, still among the flowers, somehow. We walked to the edge of the garden and sat on the low stone wall that enclosed it, taking in the movement of people, the forming and dispersing of groups—social cellular division.

Our flutes of champagne had gone warm. It felt like being a distant cousin at a family wedding, easily overlooked but somehow still necessary to the event. After a few minutes, the last rays of afternoon sun warming our skin, Rachel said, "I'm so glad you ended up here this summer."

"I am too."

"Out of all of this, at least we'll have that."

Already the August sun was setting a little earlier, and on some days, there was a crispness in the wind. Everything around us was cooling, and maybe I was too.

"If you wanted to, you could come with me up to Cambridge. Maybe get a job at the Fogg?"

We hadn't talked about what would happen when the month was over, although there was a message in my in-box from the restaurant where I worked asking me if I was coming back in September. Just seeing the name appear had made my chest constrict, a panic grip my lungs.

"Maybe," I said, sipping my flat champagne. "I'd like to stay here."

Rachel nodded. "You could always ask Aruna if she's heard of anything that might be available at the Beinecke."

We were planning an article that would reveal the discovery of the cards and a full translation of the documents Lingraf had transcribed. An article that would reveal the original, occult origins of tarot, the Renaissance's interest in parsing fate, in knowing the future. Once it was published, there was no doubt we would both be able to choose where we wanted to go. A reward for the risks I had taken that summer.

Rachel waved at the curator of the Morgan. "I'd better go say hi. Do you want an introduction?"

"No. I'm fine."

There was little else left to do but wait the event out. I pulled myself off the stone wall and made my way into the galleries, hoping I might be able to lose myself in the paintings and sculptures. Inside, I was grateful for the silence, and in front of my favorite work in the collection—a large fresco of a lion—I sat down on a bench and allowed my eyes to follow the curves of its tail. Leo and I hadn't been able to talk since that night, and the handful of text messages we'd exchanged left me with more questions than answers. But it wasn't for lack of trying; Rachel had been needier than usual in the wake of Patrick's death.

"Running away?" It was Leo.

"Taking a break," I said, facing him.

"Not in the mood to turn murder into an opportunity to leverage your next position? Good for you."

"That's unfair."

"Is it? Have you taken a look out in the gardens?"

"What else are we supposed to do?" I said. "We have to come together somehow."

Leo moved to the window in the gallery—a narrow Gothic arch of thick float glass. Lit from behind, he was just a dark outline, his features in shadow.

"And we do that by dressing up in our nicest clothes and patting ourselves on the back while the site where a man lay murdered is only steps away."

"Leo—"

"What are you getting out of his death anyway, Ann? Have you really asked yourself that?"

I had, even if I couldn't stand the answers.

"I could ask you the same thing," I said quietly.

"You know why I did it," Leo said, looping a hand, nails black with soil, around the back of his neck. "He asked me to." His voice was thin. He looked tired, his tan face pulled taut against his cheekbones. "Ann, trust yourself. There's a reason why you're in here and not out there."

But my intuition didn't work like Leo's—shrewd and quick, as much a part of him as his skin—it was harder to access. I had started to rely on the cards to guide me, to sharpen it. But Leo always had a way of standing off to the side, not because he was retiring or afraid, but because he liked to assess things, assess people. He was calculating.

"Everyone grieves differently."

"Don't make excuses for her."

"I'm making excuses for myself," I said. I meant it.

"Well don't make them for Rachel. She doesn't deserve it."

"We're friends."

He laughed. "Haven't you noticed that Rachel doesn't have friends? Just admirers. You've been to house parties full of people I consider friends, but have you ever met someone Rachel considers a friend?"

I was staring at him, angry that on some level he was right. That the world I had carefully walled myself within was beginning to show cracks.

"You haven't, have you? Now that you're thinking about it. Who did she ever introduce you to? No one, right?"

"Why does that matter?"

"Because," he said, his hands flung wide, "someone did it. Someone here killed him. Someone who is walking through the museum right now. You, me, Rachel, Moira. And you're refusing to see it."

It was a reality I wasn't prepared to face, because if I did, it would only mean one thing: more loss. And so, I had rationalized it. Compartmentalized. I hadn't, until then, at least, been willing to see Patrick's death as murder. Even through the questioning and the evidence, I had continued to believe there was another alternative, another fate that waited for Patrick. I rose from the bench and walked to where Leo stood.

"I have to get through this," I said quietly. "I can't quit. Not now."

He reached out and touched a strand of my hair, his calloused knuckles brushing against my neck as he did it. I looked up at him, willing him to lean down and kiss me. I wanted to take comfort in him, in something that seemed to be stable in a world that kept shifting around me. A world that, he was right, I couldn't see as completely as I wanted to.

"Ann," he said. "I hope you're clever enough to survive this."

Behind us, the door to the gallery groaned open. I could hear her shoes before I heard her voice.

"We should go," said Rachel. "Ann?"

"Ann and I were just discussing getting some dinner. Weren't we?"

I nodded, my face still upturned at Leo, my back to Rachel. The silence was tense, and I rolled the words I wanted to say around in my mouth until I felt sure of them.

"I think I'm going to spend the night with Leo," I said, still looking up at him.

"What?"

I turned to face Rachel. She looked fragile and washed out. Her dress, I noticed for the first time, hung awkwardly off the boniest parts of her body—her shoulders and her clavicle, her hip bones that jutted through. It was the way grief had looked on me. I didn't know when she had become even thinner, but I saw it then, her body framed between the wooden statues of Joan of Arc and Saint Ursula.

"I'm going to get dinner with Leo," I said again. "If you don't mind, that is."

"Of course I don't mind." Her arms were crossed. "We all make our own decisions."

For a minute I doubted what I was doing and said, "Do you want me to come—"

"No," she said before I could finish. "I don't."

She turned to leave, but when she reached the door that would take her out to the Bonnefont Cloister and the sun, just set below the horizon, she turned back and said, "Careful, Ann. The top of the wheel is a scary place to be."

The door closed behind her.

"What did she mean by that?" Leo asked.

"Nothing," I said, but as we walked through the galleries, I couldn't help but take one last look at the wheel of fortune and the figures lashed to it. Rachel's words burned in my mind.

CHAPTER NINETEEN

I met Laure downtown on a cramped side street where neat rows of brick apartment buildings blocked out the morning sun. The breakfast counter was tastefully finished with black and white hexagonal tiles and mirrors in oil-rubbed bronze frames, glossy wood tables accompanied by leather chairs. Plates piled with thick slices of toast and fried eggs were delivered to waiting diners, and I scanned the room for Laure before spotting her on a stool at the bar that faced the street, where walkers and cars combined to create the tissue of the day.

After a gig in Red Hook, Leo had invited me to spend the night, but I hadn't had time to wash my hair. The smell of stale cigarettes still clung to my clothes—the same clothes I had worn in the wings of the stage, watching other acts prepare for their turn. Rushing out the door to meet Laure, I had pulled my hair back into a ponytail, my curls limp; I hadn't wanted to brush them out. I wanted to remember the way Leo had wound them around his index finger before pulling them. Before telling me I was coming home with him—it was never a question.

Leo and I hadn't talked about what we were doing, and sometimes I wondered if he had other women on other nights in the same bed. But it was still easy to push those thoughts away; I didn't want Leo every night anyway. Rachel wouldn't have let me.

"You look—" Laure sipped her coffee. "Rumpled?"

I looked down at my dress that had spent the night crumpled on the floor. Leo's apartment only had a small mirror above the sink in the bathroom, but I knew Laure's assessment was right. I brushed my hand down the front of my dress, as if that would be enough to smooth out the wrinkles.

"At least you're enjoying yourself in New York," she said.

"The gardener at The Cloisters," I explained. "We've—"

Laure nodded. "I had a gardener at The Cloisters when I first moved here, too."

I looked down at the menu. I doubted Laure had brought me here to talk about my dating life or hers. Although I remembered her boyfriend at Whitman clearly—a soccer player who smoked incessantly between classes and always had a worn copy of *Howl* tucked in his back pocket. I wondered what he was doing now; I couldn't remember his name.

"So," I said after ordering a stack of pancakes that I had watched pass by only a minute before, "how are things at Yale?"

"Everything is good," said Laure, filling the silence, her shoulder pushed close against mine. "I'm sorry about Patrick." She searched my face as she said it. "I wish I'd known you were there, I would have—" She lifted her shoulders and let them fall.

I resented her trying to play the big sister when for the last two years in Walla Walla I had fended for myself, never hearing a word from her. I had even emailed Laure for advice when I received my rejection from Yale, but she never responded. It had stung, of course; I was easy to leave behind. But now that I had managed to claw my way back into her world, we were at brunch again, like nothing had ever happened.

"Rachel and I found him," I said, letting it hang between us.

"Ann—"

But I shook my head, shaking off Laure and the memory. "We're getting by. I'm getting by. It's been hardest on Rachel, I think. She knew him longest."

"And how are things going with her?"

"What do you mean?" Perhaps there was a defensiveness in my voice, because Laure held up a hand, almost placing it on my arm, before deciding to rest it back in her lap instead.

"I just mean—" She took a breath. "Has she been a good colleague? Supportive?"

"She's more than a colleague," I said. "She's a friend." After last night, I had attributed her harshness in the gallery to the fact that we were all—her, myself, Leo—under an incredible amount of stress. It wasn't enough—one interaction, one bad moment wasn't enough to undo the summer we had spent together.

"And you haven't noticed any"—she let her hand lift and wave loosely, punctuating the pause—"strange behavior?"

"Other than the death of our curator?" I didn't mean for it to come out as snide, but Laure was finding my edges.

"I'm asking because things happened when Rachel was at Yale."

I thought of her parents. I knew how a loss like that could shift the gravity of your world.

"In the middle of my first year at Yale, when Rachel was a junior, her roommate died," Laure said. "She fell out of their window. They lived on the third floor of Branford, an old historic building. Everyone was shocked because so many of the windows in that building had been painted closed for decades. It was unbelievable that someone could even get the windows open, but somehow Rachel did. And right after the Christmas holiday, her roommate jumped. Or fell." Laure took a sip of coffee and looked at me. "Or she was pushed."

"Oh my god. Poor Rachel."

"It turned out they had been roommates since freshman year. They were close, but the day after she died Rachel—"

"Everyone grieves differently," I interrupted, wanting to head off what I anticipated to be a criticism of Rachel's behavior in the wake of death.

"That's the thing, Ann. I don't think she was grieving. I think she was celebrating."

Who, I thought, was Laure to judge? I knew how impossible it was for people who hadn't experienced the loss of a loved one to understand how it remade your world in terrible, strange ways. That you couldn't judge someone for how they grieved was an understanding Rachel and I shared.

"Did she have an alibi?" I asked.

Laure nodded. "She was in the city."

"Then why are you suggesting Rachel pushed her?"

"There's more than one way to push someone," said Laure softly. I was about to say that I hadn't seen behavior like that from Rachel when Laure continued, "And it wasn't just that. She had a habit of treating other people badly. I saw her once, yelling at another student. She was screaming. Acting so loud and chaotic I could only pick up fragments, a refrain she kept saying: *you don't know, you don't know.* I asked another grad student about it, someone who had been at Yale longer than me, and he said that Rachel had a history of being difficult. Apparently, her freshman year she accused a male graduate student of artificially lowering her grade because she wouldn't sleep with him. There was no material proof, just her word against his. The student ended up having to leave Yale. Then this spring, at a department party, she outed a married professor for having an affair with his student." Laure took another sip of her coffee. "Everyone at Yale knows she's smart—really talented, actually—but . . ." Laure paused. "She's also pretty unhinged."

"We're living together." I said it as much to refute Laure's fears as to affirm my own bravery.

"Ann—"

"And we've been working together since I arrived."

"Rachel doesn't work with others."

"She does—"

"No. *You* think you're working together, but I can assure you Rachel sees it differently."

The waitress arrived with our breakfasts, but the hunger I had felt leaving Leo's was gone.

"Ann," said Laure gently, "do you ever wonder why Rachel picked you?"

"What do you mean?"

"I mean you're nice. You're new here, you're eager to please. You want to make a name for yourself. But you don't understand the kind of person you're dealing with. The world she lives in. The kind of person she is. Rachel will step on as many people as necessary to get what she wants."

On my darker days, I had bounced this thought around. Laure wasn't the first one to prove to me that I was easy to abandon, and it had struck me that it would be easy enough for Rachel to leave me out if things got tight. After all, I was the new hire—the outsider. I often wondered if I would ever be anything else. But I was also learning that it wasn't too late to look out for myself, first. Rachel and I were friends. We were conspirators and collaborators, but Laure was telling me something I already knew: I needed a contingency plan.

I studied the cutlery and white napkins that had arrived with my breakfast.

"Are people saying she had something to do with Patrick's death?" I asked.

"I don't know if people are saying it. But I'm saying it. I'm saying it to you, right now. I think she did." Laure waited a beat before she asked, "Do you?"

"No," I said. The Rachel I knew wasn't that messy. She was meticulous and methodical. Killing Patrick in front of me, in front of an entire museum of people, wasn't Rachel's style.

"You don't know her the way you think you do."

"Have you ever considered that maybe you don't?" I was surprised to hear my voice rise, a fierce and glottal catch at the back of my throat.

She put a hand on my arm. "You should get out of The Cloisters."

"What do you mean?"

"I mean working with Rachel Mondray hasn't ended well for anyone I know. If I were you, I would start looking for a new job. Today."

I almost laughed. It was impossible. Leave the cards, the work, and the manuscripts of The Cloisters? Leave my father's translations and Lingraf's papers in Rachel's hands alone? My best hope for the year ahead was to stay. Leaving now would only mean one thing: I would have to go home and leave it all behind, not just my ambitions but the objects themselves. And I wasn't willing to do that; I would stay.

"Haven't you noticed a pattern, Ann? Death clings to Rachel. It follows her everywhere. It can't all be coincidence."

"She's had some bad luck," I said. But I knew it could be something else entirely, too, something I wasn't ready to share with Laure, so I continued, "Don't you think if Rachel had systematically murdered those closest to her, someone would have noticed by now? Have you considered that she might also be a victim?"

Laure folded her hands in her lap. "I think it's possible she's both," she said. "Maybe Patrick—"

She shrugged and let the implication settle uneasily between us.

"I just want to be sure that you're going to be okay."

I couldn't resist looking at Laure while I pulled a few bills from my wallet and left them on the bar next to my uneaten breakfast. She seemed sincere, but I found it impossible to trust someone who had walked out on me when I needed them the most.

"Rachel's taught me how to look out for myself," I said, getting up from the bar.

"Ann, if you ever need anything—"

I turned before I reached the door, angry that the offer was coming now. Now that I didn't need anything from Laure.

"Isn't that the same offer you made before you left Whitman? *If I ever needed anything?* I did need something, Laure, long before I got to New York. I needed you. I needed a friend."

She started to open her mouth, but I wasn't ready to hear her excuses. "Well, I have that now."

On the subway ride uptown, I swayed back and forth across from a group of schoolgirls crowded around a single phone, laughing and pointing at whatever was unfolding on the screen. I could already see them fitting into their roles within the group—the smart one, the pretty one, the nervous one. Maybe that was why I had never managed to find a wide group of friends: none of the roles fit. And now that I was older, I wasn't plastic enough to mold myself into someone else. New York had taught me that I no longer cared if I fit; I preferred to stand out.

Walking through the entrance of The Cloisters always felt like abandoning the modern world at the door: a maze of hand-cut stone walls and Gothic arches, skeletal rib vaults and narrow hallways. It was difficult to imagine that outside these cool walls the city glittered fast and hard despite the languid summer sun. The word *cloister*, after all, derived from the Latin *claudere*, meaning to close. Here, we closed ourselves in against the rest of New York.

What Laure had said remained at the edge of my mind, needling me. And while I tried to let the research and the library pull me back into the world of discovery, I found myself glossing over pages of text before noticing what I had missed, my mind wandering down other hidden pathways. A walk through the galleries, I decided, would help clear my head.

There was something about being able to see works of art whenever the desire moved you, a series of casual, individual impressions that added up to a bigger, more complete picture. Now, when we went to other museums in the city, I found it stressful to have to take in all the details of a work in one viewing, as a visitor. Would I catch the delicate shadows on the Tintoretto, notice the way Monet built up his impasto if I only had a few minutes, one day, with the work? Working in a museum bred familiarity in the truest sense of the word—the works at The Cloisters had become like family to me.

I walked through the galleries, nodding at the security staff as I made my way into the gardens, hoping I might run into Leo. But when luck didn't put him in my path as I wandered the cobbled pathways and lingered at the lavender and lemon balm, I decided to walk under the last Gothic arch in the Bonnefont Cloister and toward the garden sheds.

When I rounded the corner, I saw them: Leo's hands stuffed in his pockets, Rachel's arms crossed, their bodies pushing away from each other despite their proximity. I was too far away to hear what they were saying, but I could tell from their faces, from the strain with which the words came out of their mouths, that they were arguing. About what, I couldn't be sure.

And for a minute, I stood there, framed in the Gothic arch, my hands holding on to either side of the jamb, watching them. The wind pressed my dress against the back of my legs, and perhaps it was that flutter that caught their eye, because just then, they turned to see me standing there. Leo didn't even offer a nod of acknowledgment, but just stalked back into the garden shed.

"What was all that about?" I asked when Rachel joined me.

"Nothing," she said. "We were just talking about the investigation. I didn't want to talk anywhere Moira might be able to hear us."

I noticed that Rachel was still carrying her bag, the one she usually dropped, first thing, in the library.

"Where have you been?" she said.

I waved a hand. "Oh, I met a friend from Whitman for coffee."

"Laure?"

"Mm-hmm."

"And Leo last night?"

"I figured it was better than coming in late and turning on all the lights."

"I wouldn't mind."

"I'll remember that."

"It gets lonely without you there." Rachel turned and looked at me while we walked, her eyes scanning my face.

"Well, I don't think Leo really wants me staying over that much," I said.

"Don't do that. Don't belittle yourself. He'd be lucky to have you there every night."

The way she said it made me feel both warm and uncomfortable, but I simply said, "Thanks."

"You know," she said, holding the door of the library open for me, "Leo is fun, but he can also be a real shit. Be aware of that fact."

I nodded. I thought I already was.

"And if you ever want to get coffee, you don't have to go all the way downtown to meet Laure. We could meet her on our way up here, or she could come to the apartment. I only know her a little bit—"

"That's okay," I said. "I don't think we're going to be seeing much more of each other."

At this Rachel smiled. "Well, the offer stands."

Back in the library, Rachel pulled the box of cards out of her bag and set them on the table.

"I'm just going to do a quick spread," I said, reaching for the cards. There was something about the readings that settled my nerves and gave me clarity. As if, in the moments when it was darkest, when I couldn't see the landscape around me, the cards could guide me.

Rachel pushed them in my direction, and I fanned them out, pulling three. The first showed a woman pouring water from an urn into a catch basin. We had associated the card with temperance, one of Aristotle's twelve virtues, because the composition focused on balance and harmony. After the temperance card, I pulled a Two of Swords and the Queen of Cups, a figure of intuition.

I had asked the cards about Rachel, and it seemed to me that every time I did, a darkness found her in the readings. Even if it was at the periphery—a single card or an inverted one. My readings were increasingly haunted by something I still wasn't fully able to grasp. And there was something there about me as well, even though I had asked them about Rachel.

When I looked up from the spread, Rachel was watching me.

"What does it say?"

"Something different for everyone," I said, rapping my knuckle against the heavy oak of the table to break the spell.

But I committed the spread to memory, the flaking paint and flecks of gold leaf lingering on my eyelids. The duality of the two, the patience and symmetry of temperance, the intuition I needed to trust but that only ever found me in unpredictable ways.

CHAPTER TWENTY

Leo's apartment had none of the clear light of Rachel's on the Upper West Side. His world was always filtered by the indirect sun that slipped past thin curtains and the haze of cigarette and weed smoke, an array of dirty jeans and work boots littering the floor, the slightly bitter smell of cheap coffee that had burned on the hot plate long before I got up. And that morning, the heat of the day had already begun to seep through the cracks in the windows and the walls. I moved my body away from his roommate's cat, who slept at the end of the bed; even that small amount of warmth too much to handle.

It was Saturday, so I called into the kitchen as I pulled on a pair of sweatpants and tied the waistband. "Can we go to the High Line?"

The last time I slept over, Leo had told me I should leave a few things, and so I had brought a bag of items to stash at the back of his closet.

"No." He was sitting on the couch in a puddle of sunlight. "Real New Yorkers don't go to the High Line."

"That can't be true."

"It is. I'm a New Yorker. I can confirm it." He was reading an interview with Tracy Letts that had been published the month before.

"It can be fun to do touristy things," I persisted.

Leo said nothing, just sipped his mug of coffee.

I decided I would take it up again once we were out for the afternoon and maybe after a few beers at lunch; in the meantime, I changed the subject.

"How did your conversation with the detective go?"

Leo had been called down to the precinct for a second time, and it seemed inevitable Rachel and I might be next. He didn't look up, but penciled a note in the margin.

"Fine. She wanted to know if anything was missing from the gardens. If I had seen anyone."

"You didn't, did you?" There was still some part of me, then, that clung to the idea that the whole investigation would resolve as an accident—an overdose, an allergic reaction.

Leo shut the magazine and set it down. "I told her I hadn't seen anyone in the gardens, except for the thousands of people who march through them every day. None of whom I think murdered Patrick."

I made myself at home on his threadbare couch and curled my knees against my chest to watch him. As much as Leo was part of The Cloisters, he wasn't of the place the way Rachel and I were, the way the curatorial staff and the preparatory staff were. He was able to keep to himself, mostly, shuttling between the sheds and the gardens. He could—and did—spend whole days climbing the trees and trimming their branches. All of it incredibly romantic. To be the keeper of medieval gardens in one of the busiest cities in the world, to spend the day moving your body and growing things that gave people joy. But Leo could be touchy about it too, this distance between our roles, our futures at the museum.

"I didn't mean—"

"I know. I'm sorry. And even though you want to go to the High Line, I thought we could do something a little more Old New York. Why don't we go down to the Village instead?"

"I'd like that. Do you think we could go to the bar where Helen Frankenthaler and Lee Krasner used to hang out?"

"The Cedar Tavern became condos in 2006. They sold the bar itself to a guy who rebuilt it in Austin."

"Oh." If that was the case, I wasn't sure why we couldn't go to the High Line.

Leo got up and poured himself another cup of coffee. "Why don't you get dressed and we'll get out of here."

I went back into the bedroom and changed into a sundress with thin straps and a spray of flowers. The things I intended to leave at Leo's I wedged between his hamper and an old amp at the back of his closet. On the top shelf were a stack of straw hats, the kind Leo wore when working. I reached up to grab one, wondering how it would look with my dress, but the stack was so high I had to stand on my toes to get a finger onto a brim. When I pulled, the entire stack came lilting down, including something that made a hard cracking sound against the wood floor.

I paused to see if Leo had heard, but he was in the kitchen, washing dishes and putting away plates from breakfast. The image of myself, emerging from the bedroom, wearing his work hat, the way some girls wore their boyfriend's shirts—a casual borrowing of apparel that seemed to reinforce intimacy—played through my head. That's what I wanted, a symbol of where we might be going. But as I restacked the hats and searched the room for something to stand on, I also found the thing that had produced the crack.

It was a delicate object, one that I was surprised to discover had made the fall intact. It was an ivory carving of a woman dressed in flowing robes, a sleeping lion curled at her feet. On her head, she wore a crown, and around her neck an intricately carved crucifix. It was no more than three or four inches tall, a private devotional figure, meant to be held by whoever owned it. Clearly it was antique. If I hadn't found it in Leo's closet, I could have easily imagined it on display at The Cloisters.

"Are you almost ready—" Leo swung into the door, his hand on the jamb. He stopped when he saw me, the carving in my hand.

"Where did this come from?" I said, holding it up in the light and turning it over, its etched areas deep and browned with age.

"Saint Daria," he said, walking over and taking the figurine from me. He placed it on the dresser.

"It's amazing."

"It was my grandmother's."

"Have you had it appraised? You should really get it insured; it looks old."

"No, I haven't."

"Do you know where she got it?" I didn't know why I was pushing. Part of me wanted to leave and head to the Village, to walk arm in arm past stately brownstones whose heavy wooden doors were inlaid with leaded glass windows. But another part of me had studied art long enough to know that this figurine was the real thing, something precious.

"I think my grandfather bought it in Europe when he finished his tour during the Second World War."

I nodded. That seemed plausible.

"My mom always wanted to take it to *Antiques Roadshow*, but she never got around to it."

"I know an antiquities dealer on East Fifty-Sixth who could appraise it for you."

Leo gave me a funny look.

"Are we going to get out of here or what?" he asked.

I threw on one of his straw hats, and he playfully dipped the brim. I wanted him to say it looked good on me, that he looked good on me.

"You should grab your stuff," he said. "I don't know if we'll be back here tonight. I have a thing."

He hadn't mentioned a thing. I thought of the bag I had just hidden at the back of his closet, of the fact that only a few days ago he had told me I had a place there too.

"Actually," he said before I could protest, "you can leave it. I'm sure you'll be back in a few days."

It wasn't the most romantic thing anyone had ever said to me, but in that moment, it felt like it. I tried to hide my smile under the brim of his hat as we walked out of the apartment.

⌁

We spent the day in a haze, moving from one bookshop to another. Visiting a store that specialized in rare vinyl and a bar that specialized in cocktails named after famous Beat writers. We walked the streets of the Village, and I was reminded again of how neighborhoody New York could be, almost suburban in these little enclaves, each with its own distinctive identity. There were flowers and thickly leafed trees. There were rich young mothers being dragged down the street to the playground by their children, the nanny on her day off. And there was the heat. The humidity and the lack of breeze, the way it amplified the smell of the bartender taking his cigarette break, the exhaust from the delivery truck, the Thai curry restaurant that was preparing for its lunch buffet. And beneath it all, the smell of hot asphalt, the metallic, earthy smell of the city in summer.

I hadn't expected to fall in love with New York, but falling in love can make a city burn brighter. I sometimes wondered if I took Leo outside of the five boroughs if he would have the same luster, if the city itself would, from a distance. But I loved the bigness and the smallness of it, the weirdness and the joy. It wasn't home, and I didn't know if it ever would be, but it was where I was supposed to be, in that moment. Then, maybe forever.

Things had never happened to me until I arrived in New York. In Walla Walla, everything was predictable—the same coffee, the same shops, the same people in line. The only discoveries to be made were those that had been made dozens, or hundreds, of times before by other people, other students, other scholars. But here, it seemed like there was nothing else to do but discover. And even when you weren't looking for them, the discoveries found you. The city had a way of making everything feel cosmic and inevitable—magical.

We were walking toward where the Cedar Tavern used to be when

Leo's phone rang. At first he ignored it, but then the ringing began again, and I could see on the screen it was a local area code. He picked it up.

"This is Leo."

While he talked, I turned to study the display of the business next to us. It sold pens and expensive stationery supplies. In the window were sheaves of embossed paper, fanned in a semicircle like playing cards. Everything, a sign in the window told me, could be monogrammed for a fee.

"Now really isn't a good time— Right, I understand."

I tried not to listen, but I thought I recognized Detective Murphy's voice. Her flat affect.

"I could come in on Monday morning? Sure. Yeah, you could meet me at the gardens."

Then a beat.

"Yes, I can walk you through what we grow. Ten would be best."

He pocketed the phone and turned to me, his shoulders up around his ears and his hands in his pockets.

"They want to talk to you again?"

"Yeah. Procedure, she said."

"I'm sure it's nothing," I said, reaching out to wrap my small hand in his. "None of us really know what Patrick did that night after we left."

"Did they mention me in your interview?"

I shook my head. "They said you had told them about Patrick and Rachel."

"What did you say?"

"Just that I'd never seen them together."

"Ann. That makes it look like I'm lying."

I took a step back. "No, it doesn't. I was telling the truth. I never saw them together. At least not in that way, not intimately." I knew how quickly this could escalate into a real fight. And I didn't want to have to expose my fault lines between Leo and Rachel, outlines that were still hazy, even to me. "I'm not trying to make you look like a liar," I said.

Leo nodded and we started walking again, shoulder to shoulder, until after a few steps he put his arm around me and pulled me in closer.

"Come on," he said. "Let's go get day drunk like the Abstract Expressionists."

We didn't end up getting day drunk, or rather, I didn't. Leo had four Manhattans and almost an entire pack of cigarettes before we parted company for the day. He never told me about the thing he had that meant I couldn't spend the night, but I heard him tell the cab to take him downtown. I walked to the subway and took it back to Rachel's apartment, which was dark and empty.

Rachel wasn't there, and I couldn't remember a time when I had been alone in the apartment. I threw my bag down on my bed, where late-afternoon sunlight spilled in, warming the parquet floors, the white bedding, the walls. I pulled out the box of tarot cards and lightly moved them around, taking care not to damage the gold leaf, and selected three cards, my eyes closed. I opened my eyes and arranged the Eight of Staves, the Queen of Swords, and the third card, a card we were considering the Chariot—with the Roman god Mercury transported in a golden chariot by a phalanx of horses—on the table. It was a spread that spoke of sharpness, dramatic change, reversal, speeding up. I held my hands over the cards for a moment, imagining how they might have glittered in fifteenth-century candlelight, before returning them to their box.

In the living room, with Rachel gone, I wanted to let my curiosity loose. I inspected every bookshelf: those that were full of medieval treatises and academic art history books, those that displayed silver-framed photos of Rachel. Several with her parents, one with a girl wearing a Yale sweatshirt. But when I took the frame off the shelf and inspected the back, where an unfamiliar name and date were tacked—Sarah, Yale, 2012—my phone rang. I let it go to voice mail and studied the image.

The girl had round cheeks and small, close-set eyes. They were both smiling. Smiling in a way I had never seen Rachel smile, open and excited. There were no other photographs with friends. Just her parents and a few solo photos: Rachel taking in the mosaics in Ravenna. Rachel in Central Park, at Tavern on the Green, blowing out birthday candles.

At the end of the hallway was Rachel's bedroom. I'd only been in it once, a few days after I moved in when I needed to ask her a question about what time we were leaving for work, but she had answered at the door and then quickly closed it. Now, I took the opportunity to open the door and peek inside. It was like mine, only larger, with four windows looking onto the park; mine looked onto the neighboring building. Her room was white and tidy, bed made neatly, folded clothes on a chair. But it was the bookcases that caught my eye. Floor-to-ceiling shelves made of rich wood that contained not only philosophical treatises but countless works of fiction.

I pulled out a copy of Irving Stone's *The Agony and the Ecstasy* only to discover it was a signed first edition. This was true of countless volumes I selected. And there were rare books too, some manuscripts, a miniature book of hours, each in a brown plastic box to protect them from the sunlight. I tried to imagine what it must be like to have so much money that I could afford to purchase the objects I studied.

Next to Rachel's bed were two side tables with clear glass lamps and cream-colored drum shades. Above the bed hung a small engraving, a copy of Dürer's drawing of the goddess Fortuna. Only after a minute did it strike me that it might be real.

From the living room, I heard a soft swoosh and rushed back down the hall to make sure Rachel hadn't arrived to catch me snooping, but it was just the door to the terrace that had slipped closed. I had forgotten to prop it open with the stone stopper.

I returned to Rachel's bedroom and pulled open the drawer of a bedside table just to see what was inside: three neatly ordered pens and a leather-bound notebook. I closed it before the temptation to open the book became overwhelming. But the truth was, I was looking for evidence—something to support what Laure said, something that could explain the edginess Leo showed when the topic of Rachel came up. Something, even, that might indicate how much she really knew about what happened to Patrick. But the only thing I discovered was that Rachel was surprisingly rigid—all her clothes were folded at right angles and her books were organized by date and theme. Her bed was made with the precision of a martinet; she had expensive taste. Rachel could be petty, ambitious, sometimes a little mean, but none of that indicated murder.

Again my phone rang. This time I picked it up, seeing my mother's name on the screen. It had been weeks since I had talked to her on the phone and not just sent a quick text in response to her increasingly alarmed inquires.

I ran my finger across the screen and answered, "Mom?"

"Oh my god, Ann. I have been trying to reach you for weeks. Are you okay? I read about the thing. At the place you work. The death." She whispered it, and I wondered who had told her. My mother, I knew, didn't read the papers.

"It's okay," I said, searching for the voice I used to use when she was like this—tiptoeing along the boundary between dizzying concern and panic. "I'm okay. The police are handling it. All of it."

"I really want you to come home, Annie. I do. I told you the city wasn't a safe place."

It was true. When I first got word from the Met that I had been admitted to their program, my mother had listed the many reasons why New York was dangerous, much more dangerous than Walla Walla, or even Seattle. But while these fears had given my mother a reason to stay, they could never have stopped me from going.

"The city is plenty safe."

"When are you coming home?"

It was the question I had been dreading, the reason I had been evading her calls and been short and noncommittal over text. I still didn't have any concrete plans, any concrete place lined up to stay.

"I don't know, Mom."

"Because I need to make plans to drive to Seattle to pick you up. You can't just expect me to drop everything when suddenly it turns out you have to give it all up. When you have to come home because there are no other options."

"There will be other options," I said, perhaps a little too forcefully.

"Don't yell at me. It's not my fault."

"I'm sorry, Mom."

"You're just like your father," she said. "I don't want you to end up like him, losing everything. I want you to come home before it comes to that."

"I will, Mom. I promise." Although I intended to do no such thing.

As the sound of her crying came through the line, I wanted to comfort her, to say something that might make her feel better. But the truth was that she couldn't know how close I had come to what had happened to Patrick at The Cloisters, that I was beginning to feel, perhaps like Rachel already did, that death followed me everywhere I went. That on my darker days, I wondered if I was the one who had brought it with me, to The Cloisters.

"This is why I didn't want you to go in the first place," she said, her voice now breaking. "Because this is what happens when you go out into the world—when we go out into the world, Ann. We lose. The deck is always stacked against us."

CHAPTER TWENTY-ONE

At the Cloisters, the staff had started to spend much of their time comparing notes—divulging the questions they had been asked by the investigating detectives, sharing their own theories as to what had happened. The silent stone hallways were now full of soft whispers and hushed conversations, words that dried up when Rachel and I walked by. It was hard not to take this reaction personally, but it was impossible to ignore the reality—we had been the ones closest to the event, to Patrick. And as long as the investigation was ongoing, we languished in its shadow.

It seemed the most pressing question was why no one had ever installed cameras in the library or Patrick's office. A question that irked Louis, who responded by saying that The Cloisters was a community of trust, and Patrick had been adamantly opposed to the surveillance of scholars; it was not our mission. This irritation had trickled down through the entire security team, who were upset to see the standard of their work being questioned by the police.

Rachel and I were busy outlining the parameters of the article we were planning on publishing about the cards, but we had also been asked by Michelle, in anticipation of a new curator and assistant curator joining us, to pull together an onboarding document outlining the status of upcoming exhibitions, collection highlights, artworks that were due to be put on display in the galleries in the fall. It was tedious work, requiring accession numbers and the inclusion of preexisting correspondence between Patrick and the Cluny Museum in Paris or the National Gallery in London.

"The search function is down," said Rachel, pushing back her chair and sighing.

We were in the process of pulling accession numbers for works that were scheduled to go on loan all around the world in the coming year. Usually this was work done by the Registrar, but Curatorial wasn't the only department to find itself short-staffed that summer.

"Let's just take the list and pull them manually." She looked at me expectantly, already standing, a pencil in one hand, a piece of paper in the other.

We walked through the galleries, noting numbers until we hit the smaller works on the list that were kept in storage. Our key cards buzzed us past the conservation rooms and into Storage, where rows and rows of shelves were kept in the climate-controlled dark. Rachel flicked on the lights and the fluorescents struggled to life.

The number of objects gifted to the Metropolitan on an annual basis was staggering. And those were only the objects they accepted. In its earliest years, the museum had become something of a repository for all paintings, sculptures, and objets d'art that didn't survive the transition from one generation to the next. Every now and then, the museum would quietly sell pieces that never managed to find their way into a gallery to make room for new things that might.

Storage, then, was like a heavily curated and conserved dustbin. In The Cloisters' storage, there were countless examples of carved capitals and pottery fragments. There were closed manuscripts in amber plastic boxes with elaborately jeweled bindings, miniatures, enamel devotionals, pieces of jewelry, reliquaries, gold-plated icons, and a single fossilized toe of a saint. We paused to take down the accession number for a reliquary of Saint Christopher.

I pulled out a shelf and looked at the exquisitely turned miniature ivory boars and unicorns while Rachel wrote down numbers on the sheet of paper. There were also, I noticed, a few slots where works were missing.

"Where did all of these go?" I asked, pointing at the empty slots.

"Probably on display," said Rachel, looking over my shoulder. "Or on loan."

I traced my finger along the labels that marked the missing objects. Each accession number began with the first three letters of the work's title, and I tried to imagine what might have been here, *RIN* for ring perhaps, a *TOU* perhaps indicating Toulouse. But the next label caught my eye. The first three letters of its accession read *DAR*. Only then did I look at its title, *Saint Daria*. The details read: *ivory, German, 1170, Weston Endowment Gift 1953*. I wrote down the accession number and followed Rachel, who had moved on to manuscripts.

The time we spent in storage seemed to drag on, and although I tried to stay focused on what Rachel was saying—*Did you see Otto III's Bible anywhere?*—all I could do was replay the way the carving in Leo's apartment had felt in my hand, the way it was both heavy and slight, the way it had been expertly incised. I had looked up the story of Saint Daria when I got home that night. She was an obscure early Christian saint who had begun her life as a priestess for the goddess Minerva. But as an apostate to the Roman religion, she had likely been given the fate awarded to unfaithful priestesses—entombment, alive, in the sand pits near the Roman catacombs. The image of myself, trapped in one of the rooms of the museum—no door, no windows, no exit—came to me.

"Are you ready?" Rachel asked, facing me and closing a storage drawer. "I think I have everything."

I nodded.

"Are you okay, Ann?"

"Fine," I said. "Just . . . a weird feeling."

"I hate that," she said, holding the door open for me to pass through.

Back in the library I waited impatiently for the search function on our intranet to be restored. When it was, I entered the accessions number and clicked return.

Of course, I had known what I would find, but that didn't change the fact that in front of me, on the screen, was the figurine I had found in Leo's closet. It had to be worth—I tried in vain to calculate the cost of something that priceless and historic—at least $50,000. True, it wasn't much by The Cloisters' standards, but it certainly would be to a gardener, an aspiring playwright.

I closed my laptop and got up, not meeting Rachel's questioning gaze. I needed some air.

Outside, the grasses of the Cuxa Cloister swayed in the breeze that made its way off the Hudson, the heads of daisies weaving and bobbing merrily as I found myself, resigned, walking toward the security offices.

"Does everyone have access to storage?" I said, popping my head in the door.

"You're letting out all the AC," complained Hal, the security guard on duty. I stepped inside.

It had never struck me that the security operation at the museum was sophisticated but casually run. There were banks of monitors and computer equipment recording a constant loop of film—a record of the movements of visitors and staff. But it was also a makeshift kitchen, stacked with boxes of pastries and an extra coffee machine. A pile of unused radios was tangled in the corner. It didn't really matter, after all; everything was wired with an alarm. Except, of course, for storage.

"I think so," said Hal. "We don't monitor it much because it's just staff. Why?"

"I was just curious."

"Something wrong?"

"No." I hadn't thought that far ahead. I hadn't thought about what I should say if they asked me why I wanted to know. But Hal returned to his monitors, and I stood there watching the flow of visitors through the galleries, their bodies like schools of fish merging and breaking apart. I wasn't ready to tell anyone anyway. I wanted to put all the pieces together first.

I decided to walk through the museum on the off chance the piece was actually on display. Each glass case, though, confirmed my suspicion. My stomach tightened into a knot, and I regretted the moment I had reached for the stack of hats.

What bad luck, I thought. No, I knew now it was something else. It was fate. The way Leo had encouraged me to take what I wanted suddenly took on a darker resonance.

Before returning to the library, I scanned my key card and went back into storage. Nodding at the conservation staff, I began to pull out shelves of objects, looking specifically for the small valuable ones. The ones that had precious stones or were made of expensive metals or materials. I also made a point to look up at each of the cameras. There were four in the storage room, each recording a separate quadrant. There was no way Leo could have been missed if he was in here, but there was little chance that the cameras were sharp enough to pick up a palmed object.

I started to notice a pattern: every third or fourth drawer had a piece missing. The accession number neatly labeled, the object space blank. I knew it was possible that some pieces were on loan; others could be down at the Met. It was even possible that Conservation was cleaning a few of them. But as I kept methodically pulling out the drawers, I noticed that none of the larger objects were so obviously absent. It was harder, I thought, to take a carved capital out of the museum than it was a pocket-size work of art. And the medieval and early Renaissance periods had no shortage of such objects.

I closed the last drawer and made my way back to the library, where Rachel looked up at me expectantly.

"Where did you go?" she said.

I wasn't ready to tell her. To admit to her—to myself—what Leo had been doing. I didn't want to expose the intimacy of the discovery, to acknowledge that the man I had slept with just a few days before had a motive for murdering Patrick. I was still too busy running through the excuses: maybe it wasn't too late to return them, maybe it was a coincidence. But that was the difficult thing about research; it was an impulse, a drive, but you could be disappointed, sometimes devastated, by the results. I was about to lie and tell Rachel that I'd just gone for a quick walk when the door swung open and Moira entered the library, trailed by Detective Murphy.

"Oh good, you're both in," said Moira. "Detective Murphy is here to talk to you."

"Thank you, Moira." Detective Murphy stood there, waiting for Moira to leave.

She lingered by the door, until finally lifting a hand and saying, "Okay, I'll be in the lobby."

Once the door closed behind her, Detective Murphy pulled out her notebook and flipped through it.

"We received an anonymous tip last night," she said, speaking directly to Rachel, "that corroborated the fact that you and Patrick were involved in an intimate relationship that may have been in the process of dissolving when he was murdered?"

Rachel looked up from her notes at both of us.

"This witness can place you arguing with Patrick in his car in The Cloisters' parking lot. The same witness says they saw you many times coming and going in the garden shed area."

"When we last spoke," said Rachel, "I informed you that I would only speak to you with my attorney present."

"In that case, I'll ask Ms. Stilwell if she has anything to add to this new information."

I started to say something when I saw Rachel shake her head, an imperceptible no.

"Ann has retained counsel as well."

"Is this true, Ms. Stilwell?"

I looked between the two of them.

"She has retained counsel," said Rachel, watching me and nodding.

"Ms. Stilwell?"

"I have," I said, even though, of course, I had not.

"I hope you didn't make this trip all the way for us," said Rachel.

"I didn't," said Detective Murphy, flipping her notes closed. "And we look forward to interviewing both of you, with your respective attorneys, of course, very soon."

Once the door had closed, Rachel returned her gaze to me.

"You don't think . . ." She let the sentence die off. The mask she usually wore—serene, smiling, assured—had slipped, if only for a moment, her eyes haunted, bloodshot. Perhaps it was the first time she looked down and saw the tightrope on which we had been walking, the vertigo overwhelming.

"Rachel," I said. "We need to go outside and talk."

We sat on a stone bench in the Bonnefont Cloister, looking out over the Hudson, our bare legs touching like schoolgirls.

"Leo's been stealing," I said. "From the museum."

For a beat Rachel said nothing, refusing to meet my gaze, until finally she exhaled and said, "Are you sure?"

I explained how I had found the figurine, how I had checked storage.

"There are other works missing," I said. "I checked. I checked the galleries and the loan logs. But there are too many missing objects for it to simply be a mistake. A disk brooch from the seventh century? A reliquary of Saint Elijah? Who would request those on loan?"

Rachel looked down onto the road that snaked below the ramparts.

I had expected her to be more surprised, but she seemed resigned at the news.

"No, you're right," she said finally. "Those are all things that would be easy to remove. Have you talked to him about it?"

"No. Absolutely not."

"Good," she said.

"It gives him a motive." I let it hang between us.

"It does. But right now they seem to think I had a motive. That's why she's here today, you know? Because she's trying to rattle me. She thinks all this poking around will make a difference." Rachel laughed, thin and hard. "When really, you're the only one who's managed to come up with a real theory. Something worth pursuing."

I hadn't thought about it like this, but she was right: I was trading Leo for her. Turning him in meant getting Rachel off the hook. It also meant more breathing room for us—for *me*—to finish our research.

"I still don't see him as the kind of person who would poison someone," I said. "Steal, yes. Murder, no."

"But it makes the most sense, doesn't it? He had the access and the opportunity. If Patrick had found out what was going on, he would have had motive too."

I thought about the way Leo and Patrick were always cordial but distant. There was a coldness between them.

"Did Patrick ever mention that he suspected Leo of anything? Even something smaller?"

Rachel shook her head.

"He didn't. But I don't know if he would have." Then she added more quietly, "Leo was always a sore subject between us."

A hummingbird buzzed us before settling on a blooming salvia plant, its purple flowers pungent and earthy in the sun.

"Who do you think the tipster was?" I finally asked.

"Don't you already know?" said Rachel, looking me in the eye.

I had already asked myself this question, and both Leo and Moira would have been happy to make that call.

"We should catch her before she goes," Rachel said, standing and offering me her hand. I took it.

"Don't you need your lawyer for that?"

"It's your story, not mine," she said.

CHAPTER TWENTY-TWO

We found Detective Murphy in the staff offices talking to the director of educational programming. She simply raised an eyebrow before following us into an empty room usually reserved for weekly staff meetings, meetings that Patrick had always led.

"Don't you need a lawyer present?" she said.

"There's something you need to know." I hadn't imagined how I would put together the next few sentences, but I reminded myself that like any good academic, I should begin with my thesis and then move on to supporting materials.

"Leo has been stealing from the museum," I said.

Detective Murphy was silent, but took out her notebook and flipped it open.

"Over the weekend, I found an object at Leo's apartment. An object that belongs to The Cloisters. An ivory carving of Saint Daria," I explained.

"Did you ask him about it?" Her pen still scratched against the paper.

"Yes. And he claimed it was his grandmother's. But while going through storage today, I noticed we were missing an identical piece from the collection."

"And you're sure it's not a replica?"

"I'm sure. But I also discovered that additional pieces were missing. Several brooches, pieces of jewelry, figurines—"

"I'm sorry," said Detective Murphy. "Are you saying that Leo's been stealing from The Cloisters? How could that be possible? It's a museum. A major museum."

"Items in storage are different," I said. "They're rarely put on display. Many of them are small. The size of your palm, or smaller. And while we have security cameras in storage, since it's only accessed by staff, they're not closely monitored. And it's normal to have a handful of items in our collections missing—traveling shows, loans, restoration, rotational display. It probably wouldn't be enough to raise a red flag at a museum as big as the Met."

Detective Murphy made additional notes.

"Has Leo mentioned to you that he's experiencing money issues? Any drug habits? Gambling? Debts?"

I shook my head. "He doesn't have a lot of money, and certainly I never see him spending it."

"How much does a gardener at The Cloisters make?"

"I don't know," I said. "Enough to get by with a roommate in New York."

"Any big purchases recently? Cars? Vacations? Jewelry?" Detective Murphy scanned my wrists, ears, and throat.

"No," I said.

"It's possible," said Rachel, from the end of the table, "that Patrick found out."

We both turned to look at her. I couldn't help but think about the cards I had seen in the library the week before—the Chariot, in particular, a symbol of rapidity, quick succession, turning of the wheels, racing through time. It felt like we were speeding up now, and I wanted to have a moment to pause, to slow us down, perhaps even rewind.

"You should check with Louis," Rachel said, "to see if they store that security footage or recycle it."

"There are no security cameras in the garden sheds," said Detective Murphy, almost to herself. Then she added, "Is Leo in today?"

I nodded.

There had always been something lawless about Leo. The way he talked and carried himself, the way he didn't care what other people thought of him. The way he played the bass not because he loved the music, but because he loved the noise—wild and chaotic, even a little violent. But I still wasn't sure it added up to murder, although I knew that under his punk ennui was a finely honed ambition, something he hid between the volumes of Sam Shepard plays, tucked in his pocket with his work gloves.

"Okay," said Detective Murphy, sliding her notes into her pocket. "I'm going to go talk to Louis. We probably won't be able to move on this until tomorrow. We need to get warrants; we need to go through the tapes. We're going to need to corroborate your story. You didn't happen to take a photograph of the item, did you?"

"No." I remembered the way Leo had drummed his fingers on my skin that morning, a quick percussion of lust. All the while, the carving of Saint Daria sat on a shelf in his closet. I shook it off. "No," I repeated.

"Okay. We're going to take it from here." Detective Murphy paused. "Thank you. For being so forthcoming."

When the door had closed behind her, Rachel reached her hand to mine and gave it a squeeze. "You did the right thing."

We tried to work that afternoon, but I struggled to focus. It was as if the speed I had experienced earlier had given way to a glacial pace, the day had become tarry. I stared at pages and reread sentences until my brain could no longer parse the easiest meanings. I realized that I had seen it. It had been in the cards—me, the Queen of Swords, using knowledge to cut others down.

I realized then that while my connection to the cards had been gradual, I trusted them. I trusted them, in many ways, more than I trusted myself. And so far, they had not been wrong. Whether that was a function of luck or something else entirely, I wasn't ready to say.

After staring at the same paragraph for twenty minutes, I decided to get up and stretch my legs. I went to the bathroom to splash water on my face, only to find Rachel standing in the hallway, waiting for me when I was done.

"You okay?"

"Fine," I said. But there was something in the way Rachel had taken comfort in this news of Leo's culpability that made me uncomfortable—a saccharine kindness that rang false.

And as much as I tried to avoid the gardens for the rest of the day, I found myself willing Leo to cross my path in other parts of the museum. Maybe I lingered too long in the kitchen or crossed the cloisters too slowly, part of me needing to see him. As if he might tell me a different story, one that would explain away my fears and absolve my guilt for turning him in. But it needed to be accidental so that I didn't explicitly impede Detective Murphy's investigation. And so, it was like fate intervened when, at the end of the day, we heard a knock on the library door and Leo popped his head in.

"We just finished trimming the flowers and have two buckets for free if anyone wants to take some home. Seems a shame to throw them out. Ann?"

Only hours ago I would have been elated by the offer, the tenderness of it. But now faced with Leo, I didn't know what to say or how to act. At least, not in front of Rachel.

"I can put them in a jar and bring them in for you, if you want?"

Rachel reached out and put her hand over my own. "We don't need any flowers, Leo," she said.

"Can I talk to you outside?" he said to me, his eyes still on Rachel's hand, on her gesture.

"I—"

"Leo," Rachel intervened, "now isn't the best time for Ann to leave."

"Okay. We can talk in here then." He slipped through the door and let it close behind him. The way he filled the space was noticeable, and for a split moment, I wondered if I should be worried.

"Leo, I think it's best if you go," said Rachel, standing.

"Can we get a minute alone?"

"Both of you, stop," I said.

"What's going on?" he asked, looking at me.

The silence in the library was uncomfortable. Through it, we could hear the steady steps of visitors as they made their way along the corridor outside. That was how The Cloisters operated, as a deeply private place for a few staff and as a spectacle for the visitors. Nothing could make me give up being on this side of the door, I realized.

"It's about the figurine," I said finally.

"What about it?" He didn't seem anxious. If anything, he was defensive, his hands shoved tightly in his pockets.

"I know you stole it. I know it came from storage."

He sighed and ran a hand through his hair. It hung limply, almost brushing the top of his shoulders.

"Ann—"

"Leo," I said, my voice gaining strength, "you *stole*. From The Cloisters. And not just plants. I've seen the storage trays. There are a handful of other things missing."

He shrugged and said nothing in response.

"Did Patrick find out?" I asked. I was facing him now, although still sitting in my chair.

At this, his head jerked up. "No. God, no. Ann. Patrick never knew. No one was even supposed to notice. You know what storage is like at the Met. *Thousands* of items. Works of art that will never see the light of day. Objects that aren't rare enough, aren't high quality enough. Objects that are too niche or from the wrong duchy. You name it. For every object in the gallery, there are two dozen in storage that have been deemed insufficient."

"Why did you do it?"

"Why not?" he said. "It's not like you're not making questionable decisions in here every day. Deciding what has value and what doesn't. When was the last time you took things without value seriously? That's right, you don't. You ignore everything that isn't anointed as special or valuable or rare. Those objects in storage, some of them have been missing for years and no one ever raised the alarm. Because those objects have been forgotten. I'm giving them a second life. And sure, I'm making some money while I do it."

It was, in a roundabout way, the same reason I had been drawn to the tarot cards, to my own work, to the objects that had been overlooked and just needed a champion. And in any case, Leo had always been honest with me. He was the kind of person, he once explained over warm beers, who believed that you could take what you wanted so long as it didn't harm anyone. He had spit out a sunflower seed shell and added, *Except for the rich. They deserve it*. At the time I had thought it was an homage to anarchism, a punk sentiment turned life motto. But I realized now—and maybe I had then, too—that he meant it.

"Don't you have debt?" he continued. "Don't you struggle to make it work in this city on what they pay us here? Sure, Rachel doesn't. But you, Ann. You haven't tried to live here, day in and day out, with so little that you share your space with dozens of roommates who come and go. All of us working three, four, five jobs to get by. I did it so I could get space to write. To be experimental. So that I wasn't getting ground down every day of my life. Isn't that something you understand, Ann? Isn't that why you're here? To try to escape being ground down?"

I said nothing, but stared at him. He was right. It was exactly why I was here.

"How many pieces did you take? Total?" I asked.

He laughed. "You don't even know, do you? You can't tell which pieces are on loan or in Conservation and which ones were converted into writer's grants and residencies. Art begetting art. It's kind of beautiful if you think about it. The symmetry. The twinning." He looked between the two of us, shaking his head. "I can't believe you don't get it."

"What happened with Patrick?" Rachel finally asked. She had been quiet the whole time, not even watching our exchange, her gaze transfixed by the stained glass window at the end of the library.

"With Patrick?" Leo said. "Nothing happened with Patrick."

Then, even if he was a little slower than we had been, I watched him realize the implications of the situation.

"You can't be serious? You don't think I—" He broke off, then started again. "No one even notices storage, least of all Patrick. He had no idea. I had nothing to do with what happened to Patrick. Nothing. I'm a thief. I have no problems stealing from people and places with all the money in the world, but I would never murder someone. Are you serious?"

"You're the only one with motive," I said, letting the statement out on an exhale, as if I had been holding it in since Leo entered the room.

"I don't have a motive," said Leo. "Patrick and I didn't always see eye to eye, but I respected him. Everyone did."

"But if he found out—" I said, as if the optics weren't already clear.

"If he found out, I knew I would go to jail. So I made sure no one found out. Admit it, Ann, you wouldn't have found out if you hadn't been in my closet that day. I was scheduled to meet with my antiques dealer the day before, but I blew him off to spend the day with you. You're the reason anyone even noticed. My weakness for you."

He was looking at me, his voice had a thickness to it I had never heard, and I could feel the pain spreading from the palms of my hands to my stomach. I believed him. Leo was a criminal—that, I suppose, I had always known—but not that kind of criminal.

"We turned the information regarding the thefts over to Detective

Murphy," I finally admitted. It felt awful, sharing that piece of information. I had been the one to let the outside world in; I was the one who ripped the veil.

"You did what?" Leo said, his eyes still fixed on my face. "Ann. Come on."

"They're going to handle it from here."

I looked up at him, part of me desperate to press my face into his chest, to feel him stroke my hair and tell me that it was okay. I longed to hear him tell me he would get away with it. The other part of me knew that would never be possible again. Out of all the secrets we kept at The Cloisters, I hadn't kept his. I hoped someday he would understand; he would understand that I had to protect my work above everything else. It was the only thing he could understand.

"All right," said Leo, "I can tell them where all the pieces went. But I need to get ahead of this thing." Again he ran a hand through his hair. "Ann, you need to know, I had nothing to do with what happened to Patrick, okay?"

I met his gaze.

"Do you believe me?"

"Yes."

He walked over to where I was sitting at the table and kneeled down in front of me so that our eyes were level.

"I'm sorry," he said, his hand wrapped around mine.

Then he let go, stood, and walked back out the door. And in his absence, I couldn't be sure what his apology was for. Was he sorry we had met, that he had spoken to me that day in the garden? That he had done it? Or that I had been the one to discover it? That he hadn't done a better job of covering it up? I wasn't sure. But it felt like time was pushing me forward in fits and starts, lurches and jumps, and I was growing nauseous, ready for the ride to stop.

I knew Leo believed that he and I were fundamentally the same. We were two people trying to make it in a world that favored everyone else, and so, we had to scramble for every advantage we could get. And he wasn't wrong. We were survivors. Climbing out of the dusty places from which we had begun, destined for bigger things. In deciding to protect myself and Rachel, that's all I had done. Made sure that I would be able to keep climbing.

The realization crystallized in me—that we were all out for our own best interests, our own goals and dreams. That here, in The Cloisters, although it was easy to forget we were in Manhattan, everyone was still out for themselves—on the come-up—and willing to do whatever was necessary to make that happen. Especially me.

I looked back at the table covered with books and notepads and thought to myself, the worst thing I could do wasn't turn in Leo. It was waste this opportunity. I would keep climbing.

CHAPTER TWENTY-THREE

The next morning, the museum remained open, despite the detectives who everywhere scribbled notes and photographed storage trays and the paints of the conservation lab, the tools in the garden shed. A search warrant had been produced early that morning and furnished to the security team on duty, who allowed them access and immediately notified the Met. But there was nothing for Fifth Avenue to do except let them dust and photograph and pry, their movements watched closely by an attorney who had been duly dispatched to observe. Moira did her best to keep them out of the lobby away from visitors, and for the most part she was successful.

Michelle had been summoned north as well to where she now stood, arms crossed, in the cool stone hallway that led to the staff offices, occasionally answering questions, but mostly, scrolling through her phone and consulting with the public relations firm the museum had hired in the event the news developed legs. Already we had heard there was a small piece planned in the *Times*. But it would run in the Arts section on Tuesday.

Enough time had passed since Patrick had been murdered that no security footage had been preserved. All we had were rumors, and for me, the awkward way one moved on after death: at first hesitantly, and then, with growing confidence, even if it was fake.

In the staff kitchen, I heard two conservators complaining to each other that the security tapes didn't go far enough back. *They're on a loop*, said the retoucher. *Can you imagine? Every seven days.* Which meant there was no recording of Leo, no hard evidence.

Outside, everything in the garden shed had been tagged and placed in thick plastic bags. The dried flowers that Leo had so lovingly gathered and hung from the hooks had been cut apart and forced into brown bags, dried petals scattered on the ground where they had been shed in the process. The greenhouse where I knew Leo kept his personal plants, those he sold for profit, had also been stripped bare, although it seemed the police didn't notice that there was anything different about that greenhouse. All plants, it appeared, were the same. Even the compost heap was being excavated, each object painstakingly photographed and catalogued.

And if the visitors to The Cloisters that day seemed oblivious to what was unfolding around them, the staff was not. With every opened door or set of footsteps on the stone passageways, we craned our heads or looked up from our work. We had been briefed by Michelle that we should not ask questions, only answer them. But the only questions we encountered that day were inquiries like, *Did you see a man with a camera come through here? Do I access the lobby through Gallery Eight or Twelve?* The forensic team seemed constantly lost in the maze of The Cloisters— they wandered from room to room, poking their heads through the next Gothic arch to see if they had finally found their way.

One of them, a young man, the botany specialist, seemed to take an interest in Rachel. He came through the library on his way to Patrick's office to notate which plants he had cultivated indoors, but he lingered longer to ask us questions.

"What's it like working here?" he said, staring up at the rib vaults that crisscrossed the ceiling above our heads.

"Like working in the thirteenth century, but with plumbing," said Rachel, not looking up from the volume she was reading.

He walked the perimeter of the library, fingering the spines of a few older volumes before smiling at us sheepishly and exiting the way he came.

Amid these distractions, I was trying to find room in our article for all the historical tidbits we had turned up in our research. Things like the list of objects that Ercole d'Este and his wife had owned: *libri*—books, 3,284; *contenitore*—vessels, 326; *calcografia*—copper plate engravings, 112; and 36 coursing hounds. Or the fact that in the summer of 1497, the city of Ferrara experienced torrential rains, flooding the duke and duchess's *studioli*, damaging letters, manuscripts, and several *cartes da trionfi*. Then there was the auction record we had found of *six douzaine cartes de tarot d'Italie pour la famille d'Este*, sold at auction for 4,000 francs to a private collector in Switzerland in 1911. Methodically, Rachel and I had built a web of information that told the story of the cards: designed in Ferrara by Pellegrino Prisciani, the astrologer of Ercole d'Este, and used by a court that itself was fascinated with the dark and capricious gods of ancient Rome. Alongside the documents from Lingraf my father had translated, we argued that the cards, like many things in Renaissance life, had a dual purpose—yes, they were used to play the game of tarot, but they were also used to divine futures. It was, I knew, the most groundbreaking contribution of Renaissance court culture to emerge in years.

But there were still gaps. Gaps in the record and our knowledge. And so, like the detectives outside who combed for evidence in the compost heap, we too had to make leaps and inferences. The only thing separating us from them, a library and six hundred years. I meticulously recorded another footnote, transcribed another translation.

Beyond the door to the library, we heard a sudden commotion, a sweeping sound and a handful of quick, pattering steps on the stone floor. Rachel and I pushed our chairs back to peek our heads out the door, where we saw Moira sprinting down the corridor, her skirt hitched as she ran after Leo, who was striding toward the garden.

"You're on a leave of absence," she called after him.

Leo didn't respond, but rather walked calmly, his long legs carrying him at a faster clip than Moira through the crowds that filled the passageway. She had her radio out and was calling for Louis to come do something, to stop him. But Leo's progress continued unimpeded.

"Leo—" she called out.

But Leo slipped around the corner, headed for the garden sheds; we followed closely behind Moira. In the back gardens, though, Leo was immediately restrained by two plainclothes officers who stepped into his path. Detective Murphy stood with a group of forensic specialists who were pushing an object deep into a plastic evidence bag; one adjusted his latex glove before pulling out a Sharpie to write on the label. She made her way over to us leisurely, kicking aside an empty black plastic potting canister as she went.

"You can't be back here," Detective Murphy said. She held her hands in front of her, clasped, like she was admonishing a child.

"I have personal items in there," Leo said, gesturing at the shed. "Years of work."

"It's all evidence."

"There were plants laid out in there that were being dried for seeds. There were hybridizations. There were—"

"Remnants of a belladonna plant whose root had been cut," Detective Murphy interjected.

"That's not possible," said Leo. "We plant belladonna in the early spring and only pull plants out before winter. If an entire plant had been removed—"

"You would have noticed?"

Detective Murphy looked at him and motioned with another hand for one of her staff to bring her the specimen in question. She held up the plastic bag, which showed a limp, patchy green plant with faded purple flowers on it. The belladonna berries still green. There was, I noticed, a small notch of root cut from the plant as well. A thick, fibrous nest with a clear patch of white across it.

"That couldn't have come from this garden. I haven't uprooted anything since the spring," Leo said.

"Follow me," said Detective Murphy, who now moved past Leo. She walked across the Bonnefont Cloister to the edge of a bed where she pulled back a canopy of thick green foliage and purple flowers. On the ground was a mussed patch of earth where something had clearly been removed, the hole hastily covered.

"Did you notice this?" she said, looking at Leo.

Leo bent down, his large frame folded against his knees. He held the greenery aside, his hands moving the dirt that was as much a part of his life as it was The Cloisters itself. He took in the surrounding plants, those he had cultivated from seedlings and guarded against the bitterness of early spring freezes. His hand lingered for only a moment on a leaf before he looked up at Detective Murphy.

"No, I didn't notice this. But don't you think if I had done it I would have done a better job of backfilling? Of disposing of the plant itself? Do you know how many items end up on the compost heap here in any given week? Mulch, leaves, trimmings. We have acres of garden that we maintain. And it's all open. To all the staff, but even to the public."

"And yet, right now, we have motive and opportunity, and both point to you," said Detective Murphy, her head cocked slightly as she studied Leo. "And now we have this." She gestured at the belladonna plants. "Maybe you'd like to save yourself some time and come with us down to the station?"

Leo looked around the gardens—the drooping grasses and blooming flowers, the pink marble columns that ringed the cloister.

"Sure," he said. "Seems like I don't have a choice."

"I'm glad we understand each other." Detective Murphy used her arm to guide Leo toward the back gate, where all their cars and vans had been parked, out of sight of the visitors.

We didn't learn until later in the day that Leo had been arrested, but by then we were in Central Park, accompanied by a picnic dinner tucked into a basket. Rachel had suggested it—*a new start*, she said. But I wasn't ready to put it all behind me. Laure was right about one thing: Rachel moved on quickly from things. The year after my father passed away, I was often on the verge of screaming or tearing apart anything friable nearby. Those moments would be followed by normal ones, but the grief came from the fact that I knew I had to keep living, even though he was gone. It was the way time kept on that was the hardest, the way my heart beat: steady and insistent, even against my fiercest desire to see it stop.

I unfurled a blue checkered blanket on the grass and smoothed its edges, flicking bits of leaf and cuttings off the felted wool. Rachel opened the basket and began arranging items: a little glass pot of terrine, a handful of cheeses wrapped in wax paper, a baguette, a knife, plates. There were also ripe nectarines and a handful of grapes, a sliver of chocolate bar. All items tenderly packed in the apartment, purchased at shocking expense from the gourmet deli on Columbus Avenue.

The text message came from Moira as the sun dipped below the wall of trees that framed the western edge of the great expanse. *Leo has been arrested. Please refer all press requests to Sarah Steinlitt, ssteinlitt@metuseum .org.* Rachel pulled off a piece of bread and meditatively ran the knife back and forth against its interior, spreading the cheese.

"Do you want some?" she said, holding it out to me, a bite missing.

"They arrested him," I said, my appetite gone.

"Of course they did."

"You don't really think he did it, do you?"

Rachel shrugged as if it didn't matter. And I realized that to her, it didn't.

"Probably," she said, slicing one of the nectarines. Its juices ran red and yellow across her thumb. "Aren't you hungry?"

She passed me a slice and I took it. Rachel licked her fingers clean.

"Eat it. It's good."

I put the fruit in my mouth, tasting its sweetness and warmth. It reminded me of home—the late-summer stone fruit that dropped from trees around Walla Walla, until the smell in the air became jammy and fermented, mixed with the dry grasses of the fields. The nostalgia rushed over me, unbidden.

"You shouldn't worry about Leo," said Rachel, breaking my reverie. "Leo rarely worries about Leo."

"I can't help it."

Rachel looked at me. "You'll grow out of it," she said, slicking a piece of bread into the glass pot of terrine to extract what remained. "Actually, I thought you already had." Rachel dusted her hands and pulled a small, wrapped package from her bag, tied neatly with yellow and white string.

"For you," she said, passing it to me.

The weight felt pleasant and substantial in my palm. But a gift hardly seemed appropriate, considering the moment in which we found ourselves. Rachel pushed on.

"Open it," she said, packing away a few of the odds and ends that remained after a picnic—the ragged pits and rinds.

I slipped the yellow and white thread off the kraft paper and peeled open its corner, where it had been primly taped, to reveal a wooden box. Inside the box was a set of tarot cards, deftly painted with watercolor fools and chariots, sets of wands and swords. The cards themselves were slightly worn, used, in fact. I pulled out the top one and fingered its corner. They had been printed on unfinished paper, which, combined with their imagery, dated them to the eighteenth or nineteenth century. The illustrations were meticulous, rendered in the typical occult style with delicate flourishes of paint and gold leaf. On the back, a light, pale blue marbling mixed in swirls of pink.

"They're French," said Rachel, brushing a handful of crumbs into the grass and not meeting my eyes. "Probably from Lyon. Early nineteenth century. Maybe 1830?"

"They're gorgeous."

"They're a gift."

"I can't accept something like this," I said, moving to hand her back the cards. A deck like this was easily a few thousand dollars, maybe more.

"You can, and you should," she said, now looking at me squarely. "It's time for you to have a deck of your own."

I pulled a few more cards to see their illustrations. "Where did they come from?" I asked, lingering over the illustration of the Hanged Man, dangling from his foot.

"You mean did I steal them?"

"No, I—"

"They're from a rare book dealer in Midtown. Not Stephen. Although, don't tell him," she said. "And their provenance is impeccable."

I spread a few on the blanket between us, noting the connections between these symbols and the fifteenth-century deck that sat at home.

"Why don't you try them?" Rachel said, lifting her shoulders a fraction with the suggestion.

I piled them together gently and shuffled. I had never believed in asking the cards specific questions; it seemed such hubris to know what to ask. Instead, it was the feeling I was after, the web they created, the impression they gave. I pulled a Two of Swords reversed, a Page of Cups, and a Ten of Swords. Only Minor Arcana in the small spread. The Page of Cups, service and instinct, the sword, as always, especially reversed, the act of cutting in half. The Ten of Swords I rarely saw, but it meant misfortune, defeat. They showed me a break, a severing, and a departure, even an overturning, a reversal. Some of this I could place, other aspects were still unrecognizable to me.

"What do they say?" said Rachel from across the blanket.

"That I should trust my intuition," I said quietly, sliding the cards back into the deck.

CHAPTER TWENTY-FOUR

The article was almost ready for submission. It would, we both knew, do more for our careers than a summer job at The Cloisters ever could. For me, it was more than a ticket to the graduate program of my choice and an assurance that I wouldn't end up back in Walla Walla. It was also proof that my father's work as a translator, long unrecognized and hidden, would have a meaningful impact. An opportunity he might never have had while he was alive.

Opportunity. That's what the article would give me—the chance to say yes or no, the chance to live in New York, the chance, almost, to re-write the past. It was a career-defining moment, a once-in-a-generation discovery, the type of discovery that rarely happened for young women, especially at the start of their careers. And while Rachel and I fretted over every footnote and double-checked every translation of fifteenth-century Latin, Leo sat in a jail cell awaiting bail.

I had, the night before, dreamt about him. I dreamt we were at the bar in the Bronx where fans tipped lazily back and forth. There, over beers, he had whispered across the table that he had done none of it. That he hadn't been the one to steal or poison Patrick.

The next day, when I told Rachel about it, she replied, "I've known him longer, and I think you'd be surprised what Leo is capable of."

We were sitting side by side at her dining table, the late-afternoon sun pooling on the parquet. I moved my cursor down the screen, doing the tedious work of formatting dates and bibliographic information.

"When I started at The Cloisters, Leo was even more feral than he is now," said Rachel, looking out the window to where the canopy of trees in Central Park swayed gently back and forth. Beneath them, families enjoying one of the last weekends of summer wandered the sidewalks. "He never talked to the staff. Patrick always said he was hired, like you, in a pinch because the long-term gardener quit unexpectedly and we needed someone. Now, after four years, it's a miracle he was never fired."

I didn't say anything but kept scrolling, adjusting.

"If you ask me, I'm not that surprised. He never thought the rules applied to him. Leo likes to believe he lives both above and below all of society's expectations. That's how he always was as a gardener: too good for the job but also happy to be in the mud."

Before coming to The Cloisters, I had long been an assiduous, if resentful, rule follower—someone who meticulously returned books on time, who followed every closing procedure at work. Seeing Leo be so joyously lawless had unlocked something in me: an enjoyment of chaos that had been building long before I came to New York. It was easy for someone like Rachel to look down on what Leo had done. The rules bent for people like her. There was invariably a workaround that could be bought or fixed with influence. It was, I thought, cowardly. What Leo had done took guts.

But I still recognized there was a gulf between stealing and murder. Leo was the type to break the law and flaunt it, but that didn't make him a murderer. I kept the thoughts to myself, letting them swirl around inside me until they became a noxious brew of paranoia, one that left me increasingly on edge and sullen, but that seemed to leave Rachel more serene than she had been at the start of the summer.

Rachel stretched her arms overhead. "Why don't we take a break? I'm tired of sitting at this table. Want to go for a walk?"

"I think I just want to finish this," I said. It was mostly true; I did want to finish. We were so close, but I needed some time apart, too.

"Suit yourself," she said, pushing back from the table.

From behind the screen of my laptop, I watched her pull her long hair into a ponytail and slip on a pair of running shoes. Then, when the door to the apartment had closed behind her, I moved to the window where I could watch her progress, waiting for her to enter the park before I picked up the phone and dialed the number on the card that Detective Murphy had given me. I stayed leaning up against the window, watching the edge of the park for the return of Rachel's swinging ponytail.

"Can I talk to Leo?" I asked when she answered the phone.

"You mean can you visit him?"

"Sure," I said. I had never known anyone who had been arrested before so I wasn't sure what I could or could not do.

"If he wants to, yes."

"Do I just come down—"

"Ann." I could hear Detective Murphy organizing papers on the other end of the line. I imagined the phone cradled against her cheek, her disorderly office. "Can I ask what is going on?"

The truth was, I didn't know what was going on, so I let the question go unanswered.

"Is there something else you want to tell me?" she asked finally.

"I don't think he did it," I said softly.

"What makes you say that."

"He doesn't have it in him."

"Sometimes we don't know what other people are capable of." She paused. "Sometimes we don't know what we're capable of."

"Do you think he did it?"

On the other end of the line, I could hear Detective Murphy mulling over the question; the telltale tap of her pencil came through the phone line, a quick staccato.

"I think he could have," she said after a beat.

"But there's a big difference between could have and did."

"Is there?"

"Of course there is." It seemed like such a silly distinction, the line between *might have* and *did*. The difference between being a murderer and just thinking how much you would like to see someone dead. "What has he been charged with?" I asked.

"Right now? Just the thefts. We don't have enough to hold him on the murder charge. But we do have enough for grand larceny."

I didn't know what else there was to say. Below me, I watched pedestrians stream in and out of the park. Had the line always been this thin? You didn't have to have been a killer to kill? Leo was nothing more than a resolution for Detective Murphy, a check mark that meant she didn't have to look any further.

"Actually, perhaps you could help me with one thing." Now I could hear Detective Murphy paging through her notes on the other end of the phone. "Leo's attorney told us who Leo had been using to fence the objects. It's rather surprising actually. We thought he might have struggled to find a broker. It's not easy to find someone so willing to move objects with such questionable provenance, but it's a place downtown. On East Fifty-Sixth Street. An antiques dealer called—"

But as she searched her notes for the name, I knew it instinctively. My breath was short and catching in my chest. A frantic lightness bubbled in my arms and legs.

"Ketch Rare Books and Antiques?" I said.

"Yes. You're familiar with it?"

"Not really. I've been there once or twice."

"With Patrick?"

"Yes. And Rachel."

On my finger, the eyes of the ram's head ring she had bought me caught the light. I tried to pull it off, but it held fast, tight around my swollen finger.

"When was this?"

"A month ago," I said. "Maybe longer?"

"Did you see any objects there that matched the description of the missing pieces."

"No. But I wasn't looking for them either."

"They have nice things?"

"Yes," I said.

"Do you know how Leo might have become familiar with the shop?"

"No."

"You never went there with him?"

"No, never."

"A few of the objects already sold," said Detective Murphy. "We're in the process of tracking those down, but it seems like a few may still be in the shop."

I thought about the beautiful brooches and rings Stephen had, about Rachel's familiarity with his inventory, about the way my arms were still tan from the afternoons we had spent on the stone wall at the museum, lounging, sharing stories.

It struck me then that no one had really told me anything. Neither Leo nor Patrick, certainly not Rachel. They had all kept the truth from me, kept it hidden for their own uses. Only Aruna had been there, Delphic in her words and her timing.

And even though it had been in front of me all summer, I had never seen the triangle between Rachel, Patrick, and Leo until now. Only, it wasn't a triangle at all. It was a wheel, and at its center, the place from which all the spokes radiated, was Rachel. *Regno, Regnavi, Sum sine regno, Regnabo*: I reign, I have reigned, I am without reign, I will reign. She turned us all like we existed on her axis. Each of us separated, mediated only by her. But of course, the details were hazy, occluded by Rachel's deft storytelling and the way she had brought me in and held me close.

"Where do I go if I want to see Leo?"

"His bond is being processed," said Detective Murphy. "As soon as that's complete, he'll be released."

"Who paid his bail?" I asked, curious.

"It looks like he did," she said.

"When will he be released?"

"Tomorrow."

I was about to say something else when the door to the apartment creaked open and I saw Rachel standing there, only lightly sweaty.

"I forgot my watch," she said, then grabbed it off the entry table and slid it across her slender wrist.

I hung up the phone and walked casually away from the window. How I missed her returning to the building I didn't know. Maybe she had cut back through the woods and run along the avenue.

"Anything exciting happening out there," she said, gesturing to where I had been standing.

"No," I said. "Just taking in the end of the day."

"When I get back, let's go to Altro Paradiso for dinner." She held the door in her hand. "I feel like Italian."

"That sounds great."

"Okay," she said, "I'll be back soon."

I waited until I saw her long, swaying ponytail enter the park for a second time before I pulled out my phone and texted Leo. *We need to talk, call me when you get out.* Then I promptly deleted the text from my phone and my computer, erasing any record Rachel could find.

The apartment was quiet, normal. Filled with books and kitchen utensils, expensive cashmere throws that were neatly folded on the backs of couches. I began to pull open the drawers in the kitchen—place mats and napkins, cutting knives and wine openers—moving methodically until I found what I was looking for: a drawer of brica-brac, Scotch tape and scissors, small screwdrivers and mostly used notepads. I felt around until I heard it, the jangle of metal on metal, a gold ring with countless keys on it. There had to be at least fifteen.

I took the ring and made my way into the hall to summon the elevator, worried as I watched it tick up from the ground level, floor by floor, that Rachel might be on it. When the elevator finally arrived, it was empty. I held the door open with my foot so no one else in the building could summon it and began to try the keys in the slot for the penthouse. The fifth one I tried clicked into place, and the button for the sixteenth floor illuminated.

When the elevator came to a stop, it opened directly into her parents' apartment, revealing a long, prewar hallway lined with paintings and drawings in gilt frames. I recognized several right away. There was a Matisse drawing from the first half of his career, an eighteenth-century Quentin de la Tour pastel, a Canaletto with views of Venice. At the end of the hallway was a two-story living room with floor-to-ceiling windows obscured by thick linen curtains, pulled perpetually against the sun. I turned on a blue-and-white chinoiserie lamp.

On tables around the room, photographs of Rachel and her parents were arrayed in sterling silver frames: photos of them sailing in the Mediterranean and her in her tennis uniform for the Spence team. There were photos of her mother and father with heads of state and at museum trustee dinners. Photos from Aspen and the Hamptons, and older family photos, from Long Lake with her grandparents on the veranda.

And then there were books, rows and rows of books, bound in leather with gold-leaf lettering—first editions, erudite pamphlets, rare manuscripts—as well as delicately upholstered couches covered with tassled pillows. I walked down another hallway, checking each bedroom until I found Rachel's.

It was tasteful and not overly big, painted pistachio green with a large sleigh bed. Rachel had her own framed photographs, and I peered curiously at the photos of her in high school, alone on the bow of a sailboat, reading on a chaise longue somewhere on the Adriatic coast. But mostly there were engravings. Rachel's bedroom was full of framed copper engravings from the sixteenth century, as well as a handful of framed medieval manuscript pages. I lingered over a few before making my way to her desk and pulling open the drawers.

Mostly, they had been stripped clean. Only a few old ballpoint pens and a blank notebook remained. There were a handful of quarters in her top drawer and bits of detritus that tended to gather in childhood bedrooms: specks of candy wrappers and an abandoned earring. I imagined she hadn't slept in here in years. But the bottom drawer of her desk was locked, and while I checked the other drawers for a key, it struck me that the key ring in my hand might have the solution. After a few failed efforts, one key fit the lock, and I pulled open the drawer.

Inside were two things: a photo of a small sailboat, the name of which read *Fortuna*, and a carved disk brooch, expertly inlaid with green stones and pearls, a cameo at its center. I recognized it instantly from the document Michelle de Forte had circulated containing images and descriptions of each missing item stolen by Leo.

As I fingered its familiar gold filigree edges, I was reminded of a Roman proverb Virgil had popularized in *The Aeneid*: *audentes fortuna juvat*, or, fortune favors the bold. Rachel, alongside Leo it seemed, had been very bold indeed.

CHAPTER TWENTY-FIVE

The offer came from Michelle via email three days later, asking me if I would stay on at The Cloisters indefinitely. The pay would be substantially more than I had been making, and they would offer me a title change to assistant curator immediately, which was ironic, considering there was still no one to assist in the main office. I kept the news to myself, reading and rereading Michelle's email until I had memorized every comma, every question mark.

Meanwhile, the crowd of visitors and last heat of summer had built to a crescendo. August saw a spike in tourists sticking to the galleries and fanning themselves with museum maps, their spent bodies slumped on stone benches, deflated and streaked with sweat. The staff felt the same. Docents had grown tired of the buses of fussy camp kids that continued to arrive, and the private concierge tour guides who usurped their position. We were tired of weaving our bodies through crowds of visitors to reach our offices and bathrooms, of the stress the volume of bodies put on the insufficient air-conditioning system. With every day that passed—sticky and thick and slow—September inched closer, even if it felt a world away.

There had been no word from Leo yet, but Rachel had gone up to Cambridge to ready her apartment for the fall semester, which began the first week of September. She'd tried to bring up the topic of me staying in her apartment, but I'd been avoiding it since finding the brooch. Instead, I'd quietly scheduled showings at the few apartments I could afford.

None of them much larger than my sublet, but all of them a year-long lease.

And even though a new curator had not yet started, they were, Michelle reported, in the final selection stages. In the same email that contained the offer, she had asked me if I wouldn't mind cleaning out Patrick's office. With little else left to do in the library, and a heavy heat blanketing the gardens, I carried a trash bag past his doors, the metal deers locked in combat, and slowly got to work.

His office had always been a calming place, and because the windows didn't have crank handles, I propped them open with books to let the fresh air circulate. Even if it was hot, it was better than the clammy, recirculated air the central system labored to produce. The majority of Patrick's books had been packed up and donated to the Yale Library weeks ago, but there were still a handful of papers, personal things, and odds and ends left in the desk drawers. Throwing away these little things—things that make up a life, make up a career—was somehow the worst of it all. And I imagined, morbidly, what would be found in my own desk someday: birthday cards from my parents, abandoned scraps of note paper, empty pens. I salvaged a few things for the library, and one thing for myself, a worn copy of *The Name of the Rose*, but placed the remaining items in the trash.

I was getting ready to go through the bank of filing cabinets behind Patrick's desk when Moira walked in.

"Do you know who's going to be hired?" She leaned against the closed door behind her, her voice barely above a whisper.

"I don't," I said, throwing the last few lingering items into the bag.

"Do you have any guesses?"

Those I had, but I did not have the patience to go through them with Moira. "Not really," I said.

Moira walked over to Patrick's desk and pulled out a drawer. "Find anything?"

"Nothing," I said.

Moira was the kind of woman who not only slowed down to take in a tragedy but also spent the rest of the week researching it, learning about the victims, and internalizing their grief as her own.

"Can you believe they granted Leo bail? He's out, you know. He could show up here anytime."

"I don't think he's allowed."

"Does that matter? Who's going to stop him? Can you imagine, him just barging in here?"

The way she said it, wistfully, as if she had played out the scenario repeatedly on her commute, made me realize I wasn't sure that Moira had really grasped the totality of the situation. She greatly enjoyed playing her role in the tragedy, bit part though it was. Leo, I knew, would never be a disgruntled worker who returned to his place of business. He'd move on, bartending for cash somewhere in the Bronx, someplace like Crystal's Moonlight Lounge where they didn't file paperwork.

"I don't think Leo will come back."

"That's right. You two had something, didn't you? I remember someone mentioning it, one of the guards maybe," Moira said, watching me from the corner of her eye.

I shrugged, hoping that if I said nothing, Moira would leave, but she looked comfortable, perched on the edge of the desk, her long leg kicking a silent rhythm.

"You know," she said, "you're better off."

"Oh?"

"Better off without Leo. I assume you two broke up, right?"

I wasn't sure we had ever been together formally enough to break up, but I nodded, stacking a few remaining books. Moira said nothing for a minute as she studied the curve of the window, until finally she said absently, "I'll never know what you girls saw in him."

It was her use of the plural: *girls*.

"What do you mean?" I asked, watching her carefully.

"Just that you and Rachel are both so nice. You're good girls. You have futures. What you were both doing with Leo, I'll never know."

Of course. I had always known it, on some level. It had been there, at the edges of the cards. It had been there in the way Rachel looked at us the day she caught us in the garden shed: exacting, calculating. I had seen it, but I had chosen to ignore it. I had made it unseen.

"What did Patrick think of them together?" I asked, unconcerned.

"Oh," she said, "I don't think he noticed. At least, not right away. I don't even know if they were together yet. It was when she first arrived. For a while, it seemed like she and Leo might really be something. But then it fell apart like all things around Leo tend to do."

"Was it ever awkward?" Although that wasn't the question I wanted answered. I wanted to know things like: how long had it gone on for, was it serious, had Leo been hurt, who broke it off, how much did Patrick know.

"Between them?"

I nodded. "Or with Patrick."

"There was a period of time when Leo and Patrick fought a lot. Little petty arguments. Things we overheard here and there. But mostly, Patrick was a gentleman about it. I can't say the same for Leo."

"When did it end?"

Moira, I thought, was enjoying this. At her core, she was a gossip, the conduit through which information moved around The Cloisters. Usually considered nonessential staff, in a moment like this, she couldn't help but love that I lingered on every word.

"I don't know," she said, picking an imaginary piece of fuzz off her skirt. "Before you came. But I don't know how long before. Rachel liked to see Patrick jealous. I think it was more that than any real interest in Leo, to be honest."

The image of Rachel and Leo together came to me in a rush, and I couldn't help but see them together in all the ways people could be. It embarrassed me that these images planted a seed of desire in my stomach, a pull that made me want to know more, to know everything, a pull that made me wish I had seen it, that it had happened in front of me.

"You know Rachel," said Moira, now watching me the way a cat would watch a fly tangled in a spider's web, with curiosity as it spun. "She never commits to much for very long. She only agreed to stay on this summer because Michael left. She was supposed to be in Berlin. She was never supposed to be here, it was just"—she waved her hand—"chance. I always wondered if she stayed because of Leo."

With that, Moira slid off the desk and walked out the door, leaving me holding a stack of books against my chest with one arm, the heavy plastic trash bag in the other. The quiet of the library, with its long oak tables and green leather chairs, its rib-vaulted ceiling and small, angular Gothic windows, seemed all at once suffocating. I felt the need to throw myself into crowds of people, to drown out the thoughts that were being knitted together in my mind.

Let's talk, came the text message from Leo.

That was all he said, but it was all it took for me to leave everything at The Cloisters behind that day. I ran down the subway steps, checking my watch while I waited for the train. At his stop, I walked as quickly as I could until I was nearly at a run by the time I reached his apartment. But I wasn't prepared to see him looking the way he did, an ankle monitor above his foot and a deep gash across his cheekbone. He held a pair of holed sweats up by the waistband, his hair pulled back, his skin pale.

He didn't say anything when I got there—no invitation or explanation—just an open door. He turned back into the apartment, where a partially eaten sandwich sat on the kitchen table.

"What do you want, Ann?"

"You slept with Rachel," I said, still out of breath.

Leo leaned against the counter, where empty coffee cups idled and crumbs from hastily prepared breakfasts collected. I wondered what he had told his roommate about the situation.

"So?"

"You didn't tell me," I said, left a little off balance by the casualness of his tone, the coolness of it. I took a seat at his table to steady myself.

"Did you tell me every person you had slept with? Was that information I needed to know?"

"No, but—"

"Come on, Ann. There's nothing cute about the babe-in-the-woods routine. You've spent a lot of time with Rachel. You know what she's like. You're not that innocent."

I wanted him to tell me everything about their relationship. I wanted to know if he thought her breasts were better than mine, how she smelled, if she liked oral sex, whether she had spent the night in the same bed he and I had slept in, deliciously high on good weed and cheap beer. He was right, I wasn't that innocent. I didn't know if I ever had been.

"I just wish you had told me." My voice came out almost a whisper.

"Why? Would it have mattered?"

"It might have."

"Really, Ann? You would have avoided me? Or maybe you would have avoided her? No. I don't think so. You've enjoyed getting involved at The Cloisters. I've watched it. Our little drama. You fit right in, like the missing piece." He paused to get a glass out of the cupboard, his back to me. "Even I felt like you were the missing piece."

I didn't know what to say, except that the way he positioned me as something necessary and interlocking with him, with Rachel, made me feel both awful and excited.

"Before you came," he said, "things always felt claustrophobic. Rachel and I. Rachel and Patrick. Moira recording every movement. The same cast of characters every day, the same monotonous work. Trim the shrubs, rake the leaves, grow the seedlings. And then you came. There was something about you. I could tell Rachel felt it right away. You broke it open, the old game, and made it into something else. You made us all believe that something new was possible."

"You talked about this, about me? You and Rachel?"

Leo nodded. "You know, she and I, we share something. We believe that doing things well sometimes means a higher cost of business. You can't be successful anymore through the old channels. There's too much competition, too much money, too many kids with trust funds that don't have to write at night between bartending shifts and day jobs. I didn't expect Rachel to get that, but she did. She knew how competitive it was, even for someone in her position. We were both willing to do what it took."

"Patrick," I said.

"Yes, for her, Patrick is what it took."

"You didn't kill him," I said.

Leo laughed. "I didn't."

"The belladonna."

"I didn't kill him, Ann. Why would I? I was selling things on the side and making pretty good money doing it. It meant I could quit my second job and write in the evenings. Rachel helped me find someone to fence them. She knew the whole thing; she was the one who suggested it. I'll never forget how she put it. *Letting them loose into the wild*, she said. We were repatriating them. And so we sold them. She never took a cut, although I offered her twenty percent. But it wasn't about the money. I think she liked the excitement of it. She liked pulling one over on Patrick, both personally and professionally. We didn't just do it at The Cloisters, either. Sure, we got caught at The Cloisters, but I've taken things from the Beinecke and the Morgan, too. Letters, manuscript pages, a handful of first editions. With Rachel's access, it was easy. But I'd like to keep the money from a few of those sales. So I've decided not to divulge Rachel's part in this side business of mine. How do you think I made bail? I wasn't even sure I was going to tell you, but—"

Leo paused and walked to the fridge and pulled out a beer, cracking it open.

"Since I may not get many more of these," he said, making a cheers gesture in my direction. "I'm impressed by how well insulated she has ended up from all this, actually."

"Why didn't you tell me?" It was a stupid question, I knew. In the end, what would knowing have meant for me? What would I have done with the information?

"You were only supposed to be temporary." The way he said it wasn't unkind or dismissive, but tender, like I was a foreign exchange student or au pair they had taken in and loved but who would inevitably, necessarily leave. "But Rachel took to you. I took to you. And then the cards, the tarot cards ruined it all."

I had never mentioned the tarot cards to him, despite the fact it had been on the tip of my tongue many times. It was a secret I had kept for Rachel; one she clearly hadn't kept for me.

"You know."

"Rachel told me about them. You know, she and Patrick had met at Yale. He was giving a lecture; she was in attendance. They were introduced, and he offered her a part-time job at the museum her senior year. I don't know how quickly they started sleeping together. Frankly, I didn't care. I've never been one to be bothered by things like that. We're all animals, after all, just trying to pass the time. But Patrick. Patrick was *into* Rachel. When he found out about us, he punched me in the face. It took two weeks for the bruising to disappear, and I had to tell everyone at work that the guitarist accidentally hit me during a set. I think Patrick thought he and Rachel were it. That she was going to get her PhD and come back to the city and move in with him in Tarrytown. But then he bought the cards. He was a big collector, you know, always buying things and just storing them around his house. She said she kept asking him to give them to her, as a gift. Then she offered to buy them from him, but he wouldn't budge. She was mad, you know? No one likes to hear the word *no* less than Rachel Mondray."

"She—"

Leo nodded.

"I'm a thief," he said, "and a moral relativist. Do I feel badly about stealing from The Cloisters? No. They are inanimate objects; I don't feel bad. But did I kill Patrick? Absolutely not. My moral relativism doesn't extend that far. Rachel's, I suspect, however, does."

"And you told this to the detective?"

"No," he said, sipping the beer. "Why would I? Who are they more likely to believe—me, a criminal, or Rachel Mondray? She set me up good, of course. Knew I couldn't turn her in because there were still a few things we'd stolen floating around, but even if I had, it wouldn't have made a difference." He shook his head. "I didn't expect her to frame me for Patrick's murder. But after the police realized it was a poisoning, I guess she had no choice."

"Didn't she worry it could all go wrong?"

"Rachel is meticulous. She's a planner. But when something goes wrong, she's always been able to come out on top. Why would this be any different?"

"We have to hold her responsible," I said, looking at Leo, a kind of desperation, an urgency to my voice, even though I knew in my bones, and the cards had told me, Leo was right.

He shrugged. "They don't have enough to convict me," he said. "At least, that's what my lawyer says. Too circumstantial. I'll do a few months in low security for the thefts before I make parole. I'll work to pay off my fine. I'm actually looking forward to it, you know. A few months to work on my writing without interruption? It's all the same to me if I do it here or upstate under a security guard. There's nothing to get Rachel on. She'll deny everything. I've seen her do it before. The day Patrick found out we'd been sleeping together, he confronted her about it. I think Moira told him. She was always hoping Patrick would get over his fixation with twenty-year-olds and date someone age-appropriate. But he confronted Rachel in the garden. I heard them arguing. She categorically denied it, even though earlier that day we had had sex in the shed. I think some of my semen was still inside her." He laughed tightly. "She's an excellent fence, that one. An incredible poker face."

When he saw the look on my face, he walked over to the table and sat down across from me.

"Oh, Ann." He touched my cheek. "I don't want you to think I did that with all the girls. Like I said, we both thought you were special from the beginning."

I stood up from the table, leaving him sitting, slightly bent forward, his hand still where he had reached out to caress my face. Part of me wanted to scream and fight. To burn it down. But the other part of me couldn't help but be excited that I had been in the middle of it all along, a buffer between them, someone they both enjoyed.

"You won't be able to catch her, you know," he called after me as I reached for the door. "You'll have to meet her on her own level. That's the only thing Rachel respects."

CHAPTER TWENTY-SIX

Leo's words stayed with me, rattled around like ice in a glass, loosely, until they dissolved into something like a plan. Which was how I found myself agreeing to go to Long Lake, when Rachel said on our way into work, at the end of her last week:

"We should take one last trip before I have to leave."

Her graduate classes started soon, and although she had offered me her place in New York, I hadn't told her yet that I'd already signed a lease in Inwood that started September first. It was easier that way. Rachel had begun to ask plaintive questions every day, things like, *You'll come visit me, won't you?* And, *We'll talk on the phone during the week, right?* This morning over coffee she had said sharply, *Don't forget me, okay?* If only I could.

As I packed my bags for the weekend, I realized there was still time for me to leave. The lease on my sublet wasn't up for four more days; I could always choose not to go to Long Lake. But as the floatplane tilted precipitously in the twilight before touching down on the dark water of the lake, I knew it wasn't a choice. It was my fate. *Audentes fortuna juvat,* Fortune favors the bold. And the city and The Cloisters had made me into someone who could be bold.

There was no one to greet us as there had been the last time, and the house was dark. Only the line of lights along the dock showed the way. By the time we made our way up the lawn and to the front door, I could already hear the plane's engine as it pulled away from the lake, leaving us alone, together, in the gathering darkness.

"No Margaret?" I asked Rachel.

"Oh, they have off through Labor Day," she said. "Usually there are people here, so there's less caretaking to do." She flicked on a switch that illuminated the living room, the honey-colored wood warm and glossy.

I had come to Long Lake so that Rachel couldn't escape the truth, so she couldn't hide behind Aruna or Michelle de Forte, or her attorneys. So she couldn't lose herself in the crowds of the city. But I hadn't anticipated Margaret and her husband being gone. They were supposed to be the backstop, the safety in case things with Rachel went off the rails, but perhaps it was better this way. She would have wanted it to be just the two of us anyway.

For days I had played out the conversation I needed to have in my mind, putting words in Rachel's mouth, letting others tumble out of my own. But the rest of the weekend I was leaving up to intuition. It would unfold, I knew, in the way it was meant to, and I didn't want the cards to tell me what to expect. Not yet. I watched Rachel pull open the refrigerator and survey the contents. The freezer, too, was mostly empty.

"We can go into town for dinner," said Rachel, opening and closing a handful of cupboards.

We carried our bags up to the rooms we had stayed in during our last trip. I walked to the window and let my fingers rest on the sill. It wasn't that The Cloisters had changed me, I realized; it was that it had sharpened me down to the slim little point of a person I had always been. New York didn't show me what I was capable of, it had left me no choice but to be that capable—the completion of a hard education begun with my father's death.

And it wasn't just the city, either. Rachel and Leo had shown me a different way of living, and for that, I had fallen in love with both of them. Standing at the edge of the window, looking across the lake, I was caught between the desire to destroy it all and hold on to it forever. The impulses were, I thought, the same.

When Rachel knocked on the door, I couldn't help but jump.

"I didn't mean to scare you," she said, walking into the room, holding a sweater in one hand and a set of keys in the other.

"You didn't."

We piled into a truck that Rachel backed out of an open garage and down a long, graded dirt driveway overhung with thickly leafed elms and oaks. After about a mile of hardwoods and marsh, we passed through an unassuming metal gate and turned left onto a two-lane highway. It only took ten or fifteen minutes until the main street of a simple, seasonal town came into focus: stands of sunglasses and little jittery coin rides for children, signs that advertised cold drinks and ice cream.

Despite the amount of time I had spent in the city that summer, some of my sharpest memories feature the main street of that downtown. It reminded me of Walla Walla and the intimacy of walking sidewalks crowded with summer tourists, weaving between parked cars, shops whose windows were full to bursting with toys and mementos—displays that hadn't changed in years—designed to entice the passerby.

"We'll eat. Then we'll get supplies," said Rachel, walking down the street in the direction of a restaurant that featured red-and-white umbrellas opened over wooden picnic tables. "I hope you like burgers because that's all we have here. The pizza place closed a year ago. It was probably for the best. It was terrible pizza, pretty shocking actually for New York."

There were only a handful of empty tables, and Rachel threw her sweater down on one before we joined the line, full of retirees and young families, a handful of teenagers who had escaped their parents' supervision for the night. We ordered from a pair of girls who stood behind windows that barely opened far enough for them to hear. They kept having to bend down, their ears almost on the counter to catch our order.

Rachel dithered about her order, but no one seemed to mind. Since Leo's arrest, her demeanor had shifted imperceptibly—she was lighter, more playful, as if any remaining concern had been lifted off her shoulders. I wondered how she justified it, because I was certain she had. What did one say to a friend who has committed murder? How was it possible to pass the time until you simply couldn't avoid the truth any longer?

Our order arrived. My burger was full of gristle and salt.

"How do you think Moira will like Beatrice?" Rachel asked between sips of soda.

Beatrice Graft had been hired to replace Patrick. A professor at Columbia and frequent lecturer at The Cloisters, she had always been a front-runner for the job.

"I think Moira believes *she* should be appointed curator," I said.

"Patrick once told me that she had been hired in her thirties. Can you imagine? She must have been there at least thirty years."

I could believe it. Moira had the look of someone who had been in the Gothic halls of the museum far too long—pale and watchful, bursting, I knew, with secrets.

"Do you think you'll be okay?" asked Rachel. There was genuine concern in her voice. "It will be like starting over. A new me, a new Leo, a new Patrick."

Those weren't necessarily bad things, I thought.

"I'll manage."

"That's what I told Michelle," said Rachel, looking past me to a table occupied by a young couple. "I told her you would be able to anchor the place with all the turmoil. Even though you haven't been there very long, I told her you could handle it. She hadn't been sure, you know, if you would be a good fit, long-term. But I reassured her."

"Thanks," I said. Although there was something in the statement I didn't like: the specter of indebtedness, of my own insufficiency.

"Don't mention it. That's what friends are for. Plus, I like knowing where you'll be in case I need you."

We ate in silence as night spread through the town, stars easily visible beyond the one streetlight. It struck me then that Rachel's generosity—the thing I had been so taken with, the thing that seemed so genuine—was actually the source of her control. She was both benefactor and micromanager, skillfully moving us through our paces, and sheltering us with privilege while we complied. And while it was clear that she liked me, she also believed she was smarter, more capable.

Before we left the city, I had called Laure and told her everything, just in case something went wrong. She believed me without question, barely an inflection in her voice as I explained it. Though she wanted to know things like, *Was I okay?* I had assured her that I was.

Rachel, I realized, had created, or been at the center of, so much loss. I knew how that changed a person. And so, I had wanted to feel around in Rachel's loss, try it on for size. I remembered the way I had cut out every article about my father's death and saved them—sometimes they were only a few lines long. His obituary had been barely the length of my thumb. It was my memory of his obituary that first caused me to go back and read articles about Rachel's parents' deaths. And there were many of them: local reports by the *Post-Star Gazette* that gave a full page to describing the recovery efforts, the damage to the boat, the state Rachel had been in when she was found. And then wanting to feel her loss even more, I moved on to articles from the *Yale Daily News* about her roommate's suicide. With every word I read, things that had once seemed unlucky, predestined, inescapable, looked less like fate and more like design.

Rachel crinkled up our paper wrappers and walked them to the trash.

On the drive back, we let our hands dangle out the window, invigorating our skin. By the time we arrived at the house, it was late. Rachel put on a record in the living room, its scratchy sound echoing through the wooden house and out the open windows onto the shores of the lake where it tried, but failed, to drown out the chorus of crickets.

She folded herself onto an old chair and opened a book, a glass of wine on the table next to her. We had spent a lot of time on our first trip to Long Lake reading, and for this trip I had packed a novel I had been meaning to read for some time—Umberto Eco's *The Name of the Rose*, the thick, worn copy I had taken from Patrick's office.

On the couch, I opened the book and fanned through its pages, until they stopped, sharply, at the end. And there, at the back, tucked against the paperback cover, was a card. I recognized the deep blue backing immediately, the scattering of gold stars that made up the constellations in the night sky. I looked up and saw Rachel engrossed in her book. I flipped the card over. It was the missing card, the Devil. The card that completed the deck. Its fake front already stripped away to reveal Janus, the god of transitions and duality. Patrick, I was shocked to discover, had always known about the hidden cards beneath.

CHAPTER TWENTY-SEVEN

I kept my discovery to myself even when, the next day, we lay on soft terry beach towels and pushed our toes into the sand. A tilted umbrella provided a sliver of shade as the sun worked its way west. At the far end, a bank of clouds was gathering. I waded out into the lake, its rocky shoreline pricking at my feet every few steps until I was far enough to dive under. The water filled my ears as my arms sliced through the air, carrying me to the old swim platform that was moored off the beach.

And as I pulled myself onto its surface, raw and full of flaking pieces of wood, I admired how brown my arms had become, the slenderness of my body courtesy of the New York summer. I had always loved the last gasps of the season. The endless drumbeat of bright August sunshine and dry grass in Walla Walla, where the return to the classroom was the first signal that fall was coming, and soon, the brooding skies of winter. I knew that the skies in New York would do more than brood. As hot as the summer had been, winter would be cold. *Biting*, Leo had said one night, leaning out onto his fire escape to exhale the joint he was smoking. Even so, I couldn't wait to feel the winter wind come off the Hudson. I lay on the platform until I felt my skin prickling and mottled with heat, then dove back into the lake, swimming ashore.

Rachel and I repeated this—swim, nap, squeeze together under the bit of shade the umbrella afforded us—until late afternoon, until the sky began to darken and the clouds shifted from white to gray, dwarfing the skyline with their height. The wind, too, had kicked up, ruffling the edges of our books and pulling at the umbrella. But as the sun dipped lower, it became clear we had waited too long. At the end of the lake, a dark band of rain was making its way toward us, the downdrafts forming whitecaps on the water. Daytime had given way to darkness—that surreal experience that only seems to happen on the hottest summer days—and while no lightning had cracked the sky, a sudden chill told me it couldn't be far away. And then, directly above us, thunder. A gust of wind knocked over our umbrella, throwing it end over end across the lawn, the towels and books tumbling after. We chased them down, the rain falling hard on our shoulders and bare legs, corralling the items as they danced in the wind before running for the veranda and the safety of the house. Already, I could hear the rain's deafening staccato hitting the roof, the boathouse, the windows.

"I don't think we'll lose power," Rachel said as soon as we were inside.

I hadn't imagined that it could become darker, but when the wind hit the broad side of the house, I took an involuntary step back. In only a matter of minutes, the afternoon had changed—irrevocably—and in that moment, I longed for the only thing that seemed to be able to hold me in place when everything else around me spun and spun—the cards. I left Rachel in the living room, watching the storm, for the bedroom where I had been sleeping; I felt around in my bag until I found it: the leather box with green ribbon that contained the cards.

Wanting to read with a complete deck, I slipped the Devil card into the center of the stack and arranged myself, cross-legged on the old woven rug facing the bank of windows, streaked with rain. I began the process of gently shuffling and laying out a spread, placing the cards with intention, arranging them in a complicated grid of ten. Five would signify what had come before, five what was still ahead. And as I laid them out, I couldn't help but be gripped by what I saw in my past. There was the Two of Cups, reversed—a card that spoke of distrust, an imbalance.

Next to it was Saturn, a card we had associated with the World in a traditional deck—the father figure. But also, in ancient Rome, Saturn had been conflated with the Greek god Cronus, a Titan who had usurped his own father and devoured his young. The Ten of Coins, reversed, focused the reading even more squarely on family, and there, too, was the Moon. That most fickle of cards, which shined a light on the error of our ways. I had to look away from the truth that the cards were trying to make clear.

"What do they tell you?" Rachel asked. She had followed me upstairs and now leaned against the doorjamb. And then so softly that I almost couldn't hear her over the rain, "What do they tell you that I can't?"

"It's not like that. It's a feeling." I looked up. "An unlocking." But I knew it could be more than that, too. The document we had translated said that the cards were prescriptive—they told the future, perhaps even *made* it.

She refused to come in the room, but stood on its threshold, watching me.

"Come on, Ann," she said. "You don't really believe that the cards can tell the future. Nothing can. Only we can make our futures."

But her voice was frail, and I remembered the story she had told me about her mother and the tea leaves, the way the reading had filled her with a fear that never fully left her.

"We all want to believe in something greater than ourselves," I said, holding the remaining cards in my hand and studying the spread. "Isn't that what Patrick always said?"

"Why would you even want to know?" Rachel said, now walking into the room and arranging herself across from me on the floor, legs crossed. "If what you're saying is true, that there's something out there waiting for us, something we might be able to see, why would you want to know that?"

It was then that I realized Rachel was actually afraid. Where I had leaned into my intuition, she had pulled away. I wondered, then, if she had actually found the tea leaves reader her mother had visited. And for a brief moment, I allowed myself to imagine her, walking into the shop, only to be cast out; the fortune-teller, pointing at her accusatorially. But the truth was, we were both right in our own ways. I *did* believe we were destined for certain things, the way I believed my father was destined to be on the side of the road that day and that nothing I could have done would have stopped his death. Because what was it like to live with the alternative? Wondering always if I could have saved him by making a different choice.

Rachel reached across the space between us, breaking my concentration, and placed a hand on my arm.

"Ann. Believing can be fun. But that's all it is—fun. It's not the work. The work is here." She pointed at the cards, a finger hovering above the illustrations. "Let's focus on that."

I looked up at her, sitting across from me, pleading. I imagined that she had once said the same to Patrick.

"Just let me read for you then," I said.

It was a dare, but also a test of how far Rachel would let me push her. It struck me, then, the distance I had put between myself and the version of who I was in those first weeks, when I tried so hard to measure up, when I tried so hard to meet her on her level. She searched my face, and for the first time, I knew we were on equal footing. She was now as uncertain as I had once been. As the sound of the rain on the windowpanes surged, she nodded.

"What do you want to ask them?" I said, holding the deck in my hand.

"Ask them about my future."

I nodded, starting to lay out the cards, a simple five-card spread. But each card that turned up was the same—the Ace, reversed. The only cards in the deck that had no illustration, save for a single image of their suit. I continued until I got to five cards, closing my eyes and feeling the softness of the vellum. When I opened them, I was shocked to learn that the remaining two cards had not changed the spread. There was the fourth Ace and the card I had slipped into the deck before Rachel had come in, before I had thought I would read for her at all—the Devil. When I looked at the cards that were supposed to sketch Rachel's future, they showed me that there wasn't one. At least, not one that I could see. There was only emptiness and sudden change. Death.

"Ann—"

Across the cards, Rachel's color had moved from her cheeks to her chest, painting her collarbones a deep, uneven crimson. Before I could say anything, she stood and left the room.

I followed her downstairs, where she stood by the window.

"Did they tell you what happened to Patrick?" she said, not turning to face me.

Looking back, I realized they had. Only I hadn't been good enough at the time to read them. "They might have."

"I never pegged you as the kind of girl who would get so wrapped up in all this," she said, now turning to face me. Her voice was thin and high. "You seemed so practical in the beginning."

"You don't understand," I said, almost to myself. I thought of the work my father had done translating the pages, how he had puzzled over them, how they had always been meant for me, had been waiting for *me*. Not Rachel.

She laughed, and it sounded like breaking glass.

"The card came for you," I said. "The Devil."

Outside, lightning cracked across the sky, shaking the house and our bodies. The strike had been close, close enough that it had struck the boathouse, where flames were now licking the end of the dock and growing. Like the Tower card, the boathouse was ablaze. The heat of the lightning had defied the rain and set fire to the structure, which was beginning to collapse into the lake.

Rachel didn't hesitate, but ran out into the storm, toward the fire. I followed, but the rain pelted my skin, and I struggled to see through the howling wind and smoke that spread low across the dock.

While Rachel knew the way instinctively, I had to keep my eyes on the planks to be sure I wasn't nearing the edge. When I finally reached the end of the dock, Rachel was standing inside the boathouse. A corner of the building still smoldered against the rain and the roof had partially fallen away. Two boats that had been winched out of the water swung in the wind.

"You knew," I said now, yelling over the noise of the storm. "You knew he had it. That he knew about the real cards underneath."

I let the implication hang between us. Patrick had known about the cards, for how long, I couldn't be sure. But I could be sure Rachel had lied to me.

She turned to face me, the wind whipping her hair. "What do you want me to say, Ann? Will it make you feel better knowing the details? Will they make a difference to you?"

"They aren't details, Rachel. They're the truth."

"Okay. Fine. Look who has decided ethics suddenly matter. Yes, he knew. But he wasn't the one to make the discovery. You were. That's the truth."

"You knew and you kept it from me."

The downdrafts and thunder had moved east, booming echoes in the distance, but the rain remained, a series of hard pinpricks that bored into my skin.

Her eyes narrowed. "Did you go see Leo, too?"

I wondered, briefly, if he had told her, but the way she said it, sharp with curiosity, made me assume he hadn't.

"I didn't need Leo to figure it out," I said. And while it was true, Leo had been asking me to see Rachel for who she was longer than anyone else.

"I thought you might. What did he tell you?"

"Nothing I didn't already know."

Rachel tipped her head back and laughed. There was no escaping the way her body shook with the movement, supple and tan. Even against a maelstrom, her beauty was a kind of refuge.

"You have no clue, Ann. How could you?"

That Rachel thought I had figured out so little gave me a pang of pleasure. I knew her better than she imagined. I had been paying attention.

"Leo has always had such an imagination. But I don't suppose they really have enough to prosecute anyway."

"No. He doesn't think so."

"Too bad, really."

"He did say you killed Patrick, though." The words had been rolling around in my mouth for days, and now they came roughly, almost misshapen to my own ears, and loud against the force of the storm.

"Now why would he think that?" Rachel took a step closer to me, and in the narrowed distance I had to fight the urge to retreat, to keep the buffer in place.

"Because he didn't. And that card"—I gestured toward the house—"that card is motive, Rachel. You had to beat him to it, didn't you? Once he had discovered the false fronts, you knew that was it."

Something passed over Rachel's face, but I couldn't be sure if it was an emotion or the rain. "It could have been an accident," said Rachel. "An overdose. A mistake. Leo has been known to make those, after all." She looked me up and down.

I knew all about Rachel's accidents and Leo's mistakes.

"Why didn't you tell me about you and Leo?" It felt like the one question I would allow myself that reached the places that hurt me the most.

"It might have ruined your fun. And Leo is very fun." She smiled, thin-lipped, strained.

I looked out across the lake, where the water was inky black, roiling like the open ocean at night. In that moment, I wanted desperately for her to be able to talk me out of it, to shift the blame to someone else, to erase her past, erase my own, as if we could start over.

"You didn't need to know," she continued. "You might never have known any of it if Patrick hadn't taken you to Stephen's that day. Did you know that I was supposed to go with him? Not you. He took you as a punishment, I think. As a way to tell me I was replaceable. But I think he saw in you what I did. Someone who could be secretive, someone who could put their success above the well-being of others, someone like me. You are like me, Ann."

"I'm not a murderer," I said.

"I hate that word," said Rachel. "Murderer. The belladonna is the real murderer. I suppose you could call me the hand of fate, actually. I prefer it to murderer. More musical."

"And what about your roommate?" I asked.

Rachel laughed. "How do you even know about that?"

"I read the reports."

"Oh my god, Ann, always the researcher. I did not kill her. She jumped from our window of her own free will."

"But Patrick—"

"But Patrick, but Patrick," Rachel mimicked. "Really, Ann. You didn't know Patrick; you didn't know what it was like before you came. I couldn't stand him. The way he pawed at me and talked to me about the future. I knew that all the work I was doing at The Cloisters was only because he liked me. If that changed, it could all be taken away at any minute. I decided to change that."

It struck me that in some sense, Rachel and I had both been at The Cloisters because of Patrick's favor, a favor that necessarily cut both ways.

"And he wasn't even a scholar," she continued. "Not anymore anyway. He was always busy buying things and hoarding them in that sad house of his in Tarrytown. And usually, it was just junk. He was a bad curator and an even worse collector. Why do you think I slept with Leo? Because I *wanted to*. Why do you think I slept with Patrick? Because I felt I had to."

I wasn't sure how much of this was true; I'd never seen Rachel do anything she didn't want to. But I knew what it was like to feel trapped. I, too, would have done anything to stay at The Cloisters, just as I would have done anything to escape Walla Walla.

"But that idiot—" She shook her head. "Years of buying second-rate manuscript pages and counterfeit reliquaries, and he finally stumbles on something good." She laughed. "Those cards. He didn't know what he had. But you knew." She took another step closer so that I could have easily reached out and touched her. "You knew what they were. What was Patrick going to do with them? Put them in frames around his house? Maybe donate them if he ever really evaluated what he had. Write an article that touched on a few narrow-minded themes. No. I wasn't going to let that happen. I did it for us, Ann. For us."

"We could have brought him in, we could have—" But as I said it, I knew it wasn't true. It wasn't what either of us wanted, and I wondered if maybe I had purposefully ignored the reality that Patrick knew, that he had figured it out.

"He didn't deserve that." Rachel almost spit out the words. "All these years, it's always great discoveries by great men. I knew that if we had shared this with him, we would have been relegated to coauthors, at best. Everyone would think the discovery was his. That he had recognized quality when everyone else, over the centuries, had been fooled. But *he* was the fool. Not us. Not you. He never would have known, but for that night in the library. He was right, you know. It turned out the drugs did give him more clarity. That night, he finally noticed there was something wrong in the feel of the cards, and he kept working them and working them trying to figure out what it was. I did my best to distract him, but he was obsessed. Until finally it clicked, and he found a way to pull apart the false front. That was when I knew it was time."

"So you poisoned him."

"I told you, I'm not a murderer. After a few hours that night, Patrick thought he needed a little more, a topper, something that would help him see more clearly, just one more dose, so I went to the garden shed and found the plant. I ground the root of the belladonna in Leo's shed and offered it to him. I watched him mix it in his water. And I sat there, quietly, as he drank it, willingly. Greedily, even. If he'd been attentive, he might have noticed how different it was, but I think, on some level, he wanted it, you know? It was his choice."

The way she justified it, as an act that could have easily been avoided, chilled me. The logic deeply flawed.

"Rachel, you're not describing choice. Patrick didn't have a choice. Your interpretation of choice is a luxury, a curtain that separates us from fate. From a fate you're authoring."

"Choice is the one thing we all share," she said, brushing off my comment. "It's the ultimate level playing field."

"It's not, Rachel. Do you think I wanted to end up at The Cloisters? Do you think I wanted to get mixed up in all this? I didn't have a choice."

"Of course you did. You could have gone back to Walla Walla. You could have left after Patrick died. You could have chosen, a million times, not to do things with me that got you deeper and deeper into this, but you did. At every turn, you did. And you know why? Because *we're the same*, Ann."

She was wrong to believe I had a choice. There were, I knew, no real choices in life. I knew this with absolute certainty, because I had not chosen to be on the road that day. Nor had my father chosen to have his car break down on his way home, its repairs long overdue, on the one blind bend between Whitman and our home. I could see the darkness in the cards now. In the face of Saturn and the milkiness of the moon—I could see what had happened that day, what I had worked so hard to forget. The way I had driven home from campus, down the country road that center-cut the wheatfields, fields whose grasses had grown high, ready for mowing. And on the bend, I hadn't seen him, hadn't seen the car through the crowded stalks of wheat. I had only felt it—the thump, the force so inconsequential against the bumper of my truck.

Only, in the rearview, had I been able to see the scene. To see his body, laid out at the edge of the gray strip of asphalt. I had run back, I remembered that now. But it was already too late. And he had told me, then, to go. To keep going. To never stop until I was far from home. *It wasn't your fault*, he had said. *Don't let this ruin your life.* Although, of course, it already had.

My father, however, had been right. It was, I now knew, not my fault. Fate had intervened to put us both on the road that day, under a blistering August sky. Rachel was wrong to believe I had ever had a choice. Choice was a fiction. Because if I'd ever had a choice, I would have veered left, I would have gone the long way, I would have done anything to prevent what happened to my father—what happened to me—that afternoon. And if choice was so easy to marshal, then I would have chosen to stop the tears that came to my eyes, to catch my breath, to stop my voice from matching the howling of the wind, the crash of the rain. The memory my mind and body had worked so hard to repress—my father, his body bloody, the blond fields and dusty soil around us, my hands on the wheel—was once again pouring out of me.

"Ann," Rachel said, closing the distance between us and wrapping her arms around me. "It's over," she said. "We can't go back."

And I cried, louder still, because she was right. We couldn't go back, and even worse, I didn't know if I wanted to. Because all of it, even my father's death, had led me here. Rachel was right, we were the same. But it wasn't a relief, that realization. It was a crushing defeat, and it was all

I could do to wrap my arms around her and slump against her body, to let her hold me up.

"I did it for us," she whispered against my neck.

And there was, somewhere inside me, something that wanted to believe her, that desperately wanted it to be true. To have it be Rachel and me from here on out—no more father figures, no more fathers, no more lovers. But I had seen in the cards what was next, and in it, through my shaking body and haunted mind, I found some relief. And just as my past had found me in the cards, I knew I couldn't escape the future they had made for me, either. I didn't have a choice.

CHAPTER TWENTY-EIGHT

By the time dawn was beginning to spread across the Adirondacks, I was already on the country road, walking in the direction of town. I held my hand out, thumb up, every time I heard a car, but with the sun barely risen, they were few and far between, mostly work trucks already full of people and loaded with ladders on their way to job sites.

When I had been walking for around an hour, a woman dressed in a housekeeping uniform pulled over and rolled down her window.

"Where you headed?" she asked.

I didn't know.

"Anywhere I can catch a bus," I said. I had slung my packed bag over my shoulder, my frame weighed down with a backpack as well.

"That'll be Johnsburg," she said, reaching across to push open the passenger door from inside. "I can take you most of the way."

We drove in silence with the hardwoods whipping by outside. Her car smelled of cigarettes, and she continually tapped the ash from the one in her hand out the edge of the window.

"You running from something?" she asked after we had been driving for a few minutes. "If you don't want to talk about it, that's fine. You just look like someone who is running from something." She gestured at my backpack on the back seat.

"Sort of."

"Is it a boy? I had to run from a boy once. When a relationship hits the skids—" She whistled and rolled her eyes.

"A bad relationship," I said.

"You'll make it. I thought I'd never fully get away, but I did. And he didn't find me, if that's what you're worried about. They always say they'll find you, but they rarely do. They get bored looking or take up with your sister—in my case, it was my sister—and then—"

She slammed on the brakes to let two deer pass in front of the car; my head nearly hit the dash. I wondered if her seat belts even worked.

"That was close," she said.

As the deer made their way into the thicket, the stag turned its head to look at me, its black eye glassy and emotionless.

"Anyway," the woman started again, "you'll be okay. I'll take you all the way to Johnsburg. We don't have to talk about it."

And we didn't. We drove the rest of the way, as the morning light went from milky to clear, just listening to the radio and driving the two-lane highway to the bus station. I hadn't left a note for Rachel. I had just left, turned off my cell phone and walked away from it, from her, from the whole thing.

There had been a bite in the air that morning when I got up before the sun. Summer was over. The world we had built at The Cloisters, the one that had kept everything else out, had crumbled, like the building in the Tower card, falling into the sea. It was, I realized, inevitable. Relationships like ours, worlds like that—they can't withstand the pressure from the outside, particularly when those pressures were from your own past. What, after all, could I tell Detective Murphy? That Rachel had created a complex morality where she felt absolved because there was always a choice for her victims, even though she had orchestrated their fates? That I, myself, was wanted for a hit-and-run in Washington? No. I knew they wouldn't understand. But I did. The cards did.

When the woman dropped me at the bus station, she pressed a few dollars into my hand.

"You're going to need this," she said.

And even though I tried to give it back to her, she insisted. There, I used a pay phone to call Laure and ask her if it would be okay if I stayed with her for the rest of the week, just until my lease started. She agreed immediately.

"Are you okay?" she said over the phone.

"Fine," I said.

"Did she do anything?"

"No."

Laure was quiet on the other end, and I could almost hear her chewing on her lower lip, trying to decide if she should push for more information.

"I'll tell you more when I get there," I said preemptively. The truth was, I didn't want to talk about it. I knew no one would understand.

It took the rest of the day to get into the city—bus transfers and trains, finally two subways and a five-block walk. It wasn't until almost 7 p.m. that I stumbled into Laure's apartment in Brooklyn where she lived with her boyfriend and two cats. I dropped both bags on the floor and collapsed on the couch.

"You can stay as long as you need," she said, bringing me a glass of water.

"I just need a week."

Laure nodded.

"Thank you," I said.

"So," said Laure, sitting next to me on the couch. "What happened?"

"It just wasn't in the cards."

And even though she tried to press me for more information, I demurred. It wasn't Laure's story. It was mine. A story that I knew very few people would believe. After I took a nap and showered, we drank too many bottles of cheap wine at a restaurant whose tables spilled onto the sidewalk, and then we walked home under the orange glow of the streetlamps. And for the first time, I saw another side of New York, the world outside The Cloisters that was still warm and buzzy, even though soon the leaves would turn colors and the air less forgiving. I breathed it all in.

The next day was Monday, and I rode the subway up to The Cloisters, enjoying again the crush of people around me, the hot, stale air. There would be a new curator at the museum, and for the occasion, I had dipped back into the clothes I had brought from Walla Walla, the scratchy polyester no longer embarrassing, just nostalgic.

When I arrived in the lobby, I noticed that Moira averted her eyes and bent down behind the desk to pull out more maps and welcome guides. The same thing happened in the kitchen, where the conservators nodded at me briskly before slipping away, leaving their sugar packets behind. In the library, Michelle found me, Beatrice Graft at her side.

"Oh, Ann. We weren't expecting you," she said. "Would you mind giving us a few minutes?" she said to Beatrice.

For a beat I worried, again, I would be let go. That she would tell me Beatrice and the museum no longer needed me. Only this time, there would be no Patrick to save me. As Beatrice slipped out the door she said, "Just come get me when you're done."

Michelle came over to the table and pulled out the chair next to mine.

"Ann," she said. "With what happened, we assumed you would want a few days off. But since you're here . . ." She trailed off. "I guess now would be as good a time as any to introduce you. You know you didn't have to do this to prove to us your commitment. We're all very aware."

"Of what?" I asked.

Then she looked at me curiously. "You have heard, haven't you?"

"Heard what?"

"Oh dear." Michelle quickly stepped outside and conferred with Beatrice before joining me again at the table. "Ann," she said, speaking slowly. "This has been a difficult summer for us here at The Cloisters, and it has been a difficult summer for you, personally. I assumed you already knew. You two were so close. But since you don't, I want to be the one to tell you. Rachel is dead. She died. A sailing accident apparently. Very tragic. Our whole staff, the whole family at The Cloisters is . . . " She let the sentence die.

"I've been staying with a friend in Brooklyn," I said. "I hadn't heard."

"Right. So you didn't know. I understand. Ann, look, I'm so sorry."

And she looked it, Michelle did. Her face was creased, and when I glanced down, I noticed she was holding my hand.

"When?" I asked.

"Yesterday. Apparently she was sailing to a small island on Long Lake. But she didn't check that the plug was in. It wasn't, and the boat took on water. She didn't have a life preserver on board. She tried to swim ashore, but a storm rolled in. It was impossible."

"Oh," I said, now looking down at the hands in my lap, Michelle's and mine, tangled together. I didn't know if she expected me to cry or not, if she needed a performance of emotion. I didn't know what I needed.

"Yes," said Michelle. "Particularly tragic because it appears to be the same way her parents passed away. Really, none of us can fathom it."

I sat in silence next to Michelle until she gave my hands a squeeze and released them, the collective mourning period ended. "Why don't you take a little time, go home, take a few days off. This will all be here for you when you get back. We need you very much, Ann Stilwell. You're doing great work here."

I thought of what a difference it was from our first meeting. The summer had changed all of us, had rearranged the fabric of our realities. *The Fates—the Moirai*—I thought, *had been busy weaving.*

"How did you find out?"

"Leo called me," said Michelle, after a moment of hesitation.

I said nothing to that.

"You should feel free to go. Why don't we agree that you'll come back on Thursday, or next week if you need the time? Really, whatever you need. After the summer you've had up here, I wouldn't blame you if you quit."

"I'm not quitting," I said, pushing back my chair and standing up. "I'd like to take a walk, but after that, I'll be back. I want to be here; I can't imagine going through this anywhere else."

Michelle looked at me and smiled.

"All right," she said.

I walked down the hill away from the ramparts of The Cloisters, their uneven outline still visible through the trees, until I stopped at a bench. Under the low, arcing limb of an elm tree, I pulled out my phone and for the first time since leaving Long Lake turned it back on. There were four messages from Rachel, but I listened to none of them. I simply scrolled until I found his name and called Leo.

"I was her emergency contact," he said, before I could even get a word out. "Can you imagine?"

I didn't say anything.

"Were you there when it happened?" he asked.

"No."

"Probably for the best."

"When did they call you?"

"Last night. I called Michelle right away."

I realized I was sitting on the very edge of the bench, one hand gripping the side so tightly my knuckles had turned white.

"What did they say?"

I could hear him readjusting the way he was sitting on the other end of the line. "That she had drowned. She probably tried to swim for shore but misjudged the distance."

I stayed silent.

"Are you okay?"

"I'm fine," I said finally. And some part of me meant it; I marveled that it might actually be true.

"Seems fitting," Leo said.

"How so?"

"That fate would intervene when no one else would."

Still, I was quiet.

"I have to go, Leo."

"Hey," he said, waiting a beat. I imagined him running his hand through his hair, a cup of coffee nearby. "Would you be interested in getting dinner or something? We're playing a gig at the—"

"Leo," I drew his name out, long and soft. "I don't know."

"Okay," he said, shifting uncomfortably again on the other end of the phone. "Well, if you change your mind—"

"I have to go. Maybe—I don't know." If things were meant to work out with Leo, I knew they would, no matter how much I resisted or he pushed.

And with that, I hung up and released my grip on the edge of the bench, flexing my hand until the blood returned. After a busy summer at The Cloisters, now, at the end of August, the park was quiet again. No groups lay sprawled on blankets, no readers dangled their sandals absently, no children chased balls. I was alone, with only the breeze off the Hudson for company and the solid rock wall of The Cloisters behind me. The grasses, I noticed, were beginning to dry—high and brown, just as they had been that day in Walla Walla. He would have been happy to see all that I had accomplished here, my father.

I thought of that day, of the way he had said to me, hard and certain: *It's not your fault.* Before I arrived at The Cloisters I didn't believe him. I couldn't. So I buried the shame and devastation and guilt as deep as possible, beyond the reaches of my memory and my life in Walla Walla, beyond even my own grief. But the summer had cracked it all open, and here, in the late-summer sun, I could finally see the truth. My father had been right all along. It hadn't been my fault. That fate had been meant for me, it was always going to find me, no matter how long I hid from it.

Ultimately, I decided not to listen to the messages Rachel left me. I deleted them all so I wouldn't be tempted to go back and listen to her voice, the lilting singsong. I erased her text messages, too, because I couldn't bear to see them. But the pictures, I kept those. I left them on my phone so I could remember what the summer had been like, what we had been like, what I had been like, before.

Back at Laure's apartment that night, after her boyfriend cooked dinner and I dried the dishes, I pulled my computer from my bag and let it sit on my lap. And then, I pulled up the article Rachel and I had worked on and highlighted her name with the cursor. After a minute of looking at her name in blue, the cursor blinking at the end, I hit Delete. Then I submitted it, without so much as a second thought. Me, listed as the sole author.

From my bag, which I had wedged under the couch that doubled as my bed, I pulled out the worn leather box wrapped in green ribbon, and opened it. Inside were the cards, the complete set. I let my finger touch the top card, the Lovers, and feel its history. The light caught the ring Rachel had bought me at Stephen's shop, the one I had worn since that day. I pulled it from my finger and walked from Laure's apartment out to the East River. There, with a view of the Manhattan skyline, I threw it into the brackish water.

CHAPTER TWENTY-NINE

The article came out in December. By then I had already been given my own office at The Cloisters—the smallest, but nevertheless, it was mine. And by the time the first snow burned the tips of the grasses in Fort Tryon Park brown, no one mentioned Rachel or Patrick anymore. Only I would remember every detail of that summer. And every spring, there would come an evening, just one, when I would walk home at night, down the glowing, sticky streets of New York, and a warm wind would bring it all back to me. Even when I stopped walking home at night in the springtime, those breezes found me—through windows or the rush of a subway train approaching—unbidden, in stillness.

I owed everything to the summer that everyone was eager to forget. In March, acceptances to doctoral programs arrived by the dozen, and countless departments hosted me and celebrated my achievements. The article had received widespread acclaim and generous reviews. No one, of course, mentioned my previous rejections. They—like me—believed that my time at The Cloisters had remade me. Indeed, I knew it had. Ultimately, I decided to go to Yale, not because it was haunted by Rachel's ghost, but because Aruna was there and she had become the closest thing I had, at that point anyway, to family.

For months, the cards sat in their box unopened, until Aruna suggested that I consider selling them to the Beinecke in a private sale, one that would quietly sweep aside the question of their provenance. The number we agreed on was large enough that I could breathe in New

Haven, knowing I wouldn't need to take on extra jobs or loans to sustain myself as a graduate student, perhaps longer.

My second year at Yale, I attended the Morgan symposium again, this time with Aruna by my side. There I met Karl Gerber, the Renaissance curator whose absence had sent me to The Cloisters, to Rachel, to Patrick, to the shadows of my past. He was gentle and kind and expressed regret at the situation he had inadvertently thrust me into.

"But," he said as we nursed coffees between sessions, "I thought you knew. Knew that I would be gone. It was arranged in advance, of course, my departure."

And it struck me that perhaps Patrick had set up the entire gambit. That the moment I thought had been fate, the moment when he knocked on Michelle's door, had in fact been orchestrated. Maybe it had been Lingraf's name on my application.

"Did Patrick arrange it?" I asked.

"Oh no," he said, voice lowered. "Rachel did. She was the one who helped facilitate my position that summer at the Carrozza Collection, in Bergamo? She said you would be coming to The Cloisters. She was sure of it. And that you would be taken care of. She was very eager to see what you might have learned working with Lingraf, you know."

He offered me a cigarette, and I took it, inhaling deeply.

Lingraf, it turned out, did not live long enough to see the publication of the article, or even the cold winds that rushed off the Cascades the winter after my summer at The Cloisters. He died of a heart attack, at home in his study, a month after my graduation. He was eighty-nine. As a result, I would never know if Rachel had reached out to him, if he had told her about me, if in all of it, she had sensed an opening, however slim. An opening that would blow open her world and mine in irrevocable ways.

The past, I now know, can tell us more than the future. It was a lesson I had learned even before I stepped foot in The Cloisters. Knowing, that day, that stretch of asphalt, would forever change me. And while the cards had told me so much, there were still some gaps to fill in. Which was how I learned, poring over microfiche at the New York Public Library, that Rachel's parents had loved to sail Lasers. Slim, shallow boats that were popular in races. Lasers, however, were occasionally problematic because their hulls contained two drain plugs: one in the stern that, if omitted, would swamp the boat immediately, and another, inside the cockpit, that would cause the boat to swamp more gradually.

Boat accidents on Long Lake, it turned out, were very common, but drownings were rare. Because of this, the investigation into Rachel's parents' deaths and her miraculous survival had occupied the police and journalists of Johnsburg for months. The biggest question was: How did the second plug, the one that should have been in the boat's cockpit, end up in the trash of the restaurant where Rachel and her parents had dined that night?

The police, naturally, interviewed everyone. But no employees or visitors could remember anyone boarding their Laser, tied alongside the wooden dock, buffeted by the wind and waves against the squeaking plastic bumpers, except, of course, for Rachel. With little in the way of motive and no witnesses, the police eventually abandoned the search. A decision, no doubt, that had been spurred by the intervention of the Mondray family attorney who had requested, in rather stern legalese, that the police allow the family time to grieve. Rachel, after all, had been a victim of the sunken boat as well. She was just, the lead investigator would say, extremely lucky.

Luck, probably from the Middle High German word *glück*, meaning fortune or happy accident. Fortune—merely another word for fate. Rachel, I knew, was not one to believe in luck. And I could see her, as I read the article, removing the life vests and leaving them behind on the dock. I could see her boarding the boat near the end of dinner to remove the plug in the cockpit. The accident had Rachel's fingerprints all over it.

By her calculus, I knew, there was still a good chance her parents would survive. But with a bit of luck, she would. And they wouldn't.

She was right, then, when she said we were the same. But I would have given anything to rewrite the fate I had authored for my father. Rachel, of course, felt no such remorse.

The cards I spread out that night in Long Lake told me how Rachel's story would end, but ultimately, I left the choice up to her. In the liquid dawn of the next morning, I had walked to the end of the dock where the Lasers were suspended above the water, masts down, sails furled, and boarded each boat, taking care not to rock it loose. From the cockpits, I pulled out the life vests and the plug, a little white disk of plastic I slipped into my pocket. I carried it all the way to Laure's apartment, and then, as we walked home from dinner, the warm wind coming off the East River, I pulled it out of my pocket and let it fall to the asphalt.

We are, you see, both masters of our fate and at the mercy of the Moirai—the three Fates who weave our futures and cut them short. And while I still believe we can control the little things in life, those small decisions that add up to the everyday, I think, perhaps, the overall shape of our life is not ours to decide. That shape belongs to fate. The Cloisters came for me and delivered me my fate that summer. But now, like Rachel, I'd rather not know how the story ends.

ANN STILWELL'S GUIDE TO
READING TAROT

✦

MAJOR ARCANA

#	TRAD CARD	FERRARA DECK CARD TITLE (AND ASSOCIATED ROMAN GOD)	ZODIAC SIGN	PLANETARY RULER	FERRARA DECK ILLUSTRATION	UPRIGHT MEANING/ INTERPRETATION	REVERSED MEANING/ INTERPRETATION
O	FOOL	NUSCE (PROMETHEUS)	AQUARIUS	URANUS	A man dressed in simple, tattered garb. Instead of holding a torch with his belongings, this figure holds a lit staff, à la Prometheus. The constellation Aquarius hangs in an orange sky behind the fool.	Beginnings and new paths. This can mean a fresh start, a new project, or a leap of faith. The card is a harbinger of change and can indicate forward-looking, creation, even magnetism.	Recklessness or incomplete projects. The inability to commit to work, family, relationships. Mercuriality. Rebelliousness or wild behavior. Stubborn independence.
I	MAGICIAN	GUSMA (MINERVA)	GEMINI	MERCURY	A woman dressed in a white robe sits upon a golden throne holding a spear. She wears a crown on her head and is flanked by twin owls. In the bright blue sky behind her, the constellation Gemini is visible.	Insight and knowledge. Ritual. Objectivity and a desire for clear communication. The ability to be a translator, between worlds or people. Wit, speed, and skill. The card is a symbol of resourcefulness and relentless pursuit.	Unrealized ambitions or elusive success. Being unprepared or standing at the edge of a beginning. An instability or restlessness that can sometimes be seen as superficiality.

#	TRAD CARD	FERRARA DECK CARD TITLE (AND ASSOCIATED ROMAN GOD)	ZODIAC SIGN	PLANETARY RULER	FERRARA DECK ILLUSTRATION	UPRIGHT MEANING/ INTERPRETATION	REVERSED MEANING/ INTERPRETATION
2	HIGH PRIESTESS	TRIXCACCIA (DIANA)	CANCER	MOON	The goddess Diana, as huntress, wearing a moon diadem, standing by a pool where a deer takes a drink of water. In the sky behind her is the constellation Cancer.	Intuition and a deep level of awareness. Empathetic and nurturing, the card can also signal psychic insight. Can signal the skill of foresight. Also a card that can mean tenacity or parental attachment.	Distraction or lack of focus. This can manifest as an exacting or touchy nature, one that blocks your ability to see or connect with your own intuition. Self-doubt and anxiety. Can indicate indulgence in self-pitying behavior.
3	EMPRESS	TRIXIMPERA (VESTA)	VIRGO	VENUS	Vesta, in a white robe, hair tied low at the nape of her neck, tending to an open hearth. Beyond the hearth is a donkey (traditional symbol of Vesta), and the constellation Virgo hangs in a daytime sky.	Tapping into femininity and fertility. An impulse toward mothering (but not always progeny). The desire to be of service. Practical, modest, and sometimes discriminating. This card signals tolerance and optimism, the ability to cultivate.	Blocked, either creatively, personally, or physically. A tendency toward being puritanical or vengeful. A healthy (or unhealthy) dose of skepticism. Criticism of yourself and others, particularly as related to realms that have been traditionally coded as feminine: the body/ the home, emotions.

#	TRAD CARD	FERRARA DECK CARD TITLE (AND ASSOCIATED ROMAN GOD)	ZODIAC SIGN	PLANETARY RULER	FERRARA DECK ILLUSTRATION	UPRIGHT MEANING/ INTERPRETATION	REVERSED MEANING/ INTERPRETATION
4	**EMPEROR**	SARIMPERA (APOLLO)	ARIES	MARS	Apollo, holding a bow and arrow, shooting at the sky, aiming directly for the sun. He wears a laurel wreath on his head and is flanked by a snake working its way toward the grass. The constellation Aries hangs in the early-evening sky.	Leadership and individuality. A paternal figure, this card can signal independence and straight-forwardness. At its best, this card can signal a soon-to-arrive source of inspiration, or a recently discovered passion.	Pettiness and egoism. Tyranny or arrogance. An unwillingness to see the truth and a preference for being indulged even when it requires deceitfulness or falseness. A tendency toward being brittle.
5	**HIERO-PHANT**	PHANTAIERO (JUPITER)	SAGIT-TARIUS	JUPITER	A bearded man seated on a throne. Cumulus clouds rise in the sky behind him, and he holds a lightning bolt in one hand. On the arms of the throne are golden eagles, and the constellation Sagittarius is visible on the dais he sits on.	Spiritual values. Tradition and knowledge. Prophesy as an ability and a right. A card that can also signal gentle initiation, or alert optimism. Also, joviality.	Self-teaching and self-sufficiency. Occasionally, a tendency toward over-confidence. A desire for rebellion against traditional structures or institutions (societal, familial, and personal). A reminder to follow your North Star.
6	**LOVERS**	TORESAMAN (VENUS)	TAURUS	VENUS	An image of Venus as a woman with long flowing hair, nude (*Venus pudica*), at sea and standing on a wisp of foam, being borne ashore by a pair of swans. The constellation Taurus, illustrated with gold stars, hangs in the sky.	Choice (of partner, but also in life). But also a desire to build, stabilize, and sustain relationships. A symbol of patience and deliberateness. Security in others, trust, and confidence.	Division or possessiveness. Also, a tendency toward lethargy. An unwillingness to make a choice that has slowed your progress. Obstinate.

#	TRAD CARD	FERRARA DECK CARD TITLE (AND ASSOCIATED ROMAN GOD)	ZODIAC SIGN	PLANETARY RULER	FERRARA DECK ILLUSTRATION	UPRIGHT MEANING/ INTERPRETATION	REVERSED MEANING/ INTERPRETATION
7	**CHARIOT**	CULUMCAR (MERCURY)	Ø	MERCURY	A winged-foot Mercury astride a chariot moving across an open stretch of Egyptian desert. His chariot is pulled by a phalanx of winged black horses.	Momentum, speed, or freedom of movement. A driving and relentless push toward a goal. But also, the card symbolizes a need to be aware of the path ahead. This card is about leading and forging the path.	A warning that things are moving too quickly. A signal that slow, deliberate progress is warranted, or even a reversal of course. In a reading: a flag or a stop sign that can be read in conjunction with other cards in the reading.
8	**JUSTICE**	TITIAGIU (JUSTITIA)	LIBRA	URANUS	A woman dressed in a flowing robe, a gold rope at her waist, holding a pair of scales. She is not blind but all-seeing. The weights on her scales are perfectly even.	Fairness and harmony. The ability to see the truth despite attempts to hide it. Idealism and the ability to be diplomatic and sincere. Firm and decisive, this card indicates an ability or willingness to negotiate objectively and with compassion.	A withholding or obscured truth. The presence of a kind of interference or insincerity. While justice is often symbolized as a woman blindfolded, only in the reverse position is the blindfold applied. This is a warning that not all is as it appears.
9	**HERMIT**	MITAERE (CHIRON)	Ø	CHIRON	The image of a centaur (Chiron) carrying a staff over a single shoulder, alone. In the landscape behind him, all that is visible is a mountain range and a cave, signaling his position as a hermit.	A turning inward or self-reflective journey. The need for aloneness and contemplation. A symbol that further study is needed.	Reclusiveness. A shying away from friends, family, or obligations. An unwillingness to be self-reflective, or a state of being too self-reflective.

#	TRAD CARD	FERRARA DECK CARD TITLE (AND ASSOCIATED ROMAN GOD)	ZODIAC SIGN	PLANETARY RULER	FERRARA DECK ILLUSTRATION	UPRIGHT MEANING/ INTERPRETATION	REVERSED MEANING/ INTERPRETATION
IO	**WHEEL**	TUNAFOR (FORTUNA)	LEO	JUPITER	A winged female figure, clothed in a deep blue dress, holding a wheel on which four figures are lashed. She spins the wheel at her leisure, with the least fortunate at the bottom.	The card of fate and fortune. A sign of felicitousness and good luck, of being chosen in love, life, or work. A very powerful card that can also mean a sudden and unexpected change that is inevitable, predestined, and already written.	Bad luck. The reversed meaning of the card aligns with the figure at the bottom of the wheel. A reversed Wheel of Fortune card means ill fortune. But not all is lost, because the wheel will turn again, and the card can signal ascendance.
II	**SRENGTH**	TUDOZA (HERCULES)	Ø	SUN	A bare-chested Hercules sits adjacent to a lion, who is lying down, tail raised mid-flick. Next to them is a forge, the heat of which is visible despite the sun, which has reached its apogee.	Determination and ferocity of will. Internal persistence and power. The act of discovering motivation and primal strength. This card signals power from within, not external power. It should not be limited to physical perceptions of power.	Vulnerability. An inability to enact change. The feeling of being hobbled or otherwise restrained by events or people around you. This can also signal frustration or an abuse of power.

#	TRAD CARD	FERRARA DECK CARD TITLE (AND ASSOCIATED ROMAN GOD)	ZODIAC SIGN	PLANETARY RULER	FERRARA DECK ILLUSTRATION	UPRIGHT MEANING/ INTERPRETATION	REVERSED MEANING/ INTERPRETATION
12	HANGED MAN	ENDOAPPE (NEPTUNE)	PISCES	NEPTUNE	A card that depicts Neptune, underwater, holding a trident. He is surrounded and encircled by a school of fish. In the watery depths behind him, the constellation Pisces is visible.	Plastic, poetic, a state of suspension. This card is lyrical in the way it signals a moment of pause, reflection, and suggestibility. This card sways with the currents. It be positive, signaling imagination and dreaminess or an unreadiness to be in and of the world.	Unstable, chaotic, otherworldly. When the tides and currents are resisted, this can cause instability or an unwillingness to make peace with or understand deeper meanings. It can also signal a brittleness of mind or will.
13	DEATH	MORS (ORCUS)	SCORPIO	PLUTO	The figure Orcus sits on a throne. Next to him sits a three-headed hydra. The landscape is barren and dark, signaling eternal night. Only in the sky above him does the constellation Scorpio, its long tail sweeping the horizon, offer illumination.	Transformation and transition. The quality of a phoenix rising from the ashes. But also, as part of that transformation, loss of the familiar. An immersion in the new, sometimes the uncomfortable. Intensity and incisiveness. A card signaling a change of seasons.	Stagnation. Bitterness or ruthlessness. An unwillingness to change or regrow. Jealous, secretive, or suspicious. Stubbornness to the point of danger. Vengeance and grudge holding.

#	TRAD CARD	FERRARA DECK CARD TITLE (AND ASSOCIATED ROMAN GOD)	ZODIAC SIGN	PLANETARY RULER	FERRARA DECK ILLUSTRATION	UPRIGHT MEANING/ INTERPRETATION	REVERSED MEANING/ INTERPRETATION
14	TEMPER-ANCE	TIATEMPER (VIRTUS)	∅	VENUS	According to Aristotle, Temperance was the most important of all virtues. Temperance is here shown as the leader of the virtues, dressed in a white dress, pouring water from an urn into a catch basin.	Modera-tion and harmony. A need to see both sides, to balance desires and wants. And in that, also a mixing and alchemy. The ability to bring two disparate elements together in compati-bility.	Over-indulgence or rigidity. Disharmony. Tension or blockage. An inability to mix or pour water from the urn. A freezing of forward progress. An inability to broker peace or work with others.
15	DEVIL	BOLUSDIA (JANUS)	∅	PLUTO	In this case, the Devil is person-ified as Janus, the two-faced god. Janus stands with his two faces showing. On one side of the card is lightness and joy and on the other, darkness and sorrow. Janus stands below an arch at the edge of the earth.	The taboo. Bondage, restriction, failure. Easily becoming enthralled or obsessed with others. Passion and the wilderness. A space outside of usual human in-teraction or inhabitance, whether real or imagined. Sexuality.	Release through chaos. Trickery. The ability to see and recognize the forces of bondage and restriction for what they are. Anxiety. A need to confront the darker forces in your life.
16	TOWER	RESTOR (VULCAN)	∅	SUN	At the bottom of a tower, we see a bearded man standing and working in a fire. However, the fire has spread to the structure itself, and the sky beyond is dark.	Unexpected or sudden change. A reversal. Release or abandon-ment of old ways of thinking, relationships, or interests. Fierce clarity or rebellion. A dramatic departure.	A signal that the time to rebuild has arrived. A period of reflection and con-struction. A warning that resistance to change is present but is unnecessary. Imprison-ment.

#	TRAD CARD	FERRARA DECK CARD TITLE (AND ASSOCIATED ROMAN GOD)	ZODIAC SIGN	PLANETARY RULER	FERRARA DECK ILLUSTRATION	UPRIGHT MEANING/ INTERPRETATION	REVERSED MEANING/ INTERPRETATION
17	STAR	ELLAST (AURORA)	Ø	VENUS	A woman dressed in a deep blue dress stands on an orb, suspended against a dawn sky. She reaches a hand up in the direction of the only remaining star left in the blue heavens.	Hope and renewal. Inspiration. Personal or divine enlightenment. Fulfillment on a deep and powerful level. A sense of calm. This card can signal smooth waters in your personal, professional, or emotional life.	Pessimism or skepticism. A loss of hope in others, the world around you, or yourself. Alienation or a feeling of being unskilled and clumsy. The feeling of being disengaged or uninspired.
18	MOON	NALU (LUNA)	Ø	MOON	A woman, dressed in a white robe, holds a crescent moon in the palm of her hand and stands suspended in the night sky. Above her, a circle of moons, signaling all the moon phases, is visible.	Fear or illusion. Deception. Not all is as it appears, and the truth is hidden. This card is a warning. An indication that there is falseness, trickery, or double-dealing in your sphere of influence. This may be in relation to those you surround yourself with, or internal, psychical.	The sensation of recognizing falseness or trickery. Small, inconsequential mistakes that are easy to move beyond. A reversed Moon card can mean you are struggling to assimilate something new into your life or identity. A reminder to record one's dreams.

#	TRAD CARD	FERRARA DECK CARD TITLE (AND ASSOCIATED ROMAN GOD)	ZODIAC SIGN	PLANETARY RULER	FERRARA DECK ILLUSTRATION	UPRIGHT MEANING/ INTERPRETATION	REVERSED MEANING/ INTERPRETATION
19	SUN	LOS (SOL)	Ø	SUN	A putto holds the sun aloft in a golden sky. He is not the traditional representation of the sun, but rather a child. He is nude, save for a cloud. Above the sun a white eagle, the insignia of the d'Este family, flies.	Positivity, success, abundance. A great return. Satisfaction or contentment. If not yet present, this card is a signal that a positive sea change is imminent. A sign of renewal or laying bare. Professional accomplishment.	Unwarranted pessimism. An inability to see the future, or clouded judgment. A warning that your decisions should not be trusted, as you are in the dark. A delay en route to success.
20	JUDGMENT	CIUMGUIDI (CERES)	Ø	EARTH	Judgment is represented as Ceres, who stands in a golden wheat field and holds a cut sheaf of wheat in one hand and a scythe in the other. In the sky above her, the morning star is visible.	A moment of accounting. Taking stock. Assessing. Shrewd clarity. It can signal forgiveness following deliberation. A clearing of personal conflicts, either within oneself or with others.	A blockage or inability to see signs. Blindness. A sign that growth is waiting but you have not yet been able to actualize it. An unwillingness to face or begin a big change.

#	TRAD CARD	FERRARA DECK CARD TITLE (AND ASSOCIATED ROMAN GOD)	ZODIAC SIGN	PLANETARY RULER	FERRARA DECK ILLUSTRATION	UPRIGHT MEANING/ INTERPRETATION	REVERSED MEANING/ INTERPRETATION
21	WORLD	DOMUN (SATURN)	CAPRICORN	SATURN	A bearded man stands holding his young in one hand, his mouth, a dark hole, open. Behind him is the world in miniature, but it is still an antediluvian world. The world just after heaven and earth have been separated.	Completion, a feeling of coming full circle. A sign of perseverance and ambition. A signal that it is your duty to close a chapter. A sense of relief, but also a sign of practicality, of being economical. Triumph and success in personal and professional realms.	Failure to reach completion. Lack of inspiration or slowness. Occasionally, a sense of severity in work or with oneself. A sign that it is time to refocus, that you may be lost.

MINOR ARCANA

Nota Bene: Reversed cards in the Minor Arcana should be assigned the opposite meaning of those indicated below

CARD	SWORDS (reason, communication: air)	STAVES (creativity, action: fire)	CUPS (emotion, intuition: water)	COINS (materiality, success: earth)
ACE	Clarity	Creation	Intimacy	Prosperity
ONE	Determination. Strength. Triumph.	Beginning. Starting anew. An adventure or enterprise.	Abundance. Fertility. Fulfillment.	Perfection. Prosperity. Bliss. Extensive wealth.
TWO	Balance, but in the case of tension, a stalemate.	Travel. Bravery to venture down new paths.	Emotional partnership. Connection with another. Union.	Occupation. Signaling skill with words. Translation and communication.
THREE	Disappointment. Rejection. Separation or betrayal.	Commerce. Practicality or useful knowledge. Specialized skill.	Resolution. Conclusion. The closing of a chapter. Celebration.	Mastery. Artistic or creative skill. Recognition or accolades.

CARD	SWORDS (reason, communication: air)	STAVES (creativity, action: fire)	CUPS (emotion, intuition: water)	COINS (materiality, success: earth)
FOUR	Rest. Filling the well. Retreat. Seclusion.	Stability. Romantic harmony. Tranquility and enjoyment.	Aversion. Disappointment. An inability to move past or through something.	Possessiveness. Hoarding. Stinginess.
FIVE	Conquest. Defeat. Self-interest.	Conflict. Competition. Rivalry or jealousy.	Emotional instability. Loss of friendship. Incomplete connection.	Financial loss or ruin. Destitute. Adversity or insecurity.
SIX	Transition or travel. Voyage. Overcoming or moving beyond.	Conquest. Triumph. The realization of a goal.	Memory. Past experiences. Nostalgia, sometimes overwhelming.	Philanthropy. Charity. Generosity. The impulse to give.
SEVEN	Perseverance. Fortitude. The ability to endure.	Success. Overcoming the odds. Winning negotiations.	Inability to realize a passion. Unrealistic expectations. Daydreaming.	Ingenuity. Inventiveness. Gain. Discovery of treasure.
EIGHT	Conflict. Restriction or limitation. Turmoil.	Swift activity. Haste toward a goal.	Abandonment of effort. Leaving behind. Departure.	Craft or skill. Apprenticeship. Handiwork. Diligence.
NINE	Despair. Heartbreak. Anxiousness.	Anticipation. Vigilance. Grit. Awareness.	Abundance. Material success or victory. Gain.	Plenty. Accomplishment. Prudence. Material comfort.
TEN	Misfortune. Defeat. Loss of energy.	Burden. Responsibility. A feeling of great pressure.	Family harmony. Contentment. Virtue.	Inheritance. Legacy. Ancestry. Affluence.
PAGE	Curious and inquisitive. Insight and discretion.	Loyalty. A sign of important news. A semaphore.	Surprise. Happy news. An offer of services or assistance.	Study. Scholarship. Reflection. A desire for learning or knowledge.
KNIGHT	Capacity and skill. Occasionally impetuousness.	Passion. Lust. Comfort with the unknown.	Opportunity or arrival. A new approach or being newly approached.	Methodical and deliberate. Persistent. Capable.
QUEEN	Perception. Keen wit.	Exuberance and enthusiasm. Graceful.	Devoted. Warmth. Feminine intuition.	Prosperity. Luxury. Opulence and generosity.
KING	Controlled, clear-headed, authoritative. Experienced. Intellect.	Visionary. Maturity. Entrepreneurship.	Emotional balance. Sound counsel. Professionalism.	Reliable. Dependable. Providing for others. Professional acumen.

ACKNOWLEDGMENTS

First, thanks go to Sarah King, who read the opening chapters of an abandoned project and insisted there was something there. (And then, enthusiastically read countless versions!) This book wouldn't exist without you.

To Natalie Hallak, my editor, whose vision and enthusiasm for this book never wavered: thank you. Working with you has been a master class on how to take a narrative from good to great, and I remain grateful for your kind, relentless pushing. To my agent, Sarah Phair, whose wise counsel and cool head are always a safe harbor: you talked me into showing you an early draft of this book and have been a champion of it ever since. Thank you for bringing big Virgo energy to all that you do!

I had no idea how lucky I was when my book landed at Atria, but as it turns out, fate was on my side once again. I have been honored and humbled by the incredible support I have received from Libby McGuire, Lindsay Sagnette, and Dana Trocker (Go Slugs!), and remain in awe of the generous work of Liz Byer. Bringing a book to readers is a complex task, one that wouldn't have been possible without Chelsea McGuckin, James Iacobelli, Halle Porter, Yvonne Taylor, Paige Lytle, Nicole Bond, Sara Bowne, Morgan Hoit, and Shelby Pumphrey. Particular thanks, as well, to Elizabeth Hitti.

Throughout my path to publication I was kept calm, buoyed, cheered on, and championed by the tireless and unstinting Maudee Genao and Gena Lanzi. I will forever live with the shame that your names were absent from the first printing of these acknowledgments. Truly, no marketing and publicity dream team has ever matched your kindness, generosity, and enthusiasm. What a joy it has been to work with you both; your authors are wildly lucky.

In the UK, *The Cloisters* had the incredible good fortune to land on the desk of Simon Taylor, who was an early and unflagging champion of the novel. There, the team at Transworld—especially, Louis Patel, Izzie Ghaffari-Parker, and Marianne Issa El-Khoury—accomplished things that authors only dream of. Thank you all for your support, humor, and kindness; I won't forget it.

Thanks, also, to two early influences on this book (although none of us knew it at the time)—Herb Kessler and Josh O'Driscoll. Many years ago you let me sit in on your medieval colloquium. All the weirdness I saw there ended up being the germ of this book. And Josh, your Instagram has been clutch.

No acknowledgments are complete without thanking the people who've gamely put up with my many interests over the years—my parents. You've never batted an eye when I've told you what outlandish thing I'm thinking about doing next. And you've greeted my writer phase with the same enthusiasm and support as everything that came before. You have always made anything seem possible, and that is a wonderful gift to give a child. You are both, simply put, the best. Thanks, also, to Bet and Wade for instilling in me a love of the arts. And to David, Karen, and Aiais, thank you for talking to me endlessly about books. And to all my extended family—I'm so lucky to have you.

But no one has heard more about this book than Andrew Hays, whose patience, love, creativity, wit, talent, good humor, and kindness are the cornerstone of our lives. Without you, nothing would be as fun, bright, or joyful. I love living with you in the shadow of the mountain that brought us together. And to our dog, Queso, who keeps us company while we type. You are a very good boy. We love you.

THE
CLOISTERS

Katy Hays

*T*his reading group guide for The Cloisters *includes an introduction, discussion questions, ideas for enhancing your book club, and a Q&A with author Katy Hays. The suggested questions are intended to help your reading group find new and interesting angles and topics for your discussion. We hope that these ideas will enrich your conversation and increase your enjoyment of the book.*

INTRODUCTION

*T*he *Secret History* meets *Ninth House* in this sinister, atmospheric novel following a circle of researchers as they uncover a mysterious deck of tarot cards and shocking secrets in New York's famed Met Cloisters.

TOPICS & QUESTIONS
FOR DISCUSSION

1. The events of *The Cloisters* take place over one summer. How do the season and summer weather reflect Ann's emotions and evolution throughout the novel?

2. Patrick and Rachel are first introduced in Chapter 2. What were your first impressions of each of them? Discuss the events that result in Ann working at The Cloisters.

3. Patrick is Rachel's mentor, but he is also her lover. How does this dynamic complicate the situation at The Cloisters? Who do you think has more power in their relationship, and what form does that power take?

4. Early on, Rachel steals a cookie from the café, and later we see her play pranks on Moira in addition to taking the tiles that identify plants in the garden and stealing a boat. What do these incidents tell us about Rachel? How do all of these "games" foreshadow revelations of the dark and dangerous choices she has made over the years?

5. What do you think motivated Ann not to share all of Lingraf's writings with Rachel and to hide the false-fronted card from Patrick?

How might the story have been different if she had shared this information with the team?

6. Loss is central to both Ann's and Rachel's stories. Discuss some of their major (and minor) losses throughout the book and how these might have shaped them as characters.

7. Laure warns Ann about Rachel's past—why do you think Ann becomes so defensive of Rachel? At this point in the book, do you think Ann and Rachel's friendship is a healthy one?

8. Discuss how Lingraf becomes central to the mystery and uncovering the truth.

9 Ann and Rachel come from very different backgrounds, but at the end of the novel, Rachel insists that they are the same. What personality traits do they share? How are they different? Ultimately, do you think Rachel is right?

10. In Chapter 4, Ann expresses how "Walla Walla would always feel like death to me." Do you think the same can be said for The Cloisters after her summer there?

11. In the end, was it fate that decided what happened to these characters or was it the choices they made?

12. In the prologue, Ann talks about how she missed "the omens that haunted The Cloisters that summer." Having finished reading the novel, what were the omens? How did the prologue foreshadow the importance (or not) of fate?

13. Both tarot and astrology play a significant role in today's discourse. These days, it seems as if everyone knows their rising sign or has a tarot deck. How do these contemporary practices relate to the historic practices outlined in *The Cloisters*? Are they different? Similar? Do you use either device, and if so, why?

ENHANCE YOUR BOOK CLUB

1. As Ann dives into her research at The Cloisters, she learns about different types of divination and fortune-telling, including augury, pyromancy, cleromancy, and tarot. Research the history of these practices. Why do you think there is a growing interest in them today?

2. Leo introduces Ann to many of the plants grown in the gardens, including some that are poisonous. List the plants mentioned, and see if you can identify any at a local botanical garden.

3. The Met Cloisters is a real museum in New York City. Learn more about the museum at www.metmuseum.org/visit/plan-your-visit/met-cloisters or plan an in-person visit!

A CONVERSATION WITH
KATY HAYS

There's a lot of history woven into the book, particularly regarding art and tarot cards. What was your research process like?

As is true for many academics, a research rabbit hole is my happy place! But surprisingly, I found very little existing scholarship on Renaissance tarot. When that happens, as a researcher, you start to look at topics that might intersect or surround the lacuna so you can set the scene. In the case of tarot, that meant turning to questions of chance (particularly as they related to card play), as well as fate, fortune, and free will. Renaissance Europe, and Italy in particular, was absolutely *obsessed* with these issues, and that literature offered me more than enough material to work with!

Is there anything you learned that you wish could have made it into the book?

I read a wonderful book by Mary Quinlan-McGrath, *Influences: Art, Optics, and Astrology in the Italian Renaissance*. In it, Quinlan-McGrath argues that anyone with a bit of power during the Renaissance (popes, aristocrats, philosophers, etc.) believed that *painted* representations of celestial bodies could impact someone's horoscope. I remember reading her book and thinking, *This is absolutely the weirdest thing I have ever read!* For example, if my Mercury is in Scorpio and I'm standing under a constellation of Taurus, just *standing under the painting* will make my communication sluggish? *What?* I wish more of that could have made it in!

Atmospheric is the perfect word to describe *The Cloisters*. How did you get in the mindset to write something so sensory?

I was working on the book during Covid, so while I had visited The Cloisters many years before, it wasn't possible to travel there while I was writing the book. To fill the gaps, I relied heavily on Google Street View, which allowed me to "walk" through Fort Tryon Park, see the exterior of the museum, and "walk" other streets in New York. Additionally, through my teaching work, I knew the Met had incredible digital resources to support their collections. That access was critical to completing the book. But also, I have to say—a playlist of Gregorian chants helped, too!

One quote from *The Cloisters* that stuck with me is: "Your interpretation of choice is a luxury, a curtain that separates us from fate." Ann and the other characters ruminate on themes of fate throughout the book. Did writing this book clarify your own thoughts on fate versus free will? If so, what are they?

I've always been fascinated by the idea of luck. Luck is a spark, a scrap of magic, something we can't control but that seems essential. In that sense, I've always considered luck and fate to be twins or, at a bare minimum, kissing cousins. I believe, like many, that choice and free will remain our primary source of power and give life shape and meaning. But there's no denying that something outside of our control—fate, luck, chance, *fortuna*—also plays a vital and sometimes outsize role in our lives.

Ann is perpetually conscious of her outsider status in the world of academia, and you pull the veil back on its uglier sides, such as how much nepotism, gatekeeping, and privilege permeate it. What do you hope readers learn about the interworkings of academic institutions?

I don't think academia has cornered the market on nepotism, gatekeeping, or being privileged! And I do have to say that I think museums like the Met are working hard to turn the page when it comes to these outmoded ways of working and hiring. But what I think remains true about academia and the art world is the extent to which a pedigree matters. It doesn't have to be familial, but it does need to be institutional—the right schools, internships, recommenders. Those elements decide the outcome of someone's career, and that quality—being anointed, almost—happens early.

Do you have a favorite tarot card? And if so, what makes it your favorite?

This will come as no surprise: the Wheel of Fortune is my favorite card. It's a deeply lucky card. That said, I primarily use a classic Rider-Waite deck, and I'm always happy to see just about any card . . . so long as it's not a sword. That suit makes me nervous!

Can you tell us a bit about what you're working on now?

Sure! I'm currently working on a novel that reimagines the House of Thebes and, particularly, the legacy of Harmonia's necklace, a cursed object in antiquity that brought misfortune to any woman who wore it. It's a family drama, set over the course of a wedding weekend in Italy, that deals with desire, social taboos, money, and creative ambition. I'm thinking of it as a cursed *Succession* meets *The Guest List*.